BILLABONG BEND

THE WILD AUSTRALIA STORIES 3

JENNIFER SCOULLAR

PILYARA PRESS

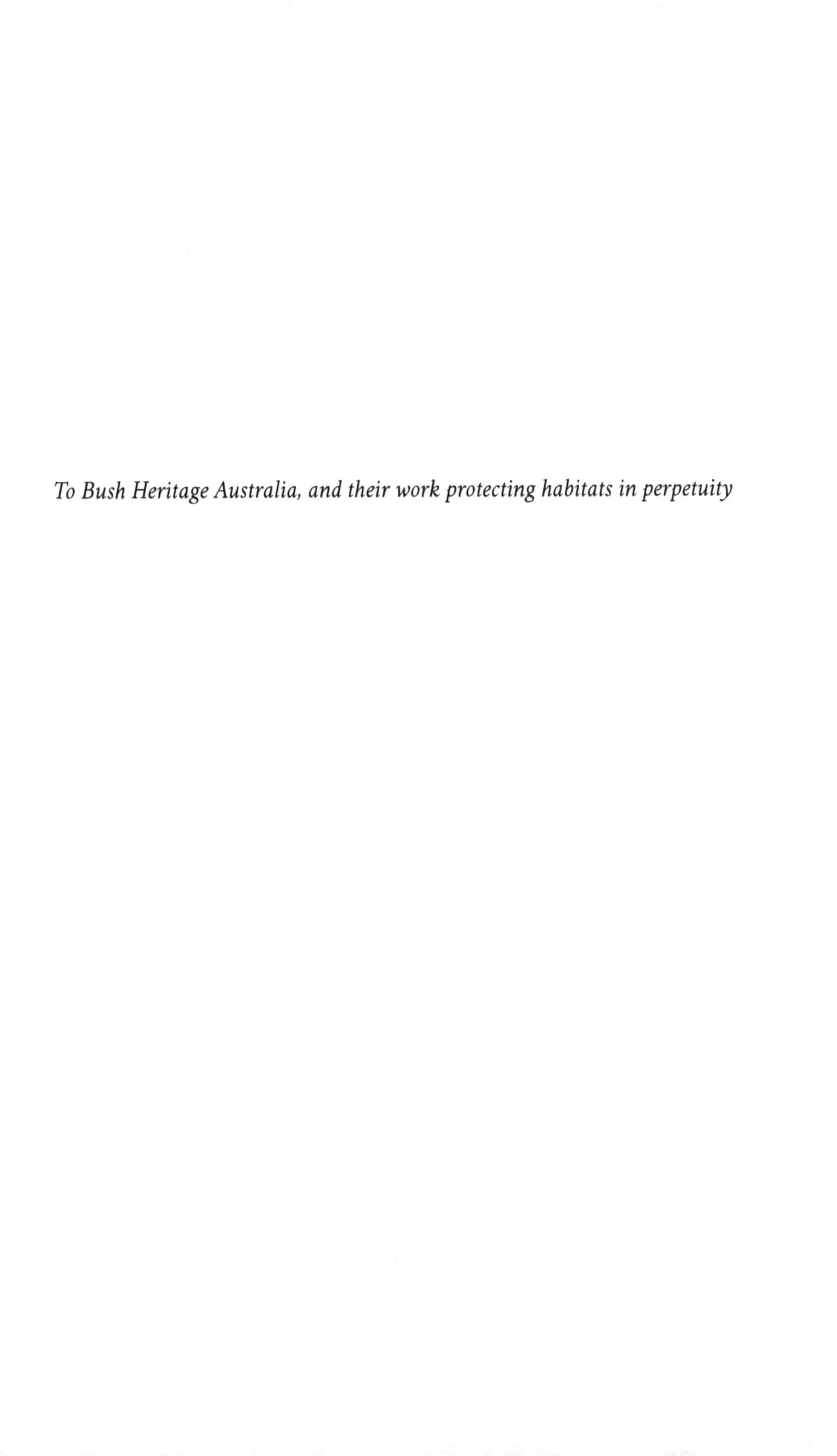

To Bush Heritage Australia, and their work protecting habitats in perpetuity

Version 1.0
ISBN: 978-1-925827-08-8

Pilyara Press
Melbourne

CHAPTER 1

Shotguns boomed and boomed again, shattering the morning peace of the marshlands, startling the roosting nankeen night heron into laboured flight. What on earth? Nina lowered her camera and steered the little runabout towards the gunshots. There, in the distance, past the bank of river red gums weeping in the heat – a tinny with two men in camo gear, weapons raised. A succession of deafening blasts echoed off the water, drowning out Nina's air horn as she powered towards them. The stench of gunpowder reached her nose and rage rose in her throat like bile. Damn them.

A mixed flock of wood ducks and teal were flapping away, well outside the fifty-metre range of an average shotgun. These men were the most incompetent poachers ever. As Nina drew near, they turned their heads at the blare of her horn. 'This is private property,' she yelled. 'Get off my land!' These wetlands belonged to her in spirit, just as she belonged to them.

One man was fat, and swigged from a beer can. The other man was taller, older, with a bushy beard. He sneered and played with his gun. 'You've got a mouth on you, sweetheart.'

A movement caught her eye, something dark floating in the water. The shadow took shape: a lifeless black swan. Nina uttered an

anguished cry and slammed on the throttle. The man's sneer turned to a look of alarm. He aimed high and pulled the trigger

Birdshot exploded overhead as she closed in, but fury made her fearless. Pelican's heavy hull rammed the tinny. Its impact launched the men, weapons and all, into the water where they floundered, gasping for air.

'You crazy bitch!' screamed the fat man as his hat floated away.

She circled the poachers grimly, checking they could swim, then went after their craft and towed it back. Using her bird- catching hook, Nina hauled their belongings from among the empty cans that littered the floor of the tinny, all the while keeping the boat just out of their reach. 'Hey . . . idiots,' she said, searching their bags. 'You watching?' She checked their wallets. 'Brodie and, ah, Shane?' An assortment of items sailed overboard to a chorus of threats and pleas: fishing rods, ammo, their lunch.

'Oh, come on. Not my car keys,' yelled the older man, adding a '*please*' for good measure.

Nina paused. 'Brodie, Shane . . . are you listening?' The men trod water and nodded furiously.

'It's hard enough for birds to breed in this drought,' she said. 'Those ducks you fired on? They have young on the water, and now you've spooked them. If they don't come back, their chicks will die of cold or starvation or get picked off by predators. And for each adult bird killed, you wound three or four with stray pellets.' The dead swan drifted closer. 'Here,' she said. 'I'll give you the same sporting chance you gave the birds.'

Nina threw the keys skywards. The men swore and thrashed hopelessly about trying to reach them. Seconds later their wallets and phones made the same trip to the bottom of the river. Nina unhitched the tinny and nudged it towards them. 'Next time' – her voice was quiet with anger – 'I won't be so friendly.' She waited until they had a hand on the side of their boat, then manoeuvred the Pelican away.

Her heart beat as loud as Pelican's engine as she wove her way upstream, through tangles of lignum and club rushes, skirting snags and overhanging branches. She didn't often encounter poachers in the wetlands, but for every rat you saw there were fifty you didn't. Duck hunting wasn't legal in New South Wales, not without a licence from the landowner, and never in breeding season. She'd seen some terrible sights this summer. A flotilla of fifty orphaned cygnets seeking the protection of a single surviving swan. A platypus drowned in a banned fish trap. A family of frightened day-old ducklings bobbing sadly in the shallows, crowded around a hunter's plastic decoy duck.

That story at least had a happy ending. She'd scooped the babies up in a net, taken them home and put them under a brooder lamp. Nina smiled to think of the peeping fluff balls, ducking and diving in the upturned dustbin lid that served as their pool. What kind of ducks were they? It was impossible to identify most waterbirds until they were fledged, and dozens of species called Billabong Bend home. She'd just have to wait and see.

Nina wiped the sweat from her eyes. Still early, yet the air was already baking. The sun blazed down from a dome of flawless blue as it had done each day for months now. She slowed to manoeuvre the boat around a leaning river cooba that almost blocked the shrunken watercourse. She'd never seen water levels this low.

Nina detoured up Langley Reach, towards the mooring of Bill-abong's homestead, keeping a sharp eye out as always. You never knew what rare waterbirds might be found in this pristine marshland. Soon the historic house appeared through the trees. With peeling paint and smashed windows, it stood like a blind sentinel above the river. She cruised around the abandoned jetty and frowned. The water was a floating carpet of vivid green, splashed with delicate purple flowers. This was worse than she thought. Water hyacinths were pretty, no doubt about it, but outside of their native Amazon they were also a curse, choking waterways.

Somebody needed to clear out the weeds here. Somebody needed to clear out the poachers. Somebody needed to repair the homestead. Nina took some photos, squared her shoulders and set her deter-mined jaw. If she had anything to do with it, that somebody was going to be her.

· · ·

Nina arrived home, moored her boat and jogged up the dusty path leading to the house. She pushed in the fly-wire door of Red Gums, checked her watch and frowned. She always lost track of time out at Billabong. Jinx, her gentle retriever, followed her inside.

'Guess you'll have to see in the new year by yourself.' Nina fondled the dog's soft ears, and he furrowed his honey-coloured brow. She felt a sudden, nervous quiver in her stomach. Her ten-year high school reunion was tonight — a masquerade ball. Nina wasn't a party person. She hated crowds and didn't do small talk. Maybe she'd lived alone in the bush for too long, or maybe she was just plain antisocial. Whatever the reason, Nina felt like a fish out of water in town these days. There were a couple of people she'd like to see, though. Dylan, for instance, and her friend Kate. It was New Year's Eve, after all.

'I don't think so,' Nina had said, when Kate first asked her. 'And anyway, Lockie can't go.'

Kate had laughed. 'Can't or won't?'

Lockie Carver managed Macquarie Station, a large pastoral property out of Moree. He and Nina had been an item for two years now. Lockie enjoyed a night at the local pub as much as anybody, but Kate was right – he wasn't much of a party animal either. Nina smiled, imagining how horrified he'd be at the prospect of having to wear a costume.

'Can't,' said Nina. 'He's spending Christmas with his folks in Queensland.'

'And you didn't go with him? Are you guys okay?'

Kate read hidden meanings into everything. 'There was nobody to look after things here, that's all,' said Nina. 'Sorry about the reunion, Katie, but I'd feel funny going by myself and anyway, I've got nothing to wear.'

'You won't be by yourself, you'll be with me, and my sister's your size. She has a gorgeous blue gown that should fit . . . Nina, I've gone to so much trouble making your mask. You just have to come.'

At the St Patrick's College reunion, guests were meant to remain masked until midnight. Nina sighed as she made herself a sandwich. 'It might be fun,' she said to the dog, who was lying politely beside the table, soft eyes trained on hers. He was an excellent listener. 'And it's about time I saw Eva. Wonder what sort of mask Kate made me? Hope it's a bird.' She tossed Jinx the last of the cheese. 'Come on, boy. We'd better do the rounds before I go.'

Nina checked her watch. Still time to take Flicka instead of the quad bike. She saddled the pretty chestnut mare, while Monty, Flicka's paddock mate, bucked and kicked around the yard. With ears back and tail up, he sounded his displeasure with long, trumpeting neighs that made his whole body quiver. 'I'll take you next time,' said Nina, 'if you behave yourself.' The rangy grey gelding calmed down long enough to take a carrot, and then went tearing around his yard again.

They were ex-racehorses, Monty too old and Flicka too slow for the track, and they were both on their way to slaughter, when Nina adopted them them from a rescue group in Moree six months earlier. Nobody had told Monty that his racing days were over. He had only one gear – top speed – and he was a wild ride. Flicka had settled better, a gentle, sensitive mare who tried hard to please. But her nerves were shot, and riding such a hyper-vigilant mount had its challenges. Nina never quite knew when Flicka might shy, so she had to keep a keen lookout and spot anything scary before her mare did.

Nina mounted Flicka and stroked her sleek golden neck, breathing in her earthy scent, proud of the growing trust between them. The lightest squeeze of her heels, and they set off on their rounds. Red Gums Station covered two thousand acres of belah and black-box floodplains. Well-bred mobs of Murray Grey cattle grazed in the paddocks, shady groves of olive and nut trees stretched out along the river, and tracts of red gum woodlands sheltered stock and wildlife alike. Neighbouring Billabong Bend might be ecologically more valuable, but Red Gums was still a top-notch grazing property.

Nina swung Flicka down towards the orchards, cantering along the wide rows of olives and pecans while Jinx ranged on ahead. She cast her eye over trunks and branches, occasionally stopping to pick a few leaves. She trotted down the laneway, checking troughs for faulty ball cocks or leaking pipes. With the drought eating into Red Gums' water entitlement, she needed to make every drop count. Hungry steers milled along the fence line, under the familiar sky of unbroken blue, bellowing for more hay. There wasn't much of that left.

Her last job was to inspect the pump station. Nina jumped down to check the new digital display that measured her water usage. Good, well below last year, and even in this drought she'd used less than half of her annual allocation. Nina stood back and surveyed the recent installation with pride. Powered by four solar panels on a tracking rack, it pumped river water up to a pair of large stock tanks. From there it flowed through to the troughs and orchards. Drip irrigators fed the root zones of her trees in precise amounts and only when required, slashing water consumption. New fences protected the fragile river edge, where native vegetation was staging a comeback. Nina held her breath as a royal spoonbill and half-grown chick stalked from the reeds. Nature was quick to heal herself, given half a chance.

The growing roar of a motor shattered the silence and sent the spoonbills dashing for cover. On the north side of the river, an approaching tractor with spray unit attached travelled along the neat crop rows. The driver, old Max Bonelli, gave her a curt wave. Nina waved back, wrinkling her nose as the acrid smell of chemicals drifted across the water.

Compared to her brown paddocks, Donnalee's cotton crop stood verdant and green. Nina scowled. She was an old-fashioned dry-land grazier. This was black-soil country and these rich, alluvial flood-plains were some of the most fertile in Australia. But just like the wetlands, they depended on water to bring them to life. When Nina was a child, the floods came every year. Visions came to her of fat cattle grazing knee-deep in waving meadows of water couch, way out in the back blocks. Of ephemeral little gilgai lakes, sparkling like jewels. Of open water and lush landscapes, and running a cow and calf every few acres. Of a dazzling profusion of wildlife. Mere memories now. There'd been no proper flood for years, not even when it rained. Not since they'd built the Hopeton Dam to tame the river, and auctioned off thousands of megalitres of water from the Bunyip to upstream irrigators.

Not more than a stone's throw across the river, a broad diversion canal led off through Donnalee's picture-perfect paddocks of green. In the distance she could see the rusty old dethridge wheels that punctuated its course — simple steel drums round an axle, fitted with eight paddle vanes. They spanned channels, spinning with the flow, operating the counters used to charge cotton farmers for their water. Dozens of these iconic water-measuring wheels still operated along the river, some with their own names and personalities: Bear Wheel, Big Cow, Old Slowpoke.

They may have been part of the river's history, but the counters were notoriously dodgy and always seemed to work in the farmers' favour. So many things could go wrong. Vanes and drums got damaged. Bearings wore out. High upstream water levels could drown wheels altogether. On top of that, the devices only functioned properly for twenty years or so, and needed their axles replaced every five. Some local dethridge wheels were over a hundred years old.

Stories abounded of farmers beating the wheels and stealing water. A cruel ruse was to jam turtles in the spokes, as the inspectors couldn't prove they hadn't become stuck and died accidentally. Irrigators once told these stories freely, but not any more. Not since the floods stopped coming.

Nina imagined the wheels, scooping up vast amounts of precious water and sending it gushing into the leaky, open channels beyond. When would this region move into the twenty-first century? Electromagnetic flow meters and flume gates were the way to go. Nobody should grow cotton along this thirsty river anyway. It just wasn't right. She hurried back up to the homestead: a modest weatherboard house with a wrap-around verandah and a rusty tin roof, standing on the only rise for miles around. Time to put aside her worries. Red Gums could manage without her for one day, and she was starting to look forward to tonight. When was the last time she'd worn anything but jeans?

Nina dropped her overnight bag near the door and took a deep breath. That was everything. Now all she needed were her keys. She searched among the bills and journals and seed lists on the table in the kitchen. Why couldn't she just put them on the hook behind the dresser like Mum always used to?

Her parents lived in Drovers Flat now, half an hour's drive east; a picturesque little town nestled on the banks of the Bunyip River. Two hotels, a central school, two churches. A general store selling everything from liquor to souvenirs, and the agricultural supply store run by Nina's parents. The place had no great claim to fame. A rodeo in November, novelty goat races in April and – before the drought, anyway – excellent fishing. Some of the state's biggest Murray cod had been caught downstream.

Her parents were fifth-generation floodplains graziers, but years of drought had crushed their passion for farming. They'd wanted to cut their losses and let Red Gums go altogether. 'This is no life for a girl,' Dad had said. 'If I had a son it might be different.' But there was no son, no other children at all. Just Nina. Eventually she'd talked them into selling Red Gums to her on vendor terms. Much as she loved running the place herself, she did miss her mother's organisational skills. Nina looked hopelessly around the messy kitchen and shrugged.

'So, I'm no housekeeper.' Jinx smiled as if to say *big deal*. She'd barely changed anything since her parents left – anything indoors, at least. Dylan teased that the old house was *'trapped in last century'*. But she didn't mind. She never noticed the old-fashioned wallpaper and faded floral curtains anyway. There was too much to be done outside.

Nina discovered her phone and keys beneath a week-old newspaper that she hadn't got around to reading. The headline caught her eye: *'Premier Tuckey brands water theft a crime – In the current drought, water theft equals environmental terrorism and will be made an indictable offence.'*

Too right. About time somebody took it seriously. Nina checked her watch. Five o'clock already. The reunion ball was at Moree, more than a hundred miles away. She turned off the fan, grabbed her bag and hurried out the door. Jinx looked disapproving and she gave him one last kiss. 'You can't come this time, boy.' The dog lay down obediently and Nina headed off, past the coolibahs in the garden, their eucalyptus scent pungent in the heat.

Through the trees beyond the river, Nina could see Max's brand new tractor pull into the house yard at Donnalee. She loved that Red Gums was the district's highest homestead. Not only did it mean protection from floods, it gave her a bird's-eye view for miles around. She hurried past the rundown lean-to that housed her own ancient tractor and her jet-black Holden Rodeo ute. Past the cattle yards and packing sheds, out the back gate. Her step grew light in anticipation of the trip.

Red Gums' rough airstrip ran down the middle of the property, dividing the young pecan orchards on the left from the mature olive groves flanking the river. Nina raised her hand, shielding her eyes from the sun's glare, relishing the shock of pleasure she always felt at the sight of Skyhawk, all hers now. The little Cessna gleamed white and tan in the afternoon sunshine.

Nina did a walk around, stroking the warm metal, admiring the custom, keen-eyed hawk design that ran the length of the striped fuselage. It was an old aircraft, a little rusty round the seams, with chipped paintwork. Tiny stress cracks showed in the wing fairings and tail cone, and she'd drilled them to stop them from worsening. It hadn't really worked, but little things like that didn't matter. What mattered was that Skyhawk unchained her from the ground, let her soar on real wings, made her an honorary bird. It was pure pleasure.

The engine muttered and coughed, then settled to its job. The propeller spun to life and Nina angled her nose into the breeze, as a boat might slant into a current. The aircraft powered up like a grounded eagle keen to be airborne, bouncing and hopping down the uneven runway until that glorious moment of lift-off.

Nina popped a mint in her mouth and settled in for the flight. She hadn't been up for a while. From the air, the extent of the drought was shockingly plain. The earth's living skin had peeled and cracked. Dry dams. Paddocks grazed so bare their fragile, black topsoil lay exposed and vulnerable. The once mighty Bunyip River snaked through the parched earth like a muddy drain. Even the trees that lined its banks looked brown and lifeless, their canopies choked with dust. The only contrast in this bleak landscape were the cotton fields, geometric shapes of vivid green, roughly following the river. Stealing its water, while the marshes and dry-land farmers died of thirst. Nina's throat tightened. Let it go, for goodness sake. This was meant to be fun. Tonight she'd connect with friends. She'd laugh and enjoy herself, safe from the loneliness that too often crept from the shadows at day's end.

On impulse, Nina banked and flew downstream. She swept over the junction where the Kingfisher met the Bunyip. No irrigators drained the wild Kingfisher River dry. No dams confined it. Faraway rains, high in its catchment, had been the saviour of this year's water-bird breeding season. Its course meandered through rugged grazing country and national parks, emerging to spill lifesaving water into the Bunyip basin, downstream from the cotton farms. The river broadened now, flanked by tracts of marsh and bushland — Billabong Bend.

Beneath her wheeled squadrons of pelicans and flocks of ibis. She flew lower. A startled white-bellied eagle took cover in a rare patch of weeping myall woodland. Lower again. Long-legged emus raced at breakneck speed through the swampy sedgeland. She could taste the vast, dry continent beneath her, hear the music of its river red gums, feel its clear, summer skies in her veins. Something prickled the back of her neck and a profound sense of excitement and joy coursed through her. She whooped out loud and dipped her wings in tribute to the wild wetlands below, all trace of depression banished. Now this, she reminded herself — this was living.

CHAPTER 2

Tonight was Nina's first school reunion and she didn't know quite what to expect. *A night of masquerade, mystery and romance* — that's how the ball had been promoted. In the town hall foyer she donned her peacock mask of feathers and rhinestones, while Kate struggled to fasten her own scarlet macaw headdress.

'Here,' said Nina. 'Let me.' She looped the elastic tight behind her friend's ears, and examined their images in the tall gilt mirror by the door. Katie had outdone herself. All those painstaking hours spent with coloured feathers, a bedazzler and a glue gun had well and truly paid off. Such lovely masks. How could a flimsy disguise make so much difference? They were both transformed, unrecognisable.

The electric blue gown that had seemed grand and overblown at Kate's house now looked stylish and sophisticated. It hung in rich, satin folds to the floor, emphasising Nina's height, hinting at the curves beneath. The beaded, strapless bodice exposed smooth, brown shoulders, the sweetheart neckline framed an actual cleavage, and the empire waist flattered her slim figure. She looked surprisingly sexy and wished Lockie was here to see it. Sometimes he treated her more like a friend than a girlfriend. There wouldn't be much chance of that if he could see her now. She stared at the mirror, trying to reconcile her elegant reflection with reality.

And she loved the mask. It hid her face, apart from her mouth and chin, affording her a delicious anonymity. Even her trademark auburn curls were out of sight, tamed in a smooth chignon.

Kate gave a spin, dissolving into a whirl of red chiffon. 'Nina, we look amazing!'

Nina took a final disbelieving look in the mirror. 'We do, don't we.' The band started up. 'Remember your promise,' said Nina. 'No bringing strangers home. I hate tiptoeing around your cottage in the morning.'

Kate grabbed her arm and whisked her through the door and into the throng. As she headed for the bar, Nina found her way blocked by a man dressed as a jester, wearing a full-face mask. He bowed and pulled her into a waltz. It was surreal to see only painted faces. No expressions to read, no smiles, no frowns – everybody hiding, herself included. Her partner's hands were smooth and white – not a farmer, this one. Reunion rules forbade using real names until midnight, although pseudonyms were encouraged. She admired his costume, wishing he would talk and maybe give himself away. 'These masks,' said Nina at last. 'They're a bit . . . freaky, don't you think?'

'Speak for yourself,' said her partner. 'Mine's a work of art.' He'd lowered his voice, but it wasn't enough to disguise the identity of her old schoolfriend. 'Dylan!'

He cackled like an evil clown. 'Let's get a drink.'

Nina took his hand and pulled him towards the bar. 'All set for your big trip?'

'*Sim, menina bonita,*' said Dylan, clicking his heels together and snapping invisible castanets. 'I'll be in Rio in time for Carnaval.'

'You'll be in your element,' she said, as they took two glasses of champagne to a quieter corner of the room. 'Your mask is a work of art, by the way.'

He cocked his bizarre head. The jester's garish, painted smile sent a sudden shiver up Nina's spine. 'This old thing? Why, this is nothing.

Wait till you see what I made for my guest. All that work and then he refuses to enter the costume competition.'

'Guest?' asked Nina. So, Dylan had brought a date? Her curiosity was piqued.

'There,' he said. 'Coming through that door.'

Nina froze. A tall, broad-shouldered man in a turquoise cape was striding towards them. He wore a kingfisher mask, all sharp jutting beak and sleek, dangerous lines. Dylan didn't introduce them. Instead he launched into an explanation of the making of the mask. 'It's papier-mâché decorated with gum leaves then painted blue, with white side stripes.' Dylan's voice rose an octave. He must have it bad for this guy. 'Then I glued on peacock feathers to imitate the plumage of an azure kingfisher. The leaves underneath support them and let them move.' As if to prove his point, a rotating fan ruffled the man's feathers in an eerily lifelike fashion. Nina feared he might fly away. 'I gave the beak a glossy, black top coat and added bronze accents at the base of each feather.' Dylan paused for breath. 'It adds a subtle richness, don't you think?'

Nina wasn't listening. Her breathing had slowed, become shallow. Her world had narrowed its focus to the figure before her. The kingfisher observed her with sharp, amber eyes, like he might impale her on his beak any second now. She looked down, grateful for the mask. But when she lifted her gaze it was as though he could see straight through her disguise, through her dress, as though she stood naked before him. The heat of a blush dampened her skin. Or was it that the room had become airless, or that her heart was for some reason refusing to beat?

Dylan tweaked a peacock feather on her own mask, and pointed to his friend. 'Birds of a feather.' Then he held the fabric of her gown against the turquoise cape and raised an eyebrow. 'A perfect match.' 'Kate did all this. I . . .' Nina's voice petered out as she lost her train of thought. The kingfisher was still watching her.

Dylan raised his arm and waved to a group of people by the bar. 'Must dash,' he said. 'Taking entries for the costume competition. I can't tempt you, no? I'll leave my two favourite chicks to get to know each other then.' There was something in Dylan's tone, like he knew a secret and she was supposed to guess it.

The man offered his arm. 'Would you like to dance?' His voice was smooth and sexy like dark chocolate, with the hint of a foreign intonation. A quiver of desire ran through her. His extended hand was sure, work-roughened and nut-brown. She took it in her own, struggling to still her trembling fingers.

He led her in a slow waltz. They moved as one. Nina shook her head to clear it, the feathers of her mask rustling softly. The arm around her was muscular, steady. Who on earth was he? Was he smiling beneath his mask? Was he good-looking? Why was her body responding to him? She was with Lockie. This man was gay and dating Dylan, one of her best friends. Talk about a dead-end attraction. 'Do I know you?' She asked.

'I don't know,' he said. 'Do you?'

The music stopped. Couples broke apart, new ones came together. The kingfisher still held her close.

Nina tried again. 'Did you go to St Patrick's?'

'No. I'm a blow-in.'

The band struck up *Rock The Casbah* by the Clash. He pulled her closer, spun her around the dance floor at such giddy speed they might have been flying. How she managed it in those heels was a miracle. Nina never wanted the music to stop, but stop it did, and she supposed she'd better return this gorgeous man to Dylan. Nina spotted him with Kate near the bar. She took her partner's hand to lead him from the dance floor. Blood pulsed in her fingertips, as if a magnet lay between the two of them. Did he feel it too?

Kate sized the kingfisher up with an approving flick of her head as he chatted to Dylan. Her macaw mask slipped sideways, but she didn't seem to notice. 'Who's that?' she whispered.

'He's Dylan's . . . friend.' Nina hoped she'd take the hint. It didn't work. Kate slunk closer to him.

'Come on, Princess Parrot,' said Nina. 'Let's get some food to line our stomachs. I have a feeling we'll need it.'

Dylan was chatting away to his date, but the kingfisher didn't seem to be listening. He seemed to have eyes only for her. Nina tossed her head and turned her back. She'd always had far too vivid an imagination.

The evening wore on. What a difference ten years made. Nina was in demand tonight, far more popular than she'd ever been in school. She danced a few dances. In spite of the masks she could pick out most people. Loud-mouthed Trevor Jackson, for instance, who'd grown so fat. Class comedian Bud Barker, whose jokes hadn't changed. She almost laughed when Shane Bond in his werewolf mask asked her to dance. She'd had a crush on him back then, and he'd never noticed. She might have been flattered, might have flung herself into the evening with gusto, if not for Dylan's mystery man. He was, unaccountably, a major distraction. And thinking about Lockie didn't seem to help.

Nina watched the kingfisher swirl a plump Catwoman around, and tried to figure out who she was. He sure knew how to move. The music ended and he left the dance floor. Nina grabbed a drink and followed him back to the corner where Kate and Dylan were scoffing champagne. She longed to hear his voice again, but was too tongue-tied to ask him a question. So instead she just tried not to stare as Kate and Dylan debated who had the worst costume. Nina feigned interest without much success.

'See Catwoman over there?' said Kate. 'That's Kathy Bell. She's pregnant. And there's Judy Cousins, our house captain.' Kate pointed to a short woman dressed like the Queen of Hearts.

'Remember how Judy said she'd never get married? She has three kids now.'

Really? So many of Nina's old classmates had settled down. What was the big attraction in having children? She didn't fit in here at all.

'I need a refill,' said Kate. She disappeared with the kingfisher to the bar.

'What's up with you?' Dylan asked her. 'Aren't you having fun?' Nina glanced at him sharply. His tone had been almost teasing.

'Tell me your friend's name.'

'No names yet,' said Dylan. 'It's the rules.'

'Stuff the stupid rules.' For some reason her emotions were very close to the surface. 'Just tell me.'

His mask seemed to smirk. 'Ricardo,' Dylan said at last, rolling his r's in a most impressive way. 'Ring any bells?'

What did he mean by that? She didn't know any Ricardos, but the name suited the man perfectly.

'This thing itches.' She scratched her ear. 'When can we take them off?'

'Midnight.'

Irritation surged through her. 'I can't wait that long.' She snatched off her mask as Kate arrived, hand in hand with a swaggering centurion. Nina couldn't place him. Where was Ricardo? Was that a flash of turquoise at the bar?

'Good idea,' said the soldier when he noticed her bare face. He removed his helmet. Bloody Geoff Baker. Whatever did Kate see in him? He still had a good body, true, but he'd been a self-absorbed egomaniac back in school, and from the look of him things hadn't changed. Did Kate intend to take him home with them, in spite of her promise? Nina squirmed at the thought of Geoff strutting around Kate's little cottage in the morning.

Then Ricardo was by her side again, casting all thought of Geoff from her mind. Nina wished that she hadn't taken off her mask. She seemed at a disadvantage, but why and in what way she wasn't sure. What did it matter if she was exposed?

'Charge your glasses,' said Dylan, as the countdown to midnight came over the sound system. 'Seven, six, five, four, three, two, one . . . Happy new year!'

Cheers and kisses and flying streamers. Nina held her breath as people's masks came off, her eyes trained on one person only, but Ricardo made no move to reveal himself.

Geoff and Kate were laughing and he was stroking her arm. Dylan removed his mask and gave them a disparaging look. 'Nina, darling, if you're ready to go home, you could come with us. Give these two lovebirds some space?'

Her head was swimming a little as she agreed. The large room felt airless, her skin clammy. The idea of going home with Ricardo, with or without Dylan, was irresistible. Nina had the strangest sense of something important ending, or beginning; she wasn't sure.

Nina grabbed her friend's hand and pulled her over to a seat in the corner. 'Is it okay with you, Katie, if I go home with Dylan tonight?'

'Sure,' said Kate, her face flushed. 'See you for breakfast?'

Nina stood up, staggering slightly, drunker than she'd imagined she was. Ricardo appeared at her side. 'You can take your mask off now,' she said, wanting to do it for him. But instead he extended a helping hand, gently grasping her upper arm, maintaining his grip even after she was solid on her feet. A charge passed between them. She sneaked a guilty glance at Dylan. Had he noticed? Would he mind? Lockie certainly would. She shook herself. What was she thinking?

They said goodbye to Kate, who barely seemed to notice, clinched tight as she was in a kiss with Geoff. Dylan led the way down the steps, across the road, along the street, around the corner to his car. Nina shivered, though the night was warm, perfumed with scented tree peonies blooming in the nearby park. She fell into the back seat. Ricardo sat in the front. Only then did he remove his mask, passing it back to her without turning around. She caught the scent of him as she laid it beside her on the seat. Nina could see the back of his head now, hair thick and dark like she'd imagined.

They took a meandering route on the short drive home, avoiding main roads and booze buses. The full moon kept pace in the window. Dylan chatted away about the costumes and complained about the people who hadn't made an effort. He gave them a comprehensive run-down on who'd broken up with who, who'd gone home with who, and why it would never work. Ricardo said nothing. Neither did Nina.

Dylan interrupted his prattle and parked the car. 'Well. We're here.'

Nina held her breath, not moving, as Ricardo unfolded himself from the front seat and stepped onto the footpath. A tall shape in the streetlight, hair gleaming blue-black, square shoulders blocking the moon. The need to properly see him overwhelmed her, made her dizzy. But when he came around to her door, reached for the handle, stooped to offer his arm, his features stayed in shadow. They walked side by side to the house, up the wooden steps to the verandah. She stumbled once, but he had her.

Dazzled moths fluttered in a bright halo cast by the porch light. At last. She turned to Ricardo and took a sharp inward breath. His dusky complexion wasn't just the result of long days outdoors. He was naturally olive-skinned, with a proud, broad forehead, narrowing to high cheekbones. Nose slightly aquiline. Prominent jaw shaded with stubble. His eyes were the colour of coffee beans and gleamed like dark mirrors. They shone with a recognition that reflected her own. She knew that face. She'd known it all her life.

CHAPTER 3

Ric. Ric Bonelli, the boy who'd grown up across the river. Once upon a time he'd been her best and closest friend. 'You.' She could barely believe the evidence of her eyes.

Ric bit his lip as though buying time to collect his thoughts. The gesture was heart-tearingly familiar. 'Nina . . .'

She didn't trust herself to speak, couldn't speak.

The door opened and Dylan appeared, sized them up. 'The penny finally dropped, did it?' He retreated into the house and Nina felt suddenly sober. Without thinking, she reached out to trace her finger down Ric's face. Her childhood sweetheart stood before her, but then again he didn't. Time had transformed him into this stunning stranger. Dylan reappeared, a bottle of champagne in hand. He popped the cork, making Nina jump. 'Come on, you two. There's more bubbly and I hate to drink alone.'

He ushered them into the lounge room. Nina didn't know where to sit, what to say, where to look. Ric's eyes were like searchlights. Dylan poured drinks and pushed a glass into her hand. She gulped it down all at once. He raised his eyebrows, refilled her glass and patted a cushion on the couch. 'Sit, Nina. This is going to be fun.'

'You're all grown up,' said Ric, staring.

Nina took another swig of Dutch courage. 'Back at the ball,' she said, 'I thought you and Dylan were an item.'

Ric said, 'Don't be stupid,' at the same time that Dylan rolled his eyes and said, 'Don't I wish.'

Ric laughed and flashed a boyish smile. For a moment he looked sixteen again. Nina searched around for something to say, anything that might bring some normality to the situation. 'I didn't know you two were friends.'

'Ric was the only kid at Drovers High who hated cricket as much as I did,' said Dylan. 'We were a natural fit.'

'I've never been much of a team player,' agreed Ric.

'No, you're more of a lone wolf,' said Dylan. 'But you stuck up for me back then, when nobody else did. Maybe because you copped a few names yourself. Problem was, you couldn't be there all the time.' He turned to Nina. 'One week in year nine, I came home from school with a bloody nose every single day. That's when Mum decided enough was enough. So she sent me to St Patrick's. Heaven compared to Drovers Central. Drama, music, a film appreciation society for the non-sporty kids. That's when Nina and I became mates, wasn't it, sweet?' Dylan put his arm around her. 'You should have seen Ric when I told him you'd be at the ball. He was desperate to go. I'd never have got him to wear that kingfisher mask and cape otherwise.'

'Shut up, Dylan.' Ric drained his glass.

Nina's heart jumped. So . . . Ric had gone tonight because of her? Her eyes held his. 'How long has it been?' she said. 'Fifteen years, maybe, since we were last down by the river?'

They'd started meeting when they were mere children. Secretly. Secretly, because their fathers had always been at odds. More than that – they'd detested each other. Sometimes Nina thought the only reason Dad had sold Red Gums was to get away from Max Bonelli. The hostility and bitterness between them had reached far and wide. As droughts had become more frequent and water issues more divisive, the men's enmity reflected people's fears. Locals had taken sides, irrigator against grazier, neighbour against neighbour. It had been like living in a war zone. Eventually Bianca, Max's patient wife, could bear it no longer. She left him, and returned to her family in Italy. The children went with her, including Ric. It had broken Nina's fourteen-year-old heart.

'Fifteen years,' agreed Ric. He looked perfect and all wrong at the same time. Time ticked by and the silence weighed heavy in the room. Dylan rolled his eyes. 'Aren't you going to tell her?'

'Tell me what?' Nina asked.

Ric shot him a furious look. Dylan heaved a big sigh and stood up. 'You know where the blankets are, Nina. The couch is quite comfy.' He collected the empty glasses. 'Goodnight, all. Have fun, but keep it down. My housemate's asleep.'

Nina felt dizzy-drunk again. She listened for the sound of Dylan's bedroom door closing. Ric was listening too, she could tell. There it was. Alone now, like in the old days down by the river. No, not like that. As children they'd known each other so well. They'd shared an easy intimacy. Now they didn't know each other at all.

'It was like you just dropped off the face of the earth,' she said. 'I thought maybe you'd had an accident. Maybe you were sick. Maybe you couldn't get to a phone, or you'd lost my number, or my address.' She swigged her drink. This was dredging up a host of hurtful memories she'd believed long-forgotten. Days spent locked away, doing nothing but wonder. Nights without sleeping, endlessly playing the *what if* game. Weeks of making excuses, blinding herself to reality. Months of fading hopes.

'I'm sorry.' He wet his lips.

'Damn it, Ric. Not a phone call? Not a text or an email or a letter?'

Ric looked at his shoes, broad neck bowed. A tendon stood out in sharp relief, and a pulse throbbed in his temple. She wanted to shake the silence out of him. 'At least tell me when you got back to Australia?'

It took him a long time to answer. 'Years ago,' he said at last. It wasn't the answer she'd expected or hoped for. Where had he been all this time?

Ric cleared his throat, still looking down. 'I wanted to come back to Drovers.' He laced his fingers together. 'But Dad was so angry.

Reckoned I'd taken Mum's side. And you know what your dad's like. He hates my guts.'

'Dad doesn't live at Red Gums any more. He runs the produce store in town now.'

Ric looked at her sideways, with a faint grin. 'Thanks for the tipoff.'

A tremor ran through her. God, he was handsome. 'So that's it?' she said. 'You didn't want to face your father or mine? It would have taken more than that to keep me away from you.'

'There was another reason.' Ric turned away, unwilling to meet her gaze. 'I heard you were with someone else.' The silence stretched for so long that Ric eventually filled it. 'So who runs Red Gums?'

'I do,' said Nina.

'What, by yourself?' He whistled through his teeth approvingly.

'Mum and Dad help out when they can, of course . . . and Lockie.'

'That'd be right,' said Ric with a soft snort. 'Bet it didn't take him long after I left.'

Something about his tone made her snap. 'You turn up out of the blue after fifteen years and now you're jealous?' Nina stood and paced the room, bristling with resentment, struggling for words. 'You meant everything to me back then,' she said, her voice rising. 'The most important person in my life, my mate, my best friend . . . my . . . How do you think I felt when you just disappeared? And now you say you've been back for years? Good grief, Ric. At least tell me what you've been doing all this time.'

A soft voice came from the hallway. 'Dad?'

Nina froze. A child stood there. A girl with large brown eyes and long dark hair, about nine years old.

The child took in the scene, sharp-eyed like a bird. She pointed at Nina. 'Who's she?'

'This is my friend, Nina,' said Ric. 'Ah . . . Nina, meet Sophie, my . . . my daughter.'

Nina blinked stupidly. Whatever was he talking about? 'It's late,' Ric said to the girl. 'You should be in bed.'

Sophie stared at Nina, like she was trying to make up her mind about something. 'That's a pretty dress,' she said. 'You look like a princess.'

'Thank you.' Nina forced a smile, her words little more than a stammer. She ran a hand over her hair, and her stomach lurched alarmingly.

The girl slipped from the hall into the lounge, sat down on the couch and tucked skinny knees beneath her pony-print nightie. 'I can't sleep,' she said. 'There's a ghost in my room.'

Nina nervously smoothed her gown. The room spun slowly. She felt as breathless as she'd been in the ballroom, but for a very different reason. She was drained, drained and sick. 'I'd better go.' She looked around for her bag.

Ric stood and laid a concerned hand on her arm. 'We've all been drinking. How will you get to Kate's?'

'I'll walk.' The thought of traipsing miles in the dark, wearing high heels and a ball gown, wasn't exactly appealing, but it was better than the alternative.

'Are you leaving?' asked Sophie. 'Don't you like it here?'

Nina ignored her and checked that her phone was in her bag. She could feel the girl's eyes upon her.

'I don't like it here either,' said Sophie. 'I hate it.'

'Go to bed, Sophie.' Ric rubbed the back of his neck. 'It's one o'clock in the morning.'

'I can't.' Sophie's eyes flashed before brimming with silent tears. 'I told you, there's a ghost.'

Ric clasped his hands behind his head. Sophie hugged her knees, and looked so small and afraid that Nina stopped fumbling with her bag. 'Where's her mother?'

Ric looked as lost as Sophie. He headed for the kitchen, beckoning Nina to follow. She stood for a moment, bag still in hand before letting it slip to the floor and going after him. 'Rachael's in a psychiatric clinic,' he said. 'With depression. Her doctor got in touch and asked me to take Sophie for the holidays.'

'Her doctor,' said Nina, trying to put the pieces together. 'You two aren't together?'

He shook his head. 'The thing with Rachael didn't last long. We lost touch. She never told me about Sophie.' He took a breath. 'Nina—'

She cut in sharply. 'When did you find out about her?'

'About a month ago.'

'Crikey, Ric. That's some story.'

'I'm going home to Donnalee,' he said. 'To sort things out with Dad and let him meet Sophie.'

'You're going home to introduce your daughter to your father.' Nina still couldn't make sense of it. Tiredness washed over her; the taste of champagne had turned sour.

'I never —' Ric began.

The girl appeared at the door, arms wrapped tightly around her. 'Your dad's going to take you back to bed,' said Nina. 'He's very good at scaring away ghosts.'

Sophie pursed her lips in doubt. 'Really? Will he stay as long as I want? Will you be here too, when I wake up?'

Nina rubbed her eyes. As betrayed as she felt, it wasn't the girl's fault. And why should she run away, when Ric was the one at fault? 'Yes and yes,' she told Sophie.

'Will you have breakfast with me?'

'I'm going to my friend's.'

Ric's eyes locked onto Nina's. 'I could make you breakfast.'

'Yes,' said Sophie. 'Ric, I mean Dad, makes really good pancakes.'

'I'm sorry, I can't.' Nina looked at him squarely. 'I just can't.'

'Nina . . .' His eyes were pleading. 'There's still more to talk about.' When she didn't answer he turned to Sophie. 'Now' – he took his daughter's hand; she let him for a moment then shook him away – 'how about we go do some ghost-busting?'

Nina gave a tight smile. 'Goodnight, Sophie.' Ric and his daughter disappeared down the hall.

Nina went to the bathroom, changed into the oversized T-shirt Dylan had left out for her, and collapsed on the couch, mind abuzz with all that had happened. Too many surprises for one evening. Too many questions still unanswered. Ric here, and with a daughter. It was a kick in the guts, in spite of the passage of time, in spite of what she and Lockie had now. Ric's return had leapfrogged her back over the intervening years. It had opened up an old wound, as raw and painful as the day he'd left. She tried to let it go, but emotion trumped reason.

Nina wiped her face and nose with the bottom of Dylan's T-shirt. Was that a footstep in the hall? She held her breath, sensing Ric's presence in the darkened doorway. So close. Part of her wanted to hear him out, hear him justify his disloyalty. Part of her would slap him if he tried. She waited, a ball of tension in the gloom, but he didn't appear. And despite exhaustion and all the booze, sleep was a long time coming.

CHAPTER 4

Nina woke to the sound of a kettle whistling in the kitchen, groggy and unsure of how to place herself in the new day. The strange events of the previous night seemed more like dreams than reality. Muted voices floated through the open door. There was Dylan, and a woman's voice – Ally, she guessed, his housemate. She strained to hear more voices, but failed. Maybe she really had dreamed the whole thing.

Dylan appeared by her side, dressed in board shorts and a Mambo singlet. He carried two mugs of tea. 'Shove over,' he said, perching beside her on the couch while Nina sat up and took the tea with faintly trembling fingers. The sweet warm liquid soothed her parched throat and revitalised her dehydrated body.

'Is he . . .? Are they . . .?' She gestured toward the kitchen.

'They sure are in there. Large as life, eating breakfast.' Dylan sipped his tea.

'I can't believe it.' She shook her head, causing her tangled auburn curls to fall across her face. 'Ric back . . . and with a daughter? You should have told me.'

'Come on,' said Dylan. 'I wouldn't have missed the look on your face last night for a million bucks.' But his brilliant blue eyes were filled with concern.

'You owe me one, mate.' Nina gave him a little kick. 'Drive me to Katie's, right now.'

'No breakfast?'

'No breakfast. And hurry, will you? There's someone I need to see.' He raised questioning brows and she kicked him again. 'As if I'd tell you anything after last night.'

'All right, all right.' Dylan studied her face. She concentrated on staying neutral, on keeping her emotions in check. He touched her arm briefly then disappeared into the kitchen. Nina closed her eyes and Ric's handsome face swam into view. Her brain whirled with conflicting emotions. Hope and disillusion, joy and sadness – love clouded with anger and a deep sense of betrayal.

She didn't want to think about how her body had disobeyed her. The way it thrilled to him, flushed for him. She didn't want to think about the small child sitting in the next room. Nina got off the couch, dressed only in the over-size T-shirt and her undies, and retrieved her bag and gown. She checked her phone. Two texts from Lockie. She dropped the phone back into her bag and peered through the kitchen door. Sophie was looking straight at her as if she'd expected her to appear right at that moment.

'Look,' she said. 'Dad made breakfast.'

Then Ric saw her too, and Nina wished she was dressed in something more than a T-shirt. 'I can't stay, I'm sorry.' Sophie's hopeful expression collapsed and she turned her attention to the pancakes on the table in front of her. Ric started to stand, but Nina waved him back down. 'Goodbye, Ric. And it was nice to meet you, Sophie.'

Dylan came in, jangling his keys. He took in the scene and shot her an enquiring look. 'Why don't you stay for breakfast, Nina?'

She was about to refuse when Sophie looked up. Something in the girl's reproachful brown eyes stopped her. 'I suppose I could stay for a little while.'

Dylan ducked into the hall while Ric pulled out a chair for her. 'I'll make you a coffee,' he said.

She advanced slowly, conscious of her bare legs, and took a seat.

'Where are you going after breakfast?' asked Sophie.

'To visit a friend, and then home.' Nina took a mouthful of pancake. Her mouth was too dry to swallow, and she was getting a headache.

'Where's home?' asked Sophie. Why did the girl have to ask so many questions?

'Nina lives just across the river from your grandfather,' said Ric. 'We're going to be neighbours.'

Sophie looked suspiciously at her father, and then back at Nina. 'Is that true?'

'Well, yes. I suppose so.'

'Do you have a farm too?'

'Yes,' said Nina.

'Are there animals?'

'Yes.'

'What sort?'

'Cows and birds, a dog. Horses.'

'Horses?' Sophie's face flushed with delight. 'Can I see them?'

The girl looked so hopeful that Nina nodded before properly thinking it through. She didn't miss the spark of pleasure in Ric's eyes. Her headache was growing. She took a last swig of coffee as Dylan came in with her bag and the blue gown draped across his arm. Nina pushed back her chair. 'I have to go.' She couldn't look at Ric, but felt his eyes on her as she followed Dylan to the door. Outside she could breathe again. The air was warm and perfumed and it felt good, so very good on her skin.

Pemberley House was a rambling, brick building that had once been a priory. Thirsty-looking roses, blooms spent, grew from two gigantic urns flanking the front door. Nina – now wearing her normal clothes, rescued from Kate's – signed in and headed for the south wing. She passed residents aimlessly wandering about, who looked expectantly at her as she approached. Past frazzled-looking nurses in charge of stainless steel trolleys, hurrying who knew where. Past a pair of bored teenagers staring at their phones in a hallway, until she came to the right room.

Eva Langley sat at a small table by the window. It was apparent, even when seated, that she was a tall woman. And despite her age and frailty, she retained a good degree of the stately elegance that had always set her apart. An aquamarine rug featuring statuesque cranes covered the floor, and a gallery of photographs lined the walls: snapshots of the homestead at Billabong Bend in its heyday; of people and horses and river scenes; of homes and house boats. Family portraits. Snapshots of a full vibrant life, well lived. Nina studied the old woman for a moment. Sunshine streaming through the glass bled the colour from her face, making her appear paler than usual. 'Knock, knock?' Nina rapped at the open door.

'Nina.' Eva looked up with a gracious smile. 'How lovely.'

'Happy new year,' said Nina. 'This is for you.' She placed the gift bag of liquorice allsorts beside the water jug on the table. Eva pressed her palms together and her blue eyes lit up. 'Ooh, such a treat.'

Nina sat on the bed. 'How are you . . . Eva?' She'd almost called her Mrs Langley, a hangover from childhood.

'Not too bad, dear. Not too bad.' Eva poured a glass of water with an unsteady hand. 'More importantly, how are things at Billabong? I never get any news from James.'

That's because your son James couldn't care less about Billabong, thought Nina. Or you. He's just waiting for you to die so he can sell the place.

'I brought you some pictures.'

Eva put on her glasses and examined the photos that Nina had taken the day before. The reach at Billabong Bend, the jetty, and a photo of the canoe tree that she'd put in a frame. The old lady sighed and smiled. 'Remember when you used to come visit me at Billabong, all by yourself, in that little boat? I'd show you where the brolgas danced, and where the little snake-necked turtles were hatching. Such happy days.'

'Of course I remember.' When Nina was a child, everyone took injured and orphaned birds to Billabong Bend. Eva had been a miracle worker, healing and restoring all sorts of waterbirds to the wild. A friendship had quickly formed between young Nina and Eva, who'd loved to pass on her knowledge of the wetlands to the eager child. It had been a magical time. Nina looked out the window to the withered garden and busy road beyond. No wonder Eva lived in the past.

'I hate this place,' said Eva, with sudden urgency. 'I'm not dead yet, but in here I might as well be. How long, do you think, before I'll go back to Billabong?' She picked up the photographs again and began looking through them. Minutes passed. It was as though she'd forgotten all about Nina's presence.

'Eva?'

Eva started, confusion clouding her features. 'This is awful.' There was a quiver in her voice. She held up a photo in her papery hand. 'Somebody must fix the jetty. And all this water hyacinth. Somebody must clear out those dreadful weeds.'

Somebody indeed. 'I could do it,' said Nina. 'Eva, why don't you sell Billabong to me, like we talked about? You know how much I love that place. I love it just like you do.'

'Don't talk nonsense, child. Where would I live?'

Normally Nina didn't have the heart to press her, but with each passing month the urgency of her mission to buy Billabong grew. Threats were mounting fast. The terrible drought. The erosion and weeds and feral animals. Hunters and irrigators and land clearers. The wetlands were copping it from all directions, and without an ally they didn't stand a chance. On top of that Eva's health was failing, a series of small strokes stealing her strength. Sometimes she was confused and didn't remember Nina's visits. Nina had to make Eva understand before it was too late.

'If you went home, you'd live at Billabong, of course,' said Nina. 'Selling to me wouldn't change that. But it would let me protect the property.'

'Protect it from what, dear?' Eva looked puzzled. She lifted the glass of water to her lips and sipped, dribbling a few drops on her blouse. 'You were always such a worrier, Nina. I'll sort everything out when I go home.'

It was no use. How could Nina explain to Eva that she was never going home? That when she died, her precious James would auction Billabong to the highest bidder? Where would Nina find the words? Instead she sat for a while, listening to Eva recount stories from the old days, until the clock on the wall told her it was time to go.

'Goodbye.' She kissed Eva's cheek. 'I'll see you again in two weeks.'

'Yes, dear.' Eva clasped her hand. 'I do look forward to your visits.'

'Me too,' sang out Nina as she slipped away. Tears pricked at her eyes. There had to be a way to convince Eva that her beautiful Billabong Bend was in peril. There just had to.

'Well, that's everything.' Nina tossed her bag onto the back seat of Kate's old Corolla, and checked the time. It was later than she thought. The dissection of their respective evenings over a late brunch had been a fascinating and protracted affair.

Kate's phone rang. 'For you.' She arched her eyebrows and handed it over. 'I think it's Ric.'

Nina frowned. 'Hello?'

'It's me, Ric,' he said. 'Dylan gave me Kate's number . . . He wouldn't give me yours.'

Clever Dylan. 'What is it?'

'The transmission's packed up in my ute . . .'

'And?'

'And I was wondering . . . could you give me and Sophie a lift to Drovers Flat? I'll pay for the petrol.' She didn't answer, her mind a kaleidoscope of competing emotions. 'Please, Nina. Sophie's been through a lot, and Dylan's house is no place for a kid. I just want to get her home to Donnalee, get her settled.'

'Okay,' said Nina. 'Meet me at the airport turn-off in twenty minutes.'

'The airport?'

'Don't keep me waiting.'

. . .

'Cool . . .' Sophie eyes shone as Nina pointed out the little Skyhawk, waiting patiently in its tie-down spot. 'I've never been in a plane before.'

'You're kidding, right?' Ric flashed Nina a nervous smile. In daylight, his movie-star good looks were even more impressive.

'Why would I be kidding?' Nina commenced her pre-flight walk-around, checked the fuel and oil levels. 'Take it or leave it.'

'Dad,' said Sophie. 'What's wrong?'

'Yes,' said Nina. 'What's wrong?'

'Nothing,' said Ric. 'Nothing at all.' But the doubt on his face belied his words. He ran his hand along the Skyhawk's pitted fuselage. 'How old is this plane?'

'It's not polite to ask a lady's age,' said Nina. 'Let's just say she's older than me.' She hauled the door open. 'It's a bit stiff.' Ric was looking over her shoulder, decidedly unimpressed. She swung the door on its hinges several times and it creaked alarmingly. 'Could use some oil.'

Sophie was clearly itching to get aboard. 'Come on, Sophie,' said Nina. 'Climb in.' The child sprang up and settled herself in a back seat. Nina smiled and showed her how to put on her seat belt. 'Is that all you've got?' asked Nina. 'That little backpack?'

'Dad left my suitcase in his car at the garage and there wasn't time to go back for it.'

Nina took in the girl's faded T-shirt and too-big shorts. Her cheap thongs. 'Tough break,' she said, stowing the bag.

'Don't worry, they'll send it on,' said Ric. He was pacing the concrete, as if wrestling with his decision.

'Are you coming or not?' asked Nina.

'Dad, get in.'

At last he climbed inside.

'Can you just pull that bit of loose carpet flat?' asked Nina. 'That's better. It rides up sometimes and gets in the way of the pedals.' Ric went a little pale, in spite of his dark complexion.

'Are you ready, Sophie?' asked Nina, as they roared up the runway.

'I can smell fuel.' Ric shifted his long legs.

'Don't worry.' Nina set her flaps. 'That's normal.'

Sophie squealed with excitement as the nose lifted and the plane took off. Nina glanced back. The girl's face was pressed hard against the window. Her first flight. What a thrill this would be for her; so new, so exciting, such an adventure. Ric cleared his throat, and she caught a glimpse of his profile, both strange and familiar. She focused on the windshield, but could still see his face. The way he looked when she first saw him. His expression when Sophie came into the lounge room. The glance at her bare legs that he'd tried to hide, and how it had made her feel. She tried to imagine Lockie's face instead, and failed.

CHAPTER 5

Rick was a bundle of nerves as they drove over the old bridge and turned into the gates at Donnalee station. He swung his bag from the back of Nina's ute and gazed around the yard of his childhood home. Here he was, back in the landscape of his past. A fierce north wind whipped his cheek and caused a line of blue shirts on the clothesline to dance and swing.

'I'd better get going.' Nina started the ute as a man emerged from the house.

'When can I come to see the horses?' asked Sophie.

'Get your dad to give me a ring.' The ute began to inch away from them.

Ric swallowed and nodded his thanks, tongue paralysed. He hadn't seen his father for fifteen years, and this meeting would not be an easy one. Dad had a temper, and had been tough on Ric and his sisters growing up. But he'd also been loving at times, and fiercely proud of them all.

Max Bonelli adhered to an old-fashioned school of thought, one where his position as head of the family had defined him as a man. He'd measured his worth by how well he could provide for his wife and kids, and on that score he'd never failed them. Then Mum had left. They all had. What would that have been like for his father? To have his family, his identity, torn away from him like that?

Ric stared at the figure on the porch and touched the shoulder of the slight girl beside him. The prospect of being a father himself, of having responsibility for this little person, was daunting. So was the idea of living with his own father for the month of Sophie's holidays. What would it be like? What might he and Sophie be walking into? The only thing he was sure of was that he wouldn't be taking any parenting tips from Max.

Sophie jammed her hands into her pockets and squinted into the baking, afternoon sunshine. He heaved a sigh. How hard must this be for her? Hard for him, too. Ric wanted to turn around and go home, wherever that was.

Nina's car had retreated in a cloud of dust. It rattled over the grid, onto the road and over the rickety bridge back to her side of the river. Max Bonelli, his father, stepped off the porch and advanced with arms outstretched. 'Ricardo.' His voice was thick with emotion. 'Happy new year. And you too, little Sophia. Welcome, welcome.'

Ric regarded his father with undisguised curiosity, amazed at how little he'd changed. Still a big man. Tall and broad-shouldered, with the body of a bull in his prime. The power and drive of him remained on full show. Grey peppered his heavy eyebrows and thick hair. Extra creases lined his weathered face, but on the whole he was as Ric remembered.

Sophie endured Max's clumsy hug. 'Sophie,' said Ric. 'This is your grandfather.'

'Poppi, please,' said Max. 'Call me Poppi.' He took Sophie's backpack and led them up the cracked concrete path. The house, framed by sunburnt camellias and a few wilting bush roses, had changed more than his father. No sign of the beautiful flower garden that Ric remembered so well. His mother, tending to each exotic bloom like it was one of a kind. His father, labouring in high summer to water it by hand. The two of them taking cuttings, laughing and arguing and working together. Their shared passion for that garden had brought out the best in them both, and now it had vanished along with their love. The only green things left were the coffee plants, growing in a tall straggly hedge along the fence. A sudden sadness came over Ric. He shrugged his shoulders as if that might cast off the gloom.

Sophie stopped and turned around. 'Where are all the animals?' She stared at him accusingly. 'You said this was a farm. I don't see any animals.'

'Donnalee is a cotton farm,' said Max, looking askance at her crest-fallen face. 'What about chickens? I have chickens. You like fat chickens?' She brightened and his broad face cracked into a grin. 'Come with me.' He put her bag down on the path and beckoned. 'And cows,' said Max, clearly delighted that he'd come up with another animal. 'I have cows too. Later, we'll see my cows.' The girl followed him around the side of the house. Ric retrieved her backpack and went on inside. So far, so good.

After dinner, he sat drinking beer with Max out on the porch, while Sophie watched television. The wind had weakened to a hot gusty breeze. Ric watched a blood-red sun sink towards the horizon. Strange, embarrassing even, to be alone with his father after all this time. He didn't know what to say. 'You live here by yourself?' he managed at last. Max nodded. 'You get lonely?'

Max stood and took a tin down from a splintered shelf. A cigar box. Ric had forgotten so much about his father. 'I have good friends,' Max said. 'Plenty of good friends along the river.' He selected a cigar and toyed with it, the way he used to when he was thinking. 'Nobody to stop me smoking in the house any more, but I still can't bring myself to do it'. He smiled to himself. 'There was a woman, after your mother left. Rosa. A good woman.'

He offered the tin. Ric shook his head. 'What happened?'

'After ten years, she tells me that she's sick and tired of playing second fiddle to a ghost. Accused me of never loving her like I loved your mother.' He grinned. 'She was right, bless her.' He snapped the cigar seal with his thumb. 'And you, Ricardo? The ladies, they like you pretty good, eh?'

'I don't know.' He looked away.

'Course they do.' Max chuckled. 'A handsome kid like you? You got that kind of wild look they go for.'

'I'm not a kid, Dad.' He kicked at the verandah post. 'I'm thirty years old. I've got my own kid now.'

Max's smile died and he used his teeth to bite off the cigar tip. 'Cramps your style, does she? There's no pride in siring a child, Ricardo, and that's all that you did.' He lit a match. 'What sort of man doesn't even know he has a daughter?'

There it was, what he'd been dreading. The meanness. Max hadn't changed. Ric frowned. 'What sort of man,' he said, jaw tensed, 'drives away his own wife and children?'

His father blew out the match. 'You want to hurt me,' he said. 'You want to fight. First time we sit and talk since you're sixteen years old, and you want to fight.'

'I didn't start it, Dad.' Ric shook his head. 'and I don't want to finish it either, but I will if I have to. I'll take Sophie and walk right out of here.' A new match flared in his father's hand. Ric finished his beer and got to his feet. 'It's up to you.'

Sophie appeared on the porch, quiet as a ghost, startling them. 'There's a movie on about a horse.'

'You like horses?' said Max.

Her eyes lit up. 'It's about two boys who are given a beautiful white horse by their gypsy grandfather. I think it might be a magic horse. It gets sold by a bad man and the boys are trying to rescue it.' She stopped like she expected them to say something. Her next words were a long time coming. 'Don't you have any horses, Poppi?'

'I'm sorry, Sophia. No horses.'

The girl ran back inside. 'Her name's Sophie,' said Ric. 'Sophie, not Sophia.'

'Sophie,' said Max. 'Sophie, of course.' He finally lit his cigar, rotating it slightly to ensure an even burn. 'Sit down, Ricardo,' he said at last. 'No more talk of women, eh? Agreed?'

A teasing breeze blew the tobacco smoke into Ric's face, a breeze that blew without cooling. He inhaled the acrid aroma, so evocative of childhood. This was his father and he was right. After all this time they had better things to do than argue. 'I'm getting another beer,' said Ric. 'Want one?'

Max breathed an audible sigh of relief from behind a puff of smoke. 'Yes, I want one. Of course I want one. Then we'll talk cotton or weather or anything you want. I step out of line, just clout me over the head, okay?'

'Okay,' said Ric. 'Let's shake on that.' Max grasped the extended hand with both of his own. His grip, tight and eager, said more than words.

'Just so we understand each other,' said Ric, 'the topic of football is also out of bounds. Women and football.' Max nodded. 'Then we should get along just fine.' Ric crushed his empty can in one hand. 'I'll go get those beers.'

Max settled his big frame back in the chair. Ric went to the kitchen, astonished by what had just happened. The ground rules had changed. He'd changed them. An echo of his father came to him, his voice like thunder. *What sort of a half-arsed job is that? Do it again, Ricardo. And remember, if I tell you to jump, you jump. Now get back out there.* He shook off the memory.

Ric cracked open a new beer and took a swig. A few weeks ago he'd been at the end of his tether. What was he supposed to do with a surprise daughter? What did he know about kids? Going home to face his father had been a last resort. But now, with room to breathe, with the beautiful Nina living across the river and with Donnalee's broad green acres stretching away to the horizon — now he knew he'd made the right choice.

CHAPTER 6

Nina stood statue-still, looking across to the north side of the river. There — an inquisitive head, staring back. In one swift motion she raised her rifle, took aim and fired. The fox dropped at the base of the red gum. 'Go,' said Nina. Jinx, who'd been waiting by her side, trembling with anticipation, launched himself into the water. He reached the opposite bank, dragged the body from beneath the twisted trunk, and started back. The tree's gnarled old roots, once submerged, now lay naked and exposed, like the clawed fingers of an ancient hand. The soil of the eroded riverbank had long ago slipped from its grasp.

Heartbreaking to see scores of the iconic river red gums, some centuries old, dying along the Bunyip. It was the same all over the Murray-Darling basin. Frightening stories abounded – that Lachlan River swamp had lost most of its trees, that flows to the Booligal marshes had halved. 'Those wetlands are like graveyards,' a neighbour had told her. 'The waterbird breeding colonies all gone.'

Jinx burst proudly from the water in a rainbow of spray. Nina crouched to examine his prize, noting with satisfaction the clean head shot. A big dog fox in the prime of life. A beautiful creature. She hated shooting anything, but foxes wreaked havoc among the small animals and ground-nesting birds along the river. Nina stood and scanned the north bank. There could well be a den hidden in those tree roots. She'd better talk to Ric.

Ric. The man was a constant distraction. She'd sit out on the verandah at night, watching the lights in the window at Donnalee homestead. And despite her best intentions, she'd imagine what he might be doing. Watching television, playing cards, laughing with his daughter? When the lights went out, she'd imagine him in bed, whispering to a lover on the phone, or talking to Sophie's mother . . . reconnecting. That's when it would hit her – an irrational wave of misery and anger that kept sleep at bay for hours. When Ric had rung this morning to ask if Sophie could visit the horses, it was almost a relief. Seeing the man might help get him out of her system. She owed it to herself – and to Lockie. Pity he'd been so busy lately. If he was around a bit more, maybe she'd stop thinking about Ric.

Nina took a final look around the sandy corner where she and Ric used to meet as children. The wide sweep of water, dappled with sunshine and shade. The twisted trees bowing to their reflections. Despite the dwindling flows, this place retained more than a hint of magic. Nina threw sticks for Jinx as she walked back to the house. What would Dad think of her inviting a Bonelli to Red Gums? He'd be pretty mad, she imagined, even after all these years.

Nina didn't know how or why the war between Max and her father had begun. No point asking Dad. She'd tried that. When she was little, he used to growl about Max being a no-good wog. She had no idea what a wog was back then, but she'd guessed from her father's tone of voice that it was something horrid.

Later she'd befriended Ric's sister, Nadia, a classmate at Drovers Central School. She'd made the mistake of asking to go to her birthday party. 'Nadia's dad is cooking pizzas in an outside mud oven,' she'd said. 'You get to put on your own toppings. And there'll be a piñata full of lollies. We're going to play bocce. It's like lawn bowls, but the balls are steel or something. You play in the dirt!'

Mum had frowned, looking past Nina to where her father stood listening in the doorway, his expression grim. She was sent to her room, and had lain on her bed, listening to the shouting in the kitchen. She never went back to school in Drovers Flat. After two days at home, she was sent to board at St Patrick's in Moree. Nina had learned the hard way that the Bonellis were out of bounds, and that she must never, ever tell anyone about her secret friendship with Ric.

It had started when she was nine years old. One summer morning she'd gone down to the river to catch tadpoles. Her dog, Buddy, had been chasing moor hens. On that particular day he'd mistaken a spreading expanse of green duckweed for dry land. Momentum took the little dog far out of his depth before he realised his mistake. 'Buddy!' she screamed, as the pup's flailing served only to take him further from the bank. 'Help!' She waded in, tearing her bare legs on sticks, slipping and sliding in the sucking mud. She called out again but the house was too far away. Nobody could hear her. Launching herself into the water's cold bite, she started after Buddy. Then Nina was struggling too, her foot somehow snagged, her body tugged by the current so she couldn't reach down to free herself. 'Help!' she yelled again, swallowing water.

And then there he was, right in front of her. A brown-skinned boy. He seemed to spring from the river itself, rising from the dark waters, lifting her sodden, spluttering pup aloft. 'Grab on,' he said. She grasped his shirt with one hand, gave an almighty kick and freed her trapped foot.

She didn't know quite how he managed it. With Buddy slung somehow around his neck and with Nina gasping for breath, dragging him down, Ric struck out for the bank in a one-armed, rhythmic crawl. The river held onto them, insistent, urging them downstream, but Ric doggedly held his course. He swam with steady determination, legs scissoring, slicing through the flow until they reached calmer, shallower water, until Nina's toes touched solid ground.

She stumbled ashore, cuddling Buddy tight, then looked around. They stood on a clean sandy bend, bordered by smooth rocks. Piles of driftwood lay about, bleached by the sun and carved into strange water-worn shapes. 'You're Ric, aren't you?' she said. 'Nadia's brother. I'm Nina.'

The boy smiled. 'I know who you are.'

'Look,' she said, 'there's a dragon.' Buddy wriggled free of her bear hug, and she picked up the dragon-shaped piece of driftwood to show Ric.

'And here's a bird,' he said, joining in the game.

Later they flung themselves down on the hot sand, surrounded by a gallery of natural sculptures, admiring their collection. "Are you a wog?' she asked. Ric nodded. 'Did you save Buddy because you like him?' Ric nodded again. 'Did you save me because you like me?'

Ric took a long time to answer. He stripped a reed and slipped it between his teeth. He patted Buddy. He doodled a picture in the sand. 'Guess so,' he said at last, with a grin.

'I'd better go.' She brushed mud and sand from herself.

'Me to.' He stood up, then bent down again and picked something up, something that flashed blue in the sun. 'For you.'

Nina examined his offering. A shining kingfisher feather. 'Thanks.'

He grinned again, then dived into the water, swimming straight as an arrow back to his own side of the river. Nina still had that feather. Year after year, she and Ric had continued to meet at the little sandy beach, sharing their secrets, their dreams, their fears.

As they grew older, the intensity of their forbidden friendship grew. They even chanced meetings in town when she was home on holidays. When she was thirteen she made them matching friendship bracelets from coloured string. 'You have to make a wish,' she said, as she tied the band to his wrist. 'Wear it until it comes off by itself. That's when your wish will come true.' She offered her arm. 'Here, tie mine on.' Ric had solemnly done the honours, but months later when her bracelet caught on a fence and snapped, the wish hadn't worked. Her father and Max Bonelli had not become friends.

When Nina was fourteen, Ric gave her a ring on the last day of summer holidays. 'It's a promise ring.' He slipped it on her finger. '*Cara mia.*' She'd never heard him speak Italian. He held out his own hand to display a matching silver band, and they'd shared their first tentative kiss.

That night, back at boarding school, when she took off the ring to examine it, she found the word *Forever* imprinted on her finger. Hidden letters inside the simple band had left a temporary impression on her skin. She wore that ring with such pride, thrilled with the impassioned secret that lay inside. Two weeks later, Ric had vanished from her life.

Nina braced against the old pain and left the sandy bank. 'Come on, Jinx,' she said. 'We don't want to be late for our visitors.'

Nina studied the girl curiously, feeling a little jealous — both of her and of her mother. She almost hoped for some reason to dislike the child. It would make things so much easier. Sophie oohed and aahed over the ducklings. She looked like she could use a good feed. Wisps of dark, unruly hair fell across her pale cheek. She must have her mother's complexion. The girl wore a baggy red T-shirt, faded to pink, and blue nylon parachute pants. It looked like she'd been dressed in an op shop. Nina searched her face for traces of Ric. The nose, perhaps, and the determined chin.

Sophie reached out a skinny arm. 'They're so cute. Dad, could we get some ducks?'

'Maybe,' he said.

Nina's mouth narrowed to a tight line. Any duck in the care of Max Bonelli would sooner or later end up on the menu. Even wild ducks weren't safe. That man regarded Billabong Bend as his own personal larder.

'Can we get some just like these?' asked the girl.

'No,' said Nina. 'Not like these. I don't know what sort of ducks these babies are yet, but they're not domestic ducks. They're wild — from the wetlands further down the river. Their mother was shot.'

Sophie turned to her with a horrified expression. 'That's awful,' she said. 'How could anybody do that?'

'How indeed?' said Nina. 'Would you like to hold one? Here, put both hands together like this, so you don't drop it.'

She placed a duckling into the child's cupped hands. 'Dad, look!' Sophie showed the duckling to Ric, who made admiring noises. 'This baby duck is the most beautiful thing I've ever seen in the whole world.'

Nina smiled. 'We'd better put this little one back with its friends.' Sophie bent down and released the duckling. When she stood up, Jinx nosed his way into her arms. 'You're the most beautiful thing in the world too.'

'How do you like living at Donnalee?' Nina asked.

Sophie gave her a guarded, guilty look and then glanced at Ric. 'It's all right, I suppose.' She hugged the dog tighter. 'I miss my mum, and it's hard getting used to a dad. I've never had one before.' Ric's jaw stiffened.

'New places always take some getting used to,' said Nina. 'Come on, there are more ducks, and some other birds as well.' She picked up the bucket of pellets and led her visitors down the hill. 'Mind you don't leave the gate open.'

Ric forged on ahead. He was wearing beat-up old jeans and a T-shirt like the boy she'd once known. But unlike that old Ric, his expression was closed to her. She felt the darkness of his mood in the bright sunshine. For a moment she wanted to ask him what was wrong, then reminded herself she didn't care. She was showing Sophie the animals, and that was all.

Six-foot fences surrounded the small paddock above the river. In the middle was a reedy dam with an artificial floating island made from planks and tyres. 'My own mini-wetlands,' said Nina. 'A place where injured birds can mend. That little windmill keeps it full.'

'There was a movie on television yesterday,' said Sophie, 'about a boy who looked after an injured pelican called Mr Percival. Do you remember, Dad?'

'Sorry, Soph,' he said. 'I wasn't paying attention.'

A shadow of disappointment crossed her face. 'It was in a beautiful place like this, except with a beach as well.'

'The Coorong,' said Nina. '*Storm Boy*.'

'That's it,' said Sophie. 'A hunter shot the pelican in the end, just for no reason. Even though the boy loved it. Even though it was his only friend. I cried.' She looked like tears weren't far away again. 'Do hunters really shoot beautiful birds like Mr Percival? Just for no reason.'

'I'm afraid they do,' Nina said. 'All the time. But don't worry. These birds are safe here. And I'll let you into a secret – when I watched *Storm Boy*, I cried too.'

A variety of ducks swam in the water: common ones like black ducks, teal and mallards, and rarer ones as well – a little pink-eared duck with its cartoon eye patches and huge square-tipped beak; a pair of bluebills. Loveliest of all was the plumed whistler, with its flank of lance-shaped feathers, and shining chestnut breast, barred in black.

Sophie beamed with delight as several ducks waddled from the water towards them. Nina gave her some pellets to throw. 'Look,' said Sophie. A white egret emerged in measured steps from behind a wattle thicket, its long neck retracted in a graceful curve. He was in full breeding plumage, his beak a crimson dagger, his noble face the softest green. A silken train of snowy plumes extended well beyond his tail. Sophie heaved a great sigh. 'That's the most beautiful thing I've ever seen in the whole world.' Nina and Ric exchanged amused glances. The little girl was certainly full of superlatives today. 'What sort of bird is it?' asked Sophie.

'That's Prince. He's an egret,' said Nina. 'He lived on a big lake near here, but somebody cut down the trees and drained the water. Prince and his family had to fly away. A piece of fishing line got wrapped round his leg and slowed him down, so he got lost. Just after sunset a farmer noticed him circling a tree full of roosting white leghorns.' Sophie looked puzzled. 'They're chickens.'

Sophie nodded. 'Keep going.'

'Prince landed on the top of the tree. You see, from the air he'd mistaken those white chickens for his family and the tree for his home. But he was lonely, and even chickens were better company than nothing. So he folded up his wings and went to sleep. In the morning, the farmer saw the fishing line was tangled in branches and Prince was stuck. He was a very kind farmer, so he rescued Prince and brought him here.'

'What will happen to him?' Sophie eyes were wide.

'When he's all healed, I'll take him to a paradise for birds called Billabong Bend, where there are other egrets. He'll miss his old mates, but he'll soon learn to love his new family, you'll see.' The beautiful bird spread his wings and bowed his head in agreement. 'And he won't have to pretend he's a chook any more.'

Sophie giggled. 'How will I see? Will you take me there?'

Nina looked at the child's excited face, remembering her own delight in the wetlands when she was no older than Sophie. She suddenly wanted to share that special pleasure with this little girl. 'What do you say, dad?'

'How about all three of us go?' said Ric. Nina's mouth dropped open. No, she hadn't meant for him to come.

'Yay!' yelled Sophie, jumping around in circles, much to Jinx's delight. He went leaping after her. 'When? When can we go?'

'Soon,' said Nina. 'But not today. Come on, I'll show you the horses next and then you can feed the parrots.'

Nina and Ric stood on the verandah, watching Sophie give carrots to Monty and Flicka. 'Does Sophie have any brothers or sisters?' Ric shook his head. 'She's a nice kid,' admitted Nina.

'Being here's good for her,' he said. 'I've never seen her so happy, so interested in things. She's not like that back at Donnalee.'

'How are you all getting on over there?'

'Good, good . . .' His voice trailed off and he played with his hat. 'How's Max?'

'All right. I can't believe how great he is with Sophie.'

'So what's the problem?'

'Is it that obvious?' He sighed. 'I'm no good at this father stuff. I don't know what to say to her, what to do with her. And Donnalee's not much of a place for a kid, especially a city kid. She's got nobody to play with, nothing to fill her time. And she's missing her mother, I guess, although today's the first time she's said so. Usually she doesn't say much of anything.'

'Are you going to stick around?'

'Until Sophie goes back to Rachael. I want her to get to know my old man. And the truth is, I don't have anywhere else to take her. I've moved round a lot. Mining camps, oil rigs . . . nowhere I'd call home.'

His fingers tightened on the rail. She wanted to ask him about these places that he wouldn't call home, wanted to ask how a boy from the riverlands ended up in a mining camp, but she didn't, wouldn't.

'What does Sophie do all day?'

'Nothing. She's on a planet of her own. Wild horses couldn't drag her away from that television.' A cloud of worry crossed his face. 'It's like she'd rather live in a fantasy world, like she believes that the movies she watches are real.'

Nina looked about at the olive groves, the nursery of native seedlings under shade cloth, the bank of red gums by the river. She looked at the sleek grey weaners butting heads on the hillside, the wide expanse of blue sky, the grand beauty all around her, and wondered how a person could want any other world but this one. Then she remembered a small girl, an only child like Sophie, sneaking away to meet the boy from the other side of the river. How lonely that girl had been sometimes, how left out she'd felt.

'Give her something to do,' said Nina. 'Even if you have to invent a job. You saw her today. She wants to look after something, she wants to feel needed.'

Ric's face softened. 'Max found a mouse in the kitchen yesterday. Sophie wouldn't let him hurt it. She said, how did we know it wasn't a mouse like Stuart Little, looking for his family. My father, my tough-as-nails father, made a home for it in a shoebox.' Ric chuckled. 'Damnedest thing I ever saw. It escaped overnight and Dad spent half the morning trying to find it for her.' Nina smiled and the gulf of years between them seemed to slip away. Ric's expression grew serious and his eyes held hers. 'Remember the hats?'

Nina turned from his penetrating, brown eyes. 'Of course.'

As children, they'd invented an ingenious signalling system for their meetings, using coloured hats hung in trees. Visiting the river to check for them had been a daily routine, whenever Nina was home from boarding school. A red baseball cap was an invitation to meet that afternoon. A beanie in response meant no. A yellow cap meant I'll come tomorrow afternoon instead. As their codes expanded, so did their hat collections. A straw hat meant let's meet the morning after tomorrow. A white cricket hat hanging beside an invitation hat, meant it was an emergency. Funny how she still remembered.

'Mum used to complain about it,' said Nina. '"Never known a girl to have so many hats," she used to say. "Shoes yes, but not hats."'

'I hid mine under the house,' said Ric. 'Don't know what Dad would have made of a boy with a hat collection.'

'And Freeman?' said Nina, caught up in the fun of remembering. 'Remember how we'd swim across to that rundown houseboat of his? What was it called?'

'Warriuka,' said Ric with a grin. 'He'd make us golden syrup pancakes and mugs of tea with about ten sugars in them.'

'What about when he took us up the Kingfisher and showed us where that big old Murray cod lived? It even had a name, Guddhu, remember? What a fish.'

Ric nodded. 'Must have been a hundred years old.'

'Freeman said it was a water guardian, and if anyone hurt it, a curse would fall on people along the river.'

'He sure was a crazy old man.'

'Not crazy,' said Nina. 'More like eccentric. And you loved his stories as much as I did. I think Freeman was the only one who knew about us.'

She jumped off the verandah, suddenly self-conscious. 'Let me show you and Sophie round. You won't know the place.'

They went down to the river track, where the banks were clothed in saplings, planted as part of her local seed project. The silvery, weeping leaves of slim borees shimmered in the sunshine. Young red gums rose strong and straight around the trunks of their dead parents. A scattering of kurrajongs, coolibahs and casuarinas sheltered thriving understoreys of lignum and goosefoot. In the shallows, chicken-wire coops protected native sedges and rushes, plants that hadn't been seen along this stretch of the Bunyip for years.

The contrast with the river's north side was stark and unavoidable. Just metres away on the opposite slope, yawning washaways scarred the bare, broken banks. Cattle had gouged deep pug-marked tracks down to the water. A series of wallows stained the mud an even darker brown, and an algal bloom coated the rocks a slimy blue-green.

Sophie and Ric stood staring. 'The river's low,' he said. 'Don't ever remember seeing it this low.'

Sophie pointed across the turbid water. 'Is that Poppi's land? Why does it look so different? It looks . . . dead.'

'Nothing a little love and care couldn't fix,' said Nina. 'Maybe you can work on your grandfather?'

'Maybe.' Sophie lifted her chin. 'Or maybe Dad could.'

Nina was liking this kid more and more. 'Come on, let's go see the pecans.'

'Not even eight years old,' said Nina as they wandered the neat rows of graceful nut trees, 'and I'll get my first full commercial crop this year, twenty-five kilos per tree I reckon.'

'That's good, right?'

She punched Ric playfully on his arm. 'Yes, it's good. Some growers don't manage that for a decade. And the market can't get enough organic pecans, here or overseas.'

'Organic,' he said. 'That sounds like a good lurk. Great marketing angle.'

'It's not an angle.' Nina frowned. 'I've joined a co-op of farmers based right here at Drovers Flat. Organic sunflowers, canola, olives, beef – even wheat. Romano has a new line of Aussie pasta products. The Bush Tucker range. They buy all their durum wheat from one of our members.'

'Any cotton farmers in your co-op?'

'No,' she said. 'No cotton farmers.'

He picked up a stone and pitched it towards the river. 'Maybe Donnalee should jump on the bandwagon.'

'Organic isn't just some buzzword you can slap on a label,' she said. 'It's a huge process to get accreditation. Took me three years after stopping the chemicals, because it takes that long for traces to disappear. Inspectors examined my entire farming process and I have to keep detailed diaries. It's hard work.'

'Sounds like it.' He tossed another stone with a restless energy. 'Is it worth all that work?'

'It's so worth it,' she said. 'I want to team up with a few more growers to press our own label. Drovers Flat Olive Oil. We could do the same with nuts. And just look around you. The whole farm looks healthier, doesn't it? Despite the drought. Loads more birds and insects, a huge diversity of native plants, and it's cheaper than buying poisons. Mulch and sub-surface watering keep the weeds down. Biological control for pests. We've got our own entomologist at the co-op.' She grasped a low-hanging branch, pulled out her *Bugs For Bugs* mini-magnifier and handed it to him. 'Look.'

Ric inspected the offered leaf through the lens. 'It's a leaf. So what?'

'Can't you see?' Nina was impatient for him to understand. 'There. That little raft of eggs. Look.' Ric squinted at the foliage obediently. 'They're green-vegetable bug eggs. See how they're going black? That's because of a parasitic wasp. It lays its eggs inside, and instead of hatching into bugs, they hatch into shiny little black wasps. If we're lucky, we might see one.' Ric pressed his lips together, nodding. 'And there's a tiny fly that does almost the same thing.'

'A fly?'

'*Trichopoda giacomellii*,' she said slowly, glad her tongue didn't trip her up. 'It targets the larvae though, not the eggs. Amazing, isn't it?' Nina felt her face flush. She'd got carried away. Not everybody found parasitic flies as fascinating as she did, but there was no trace of boredom on Ric's face.

He peered at the leaf again. 'So you don't need pesticides?' She shook her head. 'That's pretty clever. Can't imagine Dad wanting to go organic though.'

'No,' said Nina. 'I'm guessing Max doesn't skimp in the chemical department.' In her mind she could see his tractor combing the rows of cotton, she could taste the poison in the air.

Her phone rang, making her jump. 'Hi Lockie.' Ric scowled and kicked at the dusty ground. 'But I came to you last time. It's your turn to come here . . .' Ric glanced at her sideways. She lowered her voice and moved further away, feeling unaccountably guilty. 'The river pumps are playing up. I can't afford to be away overnight until they're fixed.'

Sophie ran over. 'Who are you talking to?'

'Lockie, I'll ring you back.'

'Who was that?' Sophie asked again.

'My boyfriend.' She looked squarely at Ric. 'That was my boyfriend on the phone.' It was time to wind this visit up.

At the front of the house, Ric kicked the tyre of the battered old station wagon. 'What's happening about your car?' she asked. 'The one that packed up in Moree?'

'Not worth fixing.' He wrenched open the back door.

Sophie wrinkled her nose. 'That car stinks of Poppi's cigars.'

'You're not wrong there,' he said.

'I want to sit in the front on the way home.'

'Then you'll have to hop over the seat. The front passenger door's stuck.'

Sophie took this as a challenge, and spent the next few minutes tugging at the door to no avail. Finally she gave up and climbed in.

'It's hot in here. Does this window work?'

'Nothing in this car works,' said Ric. 'Except for the motor, and I wouldn't take bets on that.'

Nina waved them goodbye, a little surprised at the old bomb of a station wagon. Quite a contrast to the brand new machinery Max had bought last season. How was Donnalee Station travelling financially, she wondered? Jinx whined and licked her hand. 'You're right,' she said. 'We've got work to do.'

Time to forget about Ric Bonelli.

CHAPTER 7

'Come with us and look at the cotton,' said Ric. 'You don't want to be staying here by yourself.'

'Yes, I do.' Sophie curled up on the couch. She aimed the remote at the television, flicked through the channels and settled on a cartoon about talking pigs and spiders.

Ric rubbed a hand over his eyes. 'So, what, you'll watch telly all morning? That sounds pretty boring.'

'Not as boring as looking at your stupid cotton.' Sophie didn't look up. 'Just a heap of flat paddocks. Not even any trees.'

'Leave her be, Ricardo.' Max was beaming as he emerged from the kitchen with a tray. It was quite amazing how indulgent he was of his granddaughter. If Ric had ever spoken to an adult so disrespectfully he would have got the belt. 'She wants to stay, so let her stay.' Max put a glass of milk and a plate of raisins and dried figs beside her. She screwed up her face, but apparently knew better than to complain, and provoke the inevitable lecture about the health benefits of dried fruit.

Ric hesitated. 'How about we go into town when I get back? We can post that letter to your mum, buy ice-creams. Monday's mobile library day. We could join you up?'

She ignored him. Eventually Ric shrugged and followed Max out the back door. This would be his first proper tour of the station since he'd been back. He shielded his eyes from the glaring sky. The sun was a demon and already the truck's cracked, vinyl seat was too hot to touch. Even the clumps of tough weeds along the track were wilting, shrinking back to their roots. They drove out past the sheds towards the river, clouds of dust boiling in their wake. Dust was everywhere. Any movement stirred it to life, whipping up fierce little willy-willies that raced away with the illusion of purpose. A mob of hungry Herefords followed the truck along the fence line, bellowing and raising a grey cloud.

Ric gazed out the window, not knowing how to feel. Fifteen years since he'd worked on this farm, whose seasons and rhythms had once been second nature to him. Field after field slipped by, a green sea reaching all the way to the brilliant blue skyline. Nothing moved out there, nothing at all. Only his eye moved, following the lonely stands of cotton to the horizon. Ric felt no itch of recognition, no yearning to reconnect with this strange, flat world. Just a vague nervousness, a throwback to childhood. As soon as the shoots were out of the ground, a cotton grower's anxiety grew along with them. You couldn't breathe easy until the harvest was in.

'What do you think?' said Max. 'Fine crop this year, eh? Best crop ever maybe.' This at least was familiar. The gamble, the wild optimism about each new season – and the sinking disappointment that so often lurked around the corner. His mother's voice came back to him, chastising his father after floods or wilt or caterpillars had devastated the cotton. 'You may as well go to the casino and lose all our money that way. It would be quicker.' There'd been good years too, and it had been easy to forget about the loss of last year's crop, when spring rolled around again.

Max stopped the truck. Ric climbed out, his boots kicking up dust as he walked. But when he crossed over into the field, over the levees framing the head ditch, the soil held his footprint and ridged in rich, dark clumps. His father's eyes shone with pride. The lush green crop stood almost waist-high. A few creamy, hibiscus-like flowers showed among the broad three-pointed leaves – big, beautiful blooms whose full glory would last for only a day. Others had withered away to dark pink. Some already boasted the green, segmented seed pods that in a few months would ripen and burst open with cotton wool.

Max gestured for Ric to follow. They picked their way carefully between the rows that had almost closed over to form a seamless green carpet. A little red flag fluttered on a stake a few rows in. 'Have a look at this.' Max reached down and gently fingered a young boll. 'See?'

Ric looked, but for the life of him he couldn't figure out what he was supposed to be seeing. His father's eyes were eager, expectant. It was the same face Nina had worn when she'd shown him the eggs on the pecan leaf. Ric examined the little green boll, scouring his memory, trying to figure out exactly what was so exceptional about it. His father's expression began to change from hope to disappointment, and then Ric had it.

'Six segments – a six-lock boll.' Knowledge came back to him in a rush. 'A bad crop might only grow three- or four-lock bolls.' He rested another one in the palm of his hand. 'This is what we want. A five-lock boll. It shows the plants are healthy and the season's been near-on perfect.'

'And we get more cotton,' said a delighted Max.

Ric nodded. 'And we get more cotton. But this –' He pointed to the rare six-lock find. 'I've never seen this before. This is really something.'

'Once a cotton man, always a cotton man. It's in your blood, eh, Ricardo?'

Ric was pretty sure it wasn't, but his father's joy was infectious, and he was pleased to have passed the test.

'Cotton's like a baby,' said Max. 'Got to keep it warm and safe, give it a drink, give it a feed. Cotton won't leave you alone, and you can't leave it alone. All the time you have to worry; it's too cold, too hot, too dry, too wet. Look around you . . . Look at the plants. What do you see?'

Ric sighed but did as he was asked. The cotton appeared to be thriving, but Max's face suggested that all was not right. He carefully inspected the closest plant. 'No sign of insect damage.'

'That's right,' said Max. 'This year I fix the little bastards once and for all with a new spray, *FirstStrike*. Never have no more trouble.'

Okay. Ric took a closer look. This field was perhaps a darker shade of green than the next one. A hot blast of wind caused the plants to clash together with a rushing, rustling sound. The leaves were the tiniest bit crinkled around the edges. 'When was the last time you irrigated this paddock?'

Max whistled approvingly. 'Nine days ago.'

'Well, you'd better water again by tomorrow,' said Ric. 'There's another scorcher forecast for Friday and leaving it any longer will affect the yield.'

'Spot on,' said Max. 'We'll flood this paddock today. Father and son, working together like in the old days. What could be better?'

Max was right. It would go a long way to cementing the tentative bond they were forming. On top of that, irrigating the paddocks had been Ric's favourite farm task, way back when, a chance to get wet in the baking summer heat. He guessed his father remembered that.

'What about Sophie?' said Ric.

'I'll walk to the dam,' said Max. 'You take the truck, go back and ask her if she wants to help us. Tell her she can cool off with a swim.'

Ric guessed that it would take more than a dip in a muddy pond to prise Sophie from the couch, but he went back anyway. She was exactly where he'd left her – eyes glazed over, staring at the screen. A goose was singing about friendship to a group of farmyard animals. He leant over the back of the couch, and tapped her on the shoulder. A jar of tadpoles sat on the cushion beside her. 'Where'd they come from?'

'Poppi.'

'Want to come for a swim?'

She brightened. 'Is there a pool at Drovers Flat?'

'I meant here,' said Ric. 'In the dam.'

'You said we'd go into town when you got back.'

So he had. He'd completely forgotten. 'We'll do it later,' said Ric. 'I have to help Poppi with some watering first.'

Sophie shrugged, turned the fan up to full and returned to the telly. 'Sure you don't want to come for a swim? I don't like leaving you here. Where's your phone?' She shrugged again. 'Go get it.' Sophie glared at him for a moment, then flounced off to her bedroom to get the phone. He checked that it was charged and had reception, then he put it on the coffee table in front of her. 'Call me if you need me,' he said. 'And answer it if it rings, okay?' The girl's attention stayed defiantly glued to the screen. He shook his head, put on his hat and left.

Ric gazed across the wide waters of the storage. This wasn't what he remembered, not at all. The area of the original dam had been massively extended and was circled by a chain of additional ponds, each one almost as big as the original. It must have cost a fortune. There was that brand-new tractor too, and late-model pickers and boll buggies in the shed. Dad must be doing all right for himself.

Max was watching him. 'What do you think, Ricardo?'

'That's a lot of water,' said Ric.

'That's a hell of a lot of water,' said Max, his weather-beaten face cracking into a grin. 'A hell of a lot of water, for the best bloody crop ever grown at Donnalee Station. Maybe the best in the whole district.' His pride and excitement was palpable. 'Mother nature and her droughts and her bugs?' he said. 'She can't touch us now.'

'I guess not,' said Ric, still stunned by the massive reservoir stretched out before him. Cotton was a plant that loved long, hot summers like this one, with low humidity and a maximum amount of sunshine. The higher the average temperatures, the greater the yield. Trouble was, long hot summers usually meant water shortages. But not this summer. It looked like Max was right. This could be the most profitable crop to ever leave the farm gate. His thoughts travelled back to the river. Its shallow water and sluggish flows. Its dead trees and exposed banks. The contrast disturbed him.

'The dream, Ricardo. Remember the dream?' Ric waited, watching the passion rise in his father's eyes. 'To buy next door, convert it to cotton, double our land?'

'I remember.' His father had tried for years to buy Billabong Bend, but was always met with a brick wall. Like most riverine graziers, the Langley's were firmly opposed to the burgeoning local cotton industry, accusing the irrigators of sucking the Bunyip River dry and diverting floodwaters into massive, unmetered storage dams. It was a debate that Ric had never taken the slightest interest in. He'd only been a kid back then, after all. But now, looking at the shining sea stretched out before him, he had to concede that the graziers might have a point.

'Old man Langley died,' said Max. 'Just a matter of time now before the place comes on the market. Maybe we'll get ourselves one of those new baler pickers for next season. Your cousin, Tony, he's got one. Never seen anything like it. Don't need no casual picking crew. Don't need to waste your money on wages. Just one picker and one bale grab for the whole harvest. That picker does everything, measures everything – tyre pressure, bale moisture, just by flicking a switch. Damn thing even steers itself.'

Ric looked suitably impressed. 'And Eva?'

Max waved a dismissive hand. 'She's an old woman, not right in the head. She won't hold on much longer. What do you think, Ricardo?'

'About what?'

'About expanding, setting up a new cotton farm? Stay here and work for me. Later on you have your own place, eh? You run Billabong. Make a good life for your daughter.'

Ric kicked at the ground. 'I've already told you, Dad, I'm not cut out for this kind of life.'

Anger flared in his father's eyes. 'I give you a chance to make something of yourself and you throw it in my face.' He checked himself and shook his head sorrowfully. 'Just think about it, okay?'

Ric cracked his knuckles. 'I'll think about it.' He had no desire to work with his father. He no longer felt the old love for these black soil plains. He was a miner now – a rigger, a driller, a blast operator.

In his line of work, the land was something to blow up and cart away.

Max pointed to the gate. 'Do the honours, please, Ricardo.'

Ric stepped onto the narrow, raised metal platform over the water. A sharp wind gust almost stole his balance. He steadied himself, arms outstretched like a tightrope walker, until he reached the rusty metal wheel at the end. There was a time when he could have run safely out there in the middle of a gale, without a second's thought, agile as a monkey. He'd always loved turning that wheel. It was a godlike feeling, to release the vast energy lurking in the main dam, to control its blind, headlong rush to lower ground, to bend it to his will.

Frothing brown water sank in a whirlpool beneath his feet, and gushed out through pipes on the other side of the dam wall, filling the dusty canal. It gobbled up the dry bed of cracked mud, carrying all before it. Dust and sticks and stones. A lizard, running for its life, was swept away. 'You go ahead,' yelled Max, over the rushing sound. 'I'll finish up here.' Ric walked back along the supply channel and raised the sluice to let the water reach the ditch at the top of the field. The cotton was watered with lengths of long black poly pipe, overbank syphons, one self-priming hose for two rows of cotton. When the head ditch was full enough Ric lifted a syphon, unsure of the technique after all this time. He plunged one end into the water a few times until the check-valve kicked in, then tossed it over the little levee into the field. Yes. A stream of water, sucked from the head ditch, was pouring from the pipe and down the length of the rows.

Ric proceeded along the crop, repeating the process over and over. Max arrived to help, but Ric waved him away. The work was as hard as he remembered. The relentless heat, the constant bending, the mind-numbing repetition. But two hours later, when he'd set the last syphon, when the thirsty cotton leaves were plumping up at the edges, when he sat nursing his blisters and waving his hat at flies — then he was happy, really happy. He could smell damp earth and hear the silence. He could feel his body spent, his restless energy drained away, replaced with a deep and unexpected sense of satisfaction.

Ric got to his feet as the truck approached with Max driving.

Something caught his eye as he climbed in – a hessian bag on the floor, moving of its own accord.

'It's for Sophia,' said Max. 'A turtle. She loves the animals, that little one.'

Nina's words came back to him. 'She wants to look after something. She wants to feel needed.' Even his father had figured that out. Everybody seemed to understand his daughter better than he did.

CHAPTER 8

'Meet Britney,' said Sophie. The little brown turtle peered at Nina through golden eyes, pupils large and round. All four webbed feet waved helplessly in mid-air. 'And these are my tadpoles.' Sophie set the jar down on the table.

Nina took the turtle from the girl's outstretched hands. 'Ah,' she said. 'A Murray River short-necked turtle.'

'How do you know?'

'See this?' Nina's finger traced the yellow stripe running from the corner of the reptile's mouth and back along the side of its head. 'And I'm afraid I don't think it's a Britney.'

'How do you mean?

Nina gently turned the turtle over, revealing its creamy-yellow under-shell. She pointed to the tail. 'See how fat and long this is? Girls' tails are smaller.' Nina got up and took a shoebox down from a shelf. 'I think he might be happier in here.'

'He's not eating,' said Sophie.

'What are you feeding him?'

'Poppi said to give him bread.'

'Bread's no good. He eats what he finds in the wild. Water weeds and snails and insects, that sort of thing.'

Sophie regarded her earnestly, clutching the shoebox to her heart. She had a pretty, turned-up nose, like a little ski jump.

Nina sat down beside her and took the girl's small hand in hers. 'Why don't we take your turtle down to the river and let him go?'

'Hold on,' said Ric. 'She loves that thing. Her grandpa gave it to her.'

'The turtle wasn't his to give.' Nina frowned. 'It belongs to the river.'

'Will he die if I keep him?' asked Sophie. 'Some of my tadpoles have died.'

'He will if you keep feeding him bread,' said Nina. 'But even if he gets the right food, do you think he'll be happy, locked up all by himself?'

Sophie looked at the turtle, scrabbling uselessly at the corner of the cardboard box. 'No,' she said, sadly. 'He won't be happy. He'll be lonely, like me.' She picked up the jar of tadpoles. 'I'm going to set them free too.'

'I think that's very kind and wise,' said Nina. 'Come on, I know the perfect place.'

'Can I speak to you?' Ric's voice had an edge to it. 'In the kitchen.'

She led him into the kitchen, conscious that it was the first time he'd been inside it, conscious of the mess.

'Sophie only wanted to find out about the turtle,' he said. 'What to feed it. And now the poor kid's going to lose all her pets?'

'Get her some proper pets, then,' said Nina. 'But don't steal animals from the wild. Frogs and turtles are having a hard enough time already with the drought.'

'Couldn't she keep them till she goes home?'

Nina shrugged. 'The tadpoles will be dead by then. And maybe the turtle too, but it's not up to me.'

Sophie appeared at the door. 'Dad, I want to let them go. They need to be free, like Elsa.'

'Who's Elsa?' asked Ric.

'The lion in the movie yesterday. Elsa couldn't be properly happy until she was set free.'

'Are you sure you want to?'

'Yes, Dad, I'm sure.' Sophie drew a giant breath. 'Let's do it.'

They all trooped down to the river. Nina noted the stick she'd dug in last week to mark the water level. It sat a good six inches above the surface.

Sophie kissed the turtle. 'Bye bye, Britney.' It scuttled down the bank and into the water with surprising alacrity. Next it was the tadpoles' turn to swim off into the reeds. Sophie looked like she'd lost her best friend.

'Ric,' said Nina. 'I promised to show you and Sophie around Billabong. We could go today?'

'Righto.' He picked up a stone, examined it briefly, then dropped it. 'How about it, Soph?'

The girl looked a little less miserable. 'Don't you have to help Poppi? You always have to help Poppi.'

'I don't have to do anything,' said Ric. 'And anyway, it's Saturday. I want to spend the day with you.' He picked up another stone, tossed it and caught it a few times, then expertly skipped it on the river — once, twice, three times.

'Can you show me how to do that?' asked Sophie.

'Sure,' said Ric. 'First you need a skinny flat rock.' They both started hunting around for something suitable. 'This'll do.' He put a stone into the girl's hand. 'Hold it with your thumb on one side and your middle finger on the other.'

The back of Nina's neck prickled to see Ric with his daughter like this.

'I'm left-handed.' Sophie's tone was matter of fact, but a slow flush of embarrassment crept upwards from Ric's jaw. How must it feel to know so little about your own child? Nina pretended to examine some freshly planted seedlings, giving Ric room to save face. His reaction had been so heartfelt, so genuine. It moved her, revived old feelings.

Ric pressed the stone into the palm of Sophie's other hand. Her fingers curled around it. 'That's right,' he said. 'You want to send it spinning in a straight line, almost flat along the water. It's all in the flick of the wrist.' With a gentle hold of Sophie's arm, he took her through the motion a few times.

Sophie threw the stone. It bounced once before sinking. 'I did it!' She looked over to Nina with excited eyes.

'Yes, you did,' said Nina. The vignette stole her breath. The stunningly handsome man and the pretty dark-haired girl, framed by the river, trees and sky. Ric saluted his daughter and then flashed Nina a smile. She bit her lip. It was a physical shock when their eyes met, as if she'd been jolted into feeling twice as alive as before.

'Can Jinx come to paradise?' The dog heard his name. He stopped nosing around a rabbit hole and trotted to Sophie's side.

'Paradise?' asked Ric.

'Nina called it a paradise for birds, remember?'

'It is a paradise,' said Nina, 'except for the mosquitoes. And yes, Jinx can come.'

The Pelican headed downriver, past where the Bunyip met the Kingfisher, past the boundary between Red Gums and Billabong Bend and out into the wetlands proper. A stiff headwind sang in the treetops, accompanied by the humming motor. Nina slowed Pelican down and switched to neutral. 'Shh.' She put her finger to her lips. 'Listen.'

A series of low trumpeting calls sounded to their left. The boat veered towards the sound, keeping to the shadows along the bank. 'There.' Two graceful grey brolgas, wings unfurled, faced each other in a green marsh meadow. They threw back their red-crowned heads and called in unison; wild, ringing cries, echoing off the water.

'What are they doing?' Sophie asked.

Nina shushed her again and grabbed her camera. 'The dance of the native companions,' she whispered. 'You're in for a treat.'

The first bird bowed, the second one curtseyed and the show began. Strut and salute, retreat and advance, piaffe and pirouette – the elegant cranes mirrored each other in an intricate ballet of measured perfection. The taller one seized a reed. He hurled it skywards, followed it into the air and parachuted back to earth on broad, still wings. His partner followed suit, and soon they were leaping in a grand celebration of life, all the while trumpeting their joy. It was a truly mesmerising sight. At last their display was done. With a final, graceful bound they took to the breeze and soared away.

'That was the most beautiful thing —' began Sophie.

'I know, I know.' Ric laughed. 'The most beautiful thing you've ever seen in your whole life.'

'Yes.' Sophie smiled at her father.

'For once I agree with you,' he said. 'I've never seen it before. Lived here half my life and I've never seen it.'

There was something in his voice. Nina looked up from checking her shots. Ric wore a look of wonder. Something fluttered in her stomach. He still got it, despite how he'd changed. He got how special these wetlands really were. As a child, he'd always loved the river, but who knew how he might feel now? One look at his face dispelled her doubts. Why it mattered so much, she couldn't tell. She just knew she wanted to sing. She wanted to whoop and leap along with the brolgas.

'Why do they dance like that?' asked Sophie.

'Nobody knows,' said Nina. 'People used to think it was a courtship ritual, but brolgas display all through the year. Sometimes a dozen together.'

'I think they just love to dance,' said Sophie. 'I would too, if I was as good as them.'

Her words reminded Nina of a story Freeman had told her and Ric, long ago. 'Once upon a time,' she said, 'there was a girl named Brolga who loved to dance. Each day she'd practise her moves, copied from the sweep of a pelican's wing or the strut of an emu or the whirl of the wind. People came from miles around to see her.'

The boat drifted into the mud. Nina handed Ric the broom handle she kept in the stern and he pushed the boat off the bank. 'I remember this story,' he said with a grin.

'Dad, don't interrupt.'

'Well, one day another tribe stole Brolga away. Her people searched and searched, day and night. When they finally found her there was a big battle and the kidnappers used magic to escape. They changed Brolga into a bird so her friends wouldn't recognise her. But when her family saw the dancing bird they knew at once who she was. Brolga was safe at last and nobody could steal her away from home again.'

Sophie looked dubious. 'I don't know if that's a happy story or a sad story.'

Close by, an unusual bird separated itself from the reeds. 'Sit still,' said Nina. In one swift movement she seized her camera, and aimed it the mottled, pot-bellied wader feeding in the shallows.

'What's that?' asked Sophie.

'That,' said Nina, as she madly snapped photographs, 'is a sharp-tailed sandpiper.'

'Is it special?' asked Sophie. 'It doesn't look very special.'

'Oh, it's special, all right,' said Nina. 'That plain-looking little bird has flown halfway around the world to get here.'

'Where from?'

'All the way from northern Siberia.' '

Siberia,' said Ric. 'Russian Siberia?'

'Yep. It breeds in the tundra of the high Arctic. Then leads its chicks in a migration flight across Kazakhstan, Mongolia, Manchuria . . .'

'No way,' said Ric, shaking his head.

'Then get this,' said Nina. 'It stops to rest in the no-man's-land between North and South Korea, smack bang in the middle of the demilitarised zone, guns pointing from both directions.' The bird turned to look at them and bowed. *Wit-wit, wit-wit.* Three other sandpipers stalked from the reeds. They greeted each other with a series of musical twitterings. 'Mum, dad and the kids,' said Nina. 'What a story they could tell.'

Nina detoured down Langley Reach and showed them the jetty and the house on the hill, its broken windows staring like blank eyes. She showed them the canoe tree, and the swan nests near the old bridge, and the egret colony in the melaleuca woodland.

'Will Prince live here one day?' asked Sophie.

Nina nodded and shushed her again. A movement in the downstream marshes had caught her eye. A single wading bird foraged furtively in the sedgeland, a bird much larger and stockier than the sandpipers. It crept along, chestnut head held low, rosy bill drawn into its body, as if trying to present a smaller target.

'I don't believe it.' Nina's voice was low and her hand reached for the camera. Impossible, surely . . . but there was no mistaking the distinctive, comma-shaped mark framing the eye. Or the white-striped crown and breast. Or the barred, metallic green of its back and wings. This was a moment she'd longed for, dreamed of. The bird disappeared behind a fallen tree. 'Everybody stay perfectly still,' she whispered. 'I have to get a photo of this bird.'

'What is it?' asked Ric.

'It's a miracle,' said Nina. 'That's what it is.'

Her passengers remained obediently quiet as Pelican drifted ever so slowly downstream. Time and time again, the elusive bird emerged from cover only to vanish just as quickly. At last her chance came. The wader paused behind a jumble of reeds. Nina could see its raised leg protruding from the thicket, could read its body language, as the bird prepared to make a break to open water. The leg pulled back a fraction, poised. Any second now.

A shot rang out, then another, startling Jinx into a flurry of barking. No! The leg withdrew and the bird took flight, just a shadowy blur obscured by the tangled lignum. Nina's mouth went dry. She clicked a few times, knowing that it was hopeless, then flicked in vain through her photos.

She couldn't speak, her throat so tight she feared she might choke. Her best chance. Her very best chance to protect Billabong and she'd ruined it. No — some moron with a gun had ruined it for her. She squeezed her eyes shut so hard they swam with dots. Jinx's consoling tongue probed her ear. 'Get off,' she said, sitting up. Her chest hurt. She couldn't breathe.

'Calm down,' said Ric, as Sophie offered her a water bottle. 'Tell us what's wrong.'

She heaved a deep breath and managed to get some oxygen into her lungs. 'That bird was a painted snipe.' Her voice sounded thin and faraway. 'It's rare, very rare.'

Sophie pointed to a magpie perched in a red gum, observing them with keen eyes.

'He's not scared. Take his photo instead.'

'You don't understand.' Nina's lip trembled. 'A photo of a magpie won't save Billabong.'

'Save it from what?' asked Sophie.

'From being sold.' Nina tried to compose herself. Despair was turning into anger and her hands curled into fists. She swept her arm wide, indicating the beauty all around. 'New owners mightn't feel the same way we do about this place.'

Another shot, and the magpie arrowed away to safety. Nina slammed the motor into life. She pointed Pelican upstream towards the gunfire, taking off so fast that Sophie almost lost her balance. Ric steadied the girl with his arm. 'Careful, Nina.'

Nina slowed to check Sophie was all right, then spun the helm and shifted gears. They were wasting precious minutes. The boat sped down a narrow channel. Caught between the bank and a fallen cooba, it whined and shuddered alarmingly, finally scraping past and breaking free.

'Nina, slow down!'

The motor roared and the bow rose as they leaped away. She scanned the water ahead. Still no sign of hunters.

A sudden wrench on her arm caused Pelican to yaw wildly. 'Stop the bloody boat!' Ric's expression, taut with anger, shocked her and brought her crashing down to earth. She straightened their course and shifted to neutral. Pelican settled quickly, like it too was sick of their wild ride.

Nina's nose ran, her head throbbed and her eyes were wet with tears. Sophie clung to the side rail, white and shaken. 'I'm sorry,' said Nina. 'I wanted to catch them so badly, I just didn't think.'

'What were you going to do if you did catch them?' asked Ric. Nina looked away. 'They could be nutters or drunk, or anything. You don't know. The only thing you do know is that they're armed.'

'Well, so am I.' Nina kicked at the rifle box bolted beneath the front seat.

'Great,' said Ric. 'So, what, you were going to shoot them?'

Sophie was trying to smother a succession of short sobs. Jinx whined in sympathy. He sat beside the girl and began to lick away her tears.

'Let's all settle down and go home,' said Ric. 'And I'll shout us a counter tea at the pub.'

'I don't think so,' said Nina.

'Please, please come,' said Sophie. 'It's boring with just Dad.'

'Thanks a lot,' said Ric with a wry smile.

Nina looked at Sophie's eager, tear-streaked face. A night out with Ric? She imagined them, sitting together in the beer garden of the Angler's Arms, music from the jukebox drifting in the warm night air. Fun for Sophie, maybe. Risky for Nina's confused state of mind. But the thought of being at home by herself wasn't what she wanted either. Not after missing that photograph. If only Lockie was coming tonight, instead of in the morning. They'd hardly seen each other in the last few weeks, and it was lonely without him. It wasn't really his fault. Lockie had been kept so busy lately: mustering, drafting, selling off cattle because of the drought. Prices were way down, but if the weather didn't break soon, she might have to do the same thing.

'Okay, I'll come,' said Nina.

Sophie's face lit up. 'Can I have a grown-up dessert, instead of ice-cream?'

'If you like,' said Ric.

'Can I have a bucket of gin and tonic?' asked Nina.

'Whatever you want,' he said. 'And you can tell me about your painted snipe while you empty your bucket. Deal?'

'Deal.' Nina managed a smile.

'Oh, and one more thing,' he said. 'Try not to kill us all on the way home.'

CHAPTER 9

Ric looked around uneasily. He'd rarely seen the inside of the Angler's Arms. The town of Drovers Flat boasted two pubs, and their patrons were historically split along party lines. Dad and his irrigator mates frequented the Royal up the road. This hotel belonged to the dry-land farmers and cattlemen.

'Is that thing real?' Sophie pointed to the huge cod mounted on the wall.

Ric nodded. This might not be his usual watering hole, but everybody knew the story of Moby Dick. 'That fish was caught sixty years ago in the Bunyip, not far from here. Weighed more than fifty kilos, apparently, when they dragged it from the water.'

'That's sad.' Sophie studied the mounted fish and the engraved plaque beneath. 'It says there's a reward,' she said. 'How can there be a reward if somebody's already caught it?'

'It's for catching a bigger one,' said Ric. 'Ever since I was a kid, there's been a reward on offer for landing a bigger cod than old Moby Dick here. Nobody's ever claimed the prize.'

'That's because there are none left,' said Nina.

Sophie pushed her dessert across to Ric and rubbed her stomach.

Half the slice of toffee cheesecake remained on the plate. 'Eyes too big for your tummy, eh?' He indicated the plate. 'Want some, Nina?'

'No thanks,' she said. 'It's all yours.' He sank his spoon into the creamy sweetness.

Sophie held out her hand. 'That will be two dollars, please.'

'Two dollars?' said Ric. 'You're going to charge me two dollars for a half-eaten piece of cake that I paid for in the first place?'

'I need more money,' said Sophie. 'Pleeease?'

Ric searched his pockets and dropped some coins into her hand. 'Here. That's the last of it.'

Sophie ran off a little way, then returned and darted in to leave a kiss on his cheek. He rubbed the spot. It tingled with pleasure and pride 'You know what?' he asked. Nina shook her beautiful head. 'That's the first time she's kissed me. Six weeks I've had her, and I finally get a kiss.'

'Reckon the pub makes more money from the games in the kids' playroom than from anything else,' said Nina, laughing. 'Parents will do anything for a bit of peace.'

'You're not wrong there.' Ric took a deep swig of beer, his gaze never leaving hers.

'Those girls at the bar,' said Nina. 'They can't keep their eyes off you.'

Ric didn't even glance in their direction. He was used to making an impression on strangers. There was only one person in the room he wanted to make an impression on, and she was sitting right there. He hadn't known what to expect, coming back. Hadn't known how he'd feel about the wild river girl, the one he'd worked so hard to drive from his thoughts. Years of forgetting had been undone at the first sight of Nina, shimmering like a bird of paradise in the Moree town hall. He wanted her back, pure and simple, Lockie or no Lockie.

'It's not fair,' she said. 'Men with children are such chick magnets. If I was to come in here with a kid, blokes would run a mile.'

'I doubt that very much,' he said.

Her green eyes darted to the bar and back again. Gorgeous green eyes flecked with amber. Filled with fire, like the rest of her. Nina might be sitting perfectly still, sipping her drink, but to Ric she was all restless sparkling energy. He felt the delicious unpredictability of her, the pent-up vitality that at times threatened to overwhelm her, and him too. He fought against touching the shining, auburn hair that sprang in waves from her temples and flowed to her bare brown shoulders. This grown-up Nina was a knockout. She bent forward, full breasts peeping from her open-necked shirt. The muscles in his abdomen clenched in frustration. Get a grip, Ric. Get a grip.

A middle-aged couple came in and sat down at a nearby table. The man had his back to them, but the woman was casting surreptitious glances their way. All evening Ric had been keeping an eye on the door, looking out for Nina's mum and dad, or for any familiar faces, friendly or otherwise. He wasn't sure if he was pleased or sorry that so far there'd been no flash of recognition.

'Who are they?' He nodded towards the couple at the next table. Nina turned a little in her chair to get a better look. 'Bert and Joan Turner,' she whispered. 'They run shorthorns out at Wonga Station.'

He recalled their names, but not their faces. The woman put a hand on her husband's arm and said something. He turned to stare, then got to his feet and approached them. 'Evening, Nina.'

'Hello Bert.'

He acknowledged her with a curt nod, all the while looking Ric up and down. 'I heard Max's boy was back.'

Ric stood up. 'Mr Turner.' He offered his hand. It hovered in mid-air, unshaken and the man crossed his arms across his barrel of a chest.

'I have a bone to pick with you and your father. With you and all your mob,' said Bert. 'A lot of us floodplain fellas do.'

'Sorry to hear —'

'It's not right what you're doing,' said Bert. 'It might be legal, but it's not right. You should understand how it affects us blokes further down the river. Max takes a thousand megs to fill his bloody great dams, that's maybe five miles downstream that won't flow when the rains come. Another cotton grower does the same thing, that's another few miles. In the end it won't even reach my fence line, won't fill the dry creeks and billabongs. What Max is doing? Well, it's flat-out stealing food off my table to put on his.'

'Bloody oath,' said another man. A low murmur of approval rippled round the room.

'Bert,' called Joan. 'Don't make a scene.'

'I'm just telling him how it is.' Bert's nostrils flared. 'Without water laying on my country once in a while, it can't grow. That's how it evolved. It needs water to lay on it or else it's just a wasteland.' And with that he returned to his table.

Ric sat down, shaking his head. 'He sure has a bee in his bonnet.'

'Bert's got a point,' said Nina quietly.

'And he made it loud and clear.' Ric swigged his beer. 'Let's change the subject. Tell me about this bird of yours. This snipe.'

'A painted snipe. Haven't you heard of it?'

Ric loved seeing the local waterbirds, but had never felt the need to know their names. He couldn't even identify the different ducks on the dams at Donnalee. His father had tried in vain to teach him when he was a boy. Max was a keen hunter, something that Ric very much hoped would not come up in the evening's conversation. His father viewed hunting as a cheap, simple way to supplement the family larder. He was an excellent shot and dispatched any wounded creature promptly. But it was still a brutal and bloody affair, and Ric had never wanted any part of it.

Growing up, there was always game hanging in the coolroom under the house. Rabbits and hares, feral goats and pigs . . . and ducks. Nothing seemed to have changed. Ric was pretty sure the lamb roast Sophie had enjoyed so much last Sunday had actually been roast kid. As a conservationist, Nina could hardly object to Dad shooting pest animals, but the ducks were a different matter. And Sophie? Well, she wouldn't understand any of it. She'd cried when Max wanted to kill one of the chickens. His tough heart had melted at her tears, and he'd solemnly promised not to harm so much as a feather on their heads. Sophie counted them each morning anyway, just to be sure. No, the secrets of the Donnalee coolroom must remain just that. He watched Nina with suspicion, as if she might somehow be reading his mind. 'Go on then,' he said. 'What's so special about this snipe of yours?'

'It could be the key to saving Billabong. A very, very rare bird, and secretive. Really hard to spot. Today was the first time I've ever seen one, although Eva always said they were there.' She finished her drink with an impatient gulp. 'It's listed as a nationally threatened species, and as an endangered migratory bird. It has a double listing. Isn't that wonderful?'

'You've lost me.'

'Under the act,' said Nina, 'it's an offence to disturb the snipe's habitat. Like, for example, constructing dams or draining wetlands. Eva's old now. If anything happens, her son James will put Billabong on the market in a split-second, and auction off its water licences. He'd sell them to anybody. Imagine if a cotton grower got hold of the place.' Ric nervously cleared his throat. 'Proving there are painted snipe at Billabong would give it some serious protection. Conservation groups like Bush Heritage might even buy it, turn it into a sanctuary. That would be a dream come true. And I had to go and miss that photograph. Can you see why I'm so upset?'

'Yep,' said Ric. 'Now I understand.' He understood a bit more than he'd bargained for. Nina and his father both had designs on Billabong Bend.

'I really need to spend tomorrow searching for snipe,' she said. 'But Mum and Dad are coming over. And Lockie. It will be great to see them but it's bloody bad timing.'

Ric shifted in his seat, bracing against a sharp stab of jealousy. 'What are they coming for?'

'To help replace some fencing that stretches along the river in the bottom paddocks. I can't keep going on the revegetation program until it's done.'

'How long are they staying?'

'Lockie can only come for the day, but Mum and Dad are staying till Tuesday. If I'm lucky, Mum will clean the house.'

He toyed with the salt shaker, spinning it with his fingers. 'I could help you with the fencing.'

'And what about your daughter?'

'Sophie wouldn't mind,' he said. 'All she does is watch television anyway. Don't know how she does it. She must be bored silly. I should have taken her on a proper holiday. Dreamworld or Seaworld or something.'

'I think it's nice you brought her home,' said Nina. 'To meet Max, to see where you grew up.'

'Maybe,' he said. 'I probably couldn't afford the theme park thing anyway.' Ric regretted the words the second they were out. Way to go to impress a girl. He should be talking himself up, not down. There were enough obstacles in his path without inventing more. Lockie Carver, for starters. He'd heard Lockie was managing Macquarie Station, fifty miles upriver. That was a nice place, a big place, and profitable. Lockie would be doing all right for himself. And then there was Jim, Nina's dad. He could imagine the look on her old man's face if he came calling.

'Tell you what,' said Nina. 'Sophie's crazy about the horses. Why not bring her round one day for a riding lesson? After Mum and Dad go home,' she added.

'Scared of me meeting the family, Nina?'

A blush travelled across her face and down her neck, down to the soft skin above her shirt. She glanced around the room, as if worried that someone might overhear their conversation.

Sophie came back to the table. 'Can we go now?'

'Run out of money?' asked Ric. She yawned and nodded. 'Come on then,' he said. 'Let's get you home.'

Half an hour later, and the rattly old station wagon pulled into the drive at Red Gums. Sophie was asleep. 'I'll walk you in,' he said to Nina. They strolled towards the house. Stars lit the sky in a silver blaze of brilliance, though the moon was just a promise, a faint glow on the eastern horizon. Ric didn't want the evening to end. He was tempted to slip an arm about her waist.

Nina's face was in shadow, but his pulse beat with awareness, as if she stood in the brightest sunshine. They stopped on the porch and she turned towards him. The smooth outline of her hair showed in the starlight, her head tilted up to him. How perfect she was, too lovely to be real. Those luminous eyes, the line of her brows, the curve of her lips. Was she feeling it too? Had she forgiven him for staying away? He wanted to explain, to tell her about the trick played on him all those years ago. No, it wasn't the right time. He would sound petty and self-serving.

'Goodnight,' she said.

'Goodnight, Nina. And thanks for today.' She waited for a few moments. What for? What should he do? He was usually so self-assured with women. Nina turned her back and went into the house. He stood a while in the darkness, longing for her, aching for her. Trembling with the memory of that blinding original love, when he'd first believed anything was possible. When he'd first believed in something more than himself.

CHAPTER 10

Ric lay in the airless bedroom, gazing out the window, as night slipped away from morning, taking the stars with it. An orange band already outlined the trees along the river, warning of the scorcher to come. He'd barely slept. When he had finally nodded off at piccaninny dawn, the big red cock had crowed, again and again, waking him and throwing his mind back into wonder and turmoil. It didn't matter how many times he went over things in his head, he always came to the same conclusion. There'd be no leaving at the end of the month when Sophie went home. He wanted Nina, and Nina was here. For the time being, at least, that meant staying on at Donnalee and working for his father, something that he'd vowed all his life never to do.

It wouldn't be for long. He'd find work on another station soon enough, get some money together. It would be a big adjustment, though, staying in one place. Ric had never felt at home back in Italy, but since returning to Australia he hadn't seemed to fit in either. So he'd drifted, always restless, always searching for a place to belong. He had an itinerant work history; fly-in fly-out jobs at mines and oil rigs, never sticking at anything for long. If he was to have a chance with Nina, that had to change. Maybe he'd rent a little place in town, put down some roots? But that was getting ahead of himself. Nobody would be hiring in this drought. Until then, he'd have to make the best of things here.

On one level it made perfect sense, it added up to a reasonable plan, a practical one. But on another level, the decision to stay disturbed Ric more than he cared to admit. Was this how it began? Wanting something so much that a man sacrificed that first little bit of his freedom to get it? Not even noticing at first, maybe, because it was such a small piece. Or maybe, because doing it got him closer to what he wanted, he reckoned it was worth it.

Years ago Dad had called him wild. Ric asked him, 'How am I wild, Dad? Because I don't want to be like you? Don't want to stay at Donnalee and grow cotton?' His father had muttered something about how one day he'd understand. Had that day come? Ric sincerely hoped that it hadn't.

The sun flared above the trees. Ric rose, pulled on shorts and a singlet and went outside. The heat was building and the whole world was thirsting for rain. He pulled on his boots and headed down to the river, like he'd done so many times before. Like he'd done when he was fourteen, fifteen, sixteen-years-old and had hungered for Nina the way he did now. Like in the days when he'd strung hats in trees to summon her.

Some silly part of him believed she might be waiting, but there was nobody there. He was all alone with the muddy ditch of a river. Any kingfishers had fled this ruined place long ago. Ric slipped down the washaway to the water's edge and stuck a stick into the sludge as a marker. With no vegetation as a buffer, the Donnalee side of the bank was collapsing into the water, clogging it with silt. Was this really the same place where he and Nina had dived and swum as children? He closed his eyes, fighting off an overwhelming sense of loneliness and loss. The contrast between the past and present was heartbreakingly clear.

He walked back to the house, unable to shake the sadness that was settling on him like a thick layer of dust, wanting suddenly to see Sophie. She wasn't in her room. She wasn't in the kitchen having breakfast. She wasn't on the faded couch watching television. He went out the back and looked around. Where was she? Ric stooped low and ventured beneath the verandah. He paused while his eyes adjusted to the dim light and soon objects emerged from the gloom. Nothing much had changed since he was a boy. It was like a time capsule. There was the old rigid inflatable boat that he'd bought for a song when he was sixteen. Nothing wrong with it, apart from a cracked hull that Dad had been going to help him mend. Maybe he'd fix it up for Sophie.

Festoons of cobwebs brushed his face. Logic told him that she wouldn't be here, that she'd never brave the dark and the spiders, but curiosity made him forge ahead. He picked his way around an assortment of bricks and planks and pipes until he reached the rusted steel doors, right at the back.

The coolroom was nothing more than an old refrigerated truck body that his father had converted. Pretty clever, really. Ric slid back the bolt, relishing the rush of cold air on his face as the double doors swung open and automatically turned on the light. He stepped inside, into the coolness that was tainted with something else. The faint, sweet tang of death. A chest freezer stood in the corner. A row of eskies and wooden boxes were stacked along the wall, together with an assortment of homemade fishing rods. A butchered sheep carcass and a side of bacon dangled from hooks in the roof. But then, knowing Dad, it was more likely to be a goat and side of feral pig, both of which could be found running wild in the neglected paddocks of Billabong Bend.

That wasn't all. Two ducks hung from the roof by their necks, and two other birds that he didn't recognise – big black-and-white ones, with domed heads like Chinese geese. Ric frowned, remembering the shots fired, the ones that had scared away Nina's rare snipe. He touched the unplucked birds. Fresh. He might have guessed. His father was almost certainly the mystery hunter in the wetlands yesterday. Ric rubbed his temple. The hard kernel of a headache was taking root deep in his skull. Curse Max and his guns.

Ric backed out of the coolroom and found his way, blinking, into the light. Sophie was running towards him, wearing a radiant smile. 'Dad, come and see.' She pulled him into the outside laundry. Max was standing beside the old incubator. It was a homemade contraption consisting of a cupboard with air holes top and bottom, a wire rack for eggs, a metal dish for water, a thermometer and two light bulbs for heat. He remembered when Max made it for Mum. She'd always hated how the cock birds harassed her hens. 'My poor girls,' she'd say. 'Never a moment's peace.' In the end she refused to have a rooster on the place, so Max had made her the incubator. Whenever they needed more chickens, friends gave them fertile eggs and Mum could hatch them out herself.

'What's going on here?' asked Ric.

'Poppi's hatching me some baby swans. He found an abandoned nest and rescued the eggs.'

Ric shot his father a sharp look and then peered into the cupboard. Nine or ten large pale eggs nestled together in the rack. Large, yes, but he'd seen plenty of swan eggs as a boy, and these ones weren't large enough. And they were off-white instead of speckled greenish-grey. He thought of the beautiful black-and-white birds hanging by their neck in the coolroom.

'When will they hatch, Poppi?'

'Any day now,' said Max. 'I've candled those eggs and they've all got fine big chicks in them, lively as you could want.' He selected an egg and held it to the girl's ear.

An astonished smile split her face. 'I can hear it, I can hear it chirping.' Sophie put her lips to the alabaster shell. 'It's all right,' she whispered, 'Mummy's here.' Sophie held the egg out to Ric, who took it gently and listened. He could hear it too, the softest peeping. 'In a few days I'll have my own baby swans,' she said. 'I can't believe it!' She threw her arms around her grandfather.

Ric returned the egg to the rack with the others. Max misted them all with a spray bottle before closing the door. Sophie dragged an old chair over in front of the incubator. 'I'm going to stay here until they hatch.'

Ric smiled. 'What, no telly?'

Sophie frowned at him, crinkling her brow and looking as stern as she could. 'I've got more important things to do than watch television. I'm going to be a mother. Poppi, could you build the swans a house outside my window?'

'Course I could,' said Max. 'And a little pond too. Do you think they'd like a pond?'

'That would be perfect,' she said, after a moment's thought. 'My swans would love a little pond.'

'Coming in for some breakfast?' Ric asked her. 'I'll make you whatever you like.'

'I said, I'm staying here.'

'Fine, suit yourself.' Ric turned and headed for the house, slowly, to ensure that Max caught up with him. 'I looked in the coolroom,' he said in a low voice. 'Those aren't swan eggs, are they? What the hell are those birds?'

'Don't know,' said Max. 'Never seen anything like them.'

When they reached the porch, Ric turned to his father. 'What did you have to go and shoot them for? Who shoots nesting birds?'

'I didn't realise. I only found the eggs afterwards.' A sheen of sweat showed on his forehead. 'At least some good's come of it. Look how happy Sophia is.'

'It's Sophie,' said Ric. 'And she wouldn't be happy if she knew the eggs were orphaned, not abandoned. If she knew you'd shot the parents.'

'Now don't you go telling her about that. Sophia's got a sweet streak, the sort of kindness your mother had.' Max frowned and examined his boots. 'I was mean sometimes, back when you were a kid. I made mistakes. Don't want to make them again.'

'Then why ever did you go and shoot those birds in the first place?'

'What am I supposed to do?' Max looked genuinely puzzled. 'Sophia won't let me eat the chickens. She's gone and named them all.'

'There's a butcher in Drovers Flat,' said Ric. 'Go and buy chickens there, like a normal person.'

'It sticks in my craw to pay out good money for meat some other fella killed, when I can get it for free.'

'Well then, go shoot the life out of the wetlands,' said Ric. 'But don't expect me to hide it from Sophie.'

Max gave him a searching look. 'That Moore girl, Nina. Bet she's behind this.'

'Maybe she is,' said Ric. 'Or maybe it's Sophie, or what Mum would say, or the plain fact that it's illegal to go shooting at Billabong. Or maybe it's that we've never seen birds like that before and they could be something rare, something special. Or that they had the right to go ahead and hatch those eggs themselves, after they went to all the trouble of mating up and laying them. Take your pick.'

His father looked stricken and took a step back.

'Hiding the truth won't work.' Ric's voice was raised and angry. 'Not if you keep on making the same mistakes. You need to stop making them, Dad. Don't pretend to stop it. Just flat-out stop it.'

Max seemed to shrink, and his broad square face caved in a little. He took off his hat, something he rarely did during the day, and twisted it in his hands. It was suddenly hard to recognise this wretched-looking man as his father. Ric was breathing fast, almost panting. He looked around to make sure Sophie wasn't in earshot.

'You know what I see when I look at Sophia?' said Max. 'I see your mother all over again — her gentleness, her softness, the parts of her I went and hurt the most. If you tell that little girl what her Poppi did, if I see that disappointment on her face, same as I did on your mama's? Well, I couldn't bear it.' He dragged his fingers through his hair with a jerky hand. 'I was hard on your mother. Hard on all of you . . . too hard.'

It was an astonishing admission, one Ric had never imagined he'd hear. 'Promise me,' said Ric, his voice fierce. 'Give me your oath that you won't go to Billabong, not even for rabbits. Swear to me that you won't even go fishing over there.'

For the briefest moment Max's face flared with anger. Then he lowered his eyes. 'All right,' he said, 'I'll stay away.'

Ric nodded. 'I'll hold you to that.' And he would, for Sophie – for Nina. He'd sink Dad's old punt if he had to, shotguns and all. But an unpleasant, nagging voice told him he was fooling himself. The promise he'd extracted from his father wasn't just about Sophie, or Nina, or protecting Billabong Bend. Part of it was about him. A big part. He'd enjoyed calling the shots for once, with the unbending, all-powerful father of his youth.

Max looked so miserable that a wave of sympathy washed away any triumph Ric felt. 'Have you had breakfast?' he asked. 'No? Come on. I'll do us bacon and eggs.'

Max brightened. 'You're on. I put a fresh piece of bacon in the fridge just yesterday.'

'I know,' said Ric. 'And I know where it came from too.'

Max laughed and clapped him on the back, leaving his hand there until they reached the house. It was the first time his father had done that since Ric was sixteen-years-old, and it felt good.

Max sank into a kitchen chair and rubbed his palms together. 'Have you considered my offer?' he asked. 'Will you stay and work with me here at Donnalee?'

Ric grabbed half a dozen eggs from the basket on the lime-washed kitchen dresser. 'Yes,' he said. 'I'll stay, even if it's just to keep an eye on you.'

'*Grazie a Dio*!' Max threw up his hands, voice cracking with emotion. 'We'll have a good life. You, me and Sophia, eh? A happy life.'

'Yeah, yeah, don't overdo it.' He didn't remind Max that Sophie would be gone in two weeks. Dad would miss her. Ric looked out the window to the laundry, to where his daughter sat hunched before the incubator. She was a strange one, all right. Stubborn too. More trouble than a cat at a dog show. But when he tried to imagine life at Donnalee without her, he failed. With a shock he realised just how much he'd miss her himself.

'I'm getting old, Ricardo.' Max had a faraway look in his eye. 'Things happen to people and, well . . . you need some sort of a stake here at Donnalee. It'll be all yours one day.'

'Cut it out, Dad,' said Ric. 'You'll probably outlast me.'

Max got up, disappeared down the hall, and returned a few minutes later with a form and a pen. 'Power of attorney, to show I'm serious.' He pushed the paper across the table. 'Sign it. You can act for me in financial matters, learn the business side of things.'

'What, so you can go fishing all day?' said Ric, sliding bacon from the pan to his father's plate. His flippant words could not disguise the unexpected pride he felt.

Max helped himself to toast. 'That's right.' He nodded in satisfaction as Ric picked up the pen. 'So I can go fishing.'

Lockie strode towards them along the half-finished fence line, hair turned to bronze by the strong light. Occasionally he tested the wire's tension with an expert flick of his finger. He looked good, fitter than ever, and since his promotion to station manager, there was a newfound authority in his bearing.

Her father acknowledged Lockie with a nod, then stared down at the shallow soupy water. 'I remember,' he said, 'before the dam up at Hopeton. Before the droughts and the carp and the irrigators . . . well, you could see the bottom of the river. Like glass, the water was. You could see the yabbies and the dragons chasing after them. You could see the catfish building nests, guarding little pebble rings on the riverbed.'

'Catfish have been gone for years,' said Nina.

'You couldn't see them in that muck, even if they were there,' he said. 'Breaks your heart to see the Bunyip sink so low. Was a time she flowed clear through the wetlands, into the Barwon, on to the Darling and down the Murray to the sea. Just look at her now.' He spat in the dust. 'Get any drier, and she'll stop flowing altogether.'

For a while they all stood silent on the bank. What was there to add? Dad had said it all. Lockie rolled a cigarette. 'We won't get anything done, moping around like this.'

It was true enough, and they got back to work. Lockie and Dad rammed pickets, dug holes and set posts, while Nina strung wire. She stopped to watch her father working. The move to town hadn't made him soft like he'd said it would. He was still lean as the fence post he was tamping in. But it had made him happier. The worry once etched into his face had faded and been replaced with smile lines.

Lockie was observing her. 'Bludger,' he said with a smile.

Dad looked up at Lockie, who was leaning on his shovel. 'Reckon that's the pot calling the kettle black.'

Nina tightened the ratchet on the strainer, watching the grips walk up the wire like magic until it was taut as a bowstring. She liked fencing. It was a hard job, but there was something immensely satisfying, almost therapeutic, about the process of connecting things together. Every fence was different, and at the end of the day you had something substantial and useful to show for your effort. It wasn't like feeding hay or watering trees or washing dishes. It didn't need doing all over again tomorrow. A well-built fence stood day in, day out, as an enduring monument to an honest day's work.

And today the job seemed easy, thanks to the extra hands on deck. Lockie had been a jackaroo at Red Gums way back when, and fitted in like one of the family. She'd missed working together like this, him crooning his country songs and Dad cracking jokes. Everything seemed much more manageable than when she was on her own. She barely noticed the sweat or the heat or the flies, and by the time Mum arrived in the afternoon with an esky full of lunch and cold drinks, they'd finished the stretch right down to the old bridge.

Nina sat in the shade, her back against a gum tree, while Mum doled out sandwiches. She was a tall woman, grown thick at the waist, solid but not fat. The colours of her sleeveless floral dress brightened up the grey-green riverbank, just like Mum's presence always brightened up any occasion. Dad took a folding chair from the ute and set it up beside Nina. Mum thanked him and settled into it. She brushed back a wisp of steel-grey hair that had escaped from the rough bun beneath her wide straw hat. On impulse Nina stood up and gave her a hug. Mum was the heart of the family, and that position bestowed on her a kind of dignity and quiet beauty that Nina loved. Jinx, who also adored Mum, trotted over to lay his head in her lap.

'How are things at Drovers, Mum?'

'Store's doing a roaring trade. We can't truck in enough feed to fill our deliveries.'

'That's good,' said Nina.

'You'd think so, wouldn't you?' Her mother smiled. 'Trouble is, half the customers can't afford to pay their accounts. And you can guess how your father takes their hard-luck stories. Straight to his heart, that's how.' Nina placed a hand on her mother's shoulder. Dad could hold a grudge, but he could also be generous to a fault, and she loved him for it. Mum placed her own hand over Nina's. 'Don't worry, darling. We're doing fine compared to a lot of people.'

Dad and Lockie leaned against trees, downing mugs of chilled lemon tea. 'How are things out your way, Lockie?' asked Mum.

'Same as everywhere,' he said. 'Paddocks darn near dried up and blown away. Lowest yields for twenty years and most of that down-graded to feed wheat. Now we're selling off cattle like crazy, in spite of rock-bottom prices.'

'That's a shame,' said Mum. 'How are your folks?'

'Good thanks, Ellen,' said Lockie. 'Went up to see them for Christmas. Asked Nina along but she wouldn't come at it.'

'Oh, Nina, why not? It would have been lovely for the two of you.'

Nina stayed silent. She'd asked Lockie to spend Christmas at Red Gums too. He'd declined, but that apparently didn't rate a mention. Why was she always the one meant to go to him? Why didn't it work the other way around? Today was the first time he'd been to Red Gums for weeks..

'I've an idea,' said Mum. 'Why not go back with Lockie for a few days, Nina? We could look after things here, couldn't we, Jim?'

Dad nodded, Lockie looked hopeful and Nina squirmed. She didn't want to go back with Lockie. She wanted to experiment with the pecans' irrigation flows, spend a whole day riding the boundaries and head back to Billabong in search of painted snipe. And then there was Sophie. She'd promised the girl a riding lesson. 'Sorry.' She hated being put on the spot like this. 'I'll be flat out this week.' Lockie's face fell. 'Perhaps you could stay on a bit longer?'

'Nah, I'm training a couple of young blokes,' he said. 'Gotta be there.'

Nina sighed. Of course he had to be there. Just like she had to be here.

'You can't expect Lockie to drop everything,' said Mum. 'Sometimes compromise is called for.'

'Except I'm the one doing all the compromising,' said Nina. 'Why is Lockie's job more important than mine?' Mum harrumphed softly and Lockie looked dark. Nina wiped the sweat from her forehead with the back of her work glove and drank the last of her tea. It had long been a sore point between Lockie and her, particularly since he'd asked her to move in with him. It wasn't like she hadn't been tempted sometimes. All the moments sitting alone on the verandah as darkness fell. When she woke by herself in the morning after a restless night. But how could she run Red Gums properly if she didn't live here?

'I meant to tell you, Nina,' said Mum. 'Eva Langley's had some sort of a fall.'

'Eva?' Nina sat forward. 'Is she all right?'

'Nothing broken, thank goodness. Just a bit shaken. She was admitted to the hospital overnight for observation, apparently, but she's back at the home now.'

'I need to see her.' Nina stood up. 'Would you mind if I flew up this afternoon?'

'If it's okay with Dad.'

'Go on,' said her father. 'Me and Lockie have got this covered, right, Lockie?'

'Reckon so.' Lockie looked down at his big flat hands for a moment. Blood seeped from a wire cut, and his nails were ragged and broken. 'I'll drive Nina back to the house if you want.'

'Would you, Lockie?' Mum fanned her rosy face with her hat. 'I fancy just sitting in the shade for a bit. There's a hint of a breeze down here by the river.'

'Righto.' Lockie climbed into his truck. 'Got your stuff?'

Nina hopped in beside him. 'Don't have any stuff,' she said. 'I travel light.'

Jinx jumped up at the cabin door, scratching and barking. Dad took hold of his collar. 'Why don't you stay with Kate tonight?' he said. 'Don't like the idea of you flying back when you're tired.'

Nina leant out the window and kissed him. 'Thanks, Dad. I'll see how I feel. Don't forget to feed Jinx. And could you give the horses some hay?'

They waved goodbye and took off, dust pluming behind them. Lockie spun the wheel to avoid a deep corrugation. 'Seems like forever since I've seen you,' he said. Nina looked out the window, thinking, *Whose fault is that?* 'And now you go haring off to Moree without me.'

'I'd hardly call visiting an old lady in a nursing home *haring off.*'

'Nah, of course not. Sorry, it's just that I've missed you.'

'And I've missed you. If only we weren't both so busy all the time.'

'How long you been running this place on your own now?' asked Lockie.

'Almost five years.'

'That long?' Lockie moved his grip on the wheel, flexing the sinews of his forearms. 'It's been a while since I had a good look round. You've worked miracles, you know that, Nina? Jim managed well enough, but you've really made the land sing. That stretch by the river, for instance. And those orchards? Going gangbusters, despite the drought, despite the irrigators sucking the Bunyip dry.'

She shot him a pleased smile. Lockie was a shrewd and experienced farmer, well respected throughout the district, someone who didn't pull any punches. He didn't often hand out praise like this, and it meant a lot.

'It's going to be tough in the future to survive out here,' said Nina. 'The climate's changing, and we have to change with it. Better ways with water, different crops like my pecans, different livestock even.'

Her words tumbled out in an enthusiastic rush. 'Carbon farming, putting native trees back on cleared land. There are big grants now for restoring riverbanks. They actually give you money.' She stopped to catch her breath. 'Problem is, people are still looking in the rear-view mirror.'

'You'll get no arguments from me,' said Lockie. 'Out Timboon way they planted ten thousand trees to reduce salinity and discovered they could claim carbon credits for them. Talk about a bonus. Hard to get your head around all the new opportunities sometimes.' They turned into the track by the dam paddock. Monty pounded along the fence like a mad thing, keeping pace with the truck, looking for all the world like he still belonged on the racetrack. 'One thing I do know,' said Lockie. 'Those bloody cotton growers are ruining it for everybody. What's the point of busting a gut to conserve water when those guys waste ten times more than we can save? They'll put us all out of business before they're through.'

Nina nodded. She looked at Lockie's rugged face in profile, the ginger stubble on his chin, the thoughtful deep-set eyes, the copper hair brightened by the sun. A handsome man, and a good and clever one. Why didn't her pulse pound for him, the way it did for Ric? Something was missing between them lately, some sort of passion. Like they'd grown too comfortable with each other and had stopped trying.

The truck pulled up at the house and they both got out. Lockie took off his hat and turned the hose in the yard on a fraction. He drank from the end and then let it trickle over his head and face, wetting his hat before plonking it back on his head.

'Want a proper cold drink?' asked Nina. 'One from the fridge?'

'I'd better get back,' he said. 'We're one man down now, remember?'

'Thanks, Lockie. I owe you one.'

'More than one actually.' He frowned and kicked aimlessly at the bone-dry ground. 'I heard Ric Bonelli's back.'

'That's right,' said Nina. 'He's moved in across the river . . . with his daughter, Sophie.'

'Yeah, his daughter. I heard about that too.' Despite Lockie's protestation about having to get back, he seemed in no hurry. What was he waiting for? But she knew. Of course she did. She just didn't want to have that conversation right now. She didn't know what she'd say.

'Seems he's got quite a reputation,' said Lockie.

'Your point?' She could hear the defiant edge to her voice. 'I can look after myself.'

'Course you can.' He pulled her close and ran a finger down her dirty cheek. 'Are you coming next weekend for the rodeo? I've got tickets for Troy Cassar-Daley Saturday night.'

She ducked from his arms. 'But the organic field day is next Saturday. You said you'd come. I'm doing a presentation on pecans.'

'Sorry, I forgot. Can't you get out of it?'

'I don't want to get out of it.'

He groaned and pulled her back to him. 'Okay, I'll come. Pity though. Those tickets are scarce as hen's teeth.'

'Go then,' she said. 'Don't waste them.'

'You sure?' He raised his brows, inspecting her face. 'You won't mind?'

'Nope.' Nina looked away. Lockie gently turned her chin and kissed her, long and slow. She closed her eyes, but the kiss was a dud. Disappointment about the field day, or something more?

He climbed behind the wheel. 'See you. Fly safe.'

The truck took off, crawling its way around the house yard so it didn't raise too much dust. Nina watched it go, turning Lockie's words over in her mind. Ric had quite a reputation, did he? Well, so what? She shook her head to clear it and hurried inside. What Ric did had nothing to do with her any more.

CHAPTER 12

It was after six o'clock by the time Nina arrived at Pemberley. Eva Langley was sitting up in bed with a thermometer in her mouth. It felt like an intrusion to enter the room, but when Nina crept in Eva greeted her with bright eyes.

'What a lovely surprise. Your timing's perfect.' Eva's voice was as strong as ever, low and tuneful. Her hair was neatly done, and in her beaded cream nightgown she looked the picture of elegance. What a relief. She actually looked better than last time. An unopened packet of liquorice sat on the corner table. Seeing it reminded Nina that she'd forgotten to bring some herself.

A nurse emerged from the small ensuite. 'Must be your day for visitors, Eva,' she said. 'I'll bring in another chair.'

'And could you order an extra dinner, Vera? That will make three.'

The nurse nodded. She smoothed the beautiful aqua bedspread over Eva's knees, the one that featured azure kingfishers. 'Chicken or fish?'

Nina looked at Eva enquiringly.

'It's one of Pemberley's little perks,' said Eva. 'My visitors are entitled to free meals. So what will it be, chicken or fish? I'd have the fish if I were you. The chicken's too dry. We'll have to eat in the room though. Darned doctor won't let me out of bed until tomorrow.'

Eva had said three dinners. Who else was coming? James? Nina couldn't stand being stuck in a room with him, not even for a few minutes. 'I don't want to impose,' she said. 'How about I come back in the morning?'

'You've only just arrived. Vera, she'll have the fish.'

What to do? Stay and put up with James? Or go and disappoint the dear old friend whom she'd just flown an hour to see? 'You look well, Eva,' said Nina. 'I was worried about you.'

'Bit of a sore ankle is all. Don't know why everybody makes such a fuss. You'd think I'd broken my hip. Yet nobody's concerned when I die of boredom every day.'

Vera returned with a second chair and set up a folding tray table. It would be rude to go now. Nina pulled a chair over next to the bed. May as well make the best of it. Perhaps she'd learn something useful in her mission to buy Billabong Bend. Perhaps she could even change James's mind. Although he wouldn't admit to wanting to sell the place, not in front of his mother.

Nina had just convinced herself that this chance meeting with James was a good thing, when a man walked in the door carrying a scruffy duffel bag. Not the man she'd expected at all. Not James. It was Freeman.

With a shock of joy she recognised the gentle, gap-toothed smile on his grizzled, bearded face. How many years since his ramshackle houseboat had meandered down the Bunyip? These days the low flows deterred all but the lightest river traffic. She'd sometimes wondered if Freeman was still alive. He'd seemed ancient even back when she and Ric were children. But rumours persisted of his turning up here and there, collecting river stories and telling them in return. And now here he was, large as life, twisting his hat and shuffling around Eva's little room.

'Nina.' His old eyes twinkled. 'It's been a long time.' Freeman was even taller than she remembered, and seemed to have hunched down to fit the room, like he somehow didn't belong under a roof.

The sleeves of his faded work shirt were rolled up over still-powerful forearms, and he wore a buttonless vest. What looked like a cut-off stirrup leather held up his ragged moleskin trousers. By contrast his boots were shiny and new, as if purchased especially for the occasion.

Nina laughed and threw her arms round his shabby shoulders. 'I don't believe it. Eva, I didn't know you and Freeman were friends.'

'There's a lot you young folks don't know.' She smiled, and the smile stayed around her eyes. 'Take my boy James, for instance. Such a sceptic. He mistakes being cynical for being wise.'

Freeman upended the three glasses sitting on the table by the water jug. He rummaged around in his bag, glanced briefly at the door, then extracted a bottle of dry ginger ale and another of brandy. Eva's eyes lit up as he poured her a generous drink. 'They treat us like children here,' she said, pouting like a girl.

Nina took a sip of the drink Freeman offered, and a delicious wave of heat moved through her. An orderly pushed in backwards through the door with a trolley of dinner trays. The three giggled and hid their drinks. Soon they were eating and laughing like old friends should. They were no longer in a room at a nursing home. This was a party, a heartfelt reunion.

'Tell Nina about your project,' said Eva.

'I collect river stories.' Freeman's ears were turning red. 'Same as always.'

'He's turned professional,' said Eva. 'Documenting life right throughout the Murray-Darling basin. People, plants, animals – everything. Photographing and recording their stories. Piecing together a priceless history of our river heritage.'

Freeman's shy smile could not disguise his pride. 'I write down what folks say, that's all.'

'Don't be so modest,' scolded Eva. 'Freeman's an author now. He sold his *Murrumbidgee Tales* to a publisher. The book's coming out next year, and they want one on the Kingfisher River after that.'

'How wonderful,' said Nina. 'What's it called Freeman, so I can buy it?'

'*Songline Stories.*' The flush deepened beneath his dark complexion. 'Beats me what they want with my old yarns, but they seem to like them. Even paid me. Enough to buy a computer, and a little runabout to tow behind the boat.' His smile turned into a grin. 'Catfish, I call her. Runs a treat up and down the shallow reaches where Warriuka can't get any more.'

'Freeman's been here all week,' said Eva. 'Bringing brandy and sweets, videoing me and my memories on his, his . . . show her, Freeman.' He pulled out a camcorder. 'On that,' she said. 'So they won't be forgotten. Here I was thinking nobody wants to listen. Then Freeman arrives and does nothing but listen, day after day.' She beamed at him. 'It's been such glorious fun.'

'And I'll go on listening, Eva,' he said. 'Listen for as long as it takes. Listen till you're done.'

Nina was intrigued. 'How do you decide where to go next?'

'It's not so easy any more,' he said. 'What with the drought, and all those dams and bridges. They've tamed the rivers something shocking. Times I've even had to truck Warriuka from place to place, but I always wind up back on the songlines.'

'Songlines?' asked Nina.

'Spirit pathways of souls who wandered Australia in the beginning,' said Eva. 'Singing out names of what they saw, of birds and trees. Of mountains and forests . . . everything. Singing the world into being, like Aslan did in *The Lion, the Witch and the Wardrobe.*'

'Do you really believe that?' Nina hadn't heard this particular creation story before. Her parents were Anglican, and proud of it.

'Oh, yes,' said Eva. 'I'm an animist. Not only people have souls, Nina. It's arrogant to think it. All of us do — animals and plants as well. So do rocks and rivers. Even wind and shadows. These spirits exist before we're born, and remain after we die. They're eternal. It's the circle of life, like in the song from *The Lion King.*'

Nina smiled. Sophie was nine and Eva was eighty-nine, but they both loved their movie allusions.

'What about you, Freeman?' asked Nina. 'What do you believe?'

'I'm a great churchgoer.' He chuckled. 'The rivers — they're my church.'

Nina laughed. 'It's so exciting,' she said. 'I can't wait to read your books.'

'I could write your story, Nina,' he said. 'Yours, and your family's. I'll come by when the river rises.'

Nina finished her drink and asked for another. What an extraordinary evening. A swift shaft of shame hit her as she realised that up until now she'd been patronising Eva. Humouring her fantasy of going home. Coming here full of pity. The true depth and breadth of this woman's life had been as invisible to her as those songlines Freeman followed.

'Eva,' said Nina. 'When you're feeling better . . .'

'You're not going to badger me about Billabong again, are you?' she said in a cross voice. 'That place will be sold over my dead body.'

'No,' said Nina quickly. 'No, I was wondering . . . would you like me to take you back there for a visit?'

Colour rushed to Eva's pale cheeks. 'Oh yes. Yes! It's high time I went home.'

Nina blinked to dam the tears that hovered behind her eyes. 'I'd better go,' she said. 'Leave you to your stories.' She embraced them both, then slipped out the door and listened. For a moment the room was quiet, then the murmur of conversation built again. The sound of Eva's musical voice followed her down the hallway. Nina swallowed hard, and hoped she'd have the courage to keep her promise.

<h1 style="text-align:center">CHAPTER 13</h1>

Ric crept into the laundry as morning fired the eastern sky. Sophie was still asleep, curled up in blankets on the dusty floor beside the incubator. She looked so tiny. He didn't know what to do, what to say, how to tell her. The early-morning phone call was seared into his memory, each word, each dreadful pause loaded with meaning.

'It's about Sophie's mother.' Hilary Harper's voice had sounded faraway and unreal. 'I'm afraid there's been an incident. Rachael overdosed yesterday and has been admitted to hospital.'

'I don't get it,' he said. 'She was getting better. Rachael was getting ready to have Sophie home.'

'Well, she's suffered a setback. A serious one, I'm afraid.'

'How serious?'

'Rachael's on a respirator. She'll recover, but it was touch and go there for a while. As her social worker, I'm hoping to readmit her to the psychiatric clinic. You'll need to keep Sophie longer than we first thought.'

'That's impossible,' said Ric. 'What about school? I'm not set up this end for a kid.'

'Ric, I don't think you quite understand. This wasn't an accidental overdose. She's in no position to care for a child.'

'Can't you find somebody else? A relative or something?'

'You're her closest relative,' said Hilary. 'And she's already settled there. Let me contact the principal at Drovers Central School. I'll forward the documents you'll need to enrol Sophie.' Ric had been speechless. 'Rachael's not well enough to talk to you or her daughter right now. The minute she is, I'll let you know.'

And that had been that. He'd lain in bed for a while, trying to get his head around the news. Then he'd pulled on a pair of shorts and crept into Sophie's room. Her bed was empty, but he'd known where to find her. She'd barely left the laundry in the two days since the eggs had arrived. She even ate her meals there. 'I can't have dinner in the kitchen any more,' she'd explained. 'What if the baby swans hatch?'

So Max had set up a card table in the corner, with a cloth and vase of red geraniums picked fresh each morning. He delivered breakfast, lunch and dinner, plus snacks. Last night Ric had sat up with Max and Sophie, playing snap and poker, using matchsticks to bet with. For once the television went unwatched, and now the laundry stank of cigars.

Might as well get it over with. Ric squatted down beside Sophie, and tapped her shoulder. No response. He gathered the bundle of girl and blankets into his arms, and carried her into the house. Sophie stirred and rubbed her eyes as he laid her on her bed. 'My eggs,' she said sleepily. 'I have to get back to my eggs.'

'There's something I have to tell you first,' he said. 'It's about your mum.'

Sophie sat up blinking. 'She's coming, isn't she? I can show her the eggs. Do you think they'll hatch before she gets here? I hope so.'

'She's not coming, Soph.' Ric hesitated. How much should he tell her? Why hadn't he asked Hilary about how to break the news? 'She's back in hospital.'

'I don't believe you.' Tears welled in her eyes. 'I want to talk to her.'

'You can't right now,' said Ric. 'She's too sick.'

'Mum said she was getting better.' Her breath came in short spurts, her eyes reproving. 'In her last letter Mum said I'd be going home soon, that things would be different.'

Ric swallowed hard. He wondered, not for the first time, how long Rachael had been ill. What Sophie had seen. Up until now, each time he'd tried to understand Sophie's world she'd pushed him away.

'You know your mum better than I do.' Ric moved slowly towards her, hand outstretched like with a startled colt. 'Does she get sick a lot?'

'Mum gets sick all the time,' said Sophie. 'Just when I think she's okay, she gets bad again. I don't know what to do. Sometimes I think she gets so sad because of me, that it's all my fault.' She collapsed in a sudden flood of tears. Ric reached her in a stride and swept her up in a protective embrace.

Max came in wearing a dressing-gown, his face a mask of concern. 'What's wrong with Sophia?'

Ric carried her to the lounge room, Max trailing after. He laid the weeping girl on the couch and sat beside her. Max put on an encouraging smile. He pulled a chair close and sat down too.

'Sophie's mother had a relapse.' Ric's voice was low. 'She's back in hospital. Sophie can't go home next week.'

Comprehension dawned in Max's eyes and his smile grew more tender. 'Your mama, she'll be fine. Lots of good people to look after her in a hospital, eh? She needs you to be brave for her.' Sophie's crying slowed to a sob. 'Can you do that?' he asked. 'Can you be brave for your mama?' Sophie nodded solemnly and Max offered his hand. 'Let's go check on your eggs. I think today — today they're going to hatch. Maybe we can take photos of the babies to send to your mama? To cheer her up.'

'Do you really think they'll hatch today?' asked Sophie in a small voice.

'Maybe not all of them. You see, mama swan, she lays one egg every day. Ten eggs, that's ten days. It takes a bit longer for those last eggs to hatch.'

'Can we go and check on them now?'

'Sure, we'll go check, and then we'll have breakfast,' said Max. 'The

three of us. I'll make your favourite omelette. Would you like that?'
Sophie nodded and managed the faintest smile. Ric looked at Max,
brows raised in admiration.

In the laundry Max opened the incubator and Sophie gasped. A
wet, wobble-headed chick stared from among a pile of broken shell. It
was like no cygnet Ric had ever seen. Pinkish head and neck and
dirty-white body. Big black bill with a little yellow egg tooth at the tip.
Its squashed-up legs and feet were yellow too.

Sophie leaned in close and it began a loud peeping. 'Don't worry,'
she cooed. 'Mummy's here.' Sophie reached in and took the baby in
her hand, raised it close to her face. It peeped louder and nibbled her
nose with its tiny bill. She giggled. 'That tickles. Dad, take a photo for
Mum.'

Now another egg was moving, and as they watched a little pip
raised on its shell. The unhatched baby joined in the peeping. Sophie's
tear-stained face had turned luminous with wonder.

'Put the chick back and leave it be until it dries off and turns fluffy,'
said Max. 'Then it can go in a brooder box. I'll set one up right in your
bedroom. Now, come and have breakfast.'

Sophie put the chick back. 'I can't leave them. Can I have breakfast
here? Can I leave the incubator door open and watch?'

'Sure you can,' said Max. 'It's warm enough for them. Ric and me,
we'll go make that omelette.'

The little girl didn't seem to hear. Max pulled a chair over for her
in front of the incubator and Sophie sat down, her eyes never leaving
the miracle of birth happening inside.

In the kitchen Ric beat eggs as Max chopped bacon and grated
potatoes. They worked for a while in silence. Ric was grateful to have
his father there, grateful to share this problem with somebody who
cared. And Dad did care; he cared a lot, that was plain. Cared about
both of them. He'd changed so much. Why couldn't he have been like
this when Mum was still here? How different things might have been.
She could have loved this man, they all could have. But change didn't
happen in a vacuum. Maybe it had taken losing everything to make
his father take stock.

'Can Sophie stay?' asked Ric. 'Don't know for how long. Don't know when Rachael will be well again.'

'You have to ask?' said Max.

'Thank goodness for those birds,' said Ric. 'Whatever they are. She'd be a wreck without them.'

'*Povero bambina*' said Max. 'Such a sweet child. Those chicks, they'll help every time she misses her mother.'

'Just make sure the goddamn things don't die on her. Then we'd really be in trouble.'

'I've raised plenty of ducks,' said Max, with a dismissive wave of his hand. 'Don't you worry. They'll be fine.'

'But they're not ducks, are they?' Ric poured egg mixture into the pan. 'And they're not swans either.' He needed to find out what those big black-and-white birds were quick-smart. Sophie's happiness depended on them surviving. Time to talk to Nina.

'Magpie geese,' said Nina, after Ric described the birds to her over the phone. 'At Billabong? I don't believe it.'

'Dad said those birds sure looked like geese . . . black-and-white, with kind of a crest on their head.'

'Doesn't sound like they could be anything else,' said Nina. 'Although magpie geese aren't strictly geese at all. They're the last of an ancient waterbird family, and they haven't lived along the Bunyip since Eva Langley was a little girl. They used to breed in the wetlands and migrate north to permanent lakes along the Paroo River in the dry season. It would be a miracle to find a pair breeding here again. And for somebody to shoot them? It's disgusting. I feel sick.'

'Me too,' said Ric. And he did, as much for the lie as for anything else. Max had been hunting rabbits, he'd said, and discovered the birds shot dead by the nest. 'At least the eggs seem okay. One's hatched already in our old incubator.'

'How exciting,' said Nina. 'You'll be able to tell straight away if it's a magpie gosling. They're very distinctive. Head and breast a kind of pinky-orange, and the rest of the body grey.'

'That's them. Now, how do I look after them? Dad says he knows, but he's only raised chickens and muscovies.'

'I imagine they wouldn't be very different from raising muscovy ducks. Muscovies are half-goose anyway . . . but wouldn't you rather bring them here?'

'No way. Sophie's had some bad news about her mum. The birds are a good distraction.'

'What's happened?'

'Nothing I want to talk about on the phone.'

'Well, tell me in person when I come to visit the goslings.' said Nina. 'I'm dying to see them, though maybe when your dad's not around.'

This was a turn-up – Nina asking to come over. Ric gave silent thanks to the little birds. 'Come round about ten,' he said. Max would be off on his regular Wednesday trip into town for supplies. The coast would be clear.

CHAPTER 14

Nina sat on the quilted blue bedspread, cradling the peeping gosling, while Sophie hovered about, anxious as any new mother. 'That's Odette,' said Sophie. 'Like in the cartoon *Swan Lake*. She's the youngest.'

'How can you tell them apart?' asked Nina, bewitched by the small marvel in her cupped hand.

Sophie gently extended the bird's leg. 'See? She has a bit of a bent toe. They're all different.'

'There's no doubt about it,' said Nina. 'These are magpie geese – the first born at Billabong in eighty years.'

'Poppi told me they were swans.'

'No, no,' said Nina. 'These babies are much more special than swans. Are they eating?'

Sophie nodded. 'They like me to feed them. Watch.' Sophie put a pinch of chick crumbles between her thumb and forefinger and tapped the gosling's bill. It stopped peeping, opened its mouth and gobbled the food down.

'Amazing. Magpie geese are the only waterfowl that feed their young beak-to-beak like that. They've imprinted on you,' said Nina. 'They believe you're their mother.'

'I am,' said Sophie proudly.

'How many are there?'

'Eight,' said Sophie. 'But there'll be ten. Two eggs still haven't hatched.'

Nina gazed down in wonder at the gaggle of little goslings, all calling for Sophie's attention. Their brooder box was spotless, their drinking water clean. Some shredded lettuce floated in a separate bowl, mimicking duckweed. The girl was doing a great job of looking after them. 'Whose idea was the lettuce?'

'Poppi's,' said Sophie. 'He knows a lot about birds.'

She had to hand it to Max. He'd done a wonderful thing rescuing these rare geese. 'Thank goodness for your Poppi,' said Nina. 'Without him, these babies didn't stand a chance.'

Sophie's eyes were shining. She lifted her chin and set her shoulders a little straighter. 'I love Poppi so much.'

'Of course you do.' What a sweet kid. 'Maybe your children have had enough excitement for one day.' Nina returned Odette to her brothers and sisters.

'Want a cuppa?' asked Ric. 'Fresh brewed. Dad grows and grinds his own coffee beans. You haven't lived till you've tasted it.'

'I'm impressed,' said Nina. 'Never thought of growing coffee.'

'Coming, Soph?' asked Ric. The girl shook her head, absorbed again with her little charges.

They slipped out of the bedroom and down the hall to the kitchen. Ric filled a stained aluminium moka pot with water. 'Dad says you should never clean it, only rinse it,' he said by way of apology. 'Theory is, the build-up of scum helps the flavour. Don't know if it's true or not. Might just be that Dad's lazy.' He added grounds to the inner chamber, and in a few minutes the kitchen was filled with the delicious aroma of fresh coffee.

'So,' said Nina, taking a seat at the table, 'why can't Sophie go home?'

'Her mother overdosed.' Ric kept his voice low. 'She's back in hospital.'

'That's awful,' said Nina. 'Poor Sophie. How's she taking it?'

'Pretty hard,' said Ric. 'It's the first time she's said anything much about Rachael to me. Then those geese started hatching and she seemed to forget all about it.'

'She's probably holding it in,' said Nina. 'Trying to hide the hurt.'

'Guess you're right, but I'm not having much luck getting through to her.' The pot bubbled over, liquid hissing and spitting on the stovetop. Ric turned it down. 'She's put up a wall.'

'Bring Sophie round this arvo for that riding lesson,' said Nina. 'Maybe she'll open up to me.'

He poured them each a coffee. 'I'd appreciate it.'

This was Nina's first time in Donnalee's kitchen. Grimy walls, cobwebbed corners, the long-time absence of a woman's touch. She studied Ric's anxious face. Their eyes met and something passed between them. Or did she imagine it?

He handed her a mug and Nina took a sip. She was normally a tea person, but the brew tasted fabulous — rich and mellow. Though anything would taste better than the stale instant coffee at her place. 'How about a favour in return?' she said. 'I'm taking Eva Langley back to Billabong Bend for a visit. Could you come along to help in case she falls or something?'

Ric looked thoughtful. 'That might be a bit of a shock for an old lady. The place is pretty neglected.'

'Yes,' said Nina. 'That's partly the idea. Maybe then she'll realise that Billabong needs looking after. Maybe then she'll sell it to me.'

'Tough call.' Ric whistled low through his teeth. 'I wouldn't want to make it.'

'Well, luckily, you don't have to,' said Nina. 'So will you come, or not?'

'Sure, I'll come.' He drained his cup. 'Be happy to. When do you want me?'

'Could you meet me at Red Gums tomorrow morning round eleven?'

Sophie ran into the kitchen. 'They're hatching,' she said. 'The last two eggs.'

'Now this I have to see.' Nina followed the girl out the back door,

Ric's words echoing in her head. Tough call, he'd said, and it was. But Eva had seen the photographs. She knew a lot already. And if *she* was Eva, she'd want to know the truth. The whole truth. Wouldn't she?

Nina had Flicka saddled and ready when Ric arrived with his daughter later that afternoon. The girl was wearing shorts and sneakers. 'Hasn't Sophie got jeans or something?'

'They're in the wash,' said Ric.

'She's only got the one pair?'

Sophie squirmed and hung her head. Oh no, she'd embarrassed the poor girl. Nina thought quickly. 'It's just . . . I was wondering if she'd like my old pony club stuff. I'm sure it's packed away somewhere. Seems a shame for it to go to waste.'

'What do you think, Soph?'

The girl gave her father a shy nod.

'Right then,' said Nina. 'Hop into the yard. I'll show you how to take off Flicka's gear. Don't want to leave her standing around all tacked up while we're up at the house.' She showed Sophie how to release the surcingle and girth, unbuckle the reins, slide off the martingale rings and run up the stirrups. 'I'd better take off the saddle,' said Nina. 'Flicka's a bit tall for you.' That was an understatement. The mare stood sixteen hands. Nina had to stand Sophie on a box to take off the bridle. What the girl needed was a pony or a nice little galloway.

Up at the house, Nina rummaged through the drawers in her old room. She'd cleared out most of them, but was sentimental about a few things. Her school blazer, her Brownie badges and her riding gear. She pulled out a tangle of green sashes and ties. Blue woollen jumpers, white shirts and fawn jodhpurs. She chose several outfits of various sizes. 'Sophie,' she called. 'Come in and try this on.'

Sophie stood before the full-length mirror, smiling, while Nina tried to brush her knotty hair.

'Ow!'

Nina gave up, fastened it back with a band, and placed the white helmet on the girl's head. 'Perfect,' she said. 'Ric, come and have a look.'

He swung into the doorway and whistled approvingly. 'Some makeover. You look great, Soph.'

Sophie smiled self-consciously and stood a little taller. Of course there was no need for the tie or the sash or the tenth-anniversary rally pin, but Sophie had insisted. She pointed to a framed photo of Nina at a similar age, riding her old piebald pony. 'Now I look like you,' she said happily. 'Dad, take a picture of me for Mum.'

Ric obliged. 'Looking like that, you should be able to ride already,' he said with a wide grin. He really did have the most charming smile. Sophie inspected the picture on the shelf, then stared down at her sneakers.

'Boots,' said Nina quickly. 'We need boots. What shoe size is she?' Ric and Sophie looked at each other and shrugged in unison. Nina fetched a tape and measured the girl's foot. 'Dad sells boots at the produce store,' she said. 'I can get a pair wholesale, if you want. Right,' said Nina. 'Now, let's get to it. There's more to riding than dressing the part.'

They trooped back down to the yards and Nina resaddled Flicka while Sophie watched, perched on a rail. 'Okay, up you go.'

Nina spent an hour showing Sophie the basics. How to sit deep in the saddle and use her legs. To keep a gentle hand on the reins. To stay tuned to the mare's body language: the angle of her ears, the set of her neck, the rhythm of her walk. Sophie tried hard and Flicka was on her best behaviour, as if she somehow appreciated the youth of her rider. Nina was proud of them both. Ric stood by taking photographs. He wasn't making a bad fist of this father caper.

'That's enough for today,' said Nina, as Sophie brought the mare to a square halt. She fell forward on Flicka's neck for a hug, startling the mare into a half-rear. Ric leaped forward and plucked his daughter from the saddle.

'Dad!' Sophie was red with embarrassment. 'I didn't need your help.'

Nina darted for the mare's head. 'Your dad did the right thing. A rearing horse is a very dangerous animal. Flicka's no pet pony. She's a high-spirited thoroughbred, only six months off the track. No more sudden movements, okay?'

Sophie looked chastened. 'Can I really keep these clothes?'

Nina smiled and shrugged. 'They don't fit me.'

'When can I have another lesson?'

Ric still had a protective hand on Sophie's shoulder. 'Soon.'

'Can I trot?'

'That's up to Nina,' he said. 'Now we'd better go home and check on those geese. You're a mother now. You have to be responsible.'

'Not all mothers are responsible. Mine's not.'

Nina's sudden intake of breath was audible. It was the matter-of-fact way Sophie said it, as much as what she'd said, that moved her. Nina suddenly felt absurdly fortunate. Two strong, loving mother figures in her life – Mum and Eva. It seemed Sophie didn't even have one.

Ric tipped his hat in that cute way he had, and escorted his daughter to the car, an affectionate arm slung around her shoulder. It was a far cry from when Nina had first met the girl at Dylan's house, when she'd twisted away from her father's touch. Despite Ric's concerns, things were changing — had changed — between him and Sophie. Nina almost envied them.

That evening Nina sat on the verandah, lights off inside as darkness fell. Most people liked dusk, liked the lengthening shadows, the winding down towards night. But for Nina it was the one time of day she felt restless and alone. And as she waited in the gloom for a phone call from Lockie, Ric and Sophie were never far from her thoughts. She couldn't help it. She missed them.

CHAPTER 15

'How marvellous to be this free,' said Eva. 'It's like I'm alive again.' The old woman turned from Skyhawk's window to Nina. Her face was flushed, her eyes bright, her voice pitched high – as excited as Sophie on her first flight. 'Don't you ever take this freedom for granted, my girl,' she said. 'There'll come a time when it's gone.' She pressed her face against the glass again. 'Will you look at those pelicans down there? Just sailing on the breeze. I'd forgotten how big they are, like squadrons of little aeroplanes. Do you know, Nina, I might go parachuting once I get settled back home. My friend Valda did. Said she was too old to be scared any more.'

Nina concentrated on the control column, the instruments, the far horizon; anything to avoid thinking about the day ahead. So many things could go wrong, so many unknown quantities. She didn't know what to worry about first. They began their descent. Keep it together, she told herself as her heart beat a little faster. Ric would be there for moral support, and who knew? Today might not be such a shock for Eva as she imagined.

Skyhawk banked and came in for landing, hopping and bumping down the rough airstrip, causing Eva to hold onto her hat and utter little cries of alarm. The ute was parked near the gate. As the plane came to a halt, Ric emerged from the shade of an olive tree and assisted Eva to disembark.

Nina unloaded the walking frame. Eva scowled as she took hold of its handles, wrists seeming too frail to bear even her slight weight. 'I won't need this darned thing when I'm settled back home,' she said. 'Not once I'm in familiar surrounds. But I suppose I should use it until then.'

'You certainly should,' said Nina. 'Don't want to risk a fall.'

Eva turned her attention to Ric. 'And who is this handsome young man?

'My neighbour, Ric, Max Bonelli's son,' said Nina. 'From Donnalee Station.'

'Donnalee . . .' Eva searched her memory. 'Your father grew cotton there.' Ric nodded. He kissed her cheek and she patted his arm. 'Hope you've put a stop to that. This is no country for cotton.'

Nina cut in before Ric could reply. 'Eva, we'll have to go by boat. Part of the Billabong track was washed away in spring and there are a few trees down.'

Eva frowned and blinked a few times. 'It's a wonder Barry hasn't got onto it. I suppose he's had a lot on his plate since Walter died. Never mind, it will be grand fun going down the river. Perhaps you can ring Barry for me when we get back, tell him the road needs clearing?'

Nina didn't respond until Eva was safely seated in the car. 'Eva, Barry lives in Sydney now. Don't you remember?'

'No.' A cloud of concern, almost of panic passed over Eva's face. 'I don't.'

'Ric, could you take Eva to the mooring, please?' asked Nina. 'I'll go back to the house for the lunches and then meet you down there.' He nodded, but his face had darkened with something close to disapproval. The ute moved away towards the river.

Nina took off at a run, her stomach churning. Was she doing the right thing? Ric obviously didn't think so. She tried to block out the image of Eva's face, tense with bewilderment. Jinx strained and barked on his chain as she approached the house. 'Shut up. You can't come.' He lay down whining, head on paws. Nina stopped to stroke his velvet ears. 'Sorry,' she said more gently. 'Seems to be my day for upsetting people.' Then she raced on to the house, grabbed the drinks and picnic basket, and headed back down to the river.

Eva was already in the boat and wearing her life jacket. What a help Ric was, what a sweetheart. He was making it very hard to hang on to her old resentments. Nina studied Eva's face. Confusion seemed to have given way to excitement, and her blue eyes were alive with expectation.

'You sit with Mrs Langley,' said Ric, positioning himself behind the wheel. 'I'll drive.' The stubborn set of his jaw still betrayed his displeasure. Nina felt another twinge of uncertainty, but pushed it aside. He had no idea how important this trip was.

They set off, the breeze from the water a refreshing counterpoint to the summer heat. At first Eva chattered away, oohing and aahing at everything, taking great gulps of the fragrant air, aromatic with the scent of eucalyptus and wild mint. But soon her brow became creased with concern. 'The river's too low,' said Eva. 'And is that cotton over there?'

'Yes,' said Nina. 'Max still grows cotton. I'm hoping now Ric's back, he can talk him out of it.'

Eva raised her voice. 'Young man, you must. You absolutely must. Just take a look around. It's either the cotton or the Bunyip.'

A hush fell on Pelican. The little boat journeyed on in silence until they reached the confluence of the Kingfisher, marking the boundary of Billabong Bend. As the river rebounded and gathered strength, so did Eva's spirit. The years seemed to slip away. Soon she was pointing out birds, mimicking their calls, explaining their nesting habits. This was the Eva Langley that Nina had known and loved as a child, the one who knew each bend in the river, each secret meander. Who greeted gum trees by name and told their stories. Nina was half-thrilled, half-despairing to hear her talk. All that knowledge. An entire lifetime of knowledge, going to waste, trapped inside a nursing home. 'I'll get James to send you my field notes and maps if you'd like, Nina.

And Walter's bird sketches. They'll be more use to you than to me now, I'm afraid.'

'Thank you, Eva. I'd love that.' Nina told her about Sophie's orphans.

'Magpie geese,' said Eva. 'I was ten years old when they last nested here. Spent a lifetime waiting for them to come back, and now you say somebody killed them? If my Walter was alive he'd have shot the man that did that.'

'If I ever find out who's responsible, Eva, I'll shoot them myself. But the eggs have hatched in an incubator. Ten healthy babies to release at Billabong. That's something at least.'

'Oh, but you can't do that,' said Eva. 'Historically, pied geese only ever came here to breed. In the dry season, when their young were fully fledged, they flew northwest to the border country, to the over-flows along the Paroo and Warrego rivers. With no adults to guide them, how will the little ones find their way? I'm afraid that knowl-edge will have died along with their parents.'

Nina's stomach lurched. She hadn't thought of that. Pelican proceeded along the dappled waterway in sombre silence. Soon the old homestead appeared above them on the hill. Eva raised her gaze to the dilapidated house. Her eyes wore an odd expression, half-way between wonder and bewilderment. The back of Nina's neck goose-bumped. She suddenly wished that she'd taken Ric's unspoken advice, and left Eva safely back at Pemberley House.

Ric cut the engine. He timed it just right, and Pelican nudged her bow through the carpet of water hyacinth and into the rundown mooring. He cast his eye over the structure, appraising its strengths and weaknesses. 'That section there.' He swung himself onto the timber and stomped around a bit. 'It's sound enough.' Nina helped Eva to her feet, and Ric half-supported, half-carried her onto the jetty. He led her across the boards, testing each one with his weight before urging her on. Nina followed with the walking frame.

They reached dry land and started up the concrete walkway. Grass and tea tree pushed through the cracks, and bush roses grew wild along the path in a profusion of blood-red blooms. Straggly blackberry canes snatched at their feet. For a fragile old woman, it was a slow and treacherous climb.

Eva stopped to rest, hand on heart, staring at the house. Goats and pigs had ruined the once beautiful gardens. Ivy formed a twisted maze up the stone walls, its tentacles dragging and splitting apart the fascia boards.

'Oh dear,' said Eva.

Ric swung her into his arms, cradling her like a child for the last few metres. He carried her up the slate steps and set her down on the bluestone verandah. Nina followed with the walker, not daring to look at either of them. Ric manoeuvred the frame in front of Eva, and she took hold with a shuddering sigh. 'I don't understand,' said Eva. 'All this damage. How long have I been away?'

'Six years.'

'Six years,' repeated Eva. 'Has it really been that long . . .' Her voice trailed off.

'Do you want to go inside?' asked Nina.

It took a long time for her to answer. 'No,' said Eva. 'No, I don't think so.' She fumbled in the wide pocket of her drop-waisted dress and extracted a set of keys. 'There's a picture . . . would you get it for me, Nina? A framed photo of Walter and me, hanging over the fireplace.'

Nina nodded. The heavy oak door was already ajar, but she thrust the keys at the lock anyway, in pretence. 'It's the big brass one,' called Eva in a faltering voice.

'I've got it.' The door begrudgingly creaked open and Nina pushed inside. Slanting shadows roamed around the hall. All was deathly still and musty with decay. Multi-coloured moulds formed patterns on the ceiling where rain had seeped through the leaking roof. Piles of smelly droppings along the architraves betrayed the presence of little bats that must, even now, be roosting between the crooked paintings and the wall. Nature was fast to reclaim what people abandoned.

She moved on through the quiet house until she reached the lounge room. A photo hung above the fireplace. It told a story, a love story. Eva as a stunning teenager, leaning against a boathouse. Posing, a coquette. She was laughing at a tall young man, teasing him. He stared at her with undisguised hunger in his eyes. Walter, her future husband. Where had that lovely young girl gone? Was she still there, trapped inside Eva's failing body?

Something moved and Nina jumped. Just a bush rat. It scuttled off through mounds of chewed-up papers strewn beneath an elegant, leather-bound desk. Nina picked up a few intact sheets. Field records and illustrations, stunning pencil sketches of wildflowers and birds. These must be the notes and drawings Eva wanted her to have. The ones supposedly safe with James. It would break Eva's heart to see them like this.

Nina eased the picture from the wall and hurried outside, resolving to return tomorrow for what remained of the notes. 'That's the one,' said Eva with the faintest smile, when she saw the photo. 'It must go on the wall in my room.' She straightened her back and regarded Nina with the clear eyes of a woman who'd lost all illusions. 'I'm weary.'

'Of course. I'll take you home.'

'And just how do you propose to do that?' asked Eva. 'Since it seems I have no home to go to.'

CHAPTER 16

Nina brought out the bottle of brandy and her best glasses. 'Didn't know until I saw you with Freeman that you liked brandy, Eva. Would you do the honours please, Ric? There's dry ginger in the fridge, and coke as well.'

Ric looked at Eva, brows raised. 'Young man,' she said. 'I'll take it straight.' He poured her a snifter. She clasped it in both hands and drank a deep draught.

Nina took a seat at the kitchen table beside her and drew a bottomless breath. 'Eva, I know it must have been a shock seeing what's happening out at Billabong.'

Eva drained her glass in one gulp and eyed Nina with a new suspicion, like she didn't quite trust her any more. And could you blame her? 'My house has been empty for six years, you say?'

'Yes,' said Nina. 'Ever since you've been at Pemberley House.' No matter how difficult, she wasn't going to pull any punches. Otherwise today's whole painful episode would have been for nothing.

'I went into that damned place after I hurt my back,' said Eva. 'Wasn't that last year?'

Ric refilled Eva's glass and poured one for himself. 'That was six years ago,' said Nina. 'Walter had a heart attack at Billabong, and you hurt your back trying to lift him.' Eva nodded. 'You both went into Moree Hospital. Walter went on to Sydney for treatment and you went into Pemberley House. Remember how upset you were that James didn't organise for you and Walter to be together?'

'I don't know,' said Eva. 'My memory lets me down. Was that really so long ago?' Nina nodded, as comprehension dawned in the old woman's eyes. 'James says my blood pressure has to drop a bit before I can go home, but I'd never manage out there on my own.'

'I'm sorry, Eva,' said Nina. 'I really am. But you needed to see for yourself, so you'd understand how important it is for me to buy Billabong.'

Eva's eyes softened. 'You love that place. You always did.' She sipped her brandy and coughed a little. 'James never had the heart for it.'

'He'll sell it, Eva.' Nina's words were urgent and low. 'When you die, he'll sell Billabong to anyone with the money.'

Eva uttered a long, knowing sigh, and reached for Nina's hand. 'Billabong Bend was settled by my family in 1830. The Langleys have nurtured and cared for that place for all this time. Protected it. Lived in harmony with its ebbs and flows, treasured its birds and animals. My father called the wetlands Billabong's crowning glory.' She squeezed Nina's fingers. 'My girl, I've been an idiot.'

'No, you haven't —'

Eva raised her hand for silence. 'When a person wants to believe something badly enough, the mind plays tricks. Deep down I knew the years were slipping past, that time was running out. I think I knew James was humouring me too, but I wouldn't face the truth. Thank you for bringing a foolish old woman to her senses.'

Nina slipped to her knees, tears in her eyes. She laid her head in Eva's lap, tasting tears as Eva stroked her hair. 'Let it out,' Eva said. It was many minutes before Nina's cries reduced to shuddering sobs, and came to a sniffing halt. 'There now,' said Eva. 'That's better.' Nina caught her breath. How she loved Eva.

'I need another drink,' said Ric. 'Anyone?'

'Dry ginger and ice this time, I think,' said Eva. 'And what about that lovely lunch you packed, Nina? We never got around to it. Haven't had roast lamb and chutney sandwiches for years. They always were my favourite.' Her good humour and courage spilled into the room, cheering them all.

'Would you stay for the night, Eva? I've made up the spare room, and there's so much I want to show you. My orphan ducklings, for instance. They're beginning to fledge. You might know what sort they are. I still can't tell. And there are the waterbirds at the dam, and the riverbank restoration.' Nina took a breath. She was rushing her words, pressing Eva too hard. 'I'm sorry. Perhaps you're tired? It's been a big day.'

'If you'd let her get a word in edgeways,' said Ric, 'she might be able to give you an answer.'

'Thank you, young man. And yes, it would be a treat to stay.' Eva took a big bite of her sandwich and gave the crust to Jinx. 'A treat to feel like I'm part of the world again.'

'You're welcome anytime,' said Nina. 'My home is your home, for as long as you like. It's not as nice as Billabong homestead, but it's all yours.'

'I wouldn't do that to you,' said Eva. 'One night is all I want. One night of living. Of drinking and talking. Maybe a board game? Maybe I could cook? I'd like to cook a meal again. Perhaps Ric will stay too?'

'Of course,' said Nina, without consulting him. 'Ric, would you go and get Sophie while we organise dinner? I'd love for her to meet Eva.'

Ric was standing by the door, his arms folded. Nina crossed the room to him, close enough to smell the brandy on his breath. 'Please?'

The corners of his mouth creased into a half smile. 'Okay,' he said in a low voice. 'We'll do this your way. You've played your trump card. I just hope it doesn't backfire on you.'

The words sent a tiny chill through her. What did he mean? Things were turning out perfectly. 'Don't be like that,' she said. 'Just go and get your daughter, will you?'

He grabbed his hat and disappeared out the door. Eva's bright, bird-like eyes inspected her, and Nina put on a sunny smile. 'Right, shall we start dinner? A roast, maybe?'

Eva patted the chair beside her. 'Plenty of time for that, my girl. Come and talk to me about that young man. Oh, and Nina?'

'Yes, Eva?'

'If I'm going to get a chance to cook, we can be a bit more ambitious than a roast, don't you think?

Nina could hardly believe it. The document on the table before her read: *Contract for Sale of Land. Vendor: Eva Margaret Langley. Purchaser: Nina Rose Moore.* A dream come true. So was the purchase price – a steal. Well, not a steal exactly, but low enough to make a big difference when it came to the bank and getting a loan. And high enough, according to Eva, to prevent James from challenging the sale. 'My finance isn't guaranteed,' said Nina. 'Just so you know.'

'For pity's sake,' said Eva. 'Just sign it. Or do you want me to change my mind?'

'No. No, of course not.' Nina's hand shook a little. She tried to steady it, overthinking the whole thing. In the end she signed her name so deliberately and self-consciously that it barely resembled her signature at all.

Eva's nurse stepped forward to witness the contract. 'Are you sure this is what you want?' she said, looking uncertain.

'Yes, Vera. Very sure.' In another moment it was done. 'Congratulations, my dear.' Eva's voice broke a fraction. Nina wrapped her in a hug, knowing how hard this decision had been, how final it really was. When she let go, Eva seemed herself again, her smile warm, her voice encouraging. 'It's a long settlement, one hundred and twenty days. I don't imagine you'll have any difficulty with the bank, not with your place going so well.'

'I've bought Red Gums on vendor terms,' said Nina. 'Will that matter?'

'Stop inventing problems.' Eva waved a hand. 'I've already had a word to my bank manager, who just happens to be Trevor Bond, your bank manager as well. He's approved your new business plan apparently. You're good for the money, Nina. The bank gets its collateral and you, God bless you, get Billabong Bend.'

Nina stared at the signed and witnessed contract, the official seal on her longstanding love affair with the marshlands. She wanted to kiss it. She wanted to dance around the room with it, and shout the good news all over the riverlands. Me and Billabong, we're a team now. We belong to each other.

A kaleidoscope of plans cascaded through her brain. She'd clear out the ferals, and she didn't just mean the poachers. She'd get rid of the pigs and goats, the foxes and rabbits and cats. She might ask Max along on their shooting trips, as a gesture of reconciliation between their families, and also because he was a bloody good shot. She'd run a few cattle on the outer floodplains, fence off the woodlands and over-flows, improve the carrying capacity and environment at the same time.

'First thing – a biodiversity survey,' said Nina. 'I'll make maps, proper survey maps. You can help me, Eva. And then there's the house. Can't afford to fix it up yet, of course, but down the line . . .' Images came to her of the homestead restored to former glory, of Eva's face when she saw it. Nina's heart hammered hard in her chest with the sheer, limitless possibilities.

When she dragged herself back to reality, Eva was studying her with a certain, sad resignation that flattened Nina's mood. She turned around, showing off the fawn suit that she'd borrowed from Kate. 'What do you think?'

'Very smart, dear, and businesslike.'

Nina kissed Eva's cheek, restless to be gone. 'I'll be back afterwards to tell you how I go.'

A sudden lethargy showed on Eva's face. 'No, no. I already know the outcome, and I don't want any more visitors today.'

'If you're sure?' Her thoughts were racing ahead to the coming meeting. Would it really be as easy as Eva suggested, a fait accompli? 'Goodbye then,' said Nina. 'Wish me luck.'

Eva smiled. 'You won't need luck, my girl. Now off you go.'

Nina swung into Moree's main street with squealing brakes. There, a spot right out the front of the bank. That blue Ford had seen it too. Nina accelerated, darting into the space ahead of the other car, oblivious to the horn blast and the rude arm gesture out the window.

Nina gathered her documents into an untidy bundle, opened the door and stepped straight into the stream of traffic. She stumbled a little, causing a car to swerve and beep. Stupid high heels. Into the bank, heading for the enquiries counter, awkward in her tight pencil skirt.

'Can I help you?'

I've an appointment with Trevor Bond.'

'Name?' The girl checked her computer screen. 'You're half an hour early.'

Half an hour. An eternity. Nina paced the room like a caged tiger. A small boy pointed at her. Nina watched the clock on the wall as she walked. The receptionist's composed expression had changed to one of pity. 'Let me see what I can do.' She made a call. Nina held her breath. 'He'll see you now.' Trevor emerged from a side room. He hadn't changed a whit in five years. A plumpish, middle-aged man with a red face and receding hairline, who'd been the Moore family bank manager forever.

Trevor gestured her into his office with a smile and an opened file sitting before him on the desk. 'Been getting reacquainted with your little farming operation.'

Was that good? Bad?

'Quite impressive.' He beamed over his glasses and she slumped a little with relief. 'You're turning a pretty profit when lots of floodplain farmers are falling over in this drought.'

Nina opened her mouth and shut it just as quickly. So far she wasn't losing here. Better just let him go until he asked a question.

'Can I see the signed contract of sale?' He ran through a few figures – her profit and loss statement, her tax returns, the rough business plan that she'd drafted to show how Billabong Bend would contribute to her bottom line. At last he said in a matter-of-fact voice, 'All approved. I'll organise a cheque for the deposit, and make the balance available at settlement in April.'

'Really? That's it?'

'I could make it more complicated if you want?' He chuckled at his own joke. 'I only wish there were more good-luck stories out your way. More clever farmers, moving with the times, adapting.' He extracted a sheaf of papers from a manila folder, and thrust a loan document before her. 'Take some time to read through it.'

The words were a blur, but she forced herself to focus on each one. When she looked up, Trevor offered her a pen. 'Sign wherever there's a cross. Here . . . and here . . . and here.' Nina did as he asked, making a conscious effort to steady her hand. There, it was done.

Nina stood out on the street in a daze. Pedestrians and cars passed by as if nothing had changed. The sun shone as before. How could everything look the same, but the world be so different? She phoned Lockie. 'I did it,' she said. 'You're speaking to the proud new owner of Billabong Bend.'

'Good job.'

Was that it? Just good job? 'Can't you be a bit more enthusiastic?'

'I'm happy for you, I am.' She could hear the *but* coming. 'But that place needs a lot of work and I won't have much time to help. The boss has bought Kilcunda Downs next door, you know that. I'll be flat out here for ages.'

Nina's elation was wilting. 'I never asked you to help.'

'No,' admitted Lockie. 'No, you didn't. But if you're tied up at Billabong, when will I ever see you?'

'So if I was to ask for help, you'd complain you're too busy, and if I don't ask for help, you complain I'm too busy? I can't win.' There was nothing wrong with her logic and Lockie knew it. He had enough sense to shut up. 'I don't suppose you could drive down tonight?' she said.

'I can't, I'm sorry,' he said. 'But you're coming up tomorrow, right? We'll celebrate then.'

'Okay. I'll go round to Mum and Dad's for a beer or something.' She disguised the disappointment in her voice. 'You are happy about me buying Billabong, right?'

'It's great news,' he said. 'So . . . see you tomorrow arvo at my place?'

'Better make it Saturday morning,' she said. 'I'm checking the boundaries tomorrow. That'll take all day.'

'Righto,' he said. 'Gotta go. Love you.'

'Love you too.' Nina's thoughts ranged about, trying to recapture her earlier euphoria, but it was no use. Without someone to share it with, her marvellous news had lost its shine.

CHAPTER 18

'I won't wear it.' Sophie stood at the door, face like thunder. She was dressed in her new Drovers Flat Central School uniform: green-checked cotton shift with a white collar, black lace-up school shoes, and a misshapen, floppy green hat. 'I look awful.'

'No . . . you don't.' Ric studied her as objectively as possible. Not that he was an expert in these matters, but he thought that Sophie might actually have a point. Something didn't look right. Her hair, for starters. Dark shocks of it stood out on either side of the hat. 'Turn around,' he said. The girl glared at him, and then spun slowly. The back view was worse, her hair a mass of tangles. He beckoned with his finger. 'Come closer.' The school dress they'd bought on Monday was too big. He knew he should have made her try things on. It hung like a sack on her skinny frame. And the crown of her new hat had somehow creased into a stiff peak. He felt a smile sneak round his lips. The overall effect was of a wild young witchling.

Sophie's eyes widened in horror. 'You think I look awful too.' She turned to run.

'Hang on.' He caught her by the arm. 'Sit down. I want to talk to you.'

Sophie collapsed in a sullen heap on the couch and hugged a

cushion tight. Ric sat down beside her, and received a swift kick. 'Cut that out.' She kicked him again, harder this time. He grabbed the cushion from her to protect his shins. 'Your hair needs brushing.'

'Don't have a brush,' said Sophie.

'Well what happened to it?'

'Dunno.'

He lifted a knotted lock of her hair. 'Why didn't you say when we were in town?'

'Dunno.'

'You can't go to school next week looking like this.' He fetched a comb and spent the next ten minutes trying to untangle his daughter's hair to a chorus of loud *ouches* and *that hurts*. 'It's no use,' he said at last. 'I think we'll have to cut it all off.'

'No!' Sophie darted out the door.

Max came in. 'What's all this screaming about?'

'I bought the wrong size school dress,' said Ric. 'Then I'm trying to comb her hair and I make a stupid joke. Now she's nicked off.' He sighed. 'I sure suck at this dad stuff.'

Max scratched his head. 'That little one, she needs her mother, I think.'

'Not much chance of that any time soon.'

Max took a wallet from his trousers and pulled out some cash. 'Take this. Buy her another dress.'

'I don't need your money.'

'Who says it's for you? Can't I do something nice for my grand-daughter?' Max pressed fifty dollars into his hand.

Ric gripped the money as if it might bite. Staying on at Donnalee and working for his father could come with unwelcome strings attached. Like Max thinking he could call the shots.

'Since it's for Sophie . . . thanks. But no more handouts, okay? I have enough put aside to last till harvest. I won't claim what I haven't worked for.'

'Always the proud one,' said Max. 'Too proud for your own good.' He put away his wallet, but not before pulling out a fat wad of notes for show. 'There's plenty more where that came from,' he said grandly.

'And when we sell that bumper crop, we'll be rolling in it. You, me and Sophia, eh?'

'Here we go . . .' said Ric. This was the old Max talking. Full of boasts and smug optimism. Better not mention Nina's purchase of Billabong just yet. The sale was bound to put his father's nose out of joint. If Ric was perfectly honest, he was a bit disappointed himself. Thrilled for Nina, of course. Absolutely thrilled that her dream had come true. But a small, wishful part of him had rather liked the idea of running Billabong Bend, of carving out some sort of a future there. He'd forgotten how satisfying it was to work on the land, forgotten the meaning cotton still held for him – and he had a daughter to provide for now.

'What will I do about Sophie?' Ric hated asking his father for advice, but Max did have a way with the girl. 'I've let her go feral.'

'No, no,' said Max. 'Sophia, she's a good girl. Let me try.'

An hour later Ric stood drinking coffee and looking out the window, barely able to believe his eyes. Sophie sat quietly on a kitchen chair on the verandah. The goslings sat around her, contentedly preening their down, and playing little bill-clacking games among themselves. Odette took pride of place on Sophie's lap.

Max stood behind the chair, gently combing conditioner into the girl's tangled hair with a little plastic comb. He stopped occasionally to painstakingly prise a knot apart with his fingers. There were no screams, no breaks for freedom – no complaints at all. Sophie was stroking Odette and chattering away as if nothing was wrong.

Max caught sight of him through the glass. 'Can you get me something, Ricardo? In my room, at the back of the wardrobe – a tin with a paddle steamer on the lid.'

'Righto.' He went down the hall and cautiously opened the door, not sure what he'd find. The last time he'd been in his father's bedroom, it had been his mother's room too. He gazed around. A lot hadn't changed. The heavy damask bedspread, the matching jade curtains, the intricately carved teak dresser that trapped the dust no matter how often it was polished. But more had changed than hadn't. No jars of make-up or jewellery on the dressing table. No colourful scarfs draped about to brighten the room. And something much more vital was missing as well. The bedroom walls had once held the fragrance of lavender, the scent of sandalwood, the subtle smell of homemade potpourri. Mum's perfume bottles were gone and, with them, the essence of her. Despite Dad's protestations that he didn't smoke in the house, Ric could smell cigars. He couldn't remember, couldn't even imagine his mother in this room any more.

A sudden, overwhelming sadness made him swallow hard and fight back the sting of tears. Get a grip. Mum was happy with her new life abroad. A new husband too, and all her children close by. All except for him. He'd been too restless for Italy, and the pull of Australia's broad acres had been too strong. He'd missed the wide skies and strong light. He'd missed driving for a thousand miles without hitting a border. And he'd missed being in love. It hadn't happened again. Perhaps his wild river girl had ruined him for anyone else.

'Have you found it?' Max's voice came down the hall, jolting Ric from his daydream. He opened the wardrobe door and pushed aside the few musty suit coats. There on the floor, in the gloom: an old tin. It looked familiar. His sisters' ribbon box. Ric lifted the lid and memories tumbled out, along with the clips and bows and bobby pins. Those beaded, crocheted scrunchies that Mum used to make. That pink sparkly one Nadia loved so much and Julia's butterfly ballet headband. He picked it up and ran the red velvet between his fingers. It would suit Sophie's dark hair.

'Hurry up,' yelled Max. 'And bring your mother's brush and mirror. In the top drawer.'

Out on the verandah, half of Sophie's hair was already combed and smoothed. Sophie turned to glare at him as he handed her the box. 'Poppi, Dad said he was going to cut all my hair off.'

'Your daddy, he's a funny guy, eh?'

'These are gorgeous.' Sophie picked up the brush, fingering its plush backing of cream linen. It featured pink and red roses in petit-point embroidery. She showed Odette the mirror. The gosling nibbled at her reflection in the glass and Sophie squealed with delight. She ran the wooden comb through the soft bristles in the brush.

Max took the comb from her and tugged at a snarl hard enough to make her wince. 'Sorry, sweetheart.' He pointed to the brush. 'Those dark, tufty bristles? Boar's hair. Very special. Makes your hair extra shiny.'

Sophie made a face. 'What's in the tin?' She oohed and aahed over the ribbons while Max finished the rest of her hair. Before long, it fell around her shoulders in a sleek, dark curtain, like heavy silk.

Ric selected a ribbon. 'I think this butterfly one would look nice.' He offered the red velvet band to his father.

Max shook his head. 'I think pigtails and the scrunchies, with tortoise-shell hair clips here . . . and here.'

'Pigtails. They're a bit outdated, aren't they?' said Ric. 'And her hair looks lovely loose.'

'That's how it got in a mess in the first place,' said Max. 'It needs tying back.'

Ric picked out a green satin headband. 'What about this?' He took the comb, swept the front section into a high ponytail, and slipped it through a hair tie. 'Then brush it back like this, and maybe a couple of bobby pins at the side.'

He and his father stepped back, tripping over a few indignant goslings, to look at Sophie. She picked up the mirror and stared at her reflection. 'That looks stupid, Dad. Let me have a go.'

'In a minute,' said Max. 'It's my turn now.' Sophie scowled but sat still. 'Now if I can just remember.' He gathered a section of hair from one side of the part and plaited it close to the scalp, working in more hair as he went. 'I've got fingers like sausages.' He ended the weave at the back of Sophie's head and secured it with a clip. Repeating it on the other side, he joined the two ends together in a thick braid down her back, leaving some hair flowing free.

Sophie smiled into the mirror, which immediately made her look prettier.

'There,' Max said proudly, rubbing his hands together as if the delicate work had been too much for stiff digits. 'Out of your eyes, but still loose at the back like your papa wanted.' He inspected the tin with great care, and chose a cream-coloured ribbon, trimmed with lace and embroidered hearts.

'That's too old-fashioned,' said Ric.

'Show me,' said Sophie. Max dangled the ribbon in front of her. 'I like it.' She shot a triumphant glance at Ric. 'It's beautiful.'

'So,' said Max, 'Sophia likes beautiful ribbons?'

She gave an emphatic nod. 'Sophia likes.'

Ric groaned. 'You're as bad as each other.'

Sophie giggled. He'd barely heard her giggle, barely heard her laugh at all. The sound warmed a place inside him he didn't know about. Now he was laughing, and his dad too, the well-remembered belly laugh of his childhood.

'You look like a human being again,' said Ric. Odette peeped in agreement. 'How about you and me drive into town? We'll change over that dress, and the silly hat as well. Post that letter to your mum. That's if Poppi can spare us?'

'Of course, go, go.' He gave Sophie a kiss. She lifted Odette from her knee and led the goslings away. Max beamed after her as she went into the house, her ten tiny fluff-balls following in single file. 'When she turns up on Monday,' he said, 'she'll be the prettiest girl in school.'

CHAPTER 19

Nina couldn't contain her excitement. The young magpie geese had come to Red Gums for their first swim in the river. Sunshine and shadows striped the Bunyip a dramatic black and gold as they approached the edge. The birds milled about, chattering to themselves, too tentative at first to dip a toe in the water.

'Don't be scared,' said Sophie. As if on a dare, the biggest one stepped in, puddling her beak in the shallows and whistling encouragement to the others. One by one the goslings slipped into the river. Their legs paddled automatically. Soon they were swimming about, nibbling at reeds, exploring the sheltered corner with excited calls. Sophie settled herself cross-legged on the bank while Nina took photos. Amazing. Magpie geese back on the Bunyip.

'Look.' Sophie giggled. One gosling was upside down, with just his tail poking up. The others watched curiously. Then they were all doing it, diving and splashing and torpedoing beneath the surface in madcap play. After twenty minutes or so they all trooped out of the water and gathered around Sophie, drying their feathers and preening contentedly. The biggest one climbed onto Sophie's lap and grumbled when Sophie stood up and dislodged her.

'Thank you for bringing them to see me.' Nina picked up two of the goslings and they peeped in loud protest.

'That's Amelia and Abigail,' said Sophie. 'They're named after the geese in *The Aristocats*, and they're very sooky.' The girl took the birds from Nina and they went quiet, snuggling into her arms.

'So they all have names now?'

'Nearly all of them.' Sophie squatted down. As many goslings as could fit scrambled onto her knee. The unlucky leftovers perched on her feet. 'There's Odette.' She pointed to the biggest one. 'You know her. This one's Melody. Then there's Ping, and Boris.'

'Boris?' asked Nina.

'I named him after the goose in *Balto*. I absolutely love that movie.'

'Of course.' Nina glanced at Ric, who shrugged and grinned. 'I should have guessed.'

'And this is Donald and Daisy and Daffy.' Sophie picked up each gosling in turn.

'How do you know if they're girls or boys?' asked Nina.

Sophie looked a little embarrassed. 'Poppi looked at their bottoms.'

'What about this little one?' Nina picked up a baby, smaller and weaker than the others. It flapped its tiny wings and cried desperately for Sophie. Nina examined it. 'Look, it's got a crooked neck.'

Sophie took the gosling protectively in her arms, soothing it with soft clicks of her tongue. 'And a crooked leg. Poppi said he was in the egg too long. He doesn't have a name yet. I haven't thought of the right one.'

'How about Quasimodo?' said Ric.

'Don't be so mean.' Sophie glared at him. 'I've seen that cartoon, Dad. Quasimodo's ugly. And he's got a giant wart that covers one eye.'

'How about Igor then?' Ric pulled a face, bent over and started lumbering around the yard.

'Stop it,' yelled Sophie, covering the little gosling's ears. 'I've seen *Frankenstein* too. I told you, he's not a monster. He's beautiful. He's just a bit crooked, that's all.'

For some reason Ric was now leaping around, scratching and

hooting like a monkey. 'You're being stupid, Dad.' Sophie looked pleadingly at Nina. 'Make him stop.'

Nina stifled a smile. 'Come and see the ducklings,' she said. 'They're freckled ducks, I've discovered. Very special. Almost as special as your babies.'

The goslings scurried after Sophie towards the duck pen, surprisingly fleet of foot with outstretched wings and wild, ringing cries. They must be a month old by now. Adult plumage was showing through their soft down. In another month they'd be flying. Historically, their parents would lead them on a flight northwest to the Queensland border or beyond, to seek out permanent water holes and see out the dry season. There was no hope of that now. Their chance for a normal life had died, along with their parents.

The goslings made friends with the ducklings through the chicken wire of their pen. Then they fanned out on the grass, using their beaks to explore, tugging and pulling at anything in their path. What would happen to them? A cloud settled on Nina as she watched the young birds. The first pied geese at Billabong for almost a century and they'd never claim their birthright.

'Sophie, I want to talk to you,' said Nina. 'About your birds. About when they grow up.'

'Poppi says he'll clip their wings, and they can live on our dam.' A certain tone in the girl's voice told Nina that she didn't entirely approve of her grandfather's plan.

'Magpie geese are protected,' said Nina. 'You're not allowed to keep them as pets. And anyway, they're wild birds. They're meant to be free, like your tadpoles, and your turtle. Free like Elsa, the lioness.'

'I know.' Sophie kissed Odette on her proud head, and looked at Nina with unhappy eyes. 'Tell me what to do.'

'I don't know myself yet,' said Nina. 'Let me do some research. Their best bet would be to join a flock of wild birds, ones who could teach them their migration route. But I've no idea where the nearest magpie geese might be. They've been locally extinct for years.'

'They think I'm their mother,' said Sophie.

'They do, and you want the best for them, don't you?' Sophie nodded. 'That's settled then. I'll work something out, and in the meantime, you just keep looking after those goslings the way you've been doing.' Sophie nodded and Nina pulled her in for a hug.

'I've been thinking, Soph,' said Ric, who'd been standing nearby listening. 'What you need is a pet. A proper one, one that Nina won't take off you.'

Sophie's eyes lit up. 'I'd never ask for anything ever again if I could have a horse.'

Nina was almost as excited as Sophie at the prospect. The girl had been having lessons for a month now. Ric dropped her off twice a week. Sophie called it *going to pony club*. She always arrived in full uniform, neat tie and all, crisply laundered, courtesy of Max. Nina found the girl to be a keen and capable student, but they spent as much time talking as riding. Sophie had started bringing her homework along. 'Will you help me? I suck at maths.'

'Why don't you ask Ric, or your grandfather?'

Sophie had hung her head. 'Don't want them to think I'm dumb.' So after the riding lesson they'd often sit on the shady riverbank and do sums or reading. Sometimes they'd draw birds. Nina enjoyed teaching Sophie what Eva had taught her. To work step by step, to be a keen observer, to keep things simple. Sometimes she helped Sophie write letters to her mother.

The child was opening up, telling Nina odds and ends about her life with Rachael. Pieced together, they formed a compelling story of hardship. Sophie's maternal grandparents were dead. She hadn't stayed in one place long enough to make lasting friendships or have any real educational continuity. Consequently she struggled at school and felt stupid. Her mother, Rachael, was often sick. There were weeks when she wouldn't get out of bed, and Sophie became the parent, making her coffee and toast and missing out on school. These episodes of illness had been growing worse. Once last year Sophie had been taken into foster care. She'd run away and found her way back home. Rachael had packed them up and moved to Queensland. There'd been a lot of boyfriends, some nice, some not so much. If anybody ever needed some love and stability – and a horse – it was this little girl.

'Sophie's making good progress,' said Nina. 'But there are limits to what I can teach her on Flicka. She really needs something smaller and safer.'

Ric turned to his daughter. 'How about a deal?' he said. 'I'll get you a horse if you behave at school.'

'It's not my fault,' said Sophie, voice rising and with a rebellious tilt to her head. 'Mrs Taylor picks on me, and the other kids are mean.'

'They're mean?' said Ric. 'They're not the ones starting fights . . . and biting, for goodness sake. Just three weeks in, and I've already been called down to the school half a dozen times. Including on your first day, no less.'

Sophie opened her mouth to argue, but must have thought better of it. 'I'll try.'

'No,' said Ric. 'If you want that horse, you won't just try. You'll do it.'

Nina frowned. Was it her place to jump in, to explain a few things to Ric? Tell him it wasn't going to be that simple for Sophie to just decide to behave?

'Will you really get me a horse?'

'Promise.' Ric held out his arm. 'Deal?'

Sophie took a while to respond, like she was weighing up the pros and cons. 'Okay,' she said. 'I do really, really want a horse, so I suppose it's a deal.' They shook hands.

'Trouble at school?' Nina asked Ric, as Sophie ran down to the horse yards to say hello to Monty and Flicka.

'Sophie picks fights. She talks back to the teacher, walks out of class whenever she feels like it. Half the time she won't go to school at all. Says she can't leave those damned geese.'

'There's a fair bit on her plate,' said Nina. 'Her mother, a new school . . . and getting used to you. Can't be easy dealing with all that.'

'Me?' Ric flashed her a melting smile. 'I'm a pushover.'

'Be serious,' said Nina. 'She's had it pretty tough. Don't expect too much too soon.'

They wandered back to the verandah. Ric leant over the rail, staring into middle distance. Nina joined him and for a moment their arms brushed together. 'Are you happy, Nina?'

The question caught her off guard. Was she happy? 'Yes, most of the time.'

Ric smiled but his eyes were sad. 'Funny how things go.' A pair of butterflies flew briefly round their heads, then danced together in the sunshine. 'Life sure is different from what you think it'll be, you know, when you're a kid.'

'Why so philosophical all of a sudden?' she asked.

'Tell me, Nina. How did you think your life would turn out, way back when?'

'Oh, I don't know,' she said. 'Not too different from what it is.' His lips pressed into a tight line. 'What about you?'

'Me?' Ric's unflinching gaze locked onto hers. 'I thought that together, you and I were going to conquer the world.'

CHAPTER 20

The bank manager's hollow words echoed down the phone. Nina shook her head. 'No, that's impossible.' A late ray of sunshine flared through the cobwebbed window and was swallowed by the evening.

'Sorry, is this the first you've heard?' asked Trevor.

'Yes,' she stammered, disbelieving, numb with the news. It couldn't be. She'd have known, wouldn't she? If Eva's heart had stopped beating, if they no longer shared this world? Why hadn't she been told? Nina's mind cast vainly about for somebody to blame. She was Eva's most regular visitor, but she wasn't a relative. The staff at Pemberley had no duty of care to inform her of anything. That precious call had belonged to James Langley. How had he reacted? With shock, with grief? Or was he indifferent, or even relieved at the news? Which emotion had topped his list? 'When did Eva die?' asked Nina, amazed such a question could leave her lips.

'Yesterday,' said Trevor. 'A heart attack. Very sudden. She died on her way to hospital. I imagined you already knew.'

A stony silence fell on the line. Nina wanted Trevor's terrible words to crawl right back up the phone and disappear. Then it struck her. 'If you thought I already knew, why did you ring?'

'Ah,' said Trevor, his discomfort plain. 'I'm afraid there's more bad news. Don't like to bother you at a time like this, but you need to know.' Nina uttered a mirthless laugh. Compared to Eva's death, what other bad news could possibly touch her?

'It's about the contract — the contract of sale for Billabong Bend . . .' He hesitated, sending a bolt of fear straight to her heart. 'It's no good, Nina. Eva's death has rendered it void.'

Nina listened, not really hearing or understanding. What was he saying? Maybe she was dreaming. She looked about her, stared out the window, bewildered. Everything seemed normal. The fluttering curtains, the darkening sky, the stately river red gums casting long shadows. All as it should be. 'Void?' she managed. 'The contract was signed and witnessed three weeks ago, the deposit paid. How can it be void?'

'Doesn't happen often,' said Trevor. 'But if the vendor dies before settlement, then the contract can't be enforced. Makes sense, if you think about it. You can't have an agreement with a dead person. Of course, in most cases the vendor's executor is happy enough to honour the spirit of the deal, to amend the contract, to carry on with the sale . . .' He paused, an awful and significant pause.

Nina's mind worked overtime, trying to anticipate where the phone call was going. Eva's executor . . . that would be James Langley. 'In most cases — but not in this case?'

'No,' said Trevor. 'Not in this case.'

'What if I talked to James myself?'

'I've already approached him on your behalf,' said Trevor. 'Told him how close you were to Eva, how badly she wanted you to have that land.'

'And?'

'No go, I'm afraid. He was quite resistant, hostile even.' Trevor stopped, as if he didn't quite know how to put it. 'James is a funny bloke — has some strange ideas.'

'Like what?'

'He has some poppycock notion that you manipulated Eva into

signing that contract. It was the purchase price that got him,' said Trevor. 'It's below market value. Not enough to upset the titles office, but enough to put a bee in his bonnet.'

'I have to talk to him.'

'I wouldn't. He's had some pretty objectionable things to say about you, Nina . . .' Another pause, long enough for her imagination to run wild. Nina ground her teeth together and tasted tears, although she didn't know she was crying. 'I'll arrange for the return of your deposit in the next few days. Word is, James will sell Billabong as soon as he can. You might be able to pick it up at auction. Be sure to send a bidder in your stead though. I wouldn't be surprised if James refused to knock the place down to you.'

'I need time to think,' said Nina.

'Course you do,' said Trevor. 'Ring me just as soon as you decide.'

Nina thanked him and put down the phone in a daze. Eva gone. Billabong Bend at risk all over again. Her body hurt like she'd been beaten black and blue. Fear and grief washed in. How could it be? Warm, brave, elegant Eva – gone. Nina reached for the phone to ring Lockie, struggling against the overwhelming tide of misery and guilt. Did the trip back to Billabong have something to do with Eva's death? Nina fought to draw breath. If she didn't share this grief with someone it would drown her.

Lockie couldn't come. 'The boss is here for the weekend. We're going over the books together, drafting a new business plan. I can't just up and leave.'

'Please.' Nina hated the cry in her voice. She was almost begging.

'I'm so sorry, babe,' said Lockie, 'but it can't be done.'

She hung silent on the phone. Surely he'd change his mind? Losing Eva and Billabong in one fell blow – he must realise how devastating that was. 'I'll come as soon as I can, but it won't be tonight,' said Lockie. 'It stinks, I know Nina, but it's the best I can do.'

'When then?'

'Don't know,' he said. 'Tomorrow maybe? I told you, I'll come as soon as I can.'

It took a while for her to speak. 'If it was you,' she said, 'I'd come.'

'If you'd just see sense and move in with me, you wouldn't have to come,' he said. 'You'd already be here. How the heck are we supposed to make this work when we never see each other? It's just too difficult.'

'I'll make it easy for you then,' said Nina, her voice hard now. 'Let's stop trying.'

'Don't be like that, babe.'

'I mean it. I'm done, Lockie. I'm not going to settle down at Macquarie Station with you. Not ever. That's what you want, right?'

'Well, yeah. That's where I thought we were heading.'

'But my heart's here, Lockie. You know that. The wetlands, the river – they're in my blood. That won't change.' Her voice was breaking. 'Find somebody else who can make you happy, because it's not me.'

'You're upset.'

'Damn straight I am. We've been drifting along, Lockie — settling. Truth is, we want different things from life,' she said. 'This break's long overdue.'

It was a while before he spoke. 'Is this about Ric Bonelli?'

'No, it's not about Ric. It's about us.' She ended the call. Things just kept falling apart. Nina pressed her knuckles against her eyes to stem the flow of tears. She'd had enough. Enough of holding tight, being tough, proving to everybody including herself that she could manage on her own. Maybe to herself more than anyone. Well, tonight she couldn't do it. Tonight she needed a friend.

She rang Kate. 'Nina?' The surprise was plain in Kate's voice when she picked up. 'It's been ages. Guess what? I'm in Sydney, with Geoff, for the weekend and we're just on our way out to dinner. We're having a fabulous time by the way . . . Is everything all right?'

Nina imagined Kate, cosied up at some city hotel, caught up in the excitement of new love. 'Everything's fine,' she said, feeling bereft. 'I won't keep you.'

Dylan, her perfect confidant, was out of reach, off in Rio. He'd been texting her photos of buff Brazilian guys, but other than that, she hadn't heard from him. The weight of her parents' kindness would be too much to bear. Who then? Any time she wasn't working at Red Gums, she usually spent with Lockie. The loneliness that sometimes came out at sunset hit her in the stark light of day. Kate had warned her, said she was losing touch all alone on the river, becoming a hermit. It seemed her friend was right. There was nobody left to call. Or was there? Memories swept in of a lonely child turning to her best friend in times of trouble. Turning to the boy across the river.

Nina rubbed her temples with her fingers. Had life ever been so bewildering? She picked up her phone and tried Dylan anyway. To her astonishment, he answered. 'Dylan, thank God. Did I wake you? I've no idea what time it is there.'

'Five-thirty in the morning,' he said. 'But don't worry, I haven't been to bed yet.' She could hardly hear him. Loud music played in the background and his voice was faint and faraway. 'What's up, chicky? My phone's almost out of charge, so be quick.'

Nina took a deep breath and began. Eva's death, losing Billabong, her growing affection for Sophie, the breakup with Lockie and her maddening, irresistible attraction to Ric Bonelli; a great, stream-of-consciousness outpouring over the shaky line.

Dylan let her finish without interrupting. 'I go away,' he said, 'and look what happens.'

'Be serious, Dylan,' she said. 'I'm so confused. What should I do?'

His voice was breaking up. She strained to hear, catching only a fragment of speech before the line went dead. 'Listen to your heart . . .'

Nina waited, sitting on the porch step, in that mysterious hour between dusk and nightfall. Time had stopped. She seemed to have been sitting there forever, in the silence, in the twilight. A wild duck called. Its lonely cry echoed off the river, before the breeze carried it downstream. When would he come? Jinx buried his cold nose in her lap, as if to say, *Won't I do?* She fondled his velvet ears. 'Not tonight, you won't.' In the waning light the windmill blades turned and turned, marking the minutes. She shivered, in spite of the balmy evening. Jinx pricked up his ears. Finally, the hum of a motor. Softer, as it slowed to take the turn. Louder now. Twin shafts of light pierced the gloom. Jinx barked and trotted to the gate.

'I'm sorry to hear it,' said Ric, visibly moved when he heard the news about Eva. He offered Nina a stubby from the six-pack of beer he'd brought over, took one for himself and put the rest in the fridge. 'Mrs Langley sure was a sweet old lady.' He took a seat beside Nina at the kitchen table. 'She meant a lot to you, didn't she?'

'Eva was the best.' It hurt to talk. Nina's throat was raw from weeping. Her reflection in the window showed wild hair, a puffy face, and eyes red and scalded from tears. 'James has no right to dishonour that contract,' she said. 'Eva wanted me to have Billabong. It was her last wish, for the wetlands to be safe.'

Nina watched Ric for any sign of disapproval. He'd been unhappy about taking Eva back to Billabong. Would he think her at fault? She couldn't bear that. But what she saw in his deep, brown eyes was open friendship with no hint of blame . . . and there was something more. Warmth, tenderness – love.

'Why didn't you keep in touch after you went to Italy?' she asked.

Ric ran a hand through his hair and took a sudden interest in the sugar bowl. He glanced up at her for a moment. A flutter of desire stirred in her stomach before he looked away again. 'You really want to know?'

Nina nodded, unsure now if she did or not.

'Someone played a stupid trick on me before I left.'

'Go on.'

He drew a deep breath. 'I was at school, hanging out with Lockie one lunchtime. Just two mates, you know, having a yarn.'

Lockie? What did he have to do with this?

'Anyway, he said he had a girlfriend. Thought he was taking the piss at first. Nothing much gets past me, and Drovers is a small town. Then he comes out with it. Nina Moore, he says. Seemed real serious about it. And I'd just made a fool of myself giving you a promise ring, kissing you.' Nina shook her head. The truth was dawning fast. 'I had to sit there,' said Ric, 'like a drongo, play-acting that I was pleased for him.' Nina thought back to that last summer before Ric left. Lockie had a holiday job at Red Gums, laying water pipes. Had he followed her down to the river? Had he seen them together?

'And you never bothered to ask me?'

'Nah.' He looked out the window. 'Suppose it was stupid, but I couldn't face you. Couldn't bear to think of you with him.' Ric was rushing now, words pouring out like it was a relief. 'Believe me, Nina, if I'd known it was nonsense I wouldn't have left. I would've stayed, no matter what Mum wanted.' He got to his feet and rubbed the back of his neck. 'When I came back to Australia, Dylan told me it wasn't true, what Lockie had said.' His eyes flew up to hers. 'But by then it was too late. Years too late,' said Ric. 'We'd missed our chance.'

Nina's head was spinning. Could this be true? Had some boastful, long-ago lie ripped apart their friendship? More than a friendship, a fledgling love affair, although they'd been only kids. But then Lockie had been a kid too, a shy sixteen-year-old boy, with a crush on the boss's daughter. A boy who must have watched her sneak off, day after day, down to the river to meet Ric. She knew Lockie so well now. Quiet. Agreeable. A man who didn't court trouble. But still waters run deep, and Lockie was also a man who took things to heart. Her clandestine friendship with Ric would have eaten away at him. She could forgive him for a foolish brag in the schoolyard, but she wouldn't forget what it had cost her.

'Maybe there's still a chance.' The phrase caught her unawares, as though it had slipped out all by itself, summoned by the power of their shared wanting.

'What about Lockie?'

'I'm through with him,' she said.

Ric wet his lips. 'Let's go down to the river.' Just six words, spoken with the tempo of a slow song. A vibration passed through her, like a giant tuning fork pressed against her body. A yearning for something unknown, and yet as familiar as breathing. Ric held out his hand. 'Will you come?'

Nina took a candle. She shut Jinx in her room, fetched a blanket and led Ric outside. Hand in hand they walked down to the river. They didn't stop at the pumps or the windmill. They didn't stop until they reached their long-ago meeting place. Memories grew large, transporting her to an earlier, innocent time. Back then it had stopped at a kiss. What about now?

Light was fading fast. A shadowy haze descended on the water, lending it a dreamlike quality, blotting out the ugliness of the opposite bank. Nina lit the candle. Ric shook out the blanket, laid it on the ground and took something from his pocket. A kingfisher feather. It shone turquoise in the gloom. 'For you.'

He pushed the feather behind her ear. Nina moved into his arms, while shadows wavered on the trunks of trees. They slow-danced for a while to the music of the river – its low murmur, its choir of crickets and frogs. This was what she needed, to be swept up in a flood of feeling. To embrace this love, lost and found. To be rendered thoughtless by Ric's kiss. They fell on the blanket, sharing one breath. The dome of light cast by the flickering candle was like a living thing, and they were its centre, its beating heart.

Each undressed the other. Her fingers explored his skin, warm and smooth beneath her touch. Honey-coloured skin, so different from Lockie's. Lockie's chest was square and white, with a thatch of dark springy hairs over his heart. Ric's heart was bare. She marvelled at his taut stomach, his contoured physique, his rigid erection. This grown Ric had the body of an athlete, an Olympian – a god. Nina arched her back, showing off a woman's body to this man who'd known her only as a girl. Some primal power had hold of her. In its grip there was no Eva, no Billabong, no tomorrow. There was only their shared need for each other.

The stars had appeared and the candle burned away long before they were satisfied. She lay at peace, head resting on Ric's arm. The night was fragrant with wild mint. Two moons, one in the sky and its dimpled twin in the river, cast a soft glow over the bush. Nina studied Ric's face. Wide brows, flared nose, square jaw. Full lips, expert lips.

She adored all of him, from the smooth brown feet pressed against her leg to the dark peak of hair at the nape of his neck. How had she lived without him, all of these years? And she knew their love lay at the heart of her existence – fundamental and undeniable.

CHAPTER 21

Sunday morning, still early. Nina took her time waking up. The events of the previous day, both terrible and wonderful, milled about her mind, and her fingers were drawn to the unfamiliar feel of the ring on her finger. Ric's promise ring from long ago, kept for all these years. She'd slipped it on before falling asleep.

Jinx nosed into the room and rested his silky head beside her pillow. She stroked his soft ears. 'Hello, Jinxy.' He jumped onto the bed and laid his warm body against her. The phone rang. Ric? She fumbled to answer it.

'Nina, darling, have you heard about Eva?'

'Yes, Mum.'

'Margie told me. Eva's heart gave out, apparently. It came as quite a shock down at Pemberley. Nobody expected it. She saw a cardiac specialist just last week and he said her heart was in good shape. It should have lasted.' Mum sighed. 'Just goes to show, you never know when your time's up.'

Mum's words rang in her ears. It should have lasted. Had losing Billabong broken Eva's heart? Or had it merely given her permission to slip away? What sort of life was it anyway, shut up in Pemberley like that, without hope? Except that up until recently she'd had hope, hadn't she – however forlorn.

'Nina?' Her mother's voice sounded anxious. 'Nina, can you still hear me?'

'Yes, Mum.'

'Your father had a word to Trevor at the bank and it looks like the sale's off. Have you heard?'

'Yes, Mum.'

'Such a terrible business. How are you holding up?' Nina didn't know how to answer that question, but thankfully a response didn't seem to be required. 'Dad's got Kevin in to run the shop. We're coming to see you.'

Nina opened her mouth to say, 'There's no need. I'm fine.' But that would be a lie. She wasn't fine. She was hollow with grief.

'Thank you.'

'Good-o.' Mum sounded pleased, and rather relieved, that their impromptu visit was going to be welcome. 'And don't worry,' she said. 'We'll bring dinner. Bye love.'

Another call came through. Ric? No, Lockie. Nina switched off her phone.

'But I wanted to surprise Poppi with breakfast in bed.'

'Well, you should have got up earlier.' Ric placed the bowl of cereal in front of Sophie. She ate a spoonful and then heaped on more sugar. 'Want more rice bubbles on your sugar?' She made a face as he poured a bowl for himself.

'Can we make Poppi dinner instead then?'

Ric nodded but his mind was elsewhere, down at the evening river with Nina. For years he'd lived with the fantasy of her naked in his arms, ready and willing beside him. He'd dreamed of her earthy scent, the taste of her mouth, the smooth-as-silk feel of her hair. The fantasy had ended more than one relationship. Last night that dream was made flesh. Everything had seemed perfect, but in the light of day he wasn't so sure. Where did things stand between them? What about Lockie? He tried to call Nina, but her phone was switched off.

'Can we give Poppi a party?' Sophie began searching through the pantry. 'Can we make him a birthday cake?'

'I suppose,' said Ric. 'Maybe Nina knows a good recipe. I'll ask her, okay?'

Sophie nodded. 'What will we give him for presents?'

'I have some cigars put away.'

Sophie screwed up her nose. 'Smoking's bad. We shouldn't encourage him. What am I going to give him?'

'Socks.'

'I'm not giving him socks. That's boring.'

'Well, that's all I've got.' Ric hadn't realised that Sophie would take Max's birthday quite so seriously.

'We have to have more presents.'

Ric grasped for an idea. What did they do for cheap homemade presents when he was a kid? Mum had been great at that. 'We'll make him a placemat with his name on it.'

Sophie considered the suggestion with a poker face. 'What else?'

'Ah . . . you could decorate a plate as well.'

'I guess . . . what else?'

'A card? You could make him a crazy card. And we've got plenty of eggs. Paint some hard-boiled eggs, and we'll give them to him in a little basket. You could make one out of paper.'

'Dad, that's Easter.'

'Oh, yeah.'

'What are you going to give him? Grown-ups don't make their own birthday presents. They buy them from the shop.'

'I'll think of something.' He was squirming a little under his daughter's interrogation.

'There's a bottle of whisky in your room,' she said. 'You could give him that. Do we have any wrapping paper?'

'I don't think so.' How did Sophie know about that whisky? He supposed he could sacrifice it to keep her happy.

'You're not very good at birthdays, are you?' she said. 'It's lucky you've got me. I'll colour in some newspaper with my school textas. We'll use that.' Boots sounded on the verandah. 'Shh, it's Poppi. Don't let him hear.'

Max came in, smiling broadly. 'Mickey's done a hell of a job on that cotton. I've checked everything west of the main channel. The whole crop's turning yellow.'

'That's good then,' said Ric.

Sophie kicked him under the table. 'Wish him a happy birthday,' she whispered.

He didn't know why, but he was embarrassed to say it. His daughter's critical glare was motivation enough, though. 'Happy birthday, Dad.'

'Thank you, my boy, thank you,' said Max, with an expansive smile.

Sophie piped in with her own 'happy birthday', and Max planted a kiss on her glowing cheek. 'With you and your dad here like this? I can't remember a happier birthday.'

'Dad and me are going to make you a cake,' she said.

He held her at arm's length and opened his eyes wide, feigning disbelief. 'You want to spoil your Poppi, eh? Is that it? Well, I'll try not to be too late home then.'

'Where are you going?' She sounded a little deflated. 'Can I come?'

Max looked at Ric, eyes alight with pride. 'Always with the questions, this little one. She's bright like a star.' He turned his attention back to Sophie. 'My friends, they're shouting me lunch at the hotel in town. Just a few old men, drinking and swapping stories. No fun for a little princess. And after that, maybe I'll go fishing.'

Sophie looked like she was about to argue, and then apparently thought better of it. 'It is your birthday, Poppi. You should do whatever you want.'

'You're a good girl,' he said. 'As nice and sweet as can be.' Sophie beamed. 'Will you do my plaits before you go, Poppi?' Max nodded. 'I'll just go tell Odette about the cake'

'Coffee?' asked Ric, shooting his father an amused smile as Sophie left. As sweet as can be? Was Dad talking about the same Sophie who'd kicked a classmate in the shins last Friday? But her behaviour had generally improved, and the phone calls from the school were becoming less frequent.

'Ricardo, today I'm truly a happy man. And Sophie? She'll soon be truly happy as well.'

'Why?' Ric handed him his coffee. 'What's up?'

'That little horse she wants so much? It may not be too far away.' Max tapped the side of his head 'I have a plan to win us some money.'

'Gambling's not a plan,' said Ric. 'It's wishful thinking.'

'No, no. Not gambling. If this plan doesn't work out, I lose nothing but my time.'

'Well, are you going to tell me?'

'A man must have his secrets, yes?'

'Fair enough.' Ric smiled. 'Good luck to you, then.'

Max sipped his coffee. 'Do something for me, Ricardo.'

'It's your birthday. What choice do I have?'

'Go check the eastern fields after breakfast. Look for green patches Mickey might have missed, and mark them on this map.' He handed Ric a rough-drawn plan of Donnalee. 'And don't worry about that cake. I'll help Sophie make it before heading into town. That way, maybe I'll be able to eat it.'

Ric grinned. 'Righto.'

Max clapped him on the back, before settling into a chair. 'A nice *pan di spagna*, with maybe a little cream and cherry liqueur.' He took a gulp of coffee. 'Haven't had a birthday cake in years. It'll be kind of nice.'

Max looked so happy, so content. A childhood memory came knocking, of another birthday. A memory locked away until now, of when their family was solid and strong, and Max had been his hero. Of him and his sisters, gathered round this same table, while Dad lit sparklers on a cake. Mum bringing plates into the kitchen, and Max claiming a triumphant birthday kiss while her hands were full. Her half-hearted protest and blush of pleasure. He'd adored his father back then, and something of that feeling was on him now. 'I want to say thanks, Dad . . . You've been great with Sophie, a big help.'

Max waved away his comment. 'You don't need my help, Ricardo. You're a fine father, much better than I was.'

Ric felt a rush of love for the old man and the words of a song came to him. *Freedom's just another word for nothing left to lose.* Here at Donnalee, with Max and Sophie . . . and yes, with Nina. Here, he was a willing captive.

CHAPTER 22

Nina lay a long time in bed, lost in thought, staring past the curtains to the sunny morning. She had to get up, get dressed, clean up a bit before her parents arrived. But her bone-weary body didn't want to move.

She'd barely slept, one moment overwhelmed by her reconnection with Ric, the next moment hijacked by grief. But as the star-shot sky had faded to dawn, her sorrow had waned along with the moonlight. Eva's own words had returned to comfort her.

'All of us have souls,' she'd said. *'Animals and plants . . . rocks and rivers. Even wind and shadows. These spirits exist before we're born, and remain after we die. They're eternal.'*

If that was true, then Eva's death wasn't the end. It wasn't something to mourn. A lingering life of suffering and loneliness, on the other hand? That surely must be dreaded, no matter what kind of spiritual belief a person might hold.

Nina yawned and sat up, hands clasped around her knees. A breeze down by the river rustled the red gums. Its whispered promise was not of death, but of life, of hope. Of life yet to be lived.

. . .

Her parents arrived mid-morning. Dad ferried in groceries, while Mum took over the kitchen, tut-tutting over the unwashed dishes and empty fridge. 'Just as I thought,' she said. 'It's a wonder you don't starve to death out here by yourself. Sit down and I'll make us a cuppa.' Nina didn't argue. It was nice to be looked after.

A cup of tea appeared before her, complete with a saucer from who knew where, along with a gigantic plate of bacon and eggs. 'You'll need to do something with these.' Mum turned over the two overripe bananas in a bowl on the bench. 'Muffins, maybe. Shame to waste them with the price of fruit the way it is.'

At first, the smell of breakfast cooking had made Nina nauseous, and she'd been sure she wouldn't be able to eat. But when she took a bite of hot, buttery toast, hunger claimed her and she wolfed it down. Her sadness wouldn't bring Eva back, and it wouldn't save Billabong either. There were things to do and plans to make.

After eating she wandered outside. The purple-flowering buddleia overhanging the verandah swarmed with swallowtails. Its fragrance hung heavy in the dry air. The sky was a sea of endless blue. Another hot day on the way. Would this drought never break? Nina went to the bathroom and stripped off. She needed cold water to pound her neck, her shoulders; shock away the tension with its chill. Instead it emerged from the low-flow water-saving showerhead in unsatisfying dribs and drabs. The sand in the little hourglass ran out, indicating her three minutes were up. Nina stepped out and tugged a brush through her tangled hair. By the time she'd slipped into underwear, she was hot all over again.

The hum of an approaching car engine broke the still morning air. Ric. She hurried to her room and pulled on her newest top. Then a pair of old jeans that she'd cut off into shorts last week, because the knees had worn out. Nina glanced in the mirror. Good. They made her legs look longer.

Would she tell her parents about Ric? Part of her wanted to keep her private life private. Mum was well-intentioned, but held strong opinions when it came to her daughter and affairs of the heart – and she was far too fond of Lockie. So much easier to keep this new relationship to herself. Or was it more than that, a hangover from child-hood maybe? From a time when Ric was her secret love, and the word *forever* lay pressed into her finger. From a time when the Bonellis were *persona non grata*, and Dad would rather have invited a tiger snake into his home than Max or one of his children.

But that time had passed. When Ric arrived, she'd introduce him, maybe ask him round for dinner, him and Sophie. Mum was a sucker for kids, and a child would help to break the ice. She hurried down the hall and onto the porch, eager to head off Ric before he ran into Dad. But it wasn't Ric coming after all. It was Lockie. He pulled up in a cloud of dust and emerged from the car wearing a worried expression.

'Why are you here?' she asked. 'I meant what I said yesterday.'

'So did I,' said Lockie. 'And I promised I'd come as soon as I could.'

He plucked a grass stem, and propped himself against the verandah post with an easy grace. His hair was longer than usual, his customary buzz cut softening into coppery curls. The look suited him. He leaned in for a kiss, but she turned her head so his lips only brushed her cheek. 'I really am sorry about Eva,' he said.

'And Billabong? Are you sorry about Billabong?'

'Course I am.'

'I thought you'd be happy the sale fell through. More time for me to play house with you at Macquarie.'

Lockie shuffled uneasily. 'Don't be like that, Nine.' He caught sight of the ring on her finger. 'What's that?'

'None of your business.' His face grew dark.

'Come on in out of the heat,' called Mum. She was buttering bread in the kitchen and had spotted him through the window. Nina groaned as they went inside. Mum was Lockie's greatest fan. She thrust a cold glass of lemonade into his hand. 'Can you stay for lunch? There's a nice bit of cold lamb here. It'll be a treat in sandwiches.'

'Any of your homemade pickles to go with it, Ellen?'

Mum beamed with pleasure and reached for the jar as Dad came in. 'Seeing as I'm here,' said Lockie, 'may as well make myself useful. Anything you need a hand with, Nina?'

'You're a good pump man, Lockie,' said Dad. 'Nina says the river pumps aren't lifting enough water.'

'No, Dad,' she said. 'I can manage.'

'Might be anything,' said Lockie. 'Worn seals, lines leaking air . . .'

'Reckon you could take a look for us?' asked Dad.

'Righto.' Lockie tipped his hat further forward on his head. 'Can I take Pelican? Might as well check the hose inlet pipes aren't clogged while I'm at it. You're bound to get problems with the river this low.'

'Thanks, mate.' Dad took the boat keys off the hook without asking and threw them to Lockie. 'I'll help Nina feed out hay and we'll be down when we're finished.'

'No worries.' Lockie disappeared out the door.

Mum dried her hands on her apron and beamed at Nina. 'Such a nice boy. Don't keep him waiting too long, sweetheart.'

'Yeah,' said Dad with a dry laugh. 'He might get away.'

Nina sank into a chair. How on earth was she going to set Lockie straight with her parents around? Here she was trying to break up with the man, and they seemed ready to marry her off.

'Will I get a bale on for you, love?'

'Thanks, Dad.'

Jim headed for the sheds, started up the old tractor and loaded a fat round bale on the rear spike, from the dwindling row along the fence. 'Hop on.'

As they bumped off down the laneway, Nina studied him in profile. Still handsome, despite the wrinkles and ruddy weather-beaten cheeks. He had the keen, clear eyes of a man who'd lived his life outdoors. The muscles of his face relaxed along newly-etched smile lines. It had been years now since she'd seen that face twisted in anger. Dad whistled a tune as he jumped down to open the gate. 'I'll do it,' she called, but he didn't seem to hear. He missed working on the farm, she could tell.

Going from paddock to paddock, hungry steers chased the tractor, bucking and kicking in excitement. Nina fed out the last of the hay and they sat for a while to watch the cattle feed. 'Why not buy in some cows and calves?' said Dad. 'I'll tell you where there's a good bull. Bert Mason's place. He'd lend it to you.'

'I'm concentrating on the orchards, Dad. Smarter farming, that's where the future lies. New crops, better use of water. In the end, I'd like to get out of cattle altogether. But in the meantime, I'm perfectly happy with my weaners.'

'There's more profit in cows and calves.'

'And more heartache. I always hated calving time. Cows down, in trouble, bellowing for dead babies. Orphans crying for their mothers.'

'Just the odd one or two,' said Dad. 'You make it sound like world war three.'

'Maybe so, but one problem calving is too many for me. I'll stick to buying in steers, healthy and already weaned.'

'Suit yourself.'

He was miffed that she didn't want his advice, she knew that. It was only natural. Dad had run the place his own way for thirty-five years. But it was still irritating when he tried to take over. One look at his crestfallen face, though, and she took pity on him. 'Let's take a look at the olives,' she said. 'There's something I want to ask you.'

It was past lunchtime before they returned to the house. Lockie was standing outside. Not in the shade. He stood instead, in the full, withering heat of the sun, legs planted wide, with balled fists and a grim face. 'Know what that bastard over the river's gone and done?' he said. 'He's rigged the wheels. Jammed some, drowned others. River water is pouring into Donnalee unmetered. I went the full length of the diversion. Not one bloody wheel is spinning. Not a one.' He cracked his knuckles. 'There's algae on the drums. The damned things haven't turned for weeks, months maybe.'

At first Nina didn't understand. Perhaps she didn't want to. She'd had her suspicions. From the air, Donnalee's expanded water storages dwarfed the river, even dwarfed the dams of other cotton farms. How had Max filled them? According to Ric, he'd been trading. Used to be that water rights and property rights went hand in hand. Water belonged to the land it was found on, which seemed only natural. But in recent years the two had been uncoupled and given a cash value independent of each other. These were tough times. The temptation was to trade licences that had lain unused in bottom drawers. Water that had never left the river was suddenly for sale. According to Ric, Max had been legitimately acquiring these sleeper licences, along with sell-offs from failed drought-stricken farmers. But now there was proof he'd been flat-out stealing water as well.

Nausea flooded right through her. She was sick with disgust and anger, sick with the hope that Lockie was mistaken. With the hope that those ugly blots on the landscape, those vast, unnatural dams, weren't filled with water stolen from the river. A suspicion crept from the shadows, lurked at the edge of her mind. What about Ric? What did he know? How could he not know? Was he complicit in this crime? For that's exactly what it is was. Theft of the most precious resource imaginable. Theft of the river itself. From the starving mud-stranded platypus to the bankrupt dry-land farmers downstream. From the ancient, ailing red gums to the vanishing egret rookeries. They were all victims of this crime.

'He won't get away with it.' Dad's voice dripped with venom. It was his old voice, the hostile voice of her childhood, back when he'd squandered so much time and energy hating Max Bonelli. It stirred a crawling fear deep in her belly.

Beads of sweat stood out on his face, and the smile lines had changed into furrows of fury. 'Give me the keys, Lockie. I'm taking a look.'

Nina shook her head.

'Give me the bloody keys.' Lockie tossed them over, and Nina shot him a furious glance.

Mum appeared in the doorway. 'Jim, what's wrong?'

Neither Lockie nor Dad acknowledged her. Mum's searching gaze fell on Nina, who ran to the verandah, taking its steps in a single stride. 'Lockie says Max has rigged the wheels along the diversion.' When Nina turned back around, Dad was striding towards the river.

'Jim.' Mum's tone was urgent. 'Come back.' He was through the gate now. 'Nina, Lockie, stop him.'

For a moment Nina couldn't move. It was like a bad dream. 'Dad, wait.' She caught up with him and grabbed his arm. He slapped it away. Nina sprinted for the jetty, with half a mind to untie the boat before he reached it. But what if Pelican drifted downstream, perhaps to be found by poachers? Better just to go with him. She was about to climb on board when strong arms gripped her. 'Jim's too hot under the collar,' said Lockie. 'I don't want you in the middle of it.'

'You're right.' Her voice was rising. 'He's angry, really angry. So why did you give him the keys?'

'I don't know,' said Lockie. 'Guess I thought he had a right to look for himself.'

'Well he doesn't. This is my place now, or have you both forgotten?' She turned to go, but he held onto her arm. 'Nina, please.' Too late. Dad had slipped by, untied and pushed off. Pelican was out of reach. The motor coughed once, then roared to life and propelled the boat out into the river.

Nina shook off Lockie's hold and sprinted back to the house. Mum was standing out on the drive, apron twisted in her hands. 'He's taken the boat,' said Nina as she passed. 'I'll ring Ric to let him know Dad's coming.'

'Hello, beautiful.' Ric's voice, a reminder of the night before – a quick flash of them down by the river. She pushed it aside.

'Ric, listen, my dad's on his way over there by boat, going up the diversion. He knows the wheels are rigged.'

'Wheels?' asked Ric. 'What do you mean?'

Her heart leaped with the hope that he really didn't know. Then that suspicion crept close again. Was his surprise genuine? She hated herself for it, but couldn't shake the doubt. 'The dethridge wheels,' she said. 'Lockie says they're rigged, the lot of them.' She paused, breathless. 'Dad's seen red. He might go after Max. Reckon you can head him off?'

'What was Lockie doing up the diversion?'

'What's that got to do with anything?'

Ric hung silent on the line for so long, she thought he'd hung up. 'I had no idea, Nina,' he said at last. 'You have to believe me.'

She wanted to say of course I believe you but the words wouldn't come. 'Can you keep Dad away from Max or not?'

'Max isn't here,' said Ric. 'It's his birthday. He's gone to the Royal with a few mates.'

'Thank goodness for that,' she said. 'Let's hope he stays there.' Nina turned to her mother as she came inside. 'Max isn't home,' she whispered.

'So what do you want me to do?' asked Ric.

'Just stay put,' said Nina. 'As long as Dad doesn't meet up with Max, he'll calm down. I'll come right over.' She finished the call and grabbed her keys.

'No,' said Mum. 'What good will that do? I don't want you caught up in this.'

'Too late for that.' She kissed her mum. 'Ring me if Dad comes back, okay?'

'Okay,' said Mum in a wavering voice. 'Was that Ric Bonelli on the phone? You sounded very friendly.'

'Don't worry.' She kissed her mother again. 'Won't be long.'

'I should have known.' Ric's dark eyes were stern and troubled as he poured her a coffee. 'If the wheels weren't turning, I should have known.'

It wasn't quite the expression of heartfelt remorse that she'd hoped for. 'There's no *if* about it,' she said. 'According to Lockie they're rigged, the lot of them, all the way down the channel.' Ric turned his head, drew his hand through his hair, did not meet her gaze. Nina studied his sombre profile as he stared out the window. She'd never seen him so withdrawn. Was he ashamed for his father, or for himself? The silence dragged on. 'You haven't seen my dad?' she asked at last.

'No,' he said. 'I was out in the back fields when you called.

Checking the crop duster hadn't missed anything. It was a bit windy when he was spraying.'

Nina frowned. She'd seen the ugly yellow air tractor, strafing the cotton. Like a clumsy cross between an aircraft and a Massey Ferguson, boxy and cumbersome, with none of the streamlined beauty of her Skyhawk. It carried built-in sprayers in massive slab wings and flew low over the crop, using its own downdraft to force a deadly mist onto the cotton. The lush young plants that had previously been so pampered, so protected, were now treated with *Strip*, a defoliant that shut down their growth and starved them to death. Last week she'd sat on the riverbank as the noisy crop duster did its work, and a stinking toxic cloud wafted over the Bunyip.

'Is that my ring?' Ric took hold of her hand.

'Yes. Do you still have yours?'

He hung his head. 'I got rid of it. Wish I hadn't.'

Nina's neck prickled uneasily. It seemed an ill omen that he'd disposed of the ring. 'Why don't you try your dad again?'

He did as she asked. 'Nothing.' Ric put down the phone. 'He won't pick up.'

Nina tried her own father. 'Mine either.' She finished her coffee, craving another, but her stomach was queasy and her head had started to ache. 'Where's Sophie?'

'Shot through somewhere with those geese.'

Nina leant forward on the table and buried her face in her arms. The firm rhythmic sensation of Ric's fingers massaged her neck, probing around her temples, soothing away the pain. Her body responded to his touch, to a memory of them together at the twilight river. Was that only last night? It seemed an age ago. 'Don't worry,' he whispered. 'We'll sort this out, I promise.'

Nina squinted her eyes tight shut. She wasn't so sure.

CHAPTER 23

Ric stood on the porch and watched Nina's ute take off out the gate, wheels spinning on gravel. She hadn't believed him, not completely. She'd needed reassurance, convincing. It shouldn't be like that. There should be complete trust between them. Ric stretched to ease his sore muscles. They were wound tight, jumping beneath his skin, coiled in readiness for . . . for what? He didn't want to argue with Nina's dad, although it sounded like Jim was spoiling for a fight. He didn't want to argue with his own father either, although it sounded like Max deserved it. That's if his dad had rigged the wheels. Nina was so certain of it. But what if it was Lockie who'd rigged them, to cast blame onto Max and onto him too? Why hadn't Nina doubted Lockie's story, the way she'd doubted his?

And what had Lockie been doing there at Nina's? After last night . . . He pushed the thought away.

Hell, Dad might have done it. Not much chance of getting caught. There was one water bailiff for the whole region – old Sam Higgins – and he'd been around since Ric was a boy. One bailiff, who had to process licence applications and keep the records on top of everything else. Sam was overworked, underpaid and browned off. He hadn't been seen down this end of the river for months. Sharp-eyed neighbours were far more likely to track down water thieves, and were liable to hand down rough justice too, long before old Sam got around to investigating their complaints.

Knowing Dad, he may have legitimately bought up water licences for miles around and still been greedy for more. Cotton growing at Donnalee was a constant battle, an endless struggle against the elements. Nina's concept of a farm working in harmony with the river's fragile ecology would seem naïve and strange to his father. For Max, farming was a contest. Each season saw a victor – either nature won, or he did. And his dream to drought-proof the farm, to dominate the river, was a long-held and passionate one. But to steal water in a drought? Ric didn't want to believe it.

These past months, connecting with Max – they'd been more special than he cared to admit. For sixteen years he'd built a wall around his heart, convinced himself that he didn't miss his father and never would. He'd edited his childhood memories, recalling the harshness and hostilities, disregarding the love and happy family times.

But that was changing. Ric was grown now, a man with a child of his own, a man with insight and understanding. The big picture lens of adulthood had panned back to reveal Max in all his colours, not just black and white. It showed him as a proud parent, a tender grandfather, a man of rich humour and uncommon resourcefulness. In his blunt, hardworking way, Dad had taught Ric a lot, had tried his best to make a man out of him. And after all these years, Ric finally appreciated that and was thankful for this second chance. Mum had told him stories about his father growing up without an education, suffering at the hands of his stepfather, risking himself to protect his sisters. Everybody was a prisoner of their past, he knew that now. Max was no more flawed than he was himself.

The hum of a motor summoned him back. Normally he wouldn't have taken much notice of the quad bike, going west down the laneway towards the dams. But a quick glance revealed that Dad's truck wasn't back and there were no other workers around on a Sunday. Who was riding it? Ric headed for the car, swinging through the gate towards the river and into the main laneway. There, up ahead. He could see the bike and make out the driver too. Ric shook his head, disbelieving — Sophie was taking her goslings for a ride. She was heading towards the storage, raising a plume of dust, her long plaits blowing in the breeze. The young geese crowded around her, some with wings outstretched like they were flying.

He beeped the horn and Sophie slowed to a stop. She turned around as he got out of the car, wearing her defiant face. 'You never said I couldn't ride the bike.'

'You're nine years old. I didn't think I had to.' A gosling jumped to the ground, then another. 'What the heck does a kid like you know about bikes?'

'I've watched you and Poppi. It's not that hard.'

'Kids are hurt all the time on those things,' he said. 'You weren't even wearing a helmet. What would your mother say if you went and got yourself killed?'

'She wouldn't care. She never even rings me.' This last point, at least, was true, so he let it go. 'Did you love my mother?' asked Sophie.

The question caught him so off guard that he forgot about her misdemeanour with the bike. What could he say? That when he and Rachael met they'd been very young. Both a bit lost, both divided from their families, with not much in common but their loneliness. They'd held together for a while, hitchhiking round, working as fruit pickers and dairy hands. Rachael had run off with a bloke headed for the prawn trawlers up north and he'd drifted west to the Kimberley oil fields. They hadn't seen each other since. Had he loved Rachael back then? In a way.

'Yes,' he said. 'I loved your mother.'

'But you don't love her any more?'

'Well . . . we lost touch.'

'And now you love Nina instead of Mum.' It wasn't a question. It was a statement.

She'd taken him by surprise again. 'Yeah,' said Ric at last, feeling unaccountably guilty. 'Maybe I do.' He had to take back control of the conversation somehow. Who was in the wrong here anyway? 'Poppi won't be happy when he finds out you've been riding the bike.'

'Poppi already knows,' she said. 'He doesn't mind.'

'How could Poppi know? He's been in town all day.'

'No he hasn't,' she said. 'He came back ages ago.'

'That's not true, Sophie. Poppi couldn't be back. His car's not there.'

'It is so true,' she said. 'Gino dropped him home. He said Poppi had too much whisky to drive. I could smell it when he kissed me.' She wrinkled her nose. Ric's eyes narrowed. Her story had the ring of truth about it, but it begged the question — where was Max? 'If you say I'm lying again,' said Sophie, 'I'll run away, and never, ever come back.'

Good, he thought uncharitably. That would solve a few problems. 'Get in the car.'

'What about my babies?'

'We'll put them in the back.' He spent the next ten minutes chasing after the young birds, without any luck, much to Sophie's amusement.

'How about I get in first?' Sophie climbed into the back of the station wagon. The goslings lined up obediently at the tailgate, flapping their stubby wings. One by one he picked them up and placed them beside her.

When they reached the house, there was still no sign of Max. 'If your grandfather came home, like you said, where is he?'

'Poppi's not ho-me, da-dee-da-dee-dum,' sing-songed Sophie. She was dancing with the geese, running in circles and waving her arms. 'He's gone fish-ing, la-la-la-la-la . . .'

Fishing? Ric plucked the girl from among the whirling birds. 'This is important, Sophie.' He kept a firm grip on her arm. 'Tell me exactly what happened.'

'I think Poppi was drunk,' she said. 'He saw me riding the bike, and I thought he'd tell me to get off, but instead he kissed me and said how clever I was.'

'And?'

'And then Poppi went down to the river with his fishing stuff. I went with him. I tried to tell him that he shouldn't catch fish, that fish want to be free and alive, just like us. Just like the whale in *Free Willy*. But he didn't listen. So then I asked him when he'd be back, because it was his birthday and we had to have the cake, and there were going to be presents. Don't you remember? You said you'd help me make Poppi presents?'

'Then what?'

Sophie played with her plaits, enjoying making him wait. 'Then Poppi said he might be back late, and he got into the punt and went off.'

'Are you sure that's all? You didn't see anybody else?'

Sophie rolled her eyes, but he kept tight hold of her. 'There was another boat,' she said at last. 'A bigger one, a little bit afterwards. I waved at the man but he didn't wave back. He followed Poppi down the river.'

CHAPTER 24

Nina put down the phone and turned to Mum and Lockie. 'That was Ric. He was wrong about Max being in town. He's gone fishing, and it looks like Dad's gone after him.'

Her mother's face paled. 'I'm worried,' she said. 'Jim's usually so level-headed, but when it comes to that man . . .'

'I'd go fetch him back,' said Lockie, 'but there's no boat. Do you think if I asked next door at Killara . . .?'

'They don't have a boat,' said Nina. 'It was stolen a few weeks ago, cut from its moorings.'

'Want me to try further afield?' he said. 'See if I can borrow one up the river?'

'If you hadn't given Dad the keys in the first place, we wouldn't need a boat.'

'Don't blame Lockie,' said Mum. 'After all, it is your father's boat.'

Nina groaned. 'No, it's not, Mum. I'm sick of this. You and Dad act like you still own Red Gums. Pelican's my boat, it came with the place when I bought it.' Frustration and a creeping fear overcame prudence and the hurt on Mum's face wasn't enough to silence her. 'Things were just fine before you all came,' she said. 'Then Lockie goes and pokes his nose where it's not wanted, and Dad jumps on the bandwagon.' She threw her hands in the air. 'Now look where we are.'

'They were just trying to help . . .' Mum said.

'Not helping,' said Nina. 'Interfering.'

Her mother left the kitchen, stiff-backed and stern-faced.

Nina avoided Lockie's gaze. He filled the kettle and put it on the stove to boil. 'You were pretty rough on your mum,' he said as he dropped teabags into cups. 'But you're right. I had no business going up the diversion, and I shouldn't have given Jim the keys when he was so wild. I'm sorry.' He took a sugar bowl down from a shelf. 'Pick the ants out first,' she said. Lockie peered into the bowl and foraged around with a teaspoon. It was hard to stay mad with Lockie. If it wasn't for him and his suspicions, Max would have got away with sucking the river dry. She really should be thanking him. Lockie thrust a mug of tea into her hand and put another on the table. 'Why don't you take this to your mother? She could probably use it.'

Nina gave a tight smile. 'I shouldn't have talked to her like that. It's all true, mind you. Mum and Dad do forget that Red Gums is mine now. But I'll go eat humble pie anyway. Lord knows Mum has enough to worry about without me adding to it.'

Mum wasn't in the lounge room. She wasn't in the bathroom or the spare room or the main bedroom. Nina knocked softly on the last door along the hall. Nothing. She knocked again, a bit harder this time. 'Come in,' said a small voice. Her mother lay on the narrow bed under the window, propped up on the cushion from the wicker-work chair, staring into space. The room had hardly changed from when Nina was a child. The same horsey curtains. The same rose-pattern wallpaper. The same sweet musty smell. Only her mother had changed.

Mum looked at her, gave a shuddering sigh, then turned away again. Nina offered her the tea. Her mother sat up a bit straighter and took the mug. 'Thank you, dear.' Jinx pushed past and went to sit beside the bed.

'My mouth runs away with me sometimes,' said Nina. 'You know that.' Mum nodded wearily and sipped the tea. Her hand trembled a little. 'Don't worry. Dad will be back any minute.' Nina settled herself into the little chair. It was too low to the ground to comfortably accommodate her long legs and her knees stuck up comically. 'What's the worst that could happen?'

Her mother wore a strange half-smile. 'Your father fell in love with me when I was just fifteen years old,' she said. 'Forty-two years, and he's never once let me down, never once looked at another woman.' Mum's hand was trembling so hard now that a little wave of tea washed over the lip of her mug. 'I couldn't bear to lose him.'

'You've worked yourself up,' said Nina soothingly. 'Dad will be fine. I'll go give him another ring.' She turned on the fan, left Mum with the tea and went back to the kitchen. For once Jinx didn't follow her. Dad still wouldn't pick up. What was the time? Four o'clock already. He'd been gone for hours now.

Lockie was leaning on the verandah post outside. He'd helped himself to a beer. Nina tipped her lukewarm tea down the sink, grabbed a beer herself and joined him outside. The air was oppressively hot.

'There's not even a breeze,' she said.

'You know Bob Carson? Grows corn out of Cunnamulla. To hear him tell it, it's so hot out there the corn's popping in the paddock before they can harvest it.' She gave him what she hoped was a withering look. 'And they have to put ice cubes in the chooks' water, or else they lay hard-boiled eggs.'

'Stop it,' she said, but a smile sneaked out just the same.

'That's better.' Lockie grinned and finished his beer. 'Did you take photos of the wheels?'

'My oath.' Lockie scrolled through his phone and handed it to her.

Dozens of shots. Wheels jammed with sticks and waterweed. Wheels drowned by high channel levels and mud, so they couldn't turn. The evidence was indisputable. Max had made a travesty of all her carefully devised water-saving measures. How long had it been going on? The wheels in the photos looked like they hadn't turned for a long time. It made her sick to think of the river's life-blood, pouring into Max's dams, night and day, maybe for months. Pouring into Max's dams even now.

She gave Lockie back the phone. His jaw was set in an angry line, his expression grim. It was hard to know how to feel, having him here after what she'd done last night. They may have broken up, but only just. She couldn't shake a creeping guilt. 'It's about time I thanked you, Lockie.' She raised her beer to him. 'Don't know why I never checked that diversion myself. Guess I didn't want to rock the boat. Didn't want to doubt my neighbour. Didn't want any more trouble.'

'Glad I could help.' Lockie's face grew soft. He moved towards her, as if for a kiss, then stopped himself. 'I'd do anything for you, Nine, you know that.' She had a sudden urge to ask him about what he'd told Ric all those years ago, about the foolish brag that had changed her life. But it wasn't the right time.

He held out his hand. 'Friends?'

Nina shook it and smiled. 'Friends, but that's all.'

'If you say so.' Lockie finished his drink. 'What do you want to do?'

'Get those bloody wheels turning,' she said. 'As soon as Dad arrives back with the boat. And afterwards, I'm telling whoever will listen. State Water Corp, Irrigation Commission, Department of Primary Industry, the Cotton Growers Guild . . . the cops. I'll shout it from the rooftops, about what a lowlife scumbag runs Donnalee. Just wait till the floodplains farmers hear about this. Max will have a war on his hands.'

Lockie cracked his knuckles. 'Suits me.'

It wouldn't suit Ric. What would he make of her conducting a campaign of accusations against his father? She swigged her beer for a little Dutch courage. Ric might not like it, but he'd bloody well have to put up with it. After all, this problem was partly of his making. If he'd had enough sense to check the dethridge wheels himself, Dad would never have taken off after Max like that. More importantly, megalitres of precious river water might have been saved. Nina squirmed as the crawling doubt returned. Ric couldn't have known, could he? Known, and not said? The thought was too unsettling. 'I'll go down to the mooring and wait for Dad,' said Nina. 'Could you stay with Mum?'

'Sure,' said Lockie. 'I'll stay.'

Jinx padded onto the jetty, whined and gazed downstream. Nina called him over to where she sat, bare legs dangling, and hugged his soft golden neck. How often had she sat like this? Nina stared at the brown Bunyip, crawling by beneath her feet. There was a time years ago, when her toes would have trailed in the river. When schools of skittering rainbow fish skimmed the water. When the red gum canopies came alive at dusk with roosting Major Mitchell's cockatoos, proud crests banded red and gold. How long had it been since she'd heard their soft whistles as they sang themselves to sleep?

Nina hauled herself to her feet, stiff and sore from sitting in one place too long. She checked her phone for the umpteenth time. According to Ric, Max wasn't back either. The knot of fear tightened in her belly. Something was seriously wrong.

The late afternoon sun hung low, firing the sky, turning the river blood-red. Sombre shadows slunk from the opposite bank and made familiar objects strange. Fallen trees became skeletons. Half-submerged logs looked like bodies. Nina turned from the river. Just a trick of the light. She hugged herself tight, skin goosebumped in spite of the heat. Somebody just walked over your grave, that's what Mum would say. Jinx whined again, louder this time, and ran to the end of the jetty. Nina followed him, ears straining. The faraway thrum of a motor. She'd recognise that sound anywhere. Pelican, and it was on its way home.

CHAPTER 25

Nina retreated down the drive, out of earshot, to make the phone call. 'Dad's back, thank God,' she said. 'But there was some sort of fight. He's all beaten up.'

'Damn,' said Ric. 'I was afraid of that.'

Was that it? No *I'm sorry for what my crazy father did.* No *Max is a lunatic.* Just 'I was afraid of that.'

'What about Max?' she asked.

'He's still not back.'

Nina hung on the phone while the silence yawned between them. She twisted the unfamiliar ring on her finger as she ended the call. That feeling was back, the unease she often felt at day's end. Her knees began to tremble with weariness and she hurried back inside. In the kitchen Mum had a washcloth and the Dettol out. She winced in sympathy with each dab at Dad's battered face. 'We'd best get your father to the doctor, Nina. I think his nose is broken.' '

You should see the other fella,' said Dad.

Mum scowled and dabbed harder. 'This is no time for jokes.'

'Who's joking? Got in a couple of good ones myself before Bonelli clocked me that last time. Went out like a light, I did. When I came to he'd shot through. No sign of the coward.'

'Stay still.' Mum sponged the dried black blood on his lips and chin. 'Hold this.' She handed Dad the bowl of antiseptic.

'Ow.' He dropped it, splashing the cloudy liquid over the table.

Mum held up his swollen right hand and peered at it. His middle finger looked crooked. 'Serves you right, Jim Moore.'

Lockie, sitting on the counter beside Nina, leaned close and whispered, 'He's dislocated the knuckle.'

'A grown man,' scolded Mum. 'Fist-fighting like a teenager, worrying us all sick.' She turned to Nina and Lockie. 'Max used to be a boxer, a middle-weight champion.' She kissed her husband tenderly on his sunburnt head. 'Nina, do you have frozen vegetables, anything like that?'

Nina got a packet of peas from the freezer. Dad's face had turned various shades of red and shiny blue. One eye was squinted shut. It must have been one heck of a fight. 'Do you want me to get Skyhawk ready?'

Mum pressed her lips together. 'No. I'll take him to Doc Bowman in Drovers. Get his opinion first. If we have to go to Moree, I'd rather drive, so I have the car.'

Nina took a few photos of Dad's smashed face. He tried to smile for the camera and failed. 'Go to the police first thing, Mum. An assault on top of theft? Max is in big trouble now.'

Her mother looked doubtful and beckoned Nina out onto the verandah. 'Let's hold off till I can talk to Max, find out if he's hurt too.' Her face shone pale in the porch light. 'It might be your father who's in big trouble here. After all, he was the one who went down that river spoiling for a fight. You heard him. Sounds to me like he started it.'

'How can you blame Dad for this? Look at him. And since when do you go talking to Max Bonelli? It'll just make things worse.'

'It won't.' There was a steely insistence in her mother's voice. 'It never hurts to hear both sides. We've got to know about Max.'

Nina was ready to argue, but something about her mother's expression made her bite her tongue. 'I'll ring Ric.'

Mum creased her brow, then nodded. 'Yes, you do that. Find out what Max is saying.'

Nina made the call. 'Ric? Max back yet?'

'No. It's gone dark and I still can't raise him. We're here with his birthday cake and I'm trying not to scare Sophie. Reckon it's time to go looking.'

'What is it?' asked Mum. 'What's wrong?'

'Max still isn't home. Ric thinks we should go look for him.'

'Yes,' said Mum quickly. 'That's a good idea. Get Ric over here and take Pelican downstream. See if you can find Max.'

'What about Sophie?' said Nina. 'Ric's little girl.'

'Isn't there someone at Donnalee who can look after her?' Nina shook her head. 'Well, I guess she'll have to come too.' Mum reached for Nina's hand and squeezed it tight. 'I sure hope Max is all right.'

Red Gums' little kitchen was getting crowded; an awkward gathering. Ric stood behind his daughter's chair, gripping its bentwood back. Jinx sat beside Sophie, licking her arm. The girl's mouth curled down, and her eyes held a sadness that not even Jinx could shift. Lockie stood in the doorway, lounging against the lintel, chewing gum with a sour expression. Dad sat with his bandaged hand on the table. Nina sat beside him, spooning a little more sugar into his coffee.

Mum pulled a tray of banana muffins from the oven, and drew in a deep breath. 'I do miss this stove,' she said. 'Things always turn out just so.' She placed a plate of muffins in the middle of the table. Lockie spat his gum outside and helped himself. 'What's the verdict, Lockie?'

'Perfect, Mrs M,' he said. 'Are you sure that's the same oven your daughter uses?'

Nina pulled a face. Ric frowned, clearly unhappy that Lockie seemed so at home in her kitchen.

'What is it you say, Nina?' Lockie continued. 'Dinner will be ready when the smoke alarm goes off.'

'Go on with you,' said Mum with the ghost of a smile. She folded her tea towel, put a muffin and glass of milk in front of Sophie, and sat down. 'Right, Jim. One more time. Just exactly where did you and Max fight? Can you think of any landmarks?'

His voice came soft and muffled through stiff lips. 'Three or four miles downstream, I guess, a bit before the Kingfisher comes in.' Nobody spoke for a while. However would they find it in the dark?

'Was it past the old jetties?' asked Nina.

'Yes, come to think of it, I think so. Somewhere round the next bend.'

'There's a big fallen red gum further along,' said Nina. 'Was it near there?'

'I don't know,' said Dad. 'So many fallen trees . . .'

'This one looks a bit like a bridge,' said Nina.

'A bridge,' said Dad. 'That rings a bell.' He flinched as he opened his mouth too wide for comfort. 'Yes, that's where we had the blue all right. That old bastard had —' Mum shook her head and indicated Sophie with a tilt of her chin. Dad started again. 'Bonelli had pulled over against the opposite bank. Looked like he was baiting hooks with yabbies.'

'I know the spot.' Nina kissed her parents swiftly. 'Let's go. There's a portable floodlight in the boat.'

Ric knelt down beside Sophie and held her shoulders. 'You stay here,' he said. 'I'm going to look for Poppi.' Sophie nodded, her eyes wide.

'We'll take care of her till you get back,' said Mum. 'And remember, no trouble, you hear me? Lockie? Ric? We have enough as it is.'

Lockie's gaze flickered to where Ric stood in the corner of the kitchen, arms folded. 'Won't be no trouble, Mrs M,' he said. 'You have my word on that.' Mum heaved a relieved sigh. 'And Ric? Do we have your word too?' He nodded assent. 'Good. Nina, you keep them to it.'

'Sure, Mum.'

'Well, you'd better all get out of here, get down that river and find Max.'

The three of them trooped from the kitchen. Nina looked back and saw her mother's dark figure framed in the bright window. She'd forgotten what a fine peacemaker Mum could be.

CHAPTER 26

They didn't find Max that night. They didn't find him the next day either. Nor did the state emergency service, or police search and rescue, or the hundreds of volunteers who combed the Billabong wetlands. It was as if he'd vanished from the face of the earth. Nina wearily washed her hands at the outside tap and followed Ric inside. Another fruitless trip down the river. They were wearing their frayed nerves on the outside of their skin. The slightest thing provoked an argument.

Nina slumped into a chair. Two full days had now passed since Max went missing. Two days of torment, of not knowing. The little town of Drovers Flat talked of little else, and was alive with speculation, some of it hateful.

'I won't be able to help search tomorrow,' Nina said. 'It's Eva's funeral.'

'Want me to come?' Ric asked.

'No, you stay here. Keep looking for Max.'

'I'll grab a coffee.' He put his hat on the table. 'Then I'll have to go home; pick Sophie up from the bus.' He gestured towards her with the kettle, brows raised. Nina nodded, studying him while he filled it, wondering what was going on in his head. How would it feel to have your father lost on the river, maybe hurt, maybe dead? She couldn't imagine. They sat without speaking until the water boiled. What had happened between them that night at the river felt very far away.

'The days are hot,' he said as he made the coffee. 'But these nights get chilly.'

'Did Max have a coat?'

'I guess. It's not hanging by the door.'

'It might be hard to spot a man,' said Nina. 'But we can't even find the tinny. It doesn't make any sense.' Ric pursed his lips together in a hard-edged frown. 'What?' asked Nina.

'It does if someone hid it. That boat's just a little thing. Fit easy into a tangle, or under a cooba thicket.'

'But why would Max hide the boat?'

'Max wouldn't.'

Nina wrestled with the implication. 'What are you saying?'

'Just what half the town's thinking.' Ric lowered his eyes. 'That maybe your dad knows more than he's letting on.'

It took a while for the full impact of his words to hit home. Her muscles coiled into knots. 'Get out.'

'Nina —'

'Get out!' She leaped from the chair, her heart racing, her breath coming in little pants.

He pushed his chair back and got slowly to his feet. 'I didn't mean —'

'How could you say that?' Her voice rose to a frantic cry. 'How could you think it? Dad told us what happened. You were there.'

He couldn't even meet her eyes. 'I'd better go.' He put on his hat and pushed out the screen door.

'Yes, go!' She worked the promise ring free and hurled it after him. He stopped to pick it up. 'Go and think your horrible thoughts somewhere else. Go, and don't come back.'

As the sound of Ric's engine faded, she subsided slowly into her chair. Jinx curled up next to her. So Ric thought Dad was hiding something and, according to him, half the town thought so too. Poor

Dad. Poor Mum. Tears were threatening but she wouldn't let them fall. 'Come on, Jinx,' she said. 'We're going to Drovers.'

'The police?' asked Nina. 'Oh, Dad.' She wrapped her arms around his shoulders. 'What happened?'

'They interviewed him.' Mum's face was drawn. 'They drove out all the way from Moree this morning. Two detectives.'

'Smart bastards, they were,' said Dad. 'Asked me about Max going missing. Reckoned I had something to do with it.'

'Oh no,' said Nina. 'They didn't – they couldn't.'

'Too right they did.' Nina looked at her mother and received a confirming nod. 'Tried to put words in my mouth,' he said.

'But you didn't do anything,' said Nina.

'The way they see it, I did plenty,' said Dad. 'Followed Max down the river, threw around accusations, started a punch-up.' He pointed to his battered face. 'This didn't help any. And since bloody Max has gone and disappeared, there's no way to prove that I copped the worst of the fight.' His face cracked into a sardonic smile. 'First time in my life I'm keen to see that man's face and he goes and disappears on me. How do you like that?' Nina sank down on the couch, stomach churning. The long-standing hatred between Max and her father was common knowledge. People were bound to talk.

There was no getting around it. Until Max was found and Dad was cleared she'd have to stay well away from Ric Bonelli. Tears welled behind her eyes and she knuckled them fiercely away. She needed to be strong, for Dad, for Mum. Maybe she and Ric could put all this behind them down the road. But a nagging little voice whined in her ear, and wouldn't let her be. Some things, it whispered, there's just no getting past.

She wanted to shout, to swear, to scream out loud. Why hadn't she seen this coming? It was her fault – her pitiful failure to stand on her own two feet. If she could just go back in time . . . There were so many points where this disaster could have been averted. When Mum had offered to come over, she should have said no. When Lockie went to check the river pumps, she should have insisted on doing it herself. When Dad wanted the keys, she should have fought harder to stop him. She should have done something, anything. But instead she'd waited around like a stunned mullet, while somewhere down the river Dad was tearing all their worlds apart.

It was time to take back control of her life. She scrolled through her phone until she found the bank manager's number. 'Trevor? It's Nina Moore. The auction for Eva's place is coming up soon. Tell me about this dummy bidder business.'

'Not a dummy bidder,' said Trevor. 'A buyer's agent. They're used when a purchaser doesn't want to be physically present at the auction.'

'Why would that happen?'

'Lots of reasons,' said Trevor. 'The buyer might be a celebrity, wanting to protect his privacy. Or he may have previously negotiated to buy the property, for example, and the deal fell through. If he shows up himself, the vendor knows exactly how much he was prepared to pay last time. So he sends an agent.'

'Or the seller might have a totally unjustified grudge against the buyer.'

Trevor chuckled. 'That too. These types of personal conflicts are surprisingly common Nina. Ex-husbands and wives, family disputes – buyers often give an agent power of attorney to bid on their behalf.'

'So if my agent winds up being the highest bidder?' asked Nina. 'What then?'

'When it comes to signing the contract, all secrecy is lost,' said Trevor. 'Your agent must inform the auctioneer that he acts on behalf of a client, and name you.'

'But you said James won't sell to me?'

'At that point he'll have no choice. Legally, once the hammer falls, the highest bidder is the purchaser. The auctioneer can't ignore your power of attorney simply because the vendor doesn't like you. James might scream blue murder, but he couldn't lawfully renege on the deal.

'That's settled, then. I'll send an agent. The auction's in two weeks. Are you sure you'll have my deposit back by then?'

'It'll be ready and waiting, along with that ten per cent loan increase we talked about. You never know, Nina. Property prices are way down with this drought and Billabong's pretty run-down. I reckon you're in with a good chance.'

Next she rang Lockie. 'You miss me terribly and want me back, right, Nine?' She recognised the pain behind his attempt at humour. It made it hard to ask for the favour. Maybe she had a nerve, but she was also pretty desperate. Nina steered their conversation away from the personal. It wasn't hard. Max's disappearance was on the tip of everyone's tongue.

'I hear Jim's been interviewed,' said Lockie. 'That stinks. You've had a rough trot, what with your dad and Eva, and losing out on that contract.'

'Were you really sorry that I lost Billabong?'

'Damn straight I was,' he said. 'The place goes up for sale soon. Maybe you should throw your hat in the ring.'

'It was a stretch buying Billabong from Eva in the first place, and that's when she was giving me a special deal. I've probably got Buckley's at open auction.'

'You never know,' said Lockie. 'That old house is derelict. Fences need replacing. The whole place is neglected. Add in the drought and the weeds, I don't reckon there'll be many takers. Not everybody loves a run-down swamp as much as you do.' He paused. 'I'd help if I could.'

'Maybe you can,' said Nina. 'Could you go to the auction in my place? You know, bid for me, so James doesn't cotton on. I know it's a lot to ask, after all that's happened . . .'

'Reckon I could,' he said. 'So you got the loan extension?'

'Yep.' She was unable to conceal the pride in her voice.

'That's bloody beautiful news,' he said. 'Bloody beautiful. You deserve that place, Nina. The way you've cared for it all your life. Seems only fitting you should have it now Eva's gone.'

His words were so sincere, so heartfelt, and she felt a great rush of gratitude. Friends like Lockie were few and far between, and she loved him, she truly did. Maybe not the way she loved Ric, but could she base her whole future on one night and a bunch of memories from when she was just a kid? She pushed the images of her and Ric at the river from her mind. Perhaps it was time to get over Ric Bonelli, once and for all.

'I wish . . .' he said.

'I know,' she said. 'You don't have to say it. Sometimes I wish it too.'

CHAPTER 27

'I won't go.' Sophie overturned her bowl with a sweep of her arm. 'I hate you, I want Poppi.'

'Sophie . . .' The girl ran from the room, the geese chasing after her. He looked around the kitchen. At the dishes piled high in the sink. At the grimy benches and poo-stained linoleum floor. At the cracked cereal bowl and spilled milk.

In the fortnight since Max's disappearance, Sophie's attitude to school had taken a turn for the worse. In fact she'd only gone for two days. Two lousy days. He couldn't blame her. Everyone knew kids could be cruel, and in this case that was an understatement. It wasn't just that she was the new kid. The problem had always been Sophie herself. She came across as brittle and defensive, even at home. I'll get you before you get me was her game plan. In the rough and tumble of the playground, this smart-alec attitude invited an unrelenting stream of taunts and hostility. And she was easily provoked, often into physical fights. Maybe Rachael had never disciplined the kid. Maybe Donnalee had made her run wild. Or maybe she'd simply inherited her grandfather's short temper. Whatever the reason, it had made it tough for her at school, right from the start.

And now this. Speculation was running high in Drovers Flat about

179

Max's fate, and wild rumours abounded. Rumours that Max had met with foul play. Rumours that it was payback for stealing water in the middle of this terrible drought. Rumours that renegade dry-land farmers had made an example of him to intimidate the irrigators and drive them out.

Sophie, of course, didn't understand any of it. All she understood was that her beloved Poppi was missing, and that kids at school were laughing about him and saying he was dead. Some had even said that he deserved it. How on earth was she supposed to put up with that? When Ric was at school he'd had mates, kids on his side when things got tough. But it wasn't like that for Sophie. She didn't have a friend in the world at Drovers. Only those damned geese . . . and Nina. She and Nina were a lot alike: stubborn and independent; obsessed with birds and horses. Those riding lessons had been the best thing ever for Sophie. But it was more than that. Nina had taken Sophie under her wing in all sorts of ways: helping her with homework, teaching her to sketch the wildlife on the river, getting her to open up about her life with Rachael. Encouraging her to go to school. His daughter listened to Nina. Well, he could really use her advice now. Trouble was, Nina wasn't talking to him.

And that wasn't his only problem. He was fast running out of money. The official search for Max had been called off. Ric still combed the river daily using a borrowed boat, but as more time passed with no sign . . . well, the possibility that Dad was dead loomed larger and larger. Ric didn't want to think about what that meant. He could hold his grief at bay for Sophie's sake. But he couldn't avoid the practical considerations any longer. What did he know about running a cotton farm? Not enough.

For the first time Ric took an interest in the calendar on the wall. Weeks of the growing season had been crossed off progressively in red ink. The last cross was labelled week 20. He looked around, found the texta and marked off another two weeks. That brought it up to date – early autumn, week 22 of a 26-week growing season. He'd toured the farm yesterday, filling in time. The defoliant had done its job. The fields of cotton were shutting down, hunching over. Leaves already curling, mottling yellow as they ran out of nitrogen. Dotted here and there with puffs of white as early cotton bolls burst open, weighing down the dying stems. Soon more and more would ripen and split, exposing the snowy bounty of fibre inside. Harvest was just weeks away. Dad had been so proud of this year's crop, the best ever grown at Donnalee.

Sixteen years since Ric had experienced a harvest. How he'd dreaded that time of year. Dad working them from dawn to dusk, and always on the brink of a meltdown. The one saving grace was the dozen or so unsuspecting backpackers that made up most of their crew. There was a lot of room for error with picking – it was a complex process, and the casuals had to learn it from scratch. Many had poor English and had never worked on a farm before. They'd always borne the brunt of Dad's temper, taking the heat off Ric and his sisters.

But this year it would be his job to get that cotton out the farm gate. Was the harvesting equipment in good order? Probably yes, knowing Dad. He'd have to find a crew somehow. How many? He couldn't remember. A couple of picker drivers, a couple of boll-buggy operators. At least four people to rake up the cotton and put tarps on the finished modules. Then someone to slash the old plants, someone to chop up the roots. That was already ten, and it didn't take account of sickies and pikers. Picking meant working twelve- hour days, six days a week for a month or more. Not every spoilt kid on a gap year could hack it.

Did Dad still house them in tents? Was that even legal any more? At the very least, he'd need to get in some porta-loos. And what about feeding people? Mum used to be the cook. She'd cook for hours, cook all day. Ric scratched his head. How the hell was he going to do this? Maybe he'd be better off getting in a harvest contractor, even if it meant leaving the picking machines idle in the shed. Dad would have a fit at the expense, but then Dad wasn't here, was he? And it would be cheaper than losing the crop altogether through some stupid mistake. Losing the crop. The thought shook him. All that ripe cotton, vast swathes of it, resembling improbable fields of summer snow. It was his duty to deliver it safely to the gin at Duggan. He shrugged a little as the unfamiliar responsibility settled uncomfortably on his shoulders.

A movement out the window caught his eye. A wind had sprung up, stirring the leaves of the browned-off camellias. Sophie was giving the geese a flying lesson, throwing bread and racing in wild circles, arms extended. Dark tangled hair whipped her face. The birds spiralled about her, wings outstretched. She looked other-worldly, like some pagan princess. Little wonder she didn't fit in at Drovers Flat Central School. He pulled down the blind. First things first. Solve their cash problems.

Ric pushed open the door of the dining room that Dad used as an office. Up until now he'd avoided going in there. The remembered fragrance of potpourri had been replaced with the acrid odour of cigars. The graceful teak table looked wrong without Mum's lace cloth and a vase of fresh flowers. Stacked papers covered its surface in a confused jumble, some piles so tall they teetered on the edge of collapse.

Ric plucked a few sheets from the table at random. A fertiliser bill from five years ago. A two-year-old letter from the bank. A flyer for the Rural Fire Service. He soon discovered there was no rhyme or reason to the piles of paper. There were sealed letters too. He flipped through them – AgriSuper, Bush Heritage, Discount Cigar World. Ric tossed them aside unopened. He'd need a lot of coffee to tackle this lot. His first instinct was to call Nina. She was always in his thoughts, her name asking to be spoken, her face in his mind's eye.

Ric hadn't seen her since she threw him out. He didn't blame her; she was sticking up for her father. But how could they fix things if she wouldn't talk to him? The police had interviewed Jim more than once now. The whole town knew it. Of course that didn't necessarily mean anything. Ric had been interviewed himself about Dad's disappearance. But Nina wanted an assurance that he didn't doubt her father. How could he give it in good conscience, with Max still missing and greater suspicion falling on Jim with each passing day?

No, he needed to forget about Nina for now. It would be a relief, to go from wanting to forgetting. If he could pull it off. If he could bear the loneliness and niggling jealousy. The idea of Lockie hanging around Red Gums . . .

Ric sighed. Might as well get on with it. He searched out an empty cardboard box and dropped it on the floor for a rubbish bin. Then he lined up the chairs along the wall and began sorting, using the seats as a filing system. Bills here: phone, power, rates. Receipts there. More bills than receipts, it seemed. Letters from seed suppliers and chemical companies over here. Correspondence more than two years old over there. Letters from the bank, the accountant and Dad's solicitor earned their own special piles on the sideboard, beside the green glass decanter and dusty liquor glasses. He found boxes of memories packed away too, letters and photographs. He put a framed photo of Max on the table, and another of Mum and Dad, just married, eyes bright with love. Hours slipped by, and a disturbing picture began to emerge.

The last few harvests had actually been pretty ordinary. It looked like Donnalee hadn't turned much of a profit for years, but you wouldn't know it from the outgoings. When it came to the farm, Dad had been spending like it was going out of fashion. There were the usual chemicals and fertilisers, but he'd also forked out a fortune on expensive varieties of transgenic cottonseed. Spent dazzling amounts on purchasing water licences and building the new dams. He'd modernised equipment. The farm operating account was in the red by hundreds of thousands of dollars. Who'd have thought Dad would turn into a massive spender in his old age? Ric smiled wryly. Not enough of one to trade in that old rust bucket of a station wagon.

Sophie came in and wandered about looking at things. She picked up the photo of Max. 'Poppi.' Her eyes lit up. 'Dad, look, it's Poppi.'

'Thought we might put it in the kitchen.'

'Who are they?' Sophie pointed to the wedding photo.

'That's Poppi when he was young.' Ric came over. 'And your grandmother, Bianca.'

'My grandmother? I always wanted a grandmother,' said Sophie softly, running a fingertip over the glass. 'She's beautiful. Is she dead?'

'No, no, she's not dead.' He felt guilty that he hadn't had this conversation with Sophie earlier. 'She lives in Italy.'

'Does she know about me?'

'Course she does.' It had taken Ric some time to pluck up the courage to tell his mother about Sophie. But he needn't have worried. She'd been excited and curious about her new granddaughter, unsatisfied with the sketchy information he'd been able to provide, and full of questions. What was Sophie's favourite colour? Her favourite thing to do, favourite song, food, subject at school . . . 'I don't know,' he'd said. 'I've just met her.'

'Your grandma's really happy to have you in the family.'

Sophie beamed with pleasure. 'Can I keep this picture in my room?'

'Sure.' She ran off with it while Ric examined the next bank statement. Dad had opened up a line of credit on Donnalee's title. And that account hadn't just been used for emergency expenses – it had also been used for day-to-day items. Cigars from the tobacconist in Moree, for example. Goddamnit, Dad had been living off the equity in the farm, running it down. They owed the bank a fortune. Ric swore and went to get more coffee. He could almost hear his mother's voice. She'd always put such great stock in the virtue of living debt-free. Used to lecture him about it all the time. 'Never spend your money before it's earned, Ricco,' she'd say. 'You get in debt? You become a slave. Soon choices aren't your own any more.'

Ric headed for the kitchen. He needed a coffee. There was no sugar in the bowl. He hunted around in the cupboards while the pot brewed, but his search came up empty. They were low on milk too. Maybe he should make a run into town for supplies? He checked his wallet. Twenty dollars. Twenty dollars and that was it. What would he do when that was gone?

His stomach grumbled. Lunch time. Since Dad disappeared, he and Sophie had been living on sandwiches. He wasn't much of a cook, except for pancakes, but it looked like he'd have to learn pretty soon. Ric opened the fridge. Not a lot left. Butter, a wilted lettuce, some eggs and a ham that was starting to go slimy. No way would Sophie eat that. Maybe if he cooked the ham for a while? He took it out and cut a few slices before wrapping it in foil and shoving it in the oven. Where was the bread? He'd taken the last loaf from the freezer just this morning. Not on the bench. Not in the pantry. He stood for a few moments in thought, and then it hit him. Sophie. She'd fed their last loaf of bread to those bloody birds. To hell with her. To hell with Dad. To hell with the lot of them.

He marched outside, calling for Sophie, yelling his displeasure to the rising wind. To the dust and the flies and empty dome of the sky. He marched across to the machinery shed, wrenched open the cabins of the tractors and pickers, searched the chicken coop and the abandoned greenhouse, scoured the haystack. No sign of her. He roared out her name, hearing the futile fury in his own voice, knowing that she wouldn't come.

There was one place he hadn't checked. He headed back to the house and caught his reflection in the cracked shaving mirror that hung from a nail beside the water tank. His father's wild, furious eyes stared back at him. It was like seeing a ghost. Ric ducked under the verandah, too rattled to think straight. He forged carelessly into the darkness before his eyes had properly adjusted. A piece of old wire snagged his boot and sent him crashing to the ground. He cracked his head on a timber crate on the way down. Ric lay there for a moment, spitting dust, the metallic tang of blood in his mouth. The fall had knocked the rage right out of him. Now tears mingled with the blood and dust, making a gluey mud that clung to his lips and cheek. Slowly he hauled himself to his feet. Just as well Sophie hadn't come when he called. He was in no fit state to deal with a child right now. He was in no fit state to deal with anyone.

Ric swung open the doors of the coolroom, squinting as the light turned itself on. Half a side of mutton still hung from the butcher hooks and two round cheeses stood in the corner, traded no doubt for fish or game. Excellent. He opened the chest freezer. The dressed carcasses of a piglet and four rabbits. Ric opened a plastic-lined box. Damn it, Dad. Full of protected catfish. Before he could chase it off, an image of Nina's horrified expression swam into his imagination.

Bunyip's iconic freshwater catfish were rare now, really rare. Everybody knew that. Nina said it was because of the carp, and the missing floods and the disappearing reed beds. Because of chemical runoff, and the freezing flows released from the base of Hopeton Dam in spring for the cotton. Cold water stopped them spawning. He never used to know this stuff, almost wished he still didn't. But there was no unscrambling the egg. The voice of Nina's conscience lived inside him now.

Ric closed the freezer lid, and his gaze fell on the eskies and boxes piled along the wall. He looked through the first box. Fish traps. The next one held nets, including illegal gillnets – rectangular panels of mesh designed to be set on the river bed. Any fish that swam into the net became entangled. They were also notorious for drowning turtles, rakali, water dragons and even platypus. Dad was incorrigible.

Ric opened the next box. A parcel wrapped in newspaper. It contained a plastic bag, and inside the bag were envelopes. Bingo. They were filled with wads of cash. Ric counted out the notes, making neat piles of different denominations. Tallied up, there was almost two thousand dollars. Plenty to live on for now. He'd forgotten about Donnalee's black market trade in beef. Dad and his friends bought and sold cattle, a few beasts at a time. They'd slaughter them privately, take what meat they needed and sell off the rest, thus avoiding the taxman. Lucky for him they operated on a cash basis only. What a relief. Ric could feel his stress levels evening out, his muscles relaxing, his mind calming down.

He took the bag, locked up the cool-room and emerged from under the verandah. Sophie was hovering over near the chook house, watching him suspiciously. 'I'm going into town,' he said. 'Want to come?'

'I won't go to school.'

'Nah, it's too late for that,' said Ric. 'Thought you might like the drive, that's all. Help me with some shopping.'

She looked more interested. 'Could we get ice-cream?'

'Sure,' he said. She still showed no sign of coming closer. 'How about layers pellets?' he asked. 'Got enough food for the hens and those geese of yours?'

'I've almost run out.'

'Well, come on then,' said Ric.

'Do you have enough money for a DVD?' asked Sophie. 'I saw *The Black Stallion* on sale at the supermarket.'

'I think we can manage that,' he said. 'Lock up those birds and brush your hair.' Feigning indifference, he walked off towards the house, watching her from the corner of his eye.

The temptation was apparently too much. After a few moment's indecision, Sophie led the geese into the pens Max had built for them, shut the gate and trotted to the back door. The birds paraded up and down the fence, protesting her departure with long honking calls. Ric turned off the oven in the kitchen, and transferred some cash from the bag into his wallet. Sophie came running from her room, hair neatly brushed. Well, that was a turn-up. Dad might still be missing, Nina might still be angry and he had a cotton harvest to organise somehow. But his cash flow problem was temporarily solved and Sophie was smiling.

Back from town and Ric was busy going through the papers again. He stopped sorting and listened. Was that laughter? He went out to the hall and peered into the lounge room. Yes, Sophie was giggling in short, high bursts. The soft, glad sound helped ease his aching heart. He hadn't heard her laugh since Dad disappeared. *The Black Stallion* was over and Sophie had moved on to *Beethoven*. They'd taken advantage of the two-for-one deal at the supermarket, but hadn't saved any money. They'd just bought double the number of DVDs. Sophie still had *Beverly Hills Chihuahua* and *FernGully* to go.

His daughter had almost been well behaved since their trip to the shop. She'd helped him wash the dishes. She'd had a shower. And after extracting a promise that she wouldn't have to go to school the next day, she'd agreed to put the geese outside for the night. All except Odette, of course. Her favourite goose was sitting beside her on the couch, but at least the bird was on a towel. Sophie giggled again as the St Bernard puppy on screen barked along to some classical music. A can of Coke and a big bowl of chips sat on the coffee table in front of her. A big improvement on milk and figs, in Sophie's estimation at least. Ric crept away before she saw him, and fetched another beer from the kitchen. He checked the time. Six o'clock, and he didn't have to worry about dinner, just pop the frozen pizzas in the oven. But not yet. Sophie was still full of chips and lollies, and he wanted to keep organising the dining room.

A wave of missing Nina crashed in on him. How perfect it would be to have her here, sharing his beer and pizza, sharing his bed. On an impulse he found her number in his phone and pressed call. Then he changed his mind just as quickly. She probably wouldn't answer and, anyway, the stolen water, her lack of faith, Dad's disappearance – those things stood squarely between them. He cast the idea of her from his mind. Right now he had more pressing responsibilities – to Dad, to Sophie, and to the cotton.

Ric resumed sorting. The table was almost empty now. Pale paper towers rose like a mini city skyline around the edges of the room. He stood with his back against the sideboard. What to tackle next? Idly he opened the drawer beside him. Once it had contained silver napkin rings and cake servers and little glass dessert bowls. Now it was filled with papers instead. He pulled out a bundle of documents with a rubber band around it. A bank statement slipped out and fell to the floor. He retrieved it and looked at the date. Just three weeks ago. That couldn't be right. An enormous injection of funds had gone into the farm operating account. Enough to put it back into credit. Where had the money come from?

Ric moved a pile from one of the seats, pulled the chair over to the table and sat down with the bundle. Somehow he had to make sense of all this. The first document was a thick sheaf of stapled pages titled *Business Plan in Support of Loan Application.* He flipped through it – balance sheets, columns of profit and loss, copies of recent income tax returns. Ric returned to the start and began reading. It was an expansion plan prepared by Dad's accountant – a proposal for the purchase of Billabong Bend. Estimated purchase price, analysis of the cost of converting it to cotton, projection of income for the next five years.

He put it down and flicked through the rest of the papers until he found a letter from the bank. Confirmation of the loan. It had been granted as per the business plan and was conditional upon the expansion of Donnalee Station, via the purchase of Billabong Bend. Beneath the letter was the actual loan agreement, signed by his father. He read through it carefully, struggling with the legalese. Why couldn't these bloody lawyers just say what they meant? He got to the repayment provisions. Impossibly large annual payments, the first one due in ten months. At least he had some time up his sleeve. Now to the conditions. Oh no, if he didn't make an offer on Billabong Bend, they'd be violating the terms of the agreement. The bank could call in the loan and demand immediate payment. But the original debt on the farm account had already swallowed up half of Dad's new advance. They couldn't afford to pay the lot back at once, not until after harvest, maybe not even then. The only way out of this mess was forward.

Ric scratched his jaw, took his empty to the kitchen and put the pizzas in the oven. He grabbed another beer and faced the window, staring into the middle distance, looking but not seeing as the red sun sank from the sky. His heartbeat echoed in his ears. The auction was next week. Dad, wherever he was, had locked them into buying Billabong and converting it to cotton. There was no way around it. And he'd doomed any chance Ric might have with Nina at the same time.

CHAPTER 28

Nina opened her eyes, instantly awake. Normally it took her a few moments to place herself in the new day, but not this morning. Today was the day of reckoning – auction day.

Lockie had arrived last night, and they'd eaten sausages rolled-up in bread out on the back porch. They'd drunk cider and talked about the remarkable heatwave that had marched unabated into autumn. They'd argued about the tricks and traps of making bids, and trawled endlessly over the events of the past few weeks.

Almost a month now since Max disappeared, and the Drovers' community was divided into two camps. Those who believed in her father's innocence – mainly dry-land farmers and their families and friends. And those who swore he was guilty of murder – mainly irrigators and their supporters. Dad had gone to school with a lot of these people, played football with them, regarded them as mates. He'd known them all his life. But that wasn't enough to protect him from the grinding rumour mill.

There was no doubting Lockie's loyalty though. It felt good to have someone so unequivocally on her side. And Nina had missed their talks. A few ciders in, and she'd tackled him on that long-ago schoolyard lie.

'It was just a joke.' Lockie's expression had belied his words. A muscle twitched in his cheek and he couldn't meet her eyes.

'So you knew about me and Ric back then. You've known all this time.' Lockie swallowed hard. 'You should have told me.' He slid further down in his chair. 'Your ears have gone red,' she said.

'Is it too late to say I'm sorry?'

Nina had let him squirm for a bit. 'Don't worry. I wouldn't want to be judged for every stupid thing I did at sixteen.' But a wave of regret had washed over her. Regret for what might have been. She'd traced the wood grain in the tabletop with her finger. His hand had crept over hers and she hadn't pulled away.

Nina yawned and stretched. Her mind had forgotten how to sleep properly, leaving her body in a constant state of fatigue. She pushed Jinx from the bed, sat up and shook her head to clear it. Today was so important. She needed to focus on the auction, on buying Billabong. On something other than bloody Max and his disappearance, and how it had ruined everything.

The police had been back. They'd interviewed her, along with half of the town. She'd tried to explain that they were wrong to suspect Dad. That he was the one who'd been hurt by Max, not the other way around. That while they were wasting time on this dead-end theory, they could have been investigating what really happened. But the detectives had just nodded and exchanged serious, knowing glances, as if her attempts to persuade them were further confirmation of her father's guilt.

On the advice of their family solicitor, Mum and Dad had made an appointment with Frank Trumble, a Moree lawyer specialising in criminal cases. Nina had gone along to their first meeting for moral support, and also because she didn't trust her parents to faithfully relay the conversation. Frank Trumble was a hawk-like man, with a thin swooping nose, sharp intelligent eyes and bony fingers. 'Don't worry,' he'd said. 'We're a long way yet from any formal investigation.'

He'd cocked his head at them. 'Missing body murders are notoriously hard to prove.'

'But not impossible?' Mum asked.

'No, not impossible. However the prosecution has the unenviable task of convincing a jury that someone is, in fact, dead. That they won't show up alive and well, months after a conviction has been returned.'

'And exactly how does the prosecution go about doing that?' asked Nina.

The lawyer shifted his gaze to her. 'First they must prove that the victim's normal behaviour has ceased, abruptly and completely. No bank transactions, no phone calls, no contact with friends or relatives, no appointments kept.'

Nina swallowed. That wouldn't be difficult. As far as she knew, nobody had seen or heard of Max since that last awful afternoon. The lawyer's casual references to murders and victims had thrown her. 'Then what?'

'Then they must present a compelling brief of circumstantial evidence. Motive, for example. They'd have a fair chance with that one.' Frank's keen eyes did not miss the glances exchanged between her parents. 'There is a history of hostility between you and the missing man, Jim, is there not? And you told me that he'd just been discovered stealing water. An unforgiveable crime, wouldn't you say, considering this dreadful drought?' Dad shifted in his chair and stayed silent. Frank had pressed his lips together in a thin smile. 'That sort of thing all goes to motive. Essentially it comes down to means, motive and opportunity. If a suspect satisfies all of these circumstances, the police may take it further.'

Frank Trumble's words played over and over in Nina's head as she pulled on a singlet and jeans. She collapsed back on the bed. Means, motive and opportunity. Dad had all three. They'd left the lawyer's office more worried than when they'd walked in.

Up until now, they'd all been so desperate to find Max. Of course they had, but what if he really was lying dead somewhere out in the wild unforgiving marshlands? Circumstances so far had conspired to make her father look guilty, but finding a body might make things far worse. Maybe it would be best if they never found Max. A sudden shaft of shame prickled her scalp. Best for Dad perhaps. Not best for little Sophie. Not best for Ric, waiting for news back at Donnalee, half mad with grief and worry.

Nina looked in the sock drawer. Empty. She pulled on the socks from yesterday. More and more, her interests and Ric's were shifting apart. What did they really have in common anyway? Nothing. Nothing except some ancient history and an irrational attraction that wouldn't put them down or let them go.

A knock came at the door, making her jump. 'Nine? I've got you a cup of tea.'

'Come in.' The mug was reassuringly warm and solid in her hand. Lockie rubbed his back. 'You're a cruel woman, making me sleep in the spare room. That bed has no springs left.'

'Sook.'

'Want breakfast?' he asked. 'Thought I'd whip up some eggs.'

'You go ahead. I don't have the stomach for it.' She trailed down the hall after him, taking tiny sips of the scalding tea.

Lockie buttered the pan and took a carton of eggs from the fridge. 'Any sausages left?' She shook her head and slumped down in a chair. He broke six eggs into a bowl and whisked them with the practised, even strokes of a man at home in the kitchen.

'I said I didn't want any.'

He grinned. 'Who said any of this is for you?'

How could he be so cheerful or so hungry? But it was nice to have him there. She realised, with a strange twinge in her chest, that she was spending more time with Lockie now that they'd broken up.

'Why don't you come with me today?' He poured the eggs into the pan. 'Stay in the car while the auction's going on. Then rub it in James Langley's face when they knock the place down to me.'

'No.' She heaved a deep, disappointed breath. 'It's safer if I stay here, in case James spots me beforehand.'

'Righto.' He tackled his breakfast, wolfing it down with astonishing speed. 'Any last-minute instructions, boss?'

'No, you know what you're doing. We've gone over it a hundred times.' She looked around her kitchen, took in all the things that were so dear to her, Lockie included. 'Thanks, Lockie. Really. I'm very grateful. Oh, and that figure I told you? That's my absolute limit. Don't get carried away and raise it, no matter what. Okay?'

'Okay.' He wiped his hands on the tea towel, drained his tea and stood up. 'But I'm not the impulsive one around here. Hate to think what'd happen if you got into a bidding war with a cotton farmer. I reckon that absolute limit would fly out the window.'

'You're probably right. Definitely best I'm not there. But just the same, the sitting around waiting's going to kill me.'

Lockie bent towards her, as if for a kiss, then paused and straightened his back. 'See you.' He put on his hat. 'Stay busy. It'll help.'

The interminable morning wore on. Stay busy. She didn't really have a choice. So much had been left undone lately. Nina collected a shovel and mattock from the tool shed, loaded them onto the bike and headed to the main pump-house. When it rained the floor always flooded. She'd been meaning to dig a drainage ditch to divert the run-off, but the idea of rain had seemed farfetched for so long . . . Still, even this mother of a drought couldn't last forever, and when it broke she intended to be ready. Nina squinted into the light, looking across the sluggish, shallow water to the north side of the river. The shadow of a movement caught her eye. Ric? No, just a steer sliding down the broken bank for a drink. But the idea of Ric wouldn't go away, like he'd set up camp in her head.

Nina grabbed the mattock, weighing the comforting heft of it, running her thumb down the smooth handle before going to work. It was hard yakka. The ground was bone dry, and the ditch needed to be a long one. After an hour of digging in full sun, raising the mattock high above her shoulder and sending it crashing down to break the earth, her back ached. She could taste dirt in her mouth and nose. Dust mixed with sweat to sting her eyes and itch her cheeks. It worked its way beneath her nails, down her T-shirt and into her pants. It got down her boots, into her socks and ground between her toes.

But Nina barely noticed how sore and filthy and tired she was because she wasn't really there any more. She was daydreaming of the evening river, of herself naked in the dim circle of light. Thought and feeling converged into one single stream of memory – down on the cool sand with Ric, his skin pressed against her, his heart within reach.

Nina hurled the mattock away. It was no good; she couldn't concentrate. Maybe she'd finish this later, inspect the olive trees instead. Leaving the tools where they lay, Nina took the bike back to the house and saddled Monty. She trotted along the rows, noting with satisfaction the healthy silver foliage and heavy crop almost ripe for harvest.

The big grey wouldn't settle, fussing and tossing his head, setting his jaw against the bit. 'You bugger,' she said, losing her hat as he cantered sideways like a crab. Impossible to check the crop like this. She swore and gave him his head. Monty straightened, accelerating into a gallop, head low and ears back. The sensation of speed, the wind whipping her cheeks, the raw equine energy surging through her legs, her seat, her entire body – everything combined to wipe out the worries of the previous few weeks. Who cared about Max, or Ric, or even Billabong? All that mattered was this moment, the adrenaline pumping through her body, and the flesh-and-blood animal racing madly beneath her.

The horse veered through the trees, forcing her to duck branches. She flattened her body along Monty's neck and spine, merging into his straining body, becoming one with her mount. Out onto the airstrip now, and Nina shut her eyes against the sun glare and urged him on. They tore blindly down the runway, still accelerating until she was sure they would take off and soar skywards. The world was nothing but a raw, moving blur of pounding hooves and straining lungs, smelling of leather and sweat. Nina whooped out loud with the sheer joy of it.

She sensed the swerve before it came. Felt it in his bunching muscles and gathering bones, saw it in the angle of his ears. She could just about read his mind. When Monty lunged sideways, Nina was ready. She gripped hard with her legs, moved with him in perfect balance, steadied his hammering heart with a reassuring hand on the reins. Her horse came to a shuddering stop, forelegs spread, sides heaving, neck lathered with sweat. A mob of grey kangaroos ahead of them bounded for cover. So that's what had made him shy. Nina let the reins go loose and leaned forward, hugging his damp neck. 'You finished?' He snorted and she took that for a yes. 'Good,' she said. 'And thank you, Monty. I needed that.'

It was getting on to noon before the phone finally rang. She took it from her pocket and stared at it, hardly daring to answer. Lockie. 'Hello?'

'No go,' he said. 'The bids went over your limit.'

Her stomach lurched and she blinked stupidly at the phone, unable to process what she was hearing.

'Nina, are you there?'

'Yes,' she said at last. 'I'm here. Who? Who bought it?'

'Two blokes went head to head, had themselves a bit of a bidding war. I dropped out early. If you ask me, it went for more than it was worth.'

'Who?' she said. 'Just tell me.'

An interminable pause. Why couldn't he just spit it out?

'Ric Bonelli,' Lockie said at last. 'Ric Bonelli bought Billabong Bend.'

The news took a while to sink in. 'That's wonderful news,' she said. 'The place is safe then.'

'Hate to burst your bubble, Nine,' he said. 'But seems to me you're taking a lot for granted. Billabong's prime cotton country.'

'You don't understand,' said Nina. 'Ric would never do anything to harm the wetlands.' She was sure of it.

CHAPTER 29

Nina and Ric sat drinking beer out on the back porch at Donnalee as the afternoon shadows lengthened. Sophie was playing circus games with the geese, tempting them with treats to make them hop through a hula hoop. Jinx tried to snatch a tidbit of bread and found himself on the receiving end of Odette's wicked beak. He yelped and made a beeline for the safety of the verandah, trying to hide himself beneath Nina's chair.

'They're so big now,' she said, admiring the graceful birds. 'Sophie's done an amazing job.'

'She has.' Ric's fingers reached for hers and they sat, side by side, holding hands like children. 'Sophie loves those birds more than me, more than anybody.'

'Any news of her mother?'

'Rachael's doing a little better.'

'Must be so hard,' she said. 'First her mother and now her grandfather. That's a lot of loss for a little girl to deal with.'

He squeezed her hand. 'Let's change the subject. No more sadness today.'

'You're right. We should be celebrating.' Nina pointed at a curved streak of cloud in the sky. 'See there? It's Eva smiling down from heaven.'

'I'll look after Billabong, Nina,' said Ric. 'I swear I will. In a year or two you won't know the place.'

'I have some ideas myself,' she said. 'I've drawn up a five-year plan. To rehabilitate the marshes. Remove the weeds and feral animals. Get a full-scale revegetation program up and running. I'd like to take a biological inventory, do some trapping too, see what we've really got.' She squeezed his hand. 'Working together like this — it's a dream come true.'

'I'll work day and night, if that's what it takes.' His voice was husky with emotion. 'For you, for Sophie. Together we'll make Billabong the best bloody farm in the whole district. Better than Macquarie Station even.'

'You can run cattle out in the back blocks,' said Nina. 'But the marshes are off limits, right?' Silence. She studied his face. Something was wrong. She repeated her question, and still there was no response. 'What's going on, Ric?'

'There'll have to be some changes at Billabong.' He couldn't look her in the eye. 'The loan to buy the place is conditional on converting it to cotton.'

Nina's mouth fell open. She couldn't believe what she was hearing.

'Hold on,' he said. 'It's not as bad as you think. I've been looking into this. There are better ways to grow cotton, more modern ways. Ways that are kinder to the land.' He shifted nervously in his seat. 'Dad's already bought a heap of a new kind of cottonseed. Genetically modified to use less water, to resist pests and diseases so you don't have to use as many chemicals. I've been reading up on the latest irrigation methods too. Some blokes are moving away from furrows to bankless channels and drip systems. And I was thinking of fencing off some parts, like you've done at Red Gums. Leaving them natural.'

Nina sat in stunned silence, a kernel of white-hot anger taking root in her heart. She tried to imagine the Ric that she'd known as a child, the river boy, doing this. No, that boy had vanished, and the person sitting next to her couldn't have hurt her more if he'd spent years in the planning. 'You'll still have to clear,' she said. 'You'll still have to drain swampland. You'll still be destroying one of the rarest inland deltas in the entire country.'

'I'll be careful, I promise,' said Ric. 'Rivers aren't rocket science.'

'No. They're a lot more complicated.'

'Nina . . . I don't have a choice.'

'That's rubbish. There's always a choice.' Her head hurt with a furious resentment that overrode her love for him. 'There's no kind way to grow cotton out here, full stop. It's bad enough what you're doing at Donnalee, but if you try it at Billabong? You'd better watch out. I'll stop you, or die trying. Come on, Jinx.' Her vision was clouding and she couldn't see properly. Everything was misty. The dog, sensing trouble, scrambled for Nina's ute.

Sophie stopped her goose show. 'Dad? Nina? What's wrong?'

'Ask your father,' said Nina over her shoulder as she reached the vehicle. What a fool she'd been. What a first-class fool. Lockie and Dad? They'd been right all along about Ric, about the whole Bonelli family. Why the hell hadn't she listened to them? Well, she wouldn't make the same mistake twice. She was done.

CHAPTER 30

'You're going to school, and that's final. Now go get dressed and pack your bag.' Sophie threw Ric a mutinous look, then disappeared down the hall. Ric went to the kitchen and made her a vegemite sandwich for lunch. He was more out of his depth than ever when it came to his daughter. Ric cling-wrapped the sandwich and added a packet of Twisties and a mandarin to the lunch box before snapping on the lid.

The geese started up an excited honking, like they did when they were let out. He dashed down the hall. Curtains waved at the open window and her room was empty. Damn it. He sank down on the bed. Don't react, he told himself. Take a moment to calm down.

When he raised his head, something caught his eye. A coloured-in envelope on the dresser, addressed in a childish scrawl. Sophie's latest letter to her mother. He picked it up, turned it over, ran his finger along the smooth, gummed edge of its unsealed flap. Then he pulled out the two sheets of paper, covered in hearts and flowers.

Dear Mum,

I miss you. Its been a long time since you sent me a letter. hope you get better soon. my geese can fly. Im glad today is friday. I hate it here. My teacher thinks I'm stupid. poppi's gone and so is nina. Its just Dad and me now and he doesn't care. He's even forgotten about my horse. Its hot in my room. Is it hot in your room? I hope you have a fan. I don't. I would run away like last time but I don't know where you are and I cant leave my geese anyway. They need on me. I love you VERY much. XXXOOO

goodbye and sweet dreams,

love from your special girl Sophie PS I lost my tooth in pizza.

Ric slipped the letter back into the envelope. Then he took it out and read it again, committing each word to memory. He dragged his hands over his hair. What a fool he'd been.

The sound of an engine starting up came through the open window. The quad bike. Ric bolted for the door, but the bike had already disappeared down the laneway. He grabbed the keys and took after it in the station wagon.

There she was, heading west towards the storage. Ric took a second look, unsure at first of what he was seeing. Dust wasn't the only thing following in the wake of the bike. Sophie's geese were racing close behind, bouncing and hopping with wings spread wide. Ric drew nearer. One goose sprang higher than the rest, and with a few uncertain wing strokes became airborne. It levelled out and soared a few inches above Sophie's head as she wrestled with the bike, skirting a pothole and slowing to negotiate the bone-rattling corrugations beyond the bull yards.

They sped up as they neared the water, and Ric hung back, captivated by the scene. Now more geese took flight, overtaking the bike, four, five . . . six of them. Hard to believe these beautiful birds were the ungainly goslings of two months ago. The bike reached the dam. In a display of synchronised grace, the flying geese folded their wings and settled on the water, sailing like miniature galleons on its rippled surface. Then they turned and swam back to Sophie, and each bowed its head in turn, as if in tribute.

Ric pulled up as the quad bike rabbit-hopped to a stop. The four earth-bound geese ran flapping and honking, up over the levee and into the water to join the others. Sophie climbed the bank and cheered, jumping up and down, clapping her hands. He wanted to join in. It was the damnedest thing he'd ever seen.

Ric dragged a boot through the dust and jammed his hands in his jean pockets. He almost wished she wouldn't turn around. It would be a shame to spoil the moment for her. But the inevitable happened, and Sophie's look of delight turned to one of sullen defiance. She'd been crying. Her red cheeks emphasised how young she really was. He forgot sometimes.

The geese waddled from the water and formed a protective ring around her. Odette hissed at him. Ric strode forward, pushing the geese away with his foot so he could reach the bike. Odette spread her wings and bit his leg as he mounted the bike. 'Get on.' Sophie climbed up behind him.

'Careful,' she said, as he reversed and headed back down the laneway. The geese honked in consternation and ran after them. Ric increased his speed. The next moment a shadow fell across his face. Looking up, he saw the long neck and head of a goose stretched out above him, just inches from his head, like the brim of some bizarre hat. He could feel the breeze of its wing strokes. Now another, and another crowded the air. They flew so close a wingtip brushed his cheek. Sophie laughed and Ric shouted with excitement. He wanted to fly properly, leave the dusty ground and lead the birds into the skies. What a buzz that would be.

They veered round the corner. The flock veered too, in tight formation. They approached the house and the geese landed all around as the bike rolled to a stop. They shook their heads, preening and calling as if nothing unusual had happened. Ric shook his head too and grinned. 'That was amazing.' He kissed Sophie's cheek and for once she didn't complain. A faint flush of pleasure coloured her face. 'How did you teach them to do that?'

'I didn't teach them,' said Sophie. 'They just do it by themselves. One time I took the bike and they weren't locked up properly. They're so clever they can wiggle the catch. Next thing they were flying after me.'

So she'd been riding the quad bike behind his back. He didn't have the heart to tell her off. He might never have the heart again. In a carefully measured tone he said, 'That was very cool, but you mustn't ride the bike. It's not safe.' She opened her mouth to protest. 'How about from now on I go with you? We can both take your geese flying.'

Sophie's eyes lit up. 'You'd come with me?'

'Sure I would. Now shut away those birds and get ready for school.'

For once she didn't argue. Ric found himself thinking about the Christmas phone call with his mother, when she'd wanted to know more about her new granddaughter. Three months on, and he still wouldn't be able to answer most of her questions. How was he going to get through to Sophie? Without Max, without Nina . . . Just the two of them, like Sophie had said in the letter. It was up to him now.

Sophie slipped into the lounge room. She wore her school dress and had made a fair attempt to brush her hair. 'What's your favourite colour?' he asked her.

'Why do you want to know that?'

'Do I need a reason?'

'Green,' said Sophie.

'Green . . . that's a very good colour.' He nodded in satisfaction and she stared at him like he was mad. 'You've missed the bus, by the way. Guess I'll have to drive you.'

'Good. I hate the bus. There's this big boy on it, Brodie. He calls me names and says Poppi was murdered. Was Poppi murdered, Dad?'

'No, of course not,' he said. 'Why didn't you tell me you've been having problems on the bus?' She shrugged. 'Would you like me to talk to the principal?'

She frowned. 'You'll make it worse.'

'Then I'll drive you to and from school until we find out what's happened to Poppi. No arguments.' Her smile was small but it was there.

Soon they were bumping down the potholed road to Drovers Flat. It seemed the perfect time for a long overdue talk. Sophie was a captive audience after all. 'I owe you an apology. We never followed up on that horse,' he said. 'I've been so distracted with looking for Poppi . . . How about I get one of those Horse Deals magazines at the general store and we go through it tonight?'

Sophie's expression brightened. 'Can I tell people at school?'

'Sure you can. But remember, no more wagging classes.' Ric slowed down to negotiate a badly corrugated section of road, then extended a hand to his daughter. 'And we're going to set aside some time each night to do your homework. Together. You never know, I might learn something. Deal?'

Sophie shook his hand. 'Deal.'

The bullet-riddled sign said Drovers Flat, population 701, elevation 130 metres. Why anybody should care about the altitude of a town marooned in these flatlands had always puzzled Ric. They drove across the river, past the dilapidated church and into the main drag. There was a garage. A post office. A little supermarket, and the produce store run by Nina's parents. When they reached the school Sophie showed no inclination to leave the car. 'Go on,' he said. 'Only one more day, then it's the weekend.'

Sophie sighed, climbed over the back seat and kicked open the stiff door. 'Don't forget to post my letter,' she said, then headed through the gate and up the concrete path to the buildings. Nobody ran to greet her. Nobody waved or said hello. She cut a lonely figure in the playground.

If only he could ask Dad's advice about Sophie. Ric missed Max with a vengeance. It was so unfair. Just when they were getting to know each other, putting the animosity of their past behind them. Just when they were properly becoming father and son.

Ric missed him on a purely practical level too. The crop was almost ready for harvest, the dying fields turning snowy white. In another week there'd be nothing but stalks, standing stark brown and dead against the everlasting blue of the sky. Groaning beneath a woolly weight of cottonseed, poised to surrender their rich bounty of fibre. With the help of his cousin Tony, Ric had hired a contracting team, but it was expensive compared to organising it himself. Very expensive. Only the prospect of such a bumper crop could justify the cost.

Ric had taken Tony, a cotton grower himself at Moree, on a tour of Donnalee. He'd surveyed the heavily-laden plants with envious eyes. 'Never seen anything like it,' he said. 'And all that water? That's Max thumbing his nose at this goddamned drought. Thumbing his nose at God himself.' There was a faraway look in his eye. 'Can't believe he's really gone, can you? That he won't be here to see this lot harvested. What a buzz he'd have got from that, eh? You've got to get this right, Ric. Got to get this harvest in. It'll be the last thing you can do for Max, kind of like a tribute.'

Thanks, Tony. Thanks for piling on the pressure. Now if he failed, it would be tantamount to dishonouring his father.

Ric drove on past the produce store, even though he needed pellets for Sophie's geese. He couldn't stomach seeing Nina's father serving customers, loading trucks — going about his day while his own father lay lost in some mosquito-infested swamp.

Oh no. Nina's black Rodeo was parked outside the general store. He hesitated, but however tough it might be, he needed to post Sophie's letter and get a few things. A deep breath and he was going in. Part of him hoped it might still work out between him and Nina. Even though she was obsessed with preserving Billabong as some kind of a shrine to nature. If he could only explain things properly. He hadn't asked for this. In fact, up until now he'd been her biggest supporter. He'd helped take Eva to Billabong. He hadn't liked the idea of taking the old woman back there, not at all. But he'd gone along with it for Nina's sake, because he loved her. Because he wanted Billabong to be hers.

Well, like it or not, the place belonged to him now. Ric got out of the car and headed down the street towards the store, tilting his hat against the glaring sun. He'd never known weather like this. Already April, and still no autumn break. Dust ruled. Clouds came and went and didn't bother trying to rain any more. Even the street trees were shrivelling, the tough little crepe myrtles lining the bitumen. The whole world seemed ready to dry up and blow away.

He was a few strides from the door now. It opened, ringing the tiny bell, and two people emerged. Nina . . . and Lockie. Bloody

Lockie. They stopped when they saw Ric, and Nina's gorgeous eyes flashed danger.

'Morning, Nina.'

She and Lockie exchanged a look and jealousy burned through him. Had Lockie's hands trailed along her skin last night? Had his lips touched hers? The idea was unbearable. Lockie's expression remained wooden, but betrayed a certain self-satisfaction around the eyes. Ric's knuckles tightened into fists. He forced his fingers open, but they had a mind of their own and clenched tight again. Perhaps his fingers were right. Perhaps all his misery would depart with a well-placed blow to Lockie's smug face.

Ric was in the way, and Nina ducked around him. Lockie followed, hand on her elbow, shouldering Ric as he went by. Ric bristled, shoved Lockie back, and the two men turned to face each other, stiff-legged, like two dogs spoiling for a fight. Nina pushed between them, close enough that he could feel her sweet breath on his face. Her eyes flew up to his and the physical pull was strong. Surely Nina felt it too? He swore that if his arms reached for her, she would be in them.

Lockie's eyes narrowed. 'What's your problem, mate?'

'Don't,' said Nina. 'He's not worth it.'

Ric stepped back like he'd been struck. She turned and walked away. Lockie shot him a poisonous glance and hurried after her.

'You poor bastard,' said Ric beneath his breath, disgusted with himself. 'You poor lovesick bastard.' Forget Nina Moore. Time to get a grip and stop mooning around. He wandered the aisles of the general store for the groceries he needed, bought a fan for Sophie's room, remembered her horse magazine. He put the shopping in the car and counted his cash. It had to last for a while longer yet. Six weeks before he'd see any harvest money.

Ric scratched the stubble on his chin. They still needed food for the chooks and geese, but he was more determined than ever not to patronise the Moore's produce store. Instead he drove to the Royal Hotel, a place where he was guaranteed to find a sympathetic ear and, with any luck, some layers pellets. He pushed in the door. Gino looked up from polishing the bar. 'Bit early for a drink, isn't it?'

'Morning, Gino. You have chooks, right?'

'Not just chooks.' Gino stood up straight. 'Show birds, mate. Bloody champions. Silkies, Old English Game bantams, Plymouth Rocks . . . Got 'em all.' He stopped polishing and his old eyes grew dreamy. 'Just moved into ducks as well. Absolutely love them.' He pulled out his wallet and showed Ric a photo of a pretty black duck with a blue-green sheen. 'Took out champion Cayuga female with this little beauty at Moree this year. Not bad for a duck beginner, eh?'

Ric tried to look suitably impressed and hide his amusement at the same time.

Gino inspected his face. 'What's up? You after some birds?'

'Not likely,' said Ric. 'I've got enough bloody birds at home as it is.' Gino harrumphed and looked slightly hurt. 'What I need is chook food. Can't stomach the idea of handing money over to Jim Moore.'

Gino nodded. 'Can't blame you there, and you're not the only one. A lot of fellas are boycotting that store.' He beckoned for Ric to follow him. The old sheds out the back were filled with sacks of feed – chaff, bran and barley. Dog biscuits and horse nuts and calf meal. A semitrailer-load of hay was parked along the back fence. Gino shooed aside the inquisitive assortment of shining poultry roaming the yard. He pointed to a pallet of layers pellets. 'Take a bag. It's on the house.' When Ric protested, Gino growled, 'You wouldn't argue with an old man, would you?' He offered his hand and Ric shook it solemnly. Gino smiled. 'Remember, the next one, you pay.' Then his expression grew serious. 'Your dad . . . still nothing?'

'No.' Ric swung the heavy bag onto his shoulders and started for the gate.

'Put that in the car, then come back and have a talk.'

Ric found Gino quarrelling with the coffee machine behind the bar, while it grumbled and hissed in protest. He sat down and took off his hat. A bottle of marsala and two little glasses stood on the countertop. Gino turned, muttering curses under his breath. 'That damn thing is more trouble than a woman.' When he saw Ric, his scowl disappeared. He raised the bottle, asking the question with his bushy eyebrows.

'Thought it was too early,' said Ric.

'Ah, *chi se ne frega*,' said Gino with a dismissive wave of his hand. He poured them both some wine. '*Salute.*' They both took a sip of the smooth, golden liquid, then another. Gino rolled his tongue about his lips, savouring each last drop. 'How are you managing?' he said. 'You and your daughter?'

'We'll get there,' said Ric. The hit of intense sweetness calmed him, loosened his tongue. 'She wants a horse. Sophie. She wants a horse and I've promised to get her one.'

Gino nodded sagely and topped up their glasses. 'Your father had the same idea. I'll tell you where there's a good horse. My sister Julia, she's got one. Bombproof black mare, sweet as can be. Her girl was all fired up about going to pony club and then she changes her mind. Wants to play netball instead. So that little horse? Just going to waste in a paddock.' He took a drink, holding it in his mouth for a moment before swallowing. 'Max already had me to talk to Julia. He was all set on getting that horse for your Sophie, God bless him.'

'Would your sister wait till the harvest's in, do you think? I'm a bit short right now.'

'I can ask her, but if you're anything like your father, you'll find a way to get hold of some cash in a hurry.'

Ric snorted. If he was anything like Max, he'd gamble the last of his cash at the TAB. Ric had never shared his father's faith in lady luck, whether it was a crop in the ground or a horse in a race; whether it was stealing water or a wife threatening to leave. Dad always believed it would work out, that he'd win in the end.

Ric thought back to the last conversation he'd had with his father, the fateful morning of Max's birthday. That little horse Sophie wants so much? It may not be too far away. I have a plan to win us some money. What had his father meant? Did this plan have something to do with his disappearance?

Ric gazed about the dim bar. Framed black and white photographs of the river in its heyday lined the walls. Old paddle-steamers. Barges piled high with wheat and wool. The dry dock at Manning. Building the Hopeton Dam. His eyes were drawn to a particular photo – a huge Murray cod, strung up to a wooden beam. They didn't grow them like that any more. It was an image from the Bunyip's glory days, when it ran wild and untamed right through to the Barwon, the Darling and on down the Murray to the sea.

And Ric suddenly yearned for the river again, the way he'd yearned for it as a boy. When its shadowy reaches and strange, shifting light had utterly bewitched him. When it was all grace and beauty and poetry, and he'd measured it in more than megalitres. 'Can you look after Sophie tonight?'

'Good as done,' said Gino. 'It'll make Enza a happy woman, to fuss over your little one. And I'll show her my birds.'

'Great. She'll like that. I'll drop her off after dinner.'

'But where are you going?' asked Gino.

'Down the river, first thing in the morning.' Ric stood up and put on his hat. 'I'm going down the river.'

CHAPTER 31

R ic rose early, before first light. Toast and a pot of coffee. Where was that thermos? He'd stowed his old fishing gear in the boat the night before. Ric fed the chooks and geese. Searched out Max's leather-bound hip flask and filled it with bourbon. Nothing left but to pack the esky and head off.

The boat sped along the dark water, transforming its tranquil surface into a choppy wake. The lantern cast a circle of light, bordered by mist. Pale stars still shone, small and faraway, and a skinny moon shivered in the sky. Ric watched the water, and hunched his shoulders against the unfamiliar chill of autumn air. Did he expect to find his father? Hardly. This trip was a pilgrimage of farewell.

Ric came upon the confluence of the Kingfisher. He turned up the wild waterway to find it rising. Rain must have fallen in the faraway southern catchments. He wanted to call Nina, tell her a fresh was on the way. But no, she'd find out for herself soon enough. No doubt she'd continue to treat Billabong Bend as her own private property. He tried to summon up some bitterness, as if it might vaccinate him against the pull of her. Who was he fooling? If she made one move towards putting things right between them, he'd be back at her side, quick as a shot.

An hour later and the sky was brightening. He loved the measured way the world lit up before sunrise. The dawn chorus of birdsong and the smell of dew-damp leaves. The steam curling from the reedy river. The hushed expectancy and mysterious early landscape of shadow and light.

Ric rounded a bend as the sun came up and he slowed the boat to a crawl. This place felt familiar. A towering twin-trunked red gum stood on the right bank. It bore the scar of a heliman, a bark shield, removed long ago with a stone axe. Years ago Freeman had shown them that tree, him and Nina. And he'd shown them something else too.

Ric countered the water's lazy flow with a nudging forward motion, nosing his bow into the weeping willows that were so ubiquitous throughout the Murray-Darling, even in this wild place. And then – there it was. The entrance to a meander, hidden by trailing branches, opening up to a chain of deep, reflective pools. Magical. Somewhere along this backwater Freeman had shown two children platypus burrows beneath the bank. Told them dreaming stories of beautiful maidens and fierce warriors. Summoned a great codfish with a clap of his hands.

Ric pushed through the willows and killed the motor. Taking up the oars, he rowed along the peaceful channel, barely raising a ripple. Past green tangles of lignum. Past cumbungi reed beds taller than a man. Nina would love this place. When he reached a wide fern-fringed pool he shipped his oars and sat awhile in silence. He tied up the boat and readied the old rod and line. What better way to remember Max than to spend a few hours fishing?

Ric attached a sinker, baited the hook, chose a lure and cast towards the bank. Then he sat down to think. Occasionally he played with the rod, mimicking the darting movement of minnows. Sunshine filtered through the treetops and he pulled off his shirt. Clouds of gnats danced above the water. A pair of bold willy wagtails skimmed the surface, hunting beetles and damsel flies. Their musical five-note call repeated over and over, soothing him into a kind of trance. *Sweet-pretty-creature . . . sweet-pretty-creature.*

Cares slipped away, there with the sun on his back, watching the cheeky antics of the bold little black-and-white birds. Time wore on. He ate his sandwiches and drank his coffee. Twice the bait was nibbled off the hook, but he didn't mind. Catching a fish was neither here nor there.

Something stirred. What was that? The boat had moved, yet no breeze stirred the gum leaf canopy above him. He scratched the four-day growth on his chin. There, it moved again, as if nudged from beneath. A submerged log, maybe? Ric went to the stern and scanned the water. Ripples ran out along its surface where there was no wind or tossed pebble. Ric held his breath as a broad shadow passed beneath the boat. And then there it was, a colossal cod, regarding him from the brown river with ancient eyes far larger than his own. There was something wise and fearless, almost friendly, about its gaze. Ric nearly dropped the rod. The next second the cod was gone, with a toss of its great head and a graceful swish of its blunt tail. The boat rocked softly as it went.

Ric remembered to breathe. What a fish! As big as a man. Was this the same cod Freeman showed them as children? Recollections of that long-lost day came back only in fragments, no matter how hard he reached for the complete memory. Murray cod this size were apex predators, lions of the river, each owning perhaps a two-hundred-metre stretch of water. Freeman's cod could live anywhere along the backwater, if it was even still alive. Ric looked for the fish again, but there was no sign. Perhaps it had been some sort of waking dream.

Ric was almost convinced he'd imagined it when something smashed his lure with enough speed and power to nearly dislocate his shoulder. The old reel sang as it let out the line. Good grief, he had it. Or did it have him? The boat strained against its tie-up until the willow branch gave way. Ric was towed up the reach, ducking over-hanging trees and struggling to maintain his grip on the rod. After ten minutes the cod changed direction, came back under the boat and slammed into the side. The impact almost catapulted Ric overboard. If he'd been in the old tinny it would have capsized for sure.

The reel played out fast again and Ric jammed the rod under the motor to help hold it. Surely the line would break any moment, but somehow it held and adrenaline took over. He'd release it, of course he would, but landing a fish this size would be the thrill of a lifetime.

Eventually the giant cod tired. It sought refuge beneath the undercut riverbank that had offered safety and protection throughout the long decades of its life. Not this time. The line wrapped itself around a snag, trapping the exhausted fish in the shallows. Ric manoeuvered close to the bank and tied up to a branch. Then he threw out the homemade gangplank, took it in two strides, and jumped ashore.

But it wasn't clean river sand like he'd expected. Ric sank knee-deep into sucking mud. He dragged his right leg clear and his boot remained stuck fast in the muck. Same thing with the left. He stepped back, feeling around for the gangplank, then kneeled down on the narrow board and lay on his stomach. With gritted teeth and closed eyes, he reached into the hole where his right leg had sunk. He was up to his shoulder in mud before his groping fingers found it. Wrenching the boot free with a sickening gurgling sound, he repeated the process to extract the other one. His wet skin was stinging, and a conversation with Nina came back to him. Acid mud was a problem along dwindling inland rivers. Sulphides in water-logged soils formed sulphuric acid when exposed to the air. At Bottle Bend near Mildura, once healthy marshes were now toxic wastelands, where nothing but microorganisms survived the steel-eating acid water. Could the Kingfisher be brewing the same deadly formula?

Ric washed off the mud, scrubbing his skin almost raw, and pulled his boots back on. He'd wasted precious minutes. A fish this size wouldn't cope well with a shallow stranding. Ric leaped into the water and waded across to the cod. It was the stuff of legends, as long as a man. A female and gravid, to judge by her bloated belly. Skin vibrant green, darkly mottled with black velvet roses. Beautiful. Her mouth yawned wide and then he saw them. Half a dozen lengths of broken fishing line, their hooks jammed tight in her jaw. One with its float and leader still attached. The nylon was frayed at the end, crimped where it snapped from the strain. Ric peered closer. Hang on, that gear looked familiar. He had to get a closer look.

With lungs bursting and muscles straining, he wrestled the struggling fish from the water and onto the bank. They lay together, heaving for breath. As his hammering heart rate slowed, he scrambled to his feet and examined her gaping mouth. The old float was a drilled wine cork. The leader, homemade from steel wire and a swivel – identical to the one on his own line. Dad's gear. Dad had caught and lost this giant cod. But when?

Ric carefully worked out his own hook, but when he tried to pull Dad's one free, the fish squirmed in pain, and was too slippery to get hold of. She grunted, squashed by her own weight. He gazed into her golden eyes. They shifted focus, but not to return his stare. They seemed to look through him, as if something stood at his back. Ric spun around, but there was nothing there. Only the trees and the river and the creaking of branches as a breeze blew up. He started as fleeting shadows fell across his face. Just a pair of whistling kites circling high above him. Their eerie cries floated down in ascending scale. Snap out of it. He was all alone on the river.

Snatches of memory merged into greater recall. Nina laughing with delight as the big cod, lazy and trusting, rose to take titbits from her hand. Freeman holding two children spellbound with a dreaming story of Ponde, the ancestral codfish who formed the winding Murray with sweeps of his enormous tail. Singsonging words in his native tongue that had sounded like a prayer. 'Guddhu is a spirit guardian,' he'd told them. 'To harm her would bring down a curse on the people of the river.'

'Guddhu,' he whispered and she moved her great gasping head. He licked his lips but they wouldn't stay wet. The shiny hooks in her aching jaw now looked like medals of courage. A sick, desperate feeling took root in his heart and he leaped for the fish, half-dragging, half-carrying her to the water. But Guddhu's colours were fading fast to grey, her gaze turning from amber to jaundiced yellow. He stumbled into deeper water, walking to force water through her collapsed gills, struggling with the dead weight of her body. It was no use. The light had died from her ancient eyes.

Ric dragged the cod back to the bank and tried to steady his breathing. The rising breeze was now a gusting southerly, blowing sharp and hard against his face. He was choking, drowning in a river of air, unable to draw the life-giving oxygen into his lungs. With a shock he tasted tears on his tongue.

Ric squeezed his eyes shut and waited until he'd calmed down enough to take stock. Guddhu was dead. He studied her massive form lying prone in the mud. Now that her life force had fled, she looked more like what she was – a giant dead fish. If he could prove that hook in her mouth was Dad's . . . well, it might offer some clue to his disappearance. It might in some small way atone for her death.

The wind was strengthening. Above him, clouds scudded into the sky, dark tendrils encroaching from the south. Dark enough, perhaps, to hold a little rain. Wasn't it always the way? Now that the crop was ripe for picking, rain would just be a nuisance.

It took a long time and all his strength to haul his catch on board: a hundred kilos of slick, muddy cod. The dozen or so sharp spines along her dorsal fin made it hard to get a grip. And there were some nasty surprises hidden in the murky water. Submerged logs with sharp snags that tore at his legs as he laboured waist-deep. The fresh was stirring the sluggish current to life, even in this backwater. Once or twice something large and soft nudged his leg beneath the surface, and he shrank away. It wasn't unusual for dead sheep or kangaroos to find their way into the river.

At last it was done. Ric pulled on his shirt and fired up the motor. A flotilla of pelicans took flight at the sound. He cruised up and down the channel a few times, then sped away, anxious to be gone from . . . from what? From the scene of the crime, was that it?

All this tangled thinking was giving him a headache. The trip home seemed to take forever. How things had changed since this morning. He no longer wanted to be alone with his thoughts on the river. Not like this. Not with Guddhu and her dead, staring eyes for company. His mind played tricks on him. Twice he killed the motor and drifted awhile, scanning the banks, certain the shadowy figure of a man moved in the swamp. But he was imagining things. What he thought was his father's battered hat behind the bulrushes turned out to be the domed head of an old man emu. And what looked like Dad's tinny ahead of him was just a floating log.

Ric remembered the hip flask. Just the thing to cure his frayed nerves. He took a big gulp of bourbon, relishing the sweetness that eased his tight throat. He looked uneasily around and whistled to cheer himself up. Ever since leaving the backwater he'd felt an atmosphere of swelling tension. Above him, dark threads of cloud had woven themselves into an unbroken blanket of grey. The wind had died, and the air was heavy and oppressive with the expectation of a storm. The cotton could stand a little rain, but a deluge would down-grade the quality. He remembered Tony's words. 'You've got to get this right, Ric. Got to get this harvest in safely. It'll be the last thing you can do for Max, kind of like a tribute.' Was the crop insured? He hadn't found anything to show that it was.

Ric swore at the black sky. He checked his phone. Getting late, almost five o'clock. There was a message from Gino. *When will you be back? Sophie wants to go home. She's worried about her geese.* Those damn geese. She'd forget about them when he presented her with a horse. What would he do with the birds then? His original plan was to give them to Nina. She'd still take them, he knew that, but he didn't want her to do him any favours. He'd have to work something out for himself.

Ric swigged back bourbon as he approached the river junction. A flash of light brightened the clouds, chased by rolling thunder. It vibrated through the water, through the boat, through his whole body. This was a teasing storm, and when it stopped playing games with him, the sky would well and truly open. Swinging right, back into the Bunyip, the first fat drops of rain hit his cheek. His hair, grown long and unkempt, soon lay plastered over his eyes. By the time he reached the mooring at Donnalee, Ric could barely see the house through sheets of rain.

Ric tied up at the little jetty, just two planks side by side, nailed to a stout red-gum log sunk in the river bed. Low flows meant the walkway was two metres above the water. No way could he lift the cod that far. He'd have to get her overboard and drag her up the bank. The prospect of jumping into the mud again, of grappling with the dead fish in the pouring rain, filled him with dread. He upended the hip flask over his mouth, his tongue collecting the last drops of bourbon. Then he used the oars to help lever the cod over the side.

Steeling himself, Ric jumped into the shallows, sinking to his knees in stinking sludge and losing his boots again in the process. He groped uselessly around in the mud for a while, hindered by his wet clothes, shivering now with cold. Damn those boots, they could stay there. He undid his belt and dragged off his waterlogged jeans. Bare feet found little purchase on the slimy bank, and he slipped time and time again. More than once he found himself flat out in the mud and rain, arms wrapped tight around the great fish, lying together in some sort of grotesque lover's embrace.

Ric finally managed to drag her up onto the bank. High but not dry. The rain had become a torrent, closing in, turning day to night. He could barely see his hands in front of him. Ric took a few moments to catch his breath. When he turned back to his task, Guddhu wasn't quite where he'd left her. She seemed to have moved closer to the water. For one unnerving moment he imagined the fish had magically returned to life. But no, she was simply sliding down the bank, as if even in death she longed for the river. He lunged for her and then screamed at the storm. In the gloom he'd grabbed the dorsal fin by mistake, and one spear-like spine had pierced his palm. Ignoring the pain he hauled at her tail, grunting with each heave, slipping and sliding in the mud and rain. At last he had the fish safe on the gravel beside the jetty. He sank to the ground to catch his breath. It was coming in short tearing gasps.

'Dad?' His ears were playing tricks on him. But when he turned around, there was his daughter, her face pale. A figure stood behind her, covered in a hat and Drizabone. The rain redoubled its efforts, pounding down in a fury. The figure moved closer and his heart dropped in his chest. Nina. She stepped forward and knelt down between him and the body of the cod, tenderly stroking the fine scales of her skin. 'Guddhu?' She looked at first like she couldn't fathom what had happened. But her expression soon changed into a mask of grief.

'She's got Dad's hook in her mouth and I wanted to take a look. I tried to release her . . . tried to put her back in the river.' He buried his face in his hands. The words sounded hollow and self-serving, even to him. He looked up, directly into Nina's accusing green eyes.

'How could you?' She swayed alarmingly, as if she didn't have the strength to remain upright. He offered his arm and she slapped it away. 'How could you?' Then she was pummelling him, raining blows down on his bare arms and chest, screaming like a wounded animal. From the corner of his eye he saw Sophie running for the house.

'I'm sorry.' He made no effort to defend himself.

The fervour of her attack was waning. 'Sophie rang me and asked for a lift. I thought we could talk,' she said. 'Thought maybe, just maybe, there was still a chance for us.' Her voice was weak now. Her finger's trailed the contours of Guddhu's face. She began to cry and he was sobbing right along with her.

'Goddamnit, Nina, I'm sorry. I'd do anything to take it back.' He was dizzy with anguish and self-reproach.

'How will you sleep?'

'Who says I will?'

'Sorry isn't enough. It will never be enough.'

She sprang to her feet and sprinted for the house through the driving rain. He ran after her, wanting to grab her, to make her listen, to make her understand. But sharp gravel under bare feet slowed him down. She was running for her ute parked out the front of the house. He reached it as the car began moving away. The Donnalee drive was awash, and the spinning wheels showered him with mud as the ute took off. It skidded wildly as Nina swung for the gate. She reached the road and swung right over the low bridge, vanishing behind a heavy curtain of rain

He thought of Nina coming to him, wanting to work things out. He thought of the cotton, cotton that this morning had been bright and fluffy as fresh snow. He dug his nails into his palms, but felt nothing. He was numb. Numb to the shame and cold. Numb to everything that had happened this last month. He turned and shuffled through fast-running rivulets of water to the house, leaving puddles on the kitchen floor.

Sophie and her geese stood in the hall doorway, regarding him with uncertain eyes. 'Are you hurt? You're bleeding.'

Ric looked at his pierced hand and shook his head. 'Nah, I'm fine.' He started towards her and she took a step backwards.

'Dad, you stink of fish.'

He caught sight of his reflection in the window and barely recognised the half-naked, filthy, wild-eyed man staring back. 'I'm sorry, Soph.'

'I know,' said Sophie. 'Now go and have a shower.' She slipped away and the sound of soft honking followed her down the hall.

CHAPTER 32

Nina burst in the door at Red Gums. Jinx, unsettled by the storm, whined in greeting. A crack of thunder sent him hurtling down the hall to his favourite hidey-hole beneath her bed. The drumming of rain on the iron roof grew to a deafening roar. A tap came at the window, like a pebble tossed against the glass. Then tapping everywhere, a rapid staccato, growing in speed and ferocity. Hail hammered the roof and walls and windows. Jinx howled from the bedroom and Nina shut the door to keep him safe. Then she went outside, her delight in the storm outweighed by her sorrow at the fact and manner of Guddhu's passing.

Surreal to think that the ancient cod, Freeman's spiritual guardian of the river, had died at Ric's hand. Incomprehensible. But then so much of Ric's behaviour was incomprehensible. His suspicions about Max's death. Buying Billabong. And yet Guddhu's death had hit her the hardest of all. Dad could still be cleared of blame. Billabong could still be saved. She'd been keen to give Sophie a lift home for that very reason, hoping to reason with Ric and change his mind. Hoping their love could be rescued along with the wetlands.

But Guddhu could not be raised from the dead. Guddhu, who was older than Nina, older than her father, older even than Freeman.

Guddhu was here when the great flood of '56 formed a vast inland sea, drowning everything in its path. She was here when the fires of' 75 raged through these plains, with eight million acres burnt and fifty thousand head of stock lost. She'd lived through a century of storms and droughts. The taming of the rivers, the Second World War. It was hard to fathom. Mandela had lived and died while Guddhu swam these same waters.

Nina's tears mingled with raindrops. A link to the living history of the floodplains had been broken today. Forks of lightning stabbed crazily across the sky, their brilliance reflected in the silver sheets of rain. Freeman said Guddhu was magical, that vengeance would fall on the people of the river if she was harmed. Superstitious nonsense? Maybe. But when Nina stared into the angry face of the sky there was no doubting Freeman's words. It seemed right, even proper that the storm should come.

She returned to the house and hunted around for matches. At this rate the power would be out soon and she didn't fancy a night alone without heating. Where was that bundle of sticks? Somewhere on the verandah. How long had it been since she'd lit a fire? November, probably. There, beneath those old tarps, a little dry kindling. Nina gathered what she needed, took it into the lounge room and shovelled out the ash from the grate into the box. Occasional hailstones found their way down the chimney. One hit the bricks and ricocheted into her cheek, drawing blood, but she didn't flinch. Nina had herself on a very short leash.

She usually enjoyed setting the first fire of the season. It meant the end of summer's gruelling heat. It meant that harvest was near, the most exciting time of the year. But as the flames wandered over the kindling, there was nothing but sadness in her heart. No, that was wrong. There was something else, something she didn't normally suffer from, even though she lived by herself in this remote corner of the river, even though she sometimes felt unsettled by the night. It was a crushing sense of loneliness, of losing the land she loved. Of finding Ric, and the truth held deep in her body and skin and memory – of wanting him, of knowing him. Then losing that too.

She moved to the window, stared at the drops of water spilling down the glass. When she turned around, enough rain had come down the chimney to extinguish her fledgling fire. She flicked on the light switch. Nothing. It could be hours before power was restored, days even. A clap of thunder shook the house, accompanied by a flurry of muted barking.

Nina went to the bedroom to calm Jinx down. 'Jinxy,' she said, stroking his golden head, grateful for his constant love. Outside the wind howled. Jinx poked his muzzle skyward and joined in. The eerie sound held her in thrall. It seemed to be saying something important, to be sharing some wisdom just outside the edge of understanding.

Nina tugged off her damp clothes and pulled on track pants and a fleecy jumper. She patted the bed and climbed beneath the blankets. Jinx jumped up and laid his warm, heavy body against her. She huddled beside him. Beyond the curtains, flashes of lightning lit up the wind-tossed trees. Too much to think about. Too many shocks, too much sorrow. Only two things gave her comfort. The gentle dog lying beside her and the beautiful, terrible storm that raged over the river, for all of that long, long night.

CHAPTER 33

Sunday morning. Ric emerged from the fog of sleep, praying the events of the previous day had happened only in a nightmare. But it was futile. Yesterday he'd killed Guddhu, and although he'd never intended it, a chunk of his humanity felt like it had died along with her. Killing the great cod was the sort of thing his father would have done, and Ric was ashamed deep in his soul. He'd ruined any chance of a reconciliation with Nina and, if you believed a superstitious old man, he'd brought down some sort of curse. And for what? The chance that an old fish hook could be important? To top it all off, a steady drumming on the roof told him that it was still raining. Ric fumbled around for his phone. His hand still hurt. He checked the time. Eight o'clock. He reset his flashing alarm. At least the power was back on.

Sophie was already watching television in the lounge room, wrapped in a blanket. She ignored him when he poked his head around the corner, asking if she wanted breakfast. Ric went in, sat beside her on the couch and paused the DVD.

'Dad, that's my favourite part.'

'This will just take a minute.' She fell back on the cushions, watching him. 'I never meant to kill that fish. I was trying to let it go.'

'Nina loved that fish. You could tell.'

'I know,' he said. 'I loved it too. And I'm terribly sorry that it died and that you were frightened. Can you forgive me?'

Sophie looked thoughtful. 'I haven't decided yet. Can I have some toast?'

'Okay.'

As he reached for the remote to put the movie back on, she kissed his cheek. 'Thanks, Dad.'

The kitchen was freezing, so he went about setting a fire in the ancient wood heater that doubled as a stove at a pinch. Who knew how long the power might last? He took Sophie her toast and glanced out the window at the sodden garden. By the look of it, the rain hadn't stopped all night. He'd better go through the office again, find out once and for all if Dad had crop insurance. Maybe give his cousin a call, get some advice on how seriously the cotton was likely to be affected. But first he'd take a look for himself.

In the drenched fields, the defoliated bushes were bowed down by the weight of waterlogged cotton. There was some hail damage, but if the rain stopped soon he could salvage most of it. The forecast promised improving weather, but forecasts could be wrong. The bureau hadn't predicted last night's storm or all this rain. He'd have to wait and hope.

This was one of the reasons he'd vowed never to follow in his father's footsteps here at Donnalee. Ric was no gambler, and yet the success of the harvest always lay in the lap of the gods.

He took his time heading home. Quite a novelty, to smell the rain, to splash through little puddles on the track. They wouldn't last long. You could almost hear the thirsty ground sucking them dry. He rang his cousin when he got back to the house.

'It's raining here too,' said Tony. 'Stopped the harvest in its tracks.'

'You've started picking?'

'Picked about fifty per cent so far. What about you? How'd you go getting a crew?'

'I've organised contractors,' said Ric. 'But they haven't started yet.'

Tony whistled through his teeth. 'That's a damn shame.'

'Will they still be right to pick, do you think?'

Tony took his time answering. 'Should be, as long as this rain stops. You'll need a few days of sunny weather first to dry the lint. Don't know where this weather blew up from. Bloody bureau got it wrong again.'

'What will be the damage?' asked Ric.

'You'll have some yellowing, no doubt about that,' said Tony. 'Some downgrade in quality. But cotton's a tough crop. You should be right — as long as it stops raining.'

Ric rang off and went to check on Sophie. She was still huddled on the couch, but the lump beneath the blanket seemed to have increased in size. Odette must be under there with her. 'Make sure you clean up any mess,' he said. Things couldn't go on like this. Those geese were wrecking the house.

Ric brewed a pot of coffee and switched on the radio for some music, but all he could find was a hissing static. And that was almost drowned out by the noise of the rain. Cotton farmers had a love-hate relationship with wet weather. They loved it at the beginning of the season and hated it at the end; it was as simple as that. He'd never learned to appreciate the sound of rain on the roof, not like Nina. For farmers like her, with their flood-dependant pastures, it was the sound of life itself.

Ric switched to the AM band. He could always get the local ABC. Their radio programs were dull, but anything was better than being alone with his thoughts this morning. He poured a coffee and sat down to listen. An environment segment, somebody talking about the Bimbimbie Zoo at Moree.

'Bimbimbie is an Aboriginal word for *place of many birds*', said the woman on the radio. 'Our wetland sanctuary gives visitors a chance to see over thirty different kinds of waterbirds in their natural surroundings. We're extending the lake, and plan to display more rare and threatened species in the future.'

Ric sipped his coffee, brain working overtime while the woman talked about Bimbimbie's scientific breeding program and qualified keepers. Problem solved. Not even Nina could argue with finding the geese a home with their very own wetland sanctuary. With their own staff, for goodness sake. He rummaged around in the kitchen drawer and found a pen in time to note down the number. Done. He rang and got straight through.

'Of course we're interested,' said the park manager. 'Magpie geese are very rare here in New South Wales. We'd be delighted to take the birds off your hands. How did you come by them?'

Ric repeated the tale he'd told Nina, and explained how Sophie had become their surrogate mother. 'Your daughter sounds like a very special girl,' said the manager. 'Her birds will get an excellent home here, you can assure her of that, but there is something you should know before we take them.'

'Yes?'

'The geese will need to be pinioned. It's a simple surgical procedure that permanently prevents them from flying. We amputate part of the wingtip by severing the second and third metacarpal bones. It lets us display the birds in large, open-air exhibits. Much kinder than keeping them in cages.'

Oh. In his mind's eye the geese rose around him once more on graceful wings, flanking the quad bike as it hurtled down the track. His skin goosebumped at the recollection. He'd been one with the flock, had shared for a moment the thrill, the primal freedom of flight that was their birthright. Could he deny them something so fundamental? But then, what choice did he have? The geese couldn't stay here, and they'd be well cared for. After a while maybe they'd forget all about flying. 'Okay,' he said at last.

'Excellent,' said the manager. 'I look forward to welcoming our new charges.'

Ric put down the phone, feeling rather empty. He wandered down the hall and into the lounge room. 'Sophie?'

'Dad, look. That girl's just like me. She has geese.' It was true. On the screen a little girl danced around in circles, followed by geese. 'They think she's their mother.'

'Well, what do you know? You're not the only nutcase in this world.' He even got a little smile for that. 'I'm going into town. Want to come?'

'Nope,' she said. 'I still haven't forgiven you for killing Nina's fish. And anyway, I want to watch this movie.'

'Righto,' he said. 'I'll bring you back some chocolate.'

Ric made a rain-soaked dash to the tool shed. Then he headed under the house to the coolroom, using a pulley to lower the giant cod to the floor. He prised the hook from her jaw with pliers and examined it. Homemade from barbed wire, just like one of Dad's. Of course Max wasn't the only person to make his own hooks or cork floats. But if it *was* Dad's gear, and he'd hooked Guddhu on that last day, it would mean Nina's father was innocent. It would mean that Dad had travelled on down the river after their fight. He hauled the cod back up and took a few photos, putting himself in for scale.

Ric went back outside and rang the Moree police station, trying to explain the significance of his discovery. 'The investigating officer won't be back till Monday,' said the voice. 'I'll pass on your message, but remember – plenty of people make their own fishing gear. Just pop the fish in your freezer for now and someone will get back to you.'

Pop the fish in the freezer. It was almost funny. Ric got in the car and tried calling Nina, but she didn't pick up. She'd be screening her calls, he guessed. Ric jumped in the car and headed for town, rumbling across the dilapidated bridge. He cast his eyes over the river. It was coming to life. For the first time since his return, the Bunyip had a visible current, rippled with a burden of sticks and leaves.

It rained all the way into Drovers Flat. The wind had died and the storm had passed, but the rain was relentless – a grey shroud hiding the sky and drastically reducing visibility. The road was treacherous, with a skin of mud. It made for a slow trip to town.

Ric pulled up at the Angler's Arms, hunched his shoulders against the weather and went around the back. A brewery truck was parked in the lane. Terry Campbell, the pub's rotund proprietor, was supervising the delivery of beer kegs. 'Safe to show my face, is it?' asked Ric.

'Fine by me,' said Terry. 'If you came here nearer to closing, when some of those bastards have already had a skinful . . . well, it might be a different story.'

'Don't worry,' said Ric. 'I'll steer clear.' The pub owner gave him a grateful nod. He didn't want any trouble, that was fair enough, but it showed how high tensions had risen in town. 'Do you have a minute, Terry?'

'Come on in. I could use an excuse to get out of this rain.'

Once inside, Ric showed him the picture of Guddhu. 'I don't believe it,' said Terry. 'I bloody well don't believe it. So Max actually pulled it off.'

'What do you mean?'

'Max came in here the day he disappeared, bragging that he'd found out where a big Murray cod lived – bigger than Moby Dick. Asked me if the reward still stood.'

Terry took another look at the photo. 'Pity he's not around to claim his money. I've never seen anything like it. There hasn't been a cod like that caught around here for seventy years.' He licked his lips. 'If this photo's fair dinkum, that monster could eat Moby Dick for breakfast. Five thousand bucks says I have to have this thing,' said Terry. 'I'll throw in an extra five hundred for good measure. What do you say?'

Ric felt a sharp twinge of resentment at Terry's use of the word monster. He tried to see past it. Five thousand dollars was a lot of money, more than enough to buy Sophie her horse. But the pain in Guddhu's ancient, dying eyes was seared into his conscience. She wouldn't be stuffed and hung on a pub wall for a lot of drunks to gawk at, not if he could help it. 'I don't think so.' Ric tipped his hat and headed for the car.

CHAPTER 34

The rain didn't stop later that day. It didn't stop that night when he and Sophie ate their Sunday roast dinner of the last of the wild pork. It didn't stop on Monday morning when he drove Sophie to school, or in the afternoon when he picked her up. On top of that, the Moree police hadn't returned his calls and Nina wouldn't even take them. When he dropped over to Red Gums, either she was out or she wouldn't answer the door. Frustration was rising like the river. The swollen Bunyip was threatening the bridge on the Donnalee road to town. When Ric did a final check on Monday evening, a muddy torrent already swirled around the struts beneath the wooden spans.

Ric woke on Tuesday morning after a restless night. It was still raining. He looked across at the alarm clock. Dead. Great. The power out again, and Dad hadn't shown him the knack of starting the dodgy generator. How late was it anyway? He couldn't judge by looking out the window. The world was a wall of grey. When he went to wake Sophie, she refused to get out of bed. 'What about our deal?'

'The deal's still on, Dad,' came her muffled reply from under the blankets. 'But I haven't seen any horse yet.' Ric let it go. She was safer at home in this weather anyway. He stood out on the porch and watched the rain. The mutter of the rising river had grown louder. Better check out the bridge.

After solid days of rain, the ground had quenched its thirst. No longer did it suck the moisture down to its heart, but instead let it lie on the surface in ever-widening puddles. Ric took the bike down the drive, dodging the brimming potholes, and turned onto the road. The mutter became a roar and his heart sank. The old bridge was awash, swallowed by the river. As he watched, the current pulled a section of decking from its support timbers. It rose to the surface then plunged downstream. Crikey, that was a first. What was he supposed to do now? This was the only road to town without taking an eighty-mile detour. And with the river this high, there was no guarantee he'd get through the back way either.

Ric sat for a while, transfixed by the angry water. A dead sheep floated past, grotesque and bloated. A tin box that might once have been somebody's pumphouse. A runaway dinghy. An entire tree, huge root ball and all, buoyed along by the current. Its trunk ploughed into another section of the damaged bridge, splintering it and ripping it from its footings. Ric tore himself away. Better get home. At this rate he'd need to move the steers to higher ground. He tried not to think about the cotton. Harvest was looking more and more like a busted flush.

Back at the house he poured himself a cup of cold coffee and lit the stove, trying to shake off his nerves. There was something sinister about the washed-away bridge, as if the river had deliberately cut them off from the rest of the world. One good thing, though – the landline still worked. He rang the school and explained, with a great deal of satisfaction, that the bridge was out. First time he'd ever had a legitimate excuse for Sophie's absence.

How was Nina faring, he wondered? Living on the other side of the river, at least she wasn't cut off from town. And the homestead at Red Gums was on a rise. Not like at Donnalee. Ric called her for the umpteenth time. He couldn't help himself. She might be in more trouble than he imagined. She might want to know about the geese or

Sophie. She might be ready to hear him apologise again. Hell, she might be missing him, like he was missing her. But the phone rang out as it always did.

Sophie emerged from the hallway, rubbing sleep from her eyes and with a blanket wrapped around her like a cape. She flicked the useless light switch and rolled her eyes. 'I'm going back to bed.'

'Soph, come into the kitchen for a minute. I want to talk to you.'

'What about?'

'About this new horse of yours.' That got her attention. She shuffled after him, blanket and all, and pulled a chair up to the flaring stove.

'We could look at that Horse Deals magazine. You can show me your favourites again.'

'I'll go get it.' She ran off. He poured a bowl of Rice Bubbles and looked in the fridge. No milk. He picked at the dry cereal with his fingers.

Sophie arrived carrying the magazine, with its dozens of book-marked pages. 'I like this one . . . and this one . . . and this one.'

He looked doubtfully at her choices. A clydesdale in Queensland. A racehorse in Melbourne. A warmblood stallion in Tasmania. 'What about this one?' He scrolled through his phone to the photo of Gino's sister's black galloway.

'It's beautiful. What's its name?'

'Midnight.'

'Boy or a girl?'

'Girl,' he said. 'A ten-year-old black mare named Midnight, just the right size for you. And she lives right here in Drovers. We can't buy her till next month, but they'll hold her for us and we can visit anytime. You can ride her, try her out'

'I wish Mum could see her . . .'

'We'll send her some photos.'

'And Nina too. She hasn't finished teaching me to ride. I haven't even cantered yet.' She gave him a stern look. 'You really should stop fighting with Nina.'

From the mouths of babes. 'I'll try.' He held up his hand. 'Scout's honour.'

She giggled. 'Were you ever a scout?'

'No,' he admitted. 'By the way, the bridge is washed out. You won't have to go to school.'

Much to Ric's surprise, Sophie looked put out. 'Can't we take the boat into town?'

'Not when the river's running so high. Too dangerous.'

'But I want to tell Shian about Midnight. She's got her own horse too. We can go riding together. Maybe she can join my pony club.'

'I thought you didn't have any friends?'

Sophie smiled. 'Maybe just one.' She let the blanket fall from her shoulders and gave him a proper hug, the first one ever. It felt very good to see Sophie happy. Lord knows, there'd been little enough happiness at Donnalee lately.

'I'm going to tell Odette and the others.' She slipped from her chair, pulled the blanket back around her, and started for the door.

'Sophie . . .'

'Guess what I've called the little goose. Igor, just like you wanted. It's actually a good name, Dad.'

He tried to remember. That's right. He'd suggested naming the runt Igor, because of its crooked neck and limping gait. 'I thought you didn't like it.'

'I do now,' she said. 'It's perfect. One of the geese in that movie was called Igor. He was little too.'

'What movie?'

'You know. That movie the other day, about the other mother-goose girl.' She turned to go.

'Sophie, wait — about your geese.' He patted the chair next to him and she sat back down. 'I've found them a new home, at a special sanctuary.' She drew her knees up to her chest. 'You'll be able to visit them whenever you want.'

'You can't take them. They're mine. Poppi gave them to me.'

'You heard what Nina said. Instinct will make them fly away in the dry season, but without parents to guide them they'll get confused and lost. You don't want them hurt, do you?'

'Can't we make them stay here somehow?'

'Not without locking them up all the time. And what's going to happen when you go home to your mum? I won't have time to wait on them hand and foot like you do.'

'Dad, you can't take them.' Her eyes welled with tears. 'I won't let you.'

'I'm sorry, Sophie.' He tried to put his arm around her but she shook him away. 'I really am, but we can't keep the geese.' He sighed and threw another log into the stove. 'I have to move the steers now. Just think about Midnight. If you want Midnight, the geese will have to go.'

'That's blackmail.' Her voice spiralled higher as she ran from the room. 'I hate you. I wish you were dead instead of Poppi.'

Ric strapped a bale of hay on the back of the bike and headed out in the pouring rain. It was easier than he'd imagined to move the cattle, much easier than managing Sophie. They crowded along the top fence line, lowing anxiously, facing the trees along the riverbank. A tall black steer with a baldy face stamped a foot and tossed his horns. He raised his head high, sniffing the air, smelling the danger.

Ric opened the gate and the cattle rushed after him. There wasn't much high ground at Donnalee, but he locked them in the top corner paddock, as far away from the threat as he could. They huddled together, still facing the river. One by one they began to bellow; a deep-throated, apprehensive bawling that jangled his nerves. Ungrateful things. They were a lot safer here, if the river kept rising, than he and Sophie would be back at the house.

CHAPTER 35

Nina sniffed the wind and smiled. She loved the scent of rain on dry earth and, even after days of wet weather, the sweet smell lingered down here by the river.

Rain had catapulted the stagnating Bunyip into wild good health. All the grief and disappointments of recent weeks could not detract from Nina's joy in the rising river. And there was more to come. They said the Hopeton Dam was breached. This was no curse; it was a blessing. Those who thought floods were just water going to waste didn't understand how this country worked. How many years since there'd been a decent overflow at Red Gums? The river had already overtaken that last peak, bursting free of its banks, and was still building. In her hat and Drizabone, Nina stood hypnotised by the spectacle. Occasionally she ran in with a stick to mark the water level as it crept incrementally higher and higher.

This was the first real test for her riparian revegetation program. At the river's edge she'd chosen low-growing rushes with matted roots to bind the bank – frogsmouth and cumbungi and other tough reeds that could withstand inundation and fast-flowing water. Higher up grew the medium-sized plants with vigorous root systems. Lignum and callistemon. Tea-tree and thyme-leaved honey-myrtle. Higher up again were the red gums, coolibahs and coobas, well established now and mature enough, she hoped, to withstand the current. As the Bunyip swelled, so did her excitement. The river's power flowed into her veins, washing away her weariness. Let it keep raining. Let the mighty waters sweep downstream to restore the dwindling billabongs, flush out the stagnant streams and breathe life back into the wetlands. Let the river reclaim its strength. A sudden heavy squall knocked her off her feet and she yelled in excitement, shouting a duet with the wailing wind.

Nina picked herself up and made her way along the bank. Further downstream, the restless water was streaming through a casuarina woodland, exploring her tree guards, gurgling into hollows and carrying away the she-oak needles it found there. Good, the young trees were holding their own. Look at that. A thrill ran through her as an elusive web-footed rakali was flushed from its hollow and darted to safety. She hardly ever saw those shy little animals. And look, a water dragon and a marsh snake swimming for the same snag. They climbed to safety, and perched facing each other in a kind of reptilian Mexican standoff.

Wherever she looked, something new and interesting was happening. It was only when a dead calf floated by that she remembered this weather could turn deadly. What about the bridge? It was bound to be flooded by now, stranding Ric and Sophie on the other side. She'd go and look later on, not that she could do much to help. Not that Ric even deserved any help, but his daughter did. Nina hurled a stick into the water. Why was everything so complicated? Her mobile phone rang, barely audible above the roar of the river. Probably Ric again. This time she just might answer it. But it wasn't Ric, it was her mother.

'Mum? Can I ring you back? I'm in the middle of something.'

'They've found Max.'

Nina's legs went weak. 'Is he … '

'He's dead Nina. They found him yesterday, floating down the Kingfisher. The rains must have flushed out his body.'

'What does this mean for Dad?'

'We don't know yet. The police aren't giving much away, but they want to talk to him again.'

'He needs a lawyer.'

'Frank Trumble will sit in on the interview.'

'I'll come as soon as I can.'

'Thank you, Nini.' There was a catch in her mother's voice. Nini. Mum hadn't used that pet name since she was little, and Nina's eyes swam with unexpected tears. Poor Mum. The family's dependable tower of strength, the embodiment of calm and humble dignity. Nina pictured her mother's kind hazel eyes. Her generous, comforting bosom that always smelt of eau de toilette. Her strong capable hands, wrinkled now and mottled with middle age. Nina thought of Sophie, across the river. Sophie, who'd never known that solid sense of family — of security and belonging.

It had come as a surprise to discover just how much she missed Sophie. More than she missed Lockie. More even than Ric. They didn't need her, not the way Sophie did. It was nice to be needed. And maybe, just maybe, she needed Sophie too. Needed to help Sophie with that new horse, if it ever happened, the way she'd promised. Needed to show Sophie the secret billabong where the snake-necked turtles hatched, and teach her how to spot a platypus. Tell her Freeman's dreaming stories. Maybe she needed to share her love of the wetlands, to pass that passion and knowledge on, the way Eva had done with her long ago. But seeing Sophie meant seeing Ric, and that was still a bridge too far.

Last night she'd sat out on the porch, watching the lights of Donnalee homestead through the trees, until one by one the windows went dark. Hoping Sophie was getting along with her father. Saying goodnight.

Nina cast another stick into the water, where it was swallowed by a whirlpool. What had happened to Max, out there in the swamp? Had he died alone, with only river red gums to witness his passing? She wouldn't want to die like that. But maybe everybody was alone at the end, no matter what their circumstances. Maybe death was always a lonely affair.

A chill ran through her. The rain had somehow found its way down her neck and she couldn't feel her fingers any more. Better get moving, stop moping around. There was plenty to do before she began the drive to town.

CHAPTER 36

The truck ground to a halt. Ric could barely see through the windscreen, even with the wipers on full. Somewhere beneath that swirling wall of water ahead of him lay the eastern irrigation channel. There'd be no getting out this way either, not even in a tractor.

'Can we go home?' asked Sophie.

Ric had spent the afternoon exploring alternative routes into town. This road had been their last option. It looked like he and Sophie were well and truly stranded.

Sophie tapped his arm. 'Dad.'

'Yeah. We can go home.' He made a three-point turn, panicking when the back wheels sank into mud at the edge of the track. They spun uselessly for a minute before finding traction. It wouldn't do to get bogged way out here. Donnalee was thirty miles away.

Ric crept back down the road, half-blinded by sheets of rain, replaying the early morning phone call over and over. The detective's words still echoed in his ears. They'd found him. They'd found Dad floating in the Kingfisher River. He hadn't told Sophie yet. He didn't have the words. Ric bit his lip and a terrible restlessness took hold of him. His father was in a Moree morgue and he was stuck out here.

They'd confirmed Max's identity by dental records. There wouldn't be a lot left of him anyway, not after six weeks in the water. No chance for a proper goodbye. The finality of his father's death slammed him in the guts, had done so all day. He'd never see him again.

Questions crowded his brain, driving him insane. Questions that might never find answers. How had his father died? His father, who'd always been as strong as an ox, who'd lived his life on the same river that had claimed him. And the most vexing question of all – what did Jim Moore have to do with it? Ric didn't want to believe in Jim's guilt. He wanted to get to town, show the detectives the evidence he'd found, the homemade float and fishhook. See if it made a difference.

Ric slowed down to negotiate a deep, fast-flowing culvert. At least Max wasn't here to see what the floods had done to the cotton. Yesterday the rising river had eaten away at the old levee, just a tiny break at first, a mere dribble. Ric had reinforced it with sand-bags, but as soon as one spot was shored up, another spot failed. Impossible. That levee had never been breached. He'd worked in a frenzy, sodden clothes clinging to his body, feet caked in sludge, heaping bags along the top of the embankment as the water edged higher. And when he ran out of sandbags he'd shovelled mud at the low spots until his muscles screamed no more. But it had kept on raining and he'd kept on working, even when he knew it was hopeless.

The water swirled around his ankles, then his calves, and the battle was lost. Dozens of trickles turned into streams and then to gushing spillways that would not be placated until the levee was washed away, and all his labour was reduced to piss in the wind. Water had inundated every field, drowning the crop of which Dad had been so proud. And still the river rose. The new dams, Dad's grand monuments to his victory over the elements, hastened the destruction of the cotton. The vast storages broke their banks, releasing raging torrents into the network of irrigation channels crisscrossing the farm, providing an efficient delivery system for the ruinous floodwaters. It would have broken Dad's heart to see his precious infrastructure used against him like this. But then who could have imagined the extent of this disaster? And their crop insurance didn't cover floods. Rain, yes, but not floods. They'd been utterly wiped out.

By the time they got home, it was prematurely dark. The clouds seemed to have sucked all the light from the sky, and water lapped just fifteen metres from the back door. Crikey, that had come up quickly, and he'd used all the sandbags on the bloody levee.

Sophie stared at the river and frowned. 'Don't worry,' said Ric. 'It won't come inside.' He kissed her before sending her in. Then he waded down to where the boat was moored and moved it higher again. At this rate he'd be tying it up beneath the house next. Ric had understood at some theoretical level that the homestead might be at risk, but he hadn't really believed it. Not until now.

He thought of Nina and how complicated it had all become. Would she ever forgive him? Where was she right now? How was she coping with the news that they'd found Max's body? It hurt to think he might never know. The unfamiliar sting of tears stabbed his eyes. At least when you hit rock bottom, things couldn't get any worse.

CHAPTER 37

By six o'clock that evening Nina was sitting in an interview room at the Moree Police Station. The air was stale and warm, and smelled faintly of perspiration. Her mind was in a whirl. Detective Inspector Reed had asked her so many questions about the day Max disappeared, often getting her to repeat things or clarify her answers. He'd warned her to try not to anticipate where the questions were going, but she couldn't help herself. What if she was somehow hurting Dad's case? The Detective Inspector took copious notes as well as recording the interview. Every sound was magnified: the scratching pen, the rustling papers, the throb of blood in her ears.

Mum went in next. Afterwards they sat together, waiting for news. It seemed like forever before Dad and his lawyer came into the room. All the colour had drained from Dad's usually ruddy face. 'I've been charged,' he said.

'Charged?' said Mum. 'What do you mean, charged? Charged with what?'

Dad sank down on the chair beside her and buried his head in his hands.

'Manslaughter, Ellen,' said Frank. 'Manslaughter, and assault causing grievous bodily harm. The autopsy on Max Bonelli shows that he drowned after suffering blunt force trauma to the head.'

'But who's to say Jim's involved?' said Mum. 'Max was drunk, wasn't he? He might have fallen and hit his head? Anything might have happened.'

'That's precisely why the charge isn't a more serious one, like murder. And Jim can claim self-defence.'

'I keep telling people,' said Dad. 'I got the worst of that fight, though I'm ashamed to say it. As far as I know, bloody Max Bonelli was fit as a fiddle when he took off in that rusted tinny of his.'

Mum put a calming hand on his arm. 'Have they found his boat?'

Frank shook his head. 'The police case is largely circumstantial. Our problem is that Jim seems to be the last person to have seen Max alive. He admits that they fought, and he has a clear motive. The hostility between Jim and Max is longstanding and common knowledge, I'm afraid. Shame that your husband was so forthcoming with the police during his earlier interviews. You really should have called me then.'

'I'm in the room,' muttered Dad. 'You don't have to talk about me like I'm not here.'

Nina went to sit by her father. She gave him a swift hug, but he shrugged her away. The room began to spin. She leaned back against the wall to steady herself and closed her eyes.

'Jim didn't do this,' said Mum. 'Can he come home?'

'Indeed he can, but he'll have to report to the police station daily.'

'Daily? That's a two-hundred-mile round trip.'

'Why don't you two find somewhere to stay here in Moree,' Frank suggested. 'We have a lot of work to do in the next few weeks.'

'We could stay with my cousin,' said Ellen. Nina could see her mum's mind working overtime, trying to organise things. By comparison, Dad just looked dazed. 'We'll drive home tonight and pick up what we need, organise Kevin to run the store,' said Mum. 'We could be back first thing tomorrow morning. Would that do?'

Frank nodded. 'Senior Sergeant Bradshaw has granted bail on Jim's own undertaking. With manslaughter there's generally a presumption against it, but frankly, Ellen, I'm not surprised your husband's been released. He has substantial standing in the community. Nobody sees Jim as a threat, and there's no danger of his interfering with witnesses because, as far as we know, there aren't any.'

A police officer came over with an air of apology and handed Frank a piece of paper. 'Can I get anyone a coffee?' She received no response and left them again. How surreal. Everybody so nice, so friendly, as if they were dealing with nothing more than a traffic offence.

Frank showed Dad the sheet of paper. 'The next thing is to sign and date the bail bond.'

Her father took up a pen and stared at the form blankly. 'What day is it?'

'The thirteenth of April.' Frank pointed something out to Dad. 'That's the date of your appearance at Moree courthouse. See? The committal mention is three weeks away. It also lists the reporting conditions. Failure to abide by any of them means bail will be revoked. Failure to appear at court is a jailable offence and will mean your security is forfeit. Understand?'

Her father nodded assent, and then her mother. But Nina didn't understand. She didn't understand any of it.

CHAPTER 38

Wednesday morning and Nina was back home. She was meant to be servicing the tractor. Instead she was down the hill watching the water again. It had been raining for five days straight now, with no sign of let-up. The wild weather was the tail end of a tropical cyclone apparently, which had turned into a rain depression. The bureau hadn't expected it to penetrate so far inland, and was hurriedly playing catch-up with river-level projections and flood warnings. It was nice to know that not everything could be explained away with science.

Nina stood with the wind in her face and the flood's low roar in her ears. She couldn't tear herself away. The river was like an awakened god – both terrible and beautiful. It was everywhere, filling up her senses, demanding worship.

The lens of her imagination swung wide. Nina saw the precious water spilling out over the plains, flowing into secret backwaters and billabongs, reviving the thirsty flood country. She saw brolgas dancing with joy; river gums drinking their fill; dry-land farmers from all over the basin celebrating as the big wet resurrected their land and livelihoods – their pastures renewed, their fallow paddocks soaking up precious moisture, ready to plant winter crops in a few months' time.

It wasn't good news for everybody, of course. The river also demanded sacrifice. Donnalee's levee banks had failed, setting the flood free. She'd watched the water spread over the flat fields, swallowing the cotton plants, drowning their black skeletons and white seed bolls beneath an unbroken sea of brown. The crop was a wipeout. Nina idly drew a cross in the damp earth with the toe of her boot. Served Ric right, didn't it? Hard not to feel something though, for a fellow farmer losing everything.

The plaintive cry of a plover sounded from the reed beds. How were Sophie's geese, she wondered? Such rare and beautiful birds. She missed having a say in their future. How would she ever know what happened to them now?

Ric picked up the telephone. Dead. The rain had been too much for the wires. With no way to charge his mobile and no landline, he and Sophie were completely cut off. It was an unnerving feeling. He emerged into the rain-soaked morning and set about moving the farm machinery from the sheds, parking the various pickers and tractors and boll-buggies further down the road on a bit of a hill. Dad still owed money on some of them. The flood wouldn't get them if he could help it.

It was a slow and thankless task. Who was to say the machines were safe anywhere in this weather? To break up the boredom he went to check on the steers. Following the sound of their hungry bellows, he discovered the unfortunate animals standing miserably with their tails to the biting wind, in a corner of their paddock that was marginally higher than the rest. The poor things were up to their knees in water. If the river kept rising at this speed, they'd be up to their necks by morning. Ric cut the fence and watched the cattle splash away. There was nothing else to do. They'd have to fend for themselves.

It was past lunchtime when he drove the last picker to the relative safety of higher ground. Ric walked the mile back to Donnalee in driving rain, so accustomed to it by now that he barely took any notice. When he arrived home, he dug another stick into the mud at the edge of the rising water. The one he'd put there two hours ago was already submerged. Ric did a lap of the house, feeling under siege. The goose pen was empty. He should have guessed it. Sophie had taken advantage of his absence to sneak her birds back into the house. But when Ric went inside there was no sign of her or the geese. He flicked on the light. Damn it, of course, no power. 'Sophie?' Not in the bedroom, not in the bathroom, nowhere inside at all. He ran to the back door and roared out her name. 'Sophie!' And then he saw something that stopped his heart from beating. The boat was gone.

Nina had turned away from the Bunyip and was making her way up to the house when a flurry of barking stopped her in her tracks. Jinx had remained at the river and something had his attention. Nina ran back down and scanned the vast expanse of water. It was hard to make anything out in the downpour. And then she heard it, the drone of a motor, growing louder. Somewhere beyond the slanting curtain of rain was a boat. Nina shook her head. Madness to try to navigate this flood.

The engine noise seemed to come from beyond the opposite bank, or at least from beyond where the opposite bank used to be. It now lay buried by metres of water. 'Shut up, Jinx,' Nina said, moving closer, shielding her eyes from the rain, trying to keep her balance on the slippery, sucking edge of the river. There, behind some red gums felled by the flood, a motorboat was making its tortuous way towards her. Nina held her breath. It might manage to hold its course out there on the overflow. But it would be in trouble when it reached the main channel, where the current ran deep and dangerous and deceptively fast.

Who was in the boat? Not Ric, and what were those shapes? Shadowy shapes moving around. The figure stood up. Oh no — Sophie. 'Go back!' screamed Nina, but the wind snatched her words away. What to do? 'Stay there!' she yelled. 'I'm coming.' Then she turned and bolted for Pelican. It wasn't far away, tied up at a temporary mooring below the dam. And the keys should still be in the pocket of her raincoat. Nina groped around with icy fingers. Yes, they were there. She reached the boat, dragged the tarpaulin off it and sprang inside. Stop fumbling, you idiot. Calm down and get that key into the ignition. Don't forget to untie her. Nina held her breath until the motor turned over, and she said a silent thanks for the trusty little vessel. Pelican had never once let her down. 'Let's go,' she said, and swung towards the river.

Damn it, there went her hat. Without the brim to shield her eyes from the rain, it was hard to see. Her own engine had drowned out the noise of the other craft, but Jinx's incessant barking told her that Sophie was close. Nina brushed away the dripping hair plastering her face. The wind had dropped, at least that was something. She steered towards the centre of the river. Already the clutching power of the current tugged at her hull. It seemed to take forever before she spotted it. There, not far from where she'd last seen it. There was the other boat, jammed in the fork of a fallen tree, held fast by the force of the flow.

The little girl sat huddled on the floor like a drowned thing, surrounded by shuffling geese. What on earth? The geese saw her first, snaking their necks in Pelican's direction and shaking their wings. 'Sophie,' screamed Nina. The girl turned a terrified face towards her and started to stand. 'No! Stay down.' Nina made a sweeping motion with her arms. Sophie stared at her for a moment and then crouched low again. Nina remembered to breathe. Ever since she was a child, Nina had loved the floods, had revelled in their wild untamed power. But now she feared the surging river with its deadly cargo of logs and debris. What chance would a child have in that water?

Nina was slowly drawing nearer. Twice she entered the main channel, and twice she changed her mind. But with each attempt she was getting a feel for the energy of the river, learning how to judge the angle. On her third attempt Nina was more sure of herself. She entered the current just right, balancing the thrust of the motor with the strength of the flow, and cutting across the main channel. After a few attempts, she manoeuvred Pelican up to the other boat, using the fallen red gum to stabilise it. 'Are you okay?'

Sophie nodded and gave the ghost of a smile. 'We're stuck.'

'Thank heavens for that.' Nina's heart thudded against her ribs. She pointed to the dark, swift-flowing water at the centre of the river. 'You wouldn't have had a hope out there.' She tied Pelican first to the tree, and then to the girl's boat. 'Come on. Let's get you lot in here with me.'

Nina reached out her arms through the sheets of rain, and Sophie took hold of her with icy hands. The next moment the girl was beside her, and the geese were coming too. With a great flapping of wings they leaped and honked their way after Sophie and onto Pelican. 'Right,' said Nina, wiping streams of water from her eyes and waiting for the birds to settle. She reached beneath the seat. 'Put on this life jacket and I'll take you home.'

'No,' Sophie said. 'Dad's going to send the geese to some sort of a zoo. I want you to have them.'

'Zoo?' asked Nina. 'What do you mean?' With a loud creaking noise, a big branch splintered away from the fallen tree trunk, loosening its hold on the other boat. Nina pulled out a pocketknife and slashed the rope that bound the two craft together. With a ripping sound the abandoned runabout tore from its anchor and was swept off, spinning wildly until it found its course and arrowed away.

She held Sophie tight and searched her face. The pleading eyes struck a chord that resonated deep within Nina. A goose nuzzled its bill against the girl's cheek and she hugged it fiercely. Nina stared at the river, at the great running stream rushing blindly along. To get back to Red Gums she'd have to cross it, brave the main channel again, where the current was fiercest and the danger greatest. But if what Sophie said was right? If these beautiful wild babies were bound for a zoo? It was unthinkable. She took another look at Sophie's expectant face and made up her mind. This girl had risked her life for the love of these birds. How could she let her down now? 'Okay.' Nina checked that the girl's life jacket was fitted correctly. 'We'll go to my place.'

'Thank you.' Sophie buried her face in Odette's rain-drenched wings.

Nina smiled and shook her head, half in wonder, half in admiration. They were going to cross the swollen river instead of turning back to the safety of Donnalee, and Sophie was thanking her? She put a hand on the girl's shoulder. How she loved this little girl.

Nina untied from the tree and aimed for the south side of the river, but it was psychologically harder this time. The added responsibility of her precious passengers caused her to second-guess herself. When she finally made her move, she was too slow, too hesitant, giving the torrent a chance to hijack Pelican's bow. Jinx had spotted them and was racing along the bank, keeping pace with the boat. Calm down, Nina told herself. Keep your nerve and work with the river. Go with the flow around the bend, and then slide off to the side where the channel was wider and the bank shallower.

The manoeuvre went as planned. But just as she escaped the grip of the current, something slammed into the boat from beneath – a submerged log. The force of the impact catapulted two of the geese overboard.

'No!' screamed Sophie, and went to dive in after them. Nina grabbed the girl's arm mid-leap. 'I've got to save them.' Sophie struggled to free herself. 'Let me go!' The madly paddling birds were swept from sight.

Nina maintained her iron grip and steered the boat one-handed to the bank. The water was moving fast even here. 'Get out,' she said. 'All of you.' Her voice was stern and commanding. Sophie climbed from Pelican and then helped the frightened geese out too. Jinx arrived and made a beeline for Sophie. The girl stooped to hug his neck, then straightened up.

'What about Odette and Igor?' asked Sophie through chattering teeth.

'I'll find them,' said Nina. 'You follow Jinx up to the house. Take off those wet clothes and find something in my room to wear. Then wrap yourself in a blanket and wait for me, okay?' The girl just stared. 'Do you want me to look for those geese or not?' Sophie nodded. 'Then do as you're bloody well told. Jinx, go home.'

The dog whined and scrambled up the shallow bank. Sophie cast one last, longing look at Nina and then started after him. The faithful young geese followed in a flurry of dark feathers.

Nina kept Pelican against the bank until Sophie was out of sight, then cast her eye downstream for any sign of the missing birds. This was how it should be. The great Bunyip running high, fast and free, as it had done in ages past, stirring her almost like a lover. She took a bottomless breath, feeling her throbbing heart, the rush of danger deep in her chest. A shock of joy cut through the last of her fear. This was what it meant to be alive.

Ric pressed the heels of his hands into his eyes until they hurt. Then he called for his daughter, shouting his misery and terror to the dark and desolate sky. 'Sophie!' But the whipping wind stole his words and hurled them into the void. Think, he told himself. Figure it out.

What would prompt her to pile her much-loved pets into a boat and risk all of their lives? He tried to put himself in her place, struggled to think like Sophie, and it was suddenly clear. She was on a mission to rescue the birds from . . . well, from him. Him and his stupid plan to give her geese away. He cupped his hands behind his head, arched his neck. He'd driven his own daughter into the treacherous floodwaters. Ric yelled out her name again. No boat, no bridge, no phone – no way to get help. It was a waking nightmare.

Ric cursed himself, cursed the rain and the river and the pitiless God above. Was he supposed to wait and do nothing while Sophie drowned? Would his dear, beautiful girl die like his father had? What could he do? Wait, what about the old inflatable? He'd already made a start on repairs, but he hadn't finished. The hull needed reinforcing, more layers of fibreglass and resin, more paint and wax. Who knew how waterproof the little boat was. It might not last ten minutes on the river, but then it again it might, and there was nothing wrong with the motor.

Ric dashed inside and found the keys, stopping briefly to look for life jackets. No luck. They must be in the missing tinny. He grabbed two buckets for bailers, found the inflatable under the house and dragged it the short distance to the water's edge. Holding his breath, he stepped in and pushed off. Barely waiting to see if the little craft floated, he started the motor and sped away. Plumes of spray fanned out behind as he zigzagged across the flood, testing the steering. So far, so good.

CHAPTER 39

Nina headed downstream, pulled by the surging current. It was harder than she'd first imagined to spot the missing birds. Visibility was dismal, and juvenile magpie geese lacked the distinctive white backs of adults. Instead they were dusky black all over, well camouflaged against the shadowy river.

All kinds of animals had sought safety in the trees along the flooded banks. Snakes and goannas, possums and rakali. Sugar gliders shared gum tree forks with surprised koalas. Even a soggy piglet had found refuge on a broad branch. Nina mentally noted the location of the trapped animals. There'd be plenty more rescues to perform after this one. Hang on, what was that? Ahead, a dead river gum had lost its balance and toppled into the main current, still anchored by its roots. Two dark birds perched on its white skeleton, the contrast making them easy to spot. Cormorants maybe, or yearling swans? No, miracle of miracles, it was Sophie's geese.

Nina angled Pelican towards them. This pick-up was going to be a bit more complicated. The fallen tree was in fast-flowing water and she couldn't count on the cooperation of the stranded birds. Still, the principle was the same. Nose into the branches and let the flow pin the boat against the trunk. Then use the catching hook and net that she always kept in the boat to grab the geese.

But Nina had misjudged the strength and direction of the flow. It swirled too swiftly around the tree, yanking at Pelican's stern, sending it shooting sideways. An overhanging bough clouted her on the head as she leaned in with the catching hook. Next minute she was in the water.

The impact stunned her, made her ears roar and rattled her brain. In her rush to go after Sophie she'd forgotten her own life jacket. An icy band tightened around Nina's chest. She clutched at the tree before being sucked underwater. The choking cold snatched at her nose and throat, trying to steal the breath from her lungs. With a mighty effort Nina tightened her grip on the branch and wrenched her head free of the swirling river, gulping down lungfuls of sweet air. Now a new danger threatened. The stern with its thrashing propeller veered towards her. She tried to clamber clear, but her limbs were like lead. The roaring in her ears grew painfully loud, making her dizzy. She couldn't move, couldn't think. Maybe she should just let go and let the river have her.

Nina's eyes swam with dots of light, like the mirrored surface of the Bunyip on a starry night. She squeezed her lids tight, and a face came unexpectedly into focus – Eva, disappointment showing in her wise eyes. The vision forced her brain into gear. She still had hold of the catching hook. Kicking her legs to get a lift, she stretched the hook towards an upper branch. It was slippery with rain and she almost lost hold, but at last she had it. She hauled herself from the water. A moment later Pelican yawed wildly, broke free of the tree and took off downstream. Nina propped with her back against a branch and watched it go with a sinking heart.

Odette edged near and snuggled in close for comfort. Nina hung the hook on a stick and stroked the rare bird's sooty feathers with both hands. Odette turned to nibble her arm. The gesture was surprisingly tender. Nina gazed at the floodwaters surrounding them and slipped her freezing fingers into Odette's feathers.

And then Nina heard it – the sound of an approaching boat. She swallowed hard and dared to hope. Yes, a man in one of those rigid inflatable dinghies. 'Help!' She waved her arms. 'Over here!' He came closer, and closer still – and then she saw. It was Ric, and he'd come to save her life.

CHAPTER 40

The dead gum tree reared its stark white head from the river. How on earth? Not Sophie marooned in its branches like Ric had feared, but Nina. His heart swelled with dread, but also with love, a love as powerful as the raging flood itself. He angled his boat towards her. It had been taking on water right from the start. He'd only got this far thanks to constant bailing, and the little inflatable wouldn't float forever.

Ric sneaked in sideways at an angle to the current until his dinghy was parallel to the tree, and Nina was almost within reach. Two of Sophie's geese were with her. How extraordinary. He nudged closer. They'd have to hurry. The dinghy wouldn't withstand being pinned by the full force of the current for long. 'Are you hurt?'

Nina shook her head. 'I found Sophie,' she managed through knocking teeth. 'She's safe at my place.'

Ric went weak with relief and almost let the boat slide off the tree. Sophie was safe. How would he ever be able to thank Nina? 'Come on.' He offered his hand. 'We need to go.'

'Wait.' Nina gathered the nearest goose in her arms. He leaned over and grabbed it from her. Trust Nina. She was as bad as Sophie when it came to those birds. The second goose was more difficult. It kept moving out of reach.

'Leave it,' he yelled. 'We've got to go. I'm sinking.' The rain was drumming harder, if that was even possible, and since he'd stopped bailing, the dinghy was taking on water fast. Nina ignored him and produced a piece of wire from nowhere. What was she, magic? She hooked the bird's leg, and after a brief struggle it gave up all resistance. Ric grabbed the goose from her and placed it beside its sibling. The two touched beaks and started dabbling in the water in the bottom of the boat. He took a deep breath. 'Your turn.'

Nina jumped across and he had her in his arms. Then they were away. Ric reversed clear of the snag, straightening up by letting the current swing the nose of the dinghy about. Nina started bailing. There was no point trying to fight the flow head-on. This was going to be a slow escape. 'Look.' Nina pointed to a red gum sliding by on their left, its trunk split by lightning. Ric nodded grimly. Until now it had been hard to place their location on the flood-changed waterway, but there was no mistaking that landmark — not far from the river junction. Once the wild waters of the Kingfisher joined the flow they'd be in real trouble. Nina bailed furiously and the dinghy gradually inched sideways, out of the main current.

Ten minutes later Ric beached the boat on the south side of the river. He jumped into knee-deep water with his eye on good tie-up spot. 'Throw me the line.' He waded towards a stout post sticking half a metre out of the water.

'You know what?' Nina's voice was excited. 'That's the corner strainer for my north paddock. I can't remember the last time the water spread so far.' She went short of cheering, but her joy was plain. The flood that had devastated the cotton and wiped him out was a boon to her. For the first time he really thought about the contradiction. 'Look.' Nina pointed downstream. A houseboat was moored in the distance, sheltering in the shallows. 'It's the Warriuka, I'm sure of it.'

Ric could barely see through the pouring rain, let alone identify a boat that he hadn't seen for sixteen years. But hey, any port in a storm.

They started towards it, wading through calf-deep water. The geese apparently saw Nina as some sort of Sophie substitute. They swam at her heels, stopping occasionally to nibble at reeds and grass. Nina picked a stalk. 'See this water couch? Good as dead a week ago. It's already greened up. Isn't it marvellous?' Ric nodded, feeling like a fraud. 'Just wait till the cows and kangaroos get a bellyful of this,' she said. 'They'll be happy as pigs in mud.'

At Donnalee the tough native couch grass was seen as a useless weed that choked irrigation channels. The answer was to poison it. He'd done it himself, plenty of times. Ric gazed around the rain-soaked corner of the river, then at Nina's euphoric expression, and something shifted quietly, softly, within him.

Nina rubbed her hands together, trying to restore feeling to her fingers. They all sat around Warriuka's little kerosene heater – Ric, Freeman, even the geese, preening and drying their feathers. The old man couldn't contain his delight upon seeing the young birds.

'You know what they say, don't you?' He whistled softly and fed Odette a crust of bread.

'No,' said Nina. 'What do they say?'

'That *nuwalgang* are birds of good fortune. That when they return to the river, they bring good luck with them.'

'That's a lovely story.' She didn't have the heart to tell him that the geese couldn't stay.

Nina moved closer to the heater. She was wearing one of Freeman's button-up shirts and a blanket wrapped around her waist like a skirt. Her own clothes were draped over an airer behind the heater. Steam rose from them in soft grey curls. Ric sat beside her, still dripping on the floor.

'I can't believe you're really here,' she said to Freeman, trying to stem the violent shivers that randomly shook her body. 'It's been years since you've been up the Bunyip.'

'Didn't I promise to come back when the river rose?'

Memories of the party in Eva's room came rushing back. 'Yes,' Nina said with a smile. 'You did indeed.'

'I'll have you know I'm a man who keeps his promises.' The whistling kettle summoned him to the stove and he returned with mugs of hot, sweet tea. Nina wrapped both hands around her chipped cup, grateful for its warmth. 'I've something else for you, Nina.' Freeman pulled a little pouch from his pocket. It held an antique cameo on a fine gold chain. 'It's a locket. Go on, open it.' For a few moments her frozen fingers fumbled with the clasp. Inside was a smiling photo of Eva. Nina stuttered her thanks, overcome with emotion.

Freeman turned his attention to Ric. 'Sorry to hear about your dad. That was a tough break. The river's deadly when she wants to be.'

Had Freeman heard the news about Nina's father being charged? She guessed that he hadn't. Nina held her breath. Would Ric say anything? She was so tired, almost too tired to leap to Dad's defence — but she would if she had to.

'Thanks, mate,' said Ric. 'Any chance you could take us back up the river? My daughter's home alone at Red Gums and I'm worried about her.'

If Freeman was surprised to hear that Ric had a daughter, he didn't show it. 'Righto,' said Freeman. 'My little Catfish, she'll handle that river, no worries.' He rose stiffly to his feet. 'But first there's something I want to show you.' Freeman took out a camcorder and fiddled with it for a bit, mumbling. 'Always takes me a while to get the hang of it . . . here we go.' He handed the device to Ric. From where she was, Nina couldn't see, but she could hear recorded voices – Freeman and . . . Max Bonelli.

Ric sat perfectly still, transfixed by the little screen. Freeman's gravelly voice was asking Max questions about his life on the river. His answers were surprisingly frank, although they had a drunken twinge to them. He'd come from Italy as a boy, he said, to stay with his grandparents. When they died he'd inherited Donnalee, and set about converting the rich grazing land to cotton. Cotton was the next big agricultural thing back then, he said, when water was free and nobody gave a thought to the possibility that one day it might run out. 'What does the river mean to you?' asked Freeman. 'She means life,' said Max. 'Life for me, and for my family. I hoard her water like a dragon hoards gold.'

The questions became more personal. Some revelations moved Nina. Max talked of bigotry, of the early prejudice against him because of his accent and heritage. He spoke of his fears for his children, his hope that they wouldn't face that same sort of intolerance. 'I was a hard bastard,' he said. 'But underneath I wanted to protect them, toughen them up, make them strong. They didn't realise that.'

'What brings you out on the river today? From the looks of it, you're going fishing.'

'That's right,' said Max. 'But I'm not after any old fish. I'm after the king of the river, that's what, a fish twice the size of old Moby Dick himself. I'll let you in on a secret.' His voice turned low and conspiratorial. Nina edged closer to hear. 'Today's my birthday, and my mate Tommo gave me the best present of all. Told me a secret he's kept for years. Told me where to find the king's cod hole.' There was a long silence, then Max continued. 'Going there now to catch the bugger.'

Nina's head was reeling. The recording had been made on Max's birthday? The same day he disappeared, the day her father was accused of murder. 'Hang on, when did you tape that?' Nina couldn't contain herself any longer. 'And where exactly?' She stood up and looked over Ric's shoulder. There was Max, his face redder than usual, although it might have been the quality of the recording.

He was happy, animated, and in the background was Warriuka's steering column. It had been videoed right here on the houseboat. The date flashed red in the corner of the screen, and a time — 4.15 p.m. Dad had been home before four o'clock that day. Herself, Mum, Lockie – they'd all seen him. And yet here was Max, alive and well at four-fifteen. Four-fifteen. She began to laugh and cry all at once.

'Look.' She shook Ric's shoulder and pointed at the time stamp. 'Do you get it? Do you know what this means? My father's innocent.'

Ric stood and swept Nina up in one swift motion, wrapping her in the strength and safety of his arms. Pushing away the pain of the last few weeks. Forgiving her, asking to be forgiven. For that brief moment she was fourteen again, down by the river, awaiting her first kiss. Their lips met in a heady mix of relief and joy.

'Will someone please tell me what's going on?' said Freeman.

'We'll need your camcorder for a while,' said Ric. 'And the police will want to take your statement.'

Nina threw her arms around Freeman's bony shoulders. 'I love you, I love you, I love you . . .' she chanted, taking hold of his gnarled brown hands and whirling him around in circles, almost losing her makeshift blanket skirt in the process. Nina danced him over to the couch, all weariness forgotten, and practically pushed him into it. 'Sit down.' She perched beside him. 'Have I got a river story for you.'

CHAPTER 41

Half an hour later they all piled into Catfish, Freeman's little runabout, and headed upriver. The rain had eased and Freeman was an expert boatman, but it still took an agonisingly long time to negotiate the powerful current. When they arrived back at Red Gums, Sophie was waiting with Jinx and the birds at the temporary tie-up place below the dam – a forlorn little figure huddled under an umbrella. Ric breathed a giant sigh of relief. Should he kiss his daughter or kill her? He wasn't sure.

When Sophie caught sight of the two geese on Catfish, her face shone with pure joy. 'Odette, Igor. You're safe!'

'What about me?' said Ric, jumping ashore and swinging her into his arms. 'Are you happy to see me?'

'Yes.' She wriggled from his grasp. 'Now give me my birds.'

Odette and Igor caught sight of Sophie. They honked in wild greeting, flapping their wings in Nina's face. Freeman helped them over the side and they ran to the girl. She knelt down, hugging the happy birds to her, while their brothers and sisters crowded round.

Freeman handed Nina the camcorder, wrapped in plastic bags to keep out the rain.

'How will you manage without it?' she asked.

'Like I used to.' He grinned and pointed to his temple. 'Keep the stories in here.'

'Are you coming inside?'

Freeman shook his head. 'Me and Warriuka, we'll be back to see you when the Bunyip calms down.' He fixed his dark eyes on Ric. 'Something's got her mighty stirred up, I reckon.'

Nina embraced him, and Freeman half-heartedly pushed her away. 'That's enough of that. Let an old man get on home, will you? There's a thunderstorm coming. I can feel it in my bones.' A final kiss and Nina jumped ashore. Freeman untied the dinghy's tow rope and threw Ric the line. 'I'll keep an eye out for them other boats,' he said. 'They'll turn up. And I'll stay put for a few days till the cops get their statement.' Then he was gone, letting the current carry Catfish downstream.

Ric sat with Sophie in front of Red Gums' roaring fire, deep in thought. 'Can my geese come in too?' Sophie asked. 'They're cold in the kitchen.' She cuddled Jinx tight, and glared at Ric when he shook his head. 'I'm not going home with you,' she said. 'You can't make me.'

He rubbed his hands together. The chill was finally leaving the marrow of his bones. 'The bridge is out and I wouldn't let you get in that dinghy, even if you wanted to,' he said. 'You'll have to stay here for now.'

'Not just for now,' said Sophie. 'I'm never going back.'

Nina rushed in, showered and changed, hair half-dry, cheeks flushed with excitement. She'd never looked more beautiful. 'I'm heading to Drovers.' She picked up the camcorder.

'Can you hold off for an hour or so?' said Ric, standing up. 'Much safer to wait till the storm passes. I need to go back to Donnalee for a bit, and don't want to leave Sophie by herself.'

'Can't it wait?'

Ric moved close and whispered something in her ear.

'Go,' said Nina. Her goodbye kiss was soft on his lips, and he was more convinced than ever of what he had to do.

· · ·

Ric shone the torch onto the body of the great cod. He'd braced himself for the smell of death but, strangely, the air in the coolroom was still sweet. He positioned a tarpaulin underneath, gently lowered her, then cut Guddhu free.

In a few minutes he'd hauled the tarp to the river's edge. The floodwaters were just a few metres from the house now. He glanced uneasily about. The sky had grown even darker, if that was possible, and the air was electric with the coming storm. Rivers of rain poured down Guddhu's body, glistening on her fine scales, bringing her once-bright colours back to life.

Ric crouched and held her head. He worked the vicious hooks loose from her jaw. Their razor-sharp points cut into his fingers, and red pearls of blood joined the raindrops on Guddhu's gleaming skin. Forks of light flashed from the clouds, followed by a thunderclap so loud it shook the ground. The sky grew blacker still, and a dreadful urgency came over him. He stripped off his clothes and stumbled thigh-deep into the lapping waters, dragging the tarp after him. The cod, at first a dead weight, grew lighter as she entered the river. Deeper and deeper he went, farther and farther into the flow, until at last she floated free. Ric gathered up the tarp and swam sideways, giving Guddhu clear passage. The current gathered her in its arms, buoyed her up, carried her downstream in a semblance of life. Lightning lit the sky, turning the water to shining quicksilver. And in that dazzling moment, he could have sworn that Guddhu swished her great tail before vanishing into the flood.

Ric swam ashore and stood naked as the wind and rain raged about him. He was one with the storm, revelling in its power, rejoicing in this display of its might. A transformation. Thanks to Nina he'd remembered who he was, and somehow, some way, he would put things right.

Ric went to the house, into the dining room, and started to search. That letter from Bush Heritage — he had to find it.

<h1 style="text-align:center">CHAPTER 42</h1>

Nina stepped onto the verandah and cocked her head. The rain had stopped. Strange, to no longer hear its steady drum on the roof. She'd flown home from Moree with clearing skies and a light spirit, having shown the police and her astonished parents the taped interview – incontrovertible evidence of Dad's innocence. The sound of Ric and Sophie bickering came through the kitchen window, and she moved closer to listen.

'I told you,' said Sophie. 'I'm going to live here with Nina. I like her old bedroom. It's got pony curtains.'

'What would your mother say?' said Ric. 'She wanted you to live with me, not with a stranger.'

Sophie's voice swelled with indignation. 'Nina's not a stranger. She's my friend, and anyway, Mum wouldn't care.' A chair squeaked inside and the little girl came running out. 'Nina, I'm so glad you're back. I have to talk to you.' Sophie's voice was high and urgent. 'It's important, a matter of life and death.'

'Well,' said Nina, 'in that case, I'm all ears.'

Sophie took her hand. 'Come into the kitchen. I want Dad to hear this too.'

Finally Sophie had them all seated at the table. She took a deep breath, fixed Nina with her big brown eyes and began. 'You said my geese couldn't stay here because they didn't have parents to teach them to migrate, right?'

Nina nodded. 'In a few weeks instinct will tell them to fly away, but they won't know where to go. They'll get lost, and if they don't find permanent wetlands . . . well, they won't survive.'

'Where would their parents take them if they were still alive?'

'I don't know for sure,' said Nina. 'But I've done some research. A few magpie geese overwintered at the Currawinya lakes last year. There's a good chance that's where they're from.'

Sophie frowned. Nina had never seen anybody think so hard. 'How far is it?'

'Hundreds of miles away. On the Queensland border, along the Paroo River.'

'Would they be safe there?' asked Sophie.

'Absolutely. It's a national park, a Ramsar wetland.'

'What's a Ramsar wetland?'

'A breeding site of worldwide importance,' said Nina. 'Listed under the Ramsar Convention. Wetlands are the only habitat in the world to have an international convention to protect them.' She looked across at Ric to make sure he heard her. 'I hope Billabong may be a Ramsar site one day, if we can talk your father out of turning it into a cotton farm.' Ric gave an enigmatic smile.

'I want my geese to go to those lakes for winter,' said Sophie.

'Well, we could drive them there,' said Nina, 'but they'd never find their way back to the Bunyip next spring.'

'Not drive them,' said Sophie. 'Fly them. Teach them to migrate.'

The idea cannoned into Nina's brain. Why not? Why shouldn't she fly them there? 'Oh, Sophie, that's a wonderful idea. What made you think of it?'

'There was this movie —'

'Of course there was,' Ric cut in.

'With a girl just like me – a mother-goose girl. She teaches them to migrate by following a little plane.'

'That's just a movie, Soph,' said Ric. 'It's not real.'

'It might be a movie,' said Nina. 'But it was based on a true story. It's been done with all sorts of birds.' Nina's head was spinning with excitement. Why hadn't she thought of it? 'Canada geese, trumpeter swans, northern bald ibis, Siberian and whooping cranes – even eagles and condors. As soon as the chicks hatch they meet a human foster parent. Then for the next few months the human stand-in spends almost every waking hour with the birds, feeding them, grooming them and playing with them – just the way Sophie's done, right? Finally the bond is so strong that the birds are willing to follow their parent anywhere. Even if that parent is sitting in an ultra-light aeroplane.'

'Could we really do it?' asked Sophie.

'It's never been done in Australia before. It would be a first, but I don't see why not.' Nina's enthusiasm for the crazy plan was building by the second. 'As long as your father agrees.' She looked across at Ric's bewildered face. 'What do you say, dad? Are you in?'

'Pleease, Dad.'

'Okay, I'm in,' he said at last. Sophie squealed so hard that Jinx began to bark.

'Right,' said Nina. 'Now all we need is the right aircraft.'

'You already have a plane,' said Sophie.

Nina shook her head. 'The Skyhawk's too big, too noisy.'

'My cousin has a trike, a two-seater,' said Ric. 'An Airborne Edge. Any good?'

'That would be perfect. Reckon you could get your hands on it?'

'Leave it to me,' he said. 'Although I've a feeling I'll regret saying that.'

Nina got up and stood behind his chair. 'You won't regret a thing. I promise.' Then she leaned over and kissed him until her toes curled. Sophie giggled and Jinx got jealous, trying to push in between them. When Nina came up for air, Ric looked like she felt – dazed with happiness.

CHAPTER 43

Two weeks on, and the flood was abating, slipping slowly off Donnalee's ruined fields. The place should be alive and bustling with the harvest by now. Instead an eerie peace ruled, disturbed only by the swans' haunting cries, and the night-time chorus of contented frogs.

Ric was replacing flood-flattened fencing along the river, enjoying the sunshine, all the while keeping an ear out for the sound of a motor. The bridge was still out, so Professor Mark Hill from Bush Heritage was coming by boat. It was lunchtime when he finally arrived, a middle-aged man with unruly grey hair poking out from under his hat, carrying a briefcase. He moored expertly at the makeshift jetty halfway up the laneway. It would be weeks before the river ran within its banks again.

Ric shook hands with his visitor and escorted him up to the house. Through the mud and smell and decay. Past the denuded paddocks, the silted-up channels, the utter absence of anything green. Donnalee looked strange and alien, even to him.

Ric brewed them a coffee and sat down to listen.

'I can't tell you how thrilled we were to get your call. When Eva Langley died I was frightened we'd missed our chance.' Ric just smiled. He was happy for Mark to do all the talking. 'We'd already assessed the ecological data with regard to rare and endangered species and eco-systems.' Mark's bushy white monobrow jumped up and down as he spoke. He stopped to clean his glasses, and a single tear glistened in the corner of his eye. 'The richness and diversity of taxa and biogeographical processes at the Billabong site is really outstanding.'

'That's good, then?' Ric poured him a coffee.

'Much, much better than good.' Mark leant forward. 'Billabong is a perfect example of an inland river delta. In its own way, it's as unique as the Coorong, and protects some endangered communities almost unknown in other reserves.' He took a phone from his pocket and scrolled through it. 'There,' he said. 'I took that photo in the wetlands two months ago.' Mark showed him a picture of a medium-sized wader with a distinctive bill.

Ric recognised it immediately – Nina's special bird. 'A painted snipe.'

Mark looked impressed. 'It's nice dealing with a man who knows what he's talking about.' He lowered his voice as if somebody was listening. 'You'd be amazed how ignorant some people are around here.' Ric nodded sagely. This was going to be a lot of fun. Mark put his briefcase on the table. 'I've drawn up the contract as discussed. Here's an irony you might appreciate. Bush Heritage acquired the funds to purchase Billabong Bend thanks to a generous bequest from Eva Langley herself. We'd finished the assessments before she died and were keen to buy, but she didn't want to sell and we didn't have the cash then anyway.' He sipped his coffee. 'Can you imagine what we thought when the place went to auction and was knocked down to a cotton grower? We thought Billabong was a goner. All those fertile river flats. Then we received the bequest money in the bank and your phone call on the very same day.' Mark reached over and shook his hand. 'Thank you, Ric.'

A warm surge of satisfaction passed through him. He'd been right — this was fun. And it was going to be even more fun telling Nina. He signed the contracts, confident he'd have the bank's blessing. Dad's pending life insurance payout had seen to that.

They walked back down to the river. 'You cotton blokes have had a bad trot with this rain,' said Mark politely, looking at the devastated fields. That's what the man said, but he was thinking that it was a crime to grow cotton here. Ric knew the drill. He'd heard it often enough from Nina.

'I'm pulling out of cotton,' said Ric. Mark's eyes lit up. 'I'm talking to the bank about a new direction, a new business plan. Reckon organic beef might be the go instead, and olives. Maybe almonds and pecans as well. What do you reckon?'

'That's a fabulous idea,' said Mark. 'Absolutely fabulous. Anything we can do to help, just ask. A working bee, for instance, to repair those riverbanks.' Mark shook Ric's hand again. 'Hope you don't mind if I head downstream for another look at Billabong,' he said. 'You have no idea how excited I am.'

'You'd be surprised.' Ric was almost fond of this strange man. The delight in Mark's eyes whenever he talked about the wetlands was the same as in Nina's. 'There's someone I must introduce you to one day, Professor,' he said. 'Someone who knows as much about Billabong as Eva did. And, by the way, I'm missing a pair of runabouts. Let me know if you see them.'

'Will do,' said Mark. 'Better yet, why don't you come with me?'

Ric shook his head. 'Nah, mate. Can't do it.' He'd had enough of the river for now. The boat slid off through the watery landscape of sunlight and shade, drawing Ric's thoughts along with it. A few days ago he'd taken a journey in memoriam to the secret cod hole, and had found the missing tinny. It had been lurking, sunken, just a hundred metres upstream from where Guddhu died. Dad must have fallen in, maybe while fighting the fish on the line, maybe too drunk to keep his balance. If the flood hadn't flushed out his body, he'd never have been found.

Old-timers loved to tell tall tales – tales of monster cod grabbing swimmers by a kicking foot and dragging them under. His mind went back to the day Guddhu died, to the memory of something heavy and soft floating in the water. His skin crawled to think of it.

He wasn't a superstitious man, but on that last trip the secluded backwater had seemed alive with ghosts. Shadows shifted at the edges of his sight, and when he looked, they were gone. Fear had slithered up his spine, playing tricks, hurrying him on with his task. Ric chose a shady spot and opened the esky. Gently does it. He lifted out the thick plastic bag, gassed with oxygen to keep the Murray codlings healthy. Then he lowered the bag into the water and let it float there for a few minutes. The baby fish gleamed like leaves of burnished bronze, but seemed sluggish. Were they okay? He removed the rubber band and let some river water into the bag. The fingerlings came to life, darting about their prison. Five minutes later he released them. A flashing blur of gold and they were gone. Ric wished them well.

Next he'd tried to retrieve the tinny, but a wide patch of dark water had taken on the dappled shape of a fish. Shaken, Ric had left the submerged boat where it lay. His disquiet had not lifted until he was safely home.

Ric wandered back to the house, thinking about what he'd said to Mark. About getting out of cotton and going organic. Why not? It would make Nina happy, but more than that, it would make him happy too. And suddenly he was looking forward to a Bush Heritage working bee down by the Bunyip. He wanted Sophie to be proud of the river at Donnalee.

His phone rang. Hilary Harper, Rachael's social worker.

'Rachael's making progress,' she said. 'I'd like to organise a time for her to ring her daughter.'

'Sophie will be stoked,' Ric said. 'How about tonight? The only thing is we're flooded out here, and staying with neighbours.' He gave her Nina's number.

'How are things going?' asked Hilary. 'Any problems, no? I'm happy to hear that . . .' He could feel a but coming. 'I've received some information from Rachael. I don't know if she even remembers telling me. She was pretty out of it at the time. Still, you need to know.'

'Yes?'

'Ric . . . I'm afraid Sophie isn't your biological daughter after all.'

Ah, he was wondering when this would come up. 'I know.'

'It seems . . . Wait, you know?'

'I sat down and did the maths a few weeks ago. Sophie was born twelve months after I last saw Rachael. It was so many years back, it took me a while to work it out.'

'But if you knew …?'

'What difference does it make?' he said. 'Sophie needs somebody and I love her. And she loves me, though you'd have a hard time getting her to admit it. She got to meet my dad and they adored each other. It was a miracle. She called him Poppi.' Ric smiled at the memory. 'Why would I want to change anything?'

It was a long time before Hilary spoke. 'You're a remarkable man, Ric Bonelli. It would be wonderful if Sophie could stay on until Rachael's more stable.'

'Sure thing.' Ric ended the call and poured himself another coffee. It was good to hear about Rachael. Sophie would get a real kick from that call. He went to the dresser and flipped open the red velvet jewellery case. Two promise rings nestled in the satin folds, Nina's original ring and a replacement band for him. Perfect. He flipped though his phone till he found Tony's number. 'Tony? Yeah, yeah, it's Ric. I need a favour, mate.'

'Ready?' asked Nina. Sophie nodded and climbed into the back seat.

Ric checked her helmet. 'Sure you're okay?'

'Dad, I'm not a scaredy-cat like you.'

Nina stifled a laugh. The geese pecked at the grass around the ultra-light, unfazed by the whir of the little engine. Daily flights behind the quad bike had desensitised them to the noise of motors. The morning was sunny and clear, without a whisper of wind. Perfect for flying. Nina crossed her fingers. She'd be as devastated as Sophie if this didn't work.

Nina had fallen in love with the little aircraft, not much more than a motorised hang-glider, on her first practice flight. She'd christened it Sparrowhawk, after discovering that its unimaginative owner had failed to name it at all. In discovering this ultra-light, she'd found a new passion. She loved everything about it: the elegant, tailored wings with their upswept tips, the stylish tail, the cute little wheels. It was beautiful to look at, and beautiful to fly – the closest thing to being a bird. Ric's cousin Tony had given her the thumbs-up after one afternoon of practice. 'That girl flies better than I do,' he'd told Ric. 'She's got the knack, like she has wings herself.'

And now they were ready. 'Good luck,' said Ric, climbing onto the quad bike. He'd be riding at their wingtip for reinforcement. Nina took a deep breath and started down the runway, the geese running after, and Ric beside, while Sophie called encouragement. And then she was airborne, praying that the geese would join her, not knowing what was happening behind. Sophie thumped her on the shoulder. Was that good or bad? And then geese filled the skies all around, falling into diagonal formation at her right wing. She tried a slow climb and they climbed too, flanking the Sparrowhawk with perfect precision. The leader, Odette, took a free ride on her slipstream, settling in with wings outstretched. Nina screamed with joy, marvelling at the bird's beauty and shining grace. They were in their element, and so was she.

Nina banked and turned, and the geese didn't miss a beat. She passed back over the runway, a hundred metres above the ground, with the sun turning everything to gold. And there was Ric below her, shouting and waving like a madman. He leaped back on the bike and took off after them. She laughed out loud and a great feeling of joy, of love, swept over her. Love for Sophie and the geese. Love for the river lands below, and love for the magnificent man, keeping perfect pace down on the ground, as she soared the wild skies, free as a bird.

ACKNOWLEDGEMENTS

With special thanks to Belinda Byrne, whose input helped make *Billabong Bend* a better story. Thanks also to Ben Ball and Sarah Fairhall, who looked after me when I needed it. Thanks to Ali Arnold, editor extraordinaire. Thanks to Caro Cooper, Arwen Summers, Clementine Edwards, and to the team at Pilyara Press who helped make this book happen.

Thanks to my lovely agent, Clare Forster of Curtis Brown. Also to my talented writing friends, the Little Lonsdale Group, for their friendship and enthusiastic support. Thanks to the Varuna Darklings, and to Peter Bishop and Clare Allan-Kamil for always believing in me. Special thanks to Dinky-Di Houseboat Holidays and the Proud Mary crew for some great times on the Murray.

Finally I'd like to thank my patient family. Thank you to Heather, Tyson and Daniel. Thanks to Samantha Roberts for proofreading help. And thanks to my brother Rod and son Matthew for their interest and willingness to brainstorm ideas. Love all you guys!

ABOUT THE AUTHOR

Bestselling Aussie author Jennifer Scoullar writes page-turning fiction about the land, people and wildlife that she loves.

Scoullar is a lapsed lawyer who harbours a deep appreciation and respect for the natural world. She lives on a farm in Australia's southern Victorian ranges, and has ridden and bred horses all her life. Her passion for animals and the bush is the catalyst for her bestselling books.

If you enjoyed this book and have a moment or two, please leave a rating or review. Reviews are of great help to authors.

www.jenniferscoullar.com